8/01

01 02 03 04

GAYLORD MG

10/01

Green River
Daydreams

ALSO BY LIU HENG:

Black Snow

Green River Daydreams

A novel by
Liu Heng

Translated from the Chinese by
Howard Goldblatt

Grove Press   New York

Published simultaneously in Canada

Printed in the United States of America

Originally published in 1993 by Wenyi Chubanshe

FIRST EDITION

Library of Congress Cataloging-in-Publication Data

Liu Heng, 1954-
    [Cang he bai ri meng. English]
    Green River daydreams : a novel / by Liu Heng ; translated from the Chinese by Howard Goldblatt.
      p. cm.
    ISBN 0-8021-1690-6
    I. Goldblatt, Howard, 1939-   II. Title.
PL2879.H38 C3613 2001
895.1'352—dc21   2001016193

DESIGN BY LAURA HAMMOND HOUGH

Grove Press

841 Broadway

New York, NY 10003

01 02 03 04 10 9 8 7 6 5 4 3 2 1

Part One
March 1992

March 1st

There's so much to tell you that I'll just start at the beginning. Humans are strange creatures. They can't remember things right in front of their eyes and can't forget incidents that have already been squashed beneath their heels. Yes, humans are strange creatures, all of them! Don't ask me what I ate at my last meal, I couldn't tell you. If you must ask something, make it interesting. If you won't, I've got nothing to say. Listen up if you don't believe me. Now where do we begin, you little shit? I've got a dirty mouth. That doesn't bother you, does it? I could tell right off you're a good boy.

That day, I can't say what year it was, maybe 1908, but anyway, I went to the Willow Township pier to wait for the mail delivery, and since I was early, I ran over to Lucky Teahouse for a bowl of Emerald Conch tea. I took it over to a seat by the window to observe the branch of the river. Nothing but small boats coming and going, with their pigs and barrels of pickled vegetables and cormorants, and, of course, women. I was sixteen at the time, and what I liked to watch most were fights, the women's faces and tits, and, of course, their asses. What's that scowl for? I suppose you never look at stuff like that. Now you're talking. Like I said, you're a good boy. Know what folks who don't like looking at women's asses like to look at? I've got a dirty mouth, but I have to say it. They like to look at their own shit in outdoor latrines! They're nothing but maggots, so let 'em look. You and me, we're humans, and we look at interesting things. What do you say, you little bastard, am I right?

A woman was standing in a boat wiggling her ass as she worked the pole, and I started dreaming, even though it was broad daylight. It was a shameful dream. I was clinging to her nice, plump ass and swaying right along with her, until we fused into a single person. Go ahead, laugh, I don't care. I had the same dream yesterday, but this time, instead of a woman, I was holding a long-tailed fox. Couldn't say if it was male or female. Fascinating, wouldn't you say?

If I'm boring you, I'll shut up. How many people in this world can claim to have reached my age? I was born in the previous '92. Eighteen ninety-two. Figure it out for yourself. Everyone else my age, they're rotting in their graves, and if someone dug up their bones, they'd probably assume they belonged to a goat or a pig. They stopped being human a long time ago. Me, I should be content with my lot. Talk, talk, talk, it's a bad sign. When old folks talk all the time, it's a sign they're on their last legs. Heaven is rushing them along!

Boy, hand me that teacup.

Thank you. Now the spittoon.

You sure have big ears.

That means good luck.

Know what people call me?

They call me Ears.

Here, touch one. What does it feel like?

That's right, a sea cucumber.

Now, where was I? So what if I talk too much? I don't care if the dead or Heaven are happy or not, they're going to have to let me speak my piece. You youngsters have got it made. You have all the time in the world to talk. You could be a mute for a year and it wouldn't make a bit of difference. But me, every sentence spoken is one less left unsaid, so I can't waste a single day. I'm not about to let a fascinating tale like mine rot away in my belly. I've got to tell it, and you can listen or not, I don't care. I've been talking to the walls for a hell of a lot longer than a year or two.

There's a woman on the wall.

Look for yourself if you don't believe me.

You must be blind!

I don't know why I waste my time talking to you.

That's not an ass, it's a water stain from last summer's rain. Don't look with your eyes, look with your mind. If your mind is focused, you can close your eyes and still see things most people can't see with their eyes open. Guess what I see right now.

You young folks are too modest. I'm not going to tell you.

I see the word lust.

You know what lust is, don't you?

Lucky Teahouse had another specialty besides selling tea: you could get your hair combed out there. As soon as you sat down, a young fellow came over, loosened your queue, and combed out your hair while you enjoyed your tea. And if you had an itch, all you had to do was point to the spot, and the teeth of his comb would take care of it. You never had to worry about dandruff falling into your teacup, because he first rubbed sesame oil all over your scalp. Who knows where Lucky came up with the idea of providing two such unrelated services, but his customers loved walking out of the place with their hair all neat and shiny, even though that little taste of elegance cost them the price of two extra cups of tea.

The teahouse was near Willow Township's Western Avenue. Once you crossed the square in front of the pier, you were on Eastern Avenue, where just about everything was for sale. The most active exchange was in the flesh market, the female flesh market. Those men whose heads reeked of sesame oil were the prostitutes' poorest customers, and once they'd finished their business, they'd come back to the teahouse, where they'd finish off a pot of tea, wipe their mouths, and brag to anyone who'd listen what they'd done and how they'd done it, all in delicious detail. If they really got going, they'd pretend that a nearby bench was the woman and reenact the event with a flurry of arms and legs. So really, Lucky Teahouse sold more than tea and hair maintenance—it was also a place that oozed sex. If not for that, I'd have picked a cheaper place to drink my tea. I later learned that Lucky's prices were reasonable compared with the tea in the whorehouses. Longtime patrons used to say you could buy a bowl of human blood for what that tea cost. So why did those men come to Lucky Teahouse before and after visiting the whorehouses? You should know the answer to that.

They were too short of cash to drink the other tea.

Me too. I was born in the countryside as a personal slave to the family of Cao Ruqi, Old Master Cao, of Elm Township. He was a famously rich member of the gentry class, and I couldn't embarrass him by drinking cheap local Green Needle tea. I always ordered Emerald Conch, which was shipped in from another province. I ignored the lewd performances all around me and concentrated on the boats outside the window, watching those women and dreaming my own dreams. But I listened, and none of the whoring customers' filthy talk escaped me. One of them bragged about how he took a bottle of foreign liquor with him and bought the favors of Black Eagle, the highest-priced whore on Willow Township's Eastern Avenue. Without spending a penny, he screwed her seven days in a row.

Lucky himself led the outcry: You lying, fucking bastard!

The braggart defended himself: If I'm lying, I'm not a man. She loves her liquor!

Lucky said: Seven days? Maybe if you killed her first, you necrophiliac!

Everyone in the teahouse roared with laughter. Now I had no idea what a necrophiliac was, but just thinking about Black Eagle, with that face and those long legs, sent prickles up my spine.

Lucky had a sharp tongue, but he treated me with courtesy, since he knew who I was. He always refilled my cup very attentively, which made me feel like I was somebody.

He asked: Ears, how's the master of your house these days?

I answered: Thank you, sir, for asking. The old gentleman's in fine shape.

He asked: Did you make another trip to the pharmacy?

I answered: The old gentleman sent me for Korean ginseng and Chinese wolfberry.

He said: So he's still using tonics, even though summer's already here, is he?

And I said: I don't know.

He asked: Are you waiting for the mail delivery? If so, you can stop waiting. Didn't you hear? There's been an insurrection by famine victims at Duckweed Bay. For the time being, no government or commercial ships are sailing the river. Unless you're willing to wait ten days or so, you can forget about mail. Go on back to Elm Township, and when you see Old Master Cao, don't forget to give him my best wishes. And be careful, don't let him take just any old tonic. You don't want to ruin his health.

Lucky sure had a way with words. The way he talked, you'd have thought he could sit at the same table with Master Cao. Truth is, if Master Cao saw him, he might not even know who Lucky was. Lucky was a decent guy, but he had no idea why I was killing time in his teahouse. Laugh if you want, but all that lewd talk had my heart racing, and I fantasized that I'd sunk into the perfume of the Eastern Avenue female flesh market. Lucky's shout interrupted my daydream: Listen up, everybody. The teahouse was still chaotic. So Lucky repeated himself: Hey, everybody, listen up! People quieted down, and were rewarded by the sound of a horn and a succession of shouts from boat trackers, lots of them, drifting over from the Green River. A ship was coming in.

The teahouse customers rushed outside to gawk, quickly filling the pier with a blanket of wobbling heads and swaying queues. Way out in front was a pack of refugees, who'd been cowering out of sight all over Willow Township, but came running out like starving dogs when they heard the commotion. A few of the painted ladies ventured out from the brothels onto the stone steps at the entrance to Eastern Avenue. All decked out in cheap, gaudy, almost see-through satins, they wore their clothes in the fashion of well-to-do ladies from downriver, not loose and baggy like the local girls. I stepped back to get a better look at them. My greedy eyes had a mind of their own and went where they wanted, like the hands of a pickpocket.

Green River was ten feet lower than years past, exposing rocks washed white on the banks; water grasses clung to the ground like a dead man's hair. The boat trackers climbed the bank, stepping on the dead grass, all the way up to the stone steps of the pier. As the ship neared the shore, it hit bottom, sending muddy bubbles to the surface. The famine refugees, acting as if they'd spotted the Emperor, fell to their knees and shouted insanely: Something to eat, Master! Please, Master, something to eat!

It was a huge ship. Not a passenger ship and not a salt ship, nor a rice transport. It was a strange-looking thing, with a mast amidships and the prow painted like a fish head with a pair of fish eyes staring out. Have you ever been to the Green River? Now that's something with no head and no tail. It goes all the way down to the county seat, the prefecture, and from there to the provincial capital. After that it flows into some other province. I didn't know anything about an ocean back then, and I figured that no matter how far the river flowed, it was just a trough in the earth that carried water round and round and never took it anywhere else. That ship from some distant province didn't interest me at all. I was too busy prying open the troughs in the prostitutes' rear ends with my eyes when the gangplank crashed against the pier.

The gunwales were lined with coolies, nobody else.

The starving refugees quickly changed their pleas: Daddy! Daddy! Give us something to eat!

I was curious to see who that daddy of theirs was, so I jerked my head around in time to see a pair of distinguished gentlemen walking down the gangplank. One was tall, the other short, and both were dressed in black Western suits with black top hats and capes. The people on the shore scared them witless. A sea of skinny arms! That and chipped beggar's bowls. The pier looked like it was overgrown with dirty mushrooms, with no room for the men to step down. The tall one took off his hat, releasing a headful of golden hair. He had a hawk nose, the eyes of a swan, and fair skin. I don't have to tell you what we were facing there.

An authentic European.

The people on shore were jolted by the sight into opening a path. The silenced refugees moved forward with outstretched beggar's bowls, into which the European tossed some coins as he threaded his way past. The shorter man also tossed coins, but with an impatience made obvious by the way he simply flung them. The wretched recipients fought over the handout, a mass of humanity that looked more like a pack of mad dogs. When he ran out of coins, the European started handing out silver dollars. The shameless refugees responded with shouts, and you'd have to be a genius to guess what they shouted this time.

Foreign Ancestor, give your hangdog grandchild one of those! When you get that hungry, you stop being human.

The shorter man wasn't a foreigner, but his complexion was lighter than the European's. He kept his eyes glued to me as he walked toward me, and even after he brushed past me, he turned back for another look. And I looked at him. I knew I'd seen that scowl somewhere before, but couldn't place the guy. Back then, anyone with a bit of education looked like that, especially schoolteachers, or scholars who hung out in wine houses, or students in advanced schools. One look at their faces told you that the sky was about to fall, and no one would get out alive.

But, hell, how could I have missed recognizing him?

He stopped about twenty feet from me and just stood there.

We were separated by famine victims and whores.

He said: Ears, is that you?

That's when it hit me. That sad look on his face almost had me in tears. I ran over, fell to my knees, and kowtowed, banging my head so hard the rocks sang out. I was numb and dizzy, but it didn't hurt at all. I tell you, those beggars and flesh-peddlers were scared witless.

Have you ever listened to a professional storyteller?

I always like the storyteller's last line.

We'll continue this—next time.

I need to go out for a walk now.

I'll tell you tomorrow who he was.

There goes another airplane. I know why they built the nursing home here. They must think that all old folks are deaf, so this is peace and quiet to us. But I'm not, and that's the thirty-eighth airplane that's flown over today. When I first moved in, I was always fussing and complaining. Every time I heard an airplane, I nearly blew my stack. But I've gotten used to it, and they're just birds to me now. I watch them the same way I used to watch the boats outside Lucky Teahouse. The Green River flowed round and round until it emptied into my head.

So I'll tell you anyway. The man's name was Cao Guanghan, Second Master of the Cao household. One of his distant uncles had served the Manchu court under the Guangxu Emperor as a diplomat, and the Old Master parlayed this connection into an opportunity to send Second Master, who was always sighing and complaining about one thing or another, to school abroad. They wanted to get him out of the Elm Township valley, where he'd likely have turned into an eccentric at best and a madman at worst. He left in 1904, when he was nineteen, so he must have been twenty-three when he came home. Not only was he dressed differently, he'd fleshed out as well. But his face hadn't changed much, still had that look that made you worry what he'd do next. Ears, is that you? he said. He sounded like a man who'd just crawled out of the bowels of Hell, and would be crawling right back in before long.

Second Master was a man to be pitied.

What was that, the thirty-ninth airplane?

Ever fly in one of those birds, youngster?

Oh, I forgot to tell you something earlier. When the foreigner was walking away from the Elm Township pier, he caused quite a stir among the whores from Eastern Avenue. One of them, in a pink dress, let out a fearful cry. It wasn't Black Eagle, it was a girl called White Horse. The way she wiggled when she said her piece, you'd have thought that Sun Wukong, the magic monkey, was prodding her from behind with that golden cudgel of his.

Yes, it was the old feudal society, so what?

A woman's still a woman.

Women are wily creatures, and that much hasn't changed.

What she said was: I'll bet that's one hell of a foreign prick!

Go on, get a good night's sleep. When you come back in the morning, I hope you'll find me still alive. All the juicy parts are

yet to come, and I want to make sure I get everything said. Go on,
get some sleep. You don't have to blush over something a woman
said.

Word for word, that's exactly what she said.

Now I'm tired.

March 2nd

Elm Township is located in a huge valley behind two mountain
ranges. The Black River flows through it moving fast, and is so
shallow it only takes rafts, no real boats or ships, no matter how
light they are. There are house-sized rocks in the middle of the
river, and you can hear the water crash into them. The river makes
forty-nine turns through the mountains before it reaches the western edge of Willow Township and becomes a branch of the Green
River.

Back then, for the convenience of rafts, there were no low bridges
across the river, just a single suspension bridge. Where there was
no bridge, you had to wade across. The distance from the pier to
Elm Township was three miles, the road sometimes on this side of
the river and sometimes on that side. People who didn't have the
wherewithal to ride in a sedan chair or on horseback walked barefoot, shoes in hand, and during the summer floods, the road
disappeared altogether. But so what, since traffic between Elm
Township and places on the other side of the mountains was frequently disrupted anyway? People in Elm Township prospered,
with food to eat and clothes to wear. What did we have to be afraid
of? Compared to countless little villages and townships all up and

down the Green River, in the eyes of its residents, Elm Township was heaven on earth.

Now that I think of it, all that self-satisfaction was ridiculous. There were only two kinds of people in the whole valley: members of the Cao family and their tenant farmers and servants. Elm Township may have been heaven on earth for the Cao family, but it was just another place for the rest of us, the slaves. What was I, after all? I considered myself a man, but when all was said and done, I was just another Cao family mutt, one they'd saved from starvation.

Back then, if you want the truth, I was happy to be a mutt, just for the privilege of serving the Cao household. The reason's simple: they treated me like one of their own. I had no father and no mother. At the age of three I was feeding the Caos' chickens, at five I was slopping their hogs, and at nine I was taking care of their horses. When other people reached the age of sixteen, they became coolie laborers, working in the family's slaughterhouse or paper mill or fan factory; but when I turned fourteen, Old Master Cao made me his personal attendant, and from then on, I ate well, dressed well, and had things other people didn't. What more could I ask for? From the time I started hobnobbing with the Caos' chickens, I stopped considering myself an outsider. All those years of muddling along had me feeling I was the next thing to one of Master Cao's sons. Who cared what he thought, so long as I stayed convinced? Now what would you call somebody who sneaks around pretending he's the son of an old landlord?

A tragic figure, you got that right.

So why did I weep and kowtow to Second Master when I saw him at the pier? That's where the secret lies. The worried look on his face made me feel close to him. So I ran interference and asked him to take hold of my shoulder. Which, after a moment's pause, is what he did. I was content to serve as his crutch as I plowed through the human barrier of refugees. But they never stopped begging: Dear Daddy! Save us! Boy, wouldn't I have liked to give them a swift kick! If they were so hungry, why not dine on the flesh on their own legs? What right did that scum have to live in the same

world as him? Second Master looked sad, but I couldn't tell for sure
if he pitied or resented them. He threaded his way through the
crowd like a man fleeing for his life.

He asked: What has this place become?

I said: Last year floods, this year drought.

He asked: How about the Elm Township rice granaries?

I said: They're full.

He asked: Why not give out some for relief?

I said: They've already given out quite a bit. The family runs a
soup kitchen at the county seat. They serve meals every five days.
Elder Master goes into town a couple of times every month.

He asked: Why isn't it open every day?

His indignation dumbfounded me.

And he wasn't finished: Do people only have to eat every five
days? he asked.

I said: If the government can't do anything about it, what are
we supposed to do? And what do we eat if we give all our rice
away?

He said: Share and share alike.

Second Master was as eccentric as ever, and I cautioned myself
to be careful. Once we were on the road, I begged him to let me
carry him up the mountain on my back, but he said no. I tried again,
but he still wouldn't allow it. He relented a bit by resting his arms
on my shoulders. But I was afraid his arms would get tired that way,
so I hunkered down and bent over to make myself as short as possible. My face was so close to the ground I could have crawled up
the mountain.

The foreigner never left our side, listening to everything I said
to Second Master and watching our lips move. When we weren't
talking, he whistled, loud as a flute. Second Master was in too foul
a mood to talk much, and when he did it was little more than a
mumble. But the foreigner nodded his head each time. He had a
kind, honest face, just not terribly smart. He walked over to some
trees by the side of the road and let loose a shockingly powerful
stream of piss. I was so sharp-eyed that nothing got past me, and
I recalled what that whore had said. That shows what kind of per-

son I was. I started dreaming again about women bending to pole their boats with their asses sticking up in the air.

Take a good look at my face. Would you call it loathsome?

You know, you can't tell if a person's loathsome just by looking at him. Take you, for instance. You look like a good boy, but I have no idea what's going through your mind.

You wouldn't be thinking of removing some girl's pants, would you?

Well, I did a lot of that when I was young.

In my dreams, of course.

That's right. In dreams only.

As for the other stuff, I'll tell you about that later.

We didn't get home till late that night, accompanied by hundreds of starving refugees, who fought to help Second Master with his baggage. There was no getting rid of them. Along with the baggage, there were five or six wooden crates, the largest about the size of a small melon shed, the smallest as big as a henhouse. I later discovered that they were filled with used machinery for manufacturing matches. He'd planned on hiring porters for the task, but the refugees swarmed up and carried off the machinery like an army of ants. I told Second Master he was just asking for trouble letting those people hang around Elm Township and live on handouts, but he ignored my warning, except for an angry stare.

He said: What's wrong with doing it this way?

The refugees were smart enough to spare no effort and to handle the chests with care. By the time we'd made it halfway up the mountain, they were already at the top, where they were met by Cao family menials whose job it was to keep refugees out and stop them from stirring up trouble. This time they weren't successful. Backed up by Second Master, the procession marched into Elm Township like a flock of sheep, transporting the wooden crates right down the main street of town, like a column of holiday revelers.

Word of our arrival had preceded us up the mountain, and we were met by Cao family servants with lanterns and torches. The whole township had been roused by the commotion. I heard the voice of Elder Master, Second Master's brother, Cao Guangman, over the din and saw him standing on the steps of the Cao estate gate tower, his face glowing red in the torchlight. He and Second Master were opposites in just about every respect. His boisterous laughter could send roof tiles crashing to the ground.

He said: Guanghan! Guanghan! Where are you?

It took some doing, but we finally managed to elbow our way up front, where Elder Master grabbed his younger brother by the arms. Just looking at them together, one hot and one cold, gave me the creeps.

The older brother said: I wouldn't have recognized you.

The younger one said: Is that so?

The older brother asked: What's that foreigner doing here?

The younger one said: He's a mechanical engineer, and my friend.

Second Master babbled something to the foreigner.

The foreigner said: How do you do.

His voice cut the air like the screech of a cat.

I knew something was wrong as soon as I walked through the gate. Second Master appeared to be having second thoughts about the refugees, who surged in behind him like a pack of madmen. As they banged on the wooden crates they began to chant: One, two, three, give us something to eat! Four, five, six, bring out the meat! Seven, eight, nine, give us some wine! Give us some wine!

Second Master turned pale. Now it was time to pay the piper.

If somebody calls you Daddy, don't ever take it seriously.

Never believe people who praise you to the skies.

March 3rd

Second Master looked like an infant at the tit. Burying his face in his mother's bosom, he fell to his knees and stayed there without moving. But you can't blame him, because it was she who'd called him over, grabbed him, and hugged him so tightly he could barely move. It was something we'd seen often before he went abroad. That was just the way they were. Second Master wasn't weaned until the age of nine. With him willing to keep sucking and her willing to let him, we were hard put to know where to fix the blame.

Second Master didn't stand up for the longest time, maybe because his nostrils were filled with a scent he'd been missing for years. Mrs. Cao, of the Zhang family, who wasn't yet fifty, was a strict vegetarian and a devout Buddhist. Tears were streaming down her still-young face.

She said: Hanhan, now that you're home, don't ever leave again!

Second Master just sobbed and buried his face deeper, like a suckling pig.

They acted as if they were alone in the spacious room that served the family for greeting visitors. Old Master Cao, Second Master's father, was seated in an armchair at the head of the room, flanked by Elder Master on one side and the foreigner on the other. I was standing by the window. No one said a word. We were bowled over, especially the foreigner, who must have thought they were a very unusual mother and son. Old Master and Elder Master were bowled over by something quite different.

Me too.

I figured he'd coiled it up under his hat. But when he ran into his mother's arms, his hat fell to the floor, like a lopped-off head. Only people who opposed the Manchu dynasty cut off their queues. Was Second Master a rebel?

Mrs. Cao wept and wept.

Old Master Cao didn't say a word. He appeared to be asleep.

Elder Master smiled at the foreigner and nodded. The foreigner returned the smile and nodded back. That happened a few more times, until finally they stopped looking at each other altogether and turned their attention elsewhere, afraid to make eye contact. Mother and son gave no indication that they were about to let each other go. I could tell that the foreigner was getting antsy, and that if something didn't happen soon, his friend might actually go for his mother's nipple. Now wouldn't that have been something!

He had reason to worry.

I'd seen it with my own eyes. It happened the year before Second Master went abroad, in Mrs. Cao's meditation room, in the middle of summer, when her window was opened halfway. The back of Second Master's head and one of Mrs. Cao's tits were in plain view. Her tit looked like a milky white gourd, except not as firm. Second Master was eighteen at the time. I was eleven.

Since I was in the habit of strolling around the estate, I saw lots of eye-opening things. Sometimes, when I was still little, I climbed up onto the roof to retrieve nervous hens that had flown up there. Later, when I was a little bigger, I went up there to gaze at the stars and count them. Later still, my reasons were more complex. I don't have to tell you what they were, if you get my drift.

That day, the foreigner was given the cold shoulder. The Caos were an urbane family who'd had plenty of contact with foreigners before. The priest from the Catholic church at Acacia Township often came to Elm Township, not in a sedan chair and not on horseback, but always on a donkey, a creature that was taller than a horse and brayed all the time. He didn't come to preach the gospel, but to buy hog bristles from the Cao slaughterhouse and lumber from its timber mill. He spoke Chinese and was an accomplished bargainer. If he was pressed, he'd shrug his shoulders, smile, and say to Elder Master: Fuck your old lady!

Elder Master would smile right back and say: Fuck your old man!

Then, once the bargain was struck, they'd pat each other on the shoulders like two old friends.

There was an agreement between the priest and the Cao family that he wouldn't preach the gospel in Elm Township, since the local residents were all Buddhists. The Caos weren't afraid to have dealings with him; in their eyes he was just another businessman, like all foreigners, including the latest on the scene. I'm sure that's what Old Master and his elder son were thinking.

I felt sorry for our big-nosed guest, so when I brought him tea, I knelt on one knee and held the cup over my head with both hands. He reacted to my expression of courtesy for an honored guest by fumbling anxiously to take the cup from me. You'd have thought he was witnessing Mrs. Cao flop out her tit.

He didn't act like a man of much importance.

A while later, I followed Old Master to his room, where he had me open the latest packet from the pharmacy and show it to him. I told him they were out of five-legged Korean ginseng, and had only the four-legged and three-legged varieties. But there were plenty of tassels, and each root had thirty or more shoots. He picked up one and made a careful count.

He asked: Did the Chinese wolfberry grow in a place with sandy soil?

I said: That's what the pharmacist told me.

A little brazier burned in Old Master's room the year round, and there was always something stewing in the cauldron on top of it. He never let his servants get near it, always attending to it himself. Where his health was concerned, he was diligent to the point of obsession. No one but him could bear up under the peculiar odor that filled the room. Mrs. Cao had moved out and taken up residence in her meditation room, where she ate, drank, shat, pissed, and slept, probably to avoid the odor of Old Master's concoctions. But then she had obsessions of her own—the Buddha and ghosts

and goblins. She had early on begun seeing herself as a future
immortal!

Her coming to the guest room to greet Second Master was no
minor event.

Old Master Cao was happy with this arrangement. His daily
pleasures consisted mainly of stirring his medicinal concoction
with a wooden chopstick. He also read, he practiced Tai Chi, and
he adorned fans from the family factory with his own calligraphy
and paintings. He couldn't have been happier. Except when visited
by thoughts of his own mortality. Although he never admitted it, I
knew the depth of his fears. Every time this thought weighed him
down, he redoubled his efforts in stewing up exotic ingredients:
he had ingested ants and wasps, silkworm pupas and hornets, even
a batch of centipedes stewed in honey. He couldn't begin to say
how many different things he'd consumed. Outsiders knew only
that he prepared things like ginseng and antlers as tonics, and had
no idea just what he was up to. No one in his family knew as much
as I did, because it was me who caught dragonflies and crickets
for him, even baby mice!

He entrusted all the family's enterprises to his elder son.

Elder Master liked things just the way they were. A man of
unlimited energy, he felt there was nothing in the world he couldn't
accomplish. He hadn't batted an eye when hundreds of famine
victims formed a barrier out at the gate. All he did was rouse six
family cooks from their sleep and have them work all night preparing pots of congee and steamed rolls; then he personally helped
carry the food out to the gate tower steps and began tossing the
rolls to the crowd, like skimming rocks on the surface of the Black
River.

He said: Go up the mountain and take some timber over to
Willow Township. I'll make sure you have food to eat. Get started
at daybreak, and I promise you three square meals.

What happened later proved he'd arranged for food, all right—
one meal. When they finished their work and returned to the estate, they were met by a contingent of servants armed with fowling
pieces, domestic shotguns, and rifles, and forced at gunpoint back

to the foot of the mountain. Peace returned to Elm Township. Elder Master was every bit the Elder Master! His intelligence and decisiveness far outstripped that of his brother.

What was Second Master good at?

He was good at suckling at his mother's tit.

That night he and the foreigner bedded down in a building in the left-hand-corner compound. The Old Master and Mrs. Cao lived in the main house, Elder Master and his family lived in the buildings in the right corner. The buildings on the left had been left vacant all those years, even though they were kept neat and clean; there was a pond, a man-made hill, and wisteria trellises. It was fascinating the way they wound around, making it a great place to be in. The Old Master told me to move in with Second Master and the foreigner.

He said: You can have the side room next to the gate.

As he gave me my orders he dumped some ginseng roots into the cauldron.

He added: Keep an eye on them for me.

I didn't know exactly what he meant.

He said: Guanghan's a madman.

Old Master fished the stewed head of a sparrow out of the cauldron, put it into his mouth, and crunched away. A bunch of feathers floated on the top of the mixture. Old Master dumped the rest of the ginseng into the concoction.

The last thing he said to me was: That barbarian is a thief!

Now I was really confused.

I ask you, how could I not be?

Crunch crunch crunch!

I can't go on.

I've got a headache.

A splitting headache.

I shouldn't have told you about climbing onto the roof. For all these years, that's been my one and only secret. I hope you don't get any wild ideas. My face is turning red. Whether you understand me or not is of no concern to me. The experiences of my life are my

riches, and some of them are accumulations of activities on that
rooftop. You can't expect this old face not to turn red, can you?

Have you ever gotten excited over something like that?

Are you just trying to reassure me?

You're right! The problem with modern buildings is they don't have enough spy holes.

You've made me very happy, young man. Thank you for linking the tale I'm telling to my roof-climbing. I should have thought of that long ago. The years have softened my brain.

The man-made hill was right next to the eaves.

I could climb up there lickety-split.

After all, I'd been in charge of the Cao family horses for five years!

Everything's easy when you're young.

Have you ever thought about using a telescope?

I saw something about them in a tabloid once.

Shit!

What a loss of face, ancient as it is!

March 4th

I changed from being a main-house attendant to a left-corner compound escort. I was also Old Master Cao's medicine boy and spy. I had my hands full, but I knew where to start and where to go from there. The foreigner had trouble adapting to the food at the Cao home, but that didn't worry me much. If he didn't want to eat, let him go hungry for a while. After secretly measuring the sweatband of Second Master's hat, I went to have a queue made for him.

At a village in Willow Township I rounded up eight tenant farmers whose hair was about the same color as his, gave them each a few coins, and harvested enough hair for my purposes. Then I went to see a man who wove baskets. After washing the hair in a mixture of vinegar and spices, he wove it into a shiny black queue. Of course, he asked me who it was for, and whether it was a case of somebody having shaved his head.

I said: It's for a monk who's giving up his vows, a relative of mine.

I took it home and showed it to Old Master.

Old Master said: No lice, I assume.

He was pleased, and told me to summon Second Master, who was in the sedan chair shed out front, polishing some machinery. He was covered with grease. When he saw the fake queue, all he did was snort loudly. The room grew tense.

He said: These are shackles the Manchus put around our necks. Just because you don't want to breathe fresh air, why won't you let others do it?

Old Master said: I told you to wear it, so wear it. It won't choke you.

Second Master asked: Why do you have to deceive yourself and everyone else?

Old Master said: You may have studied foreign ways, but don't forget who you are.

Second Master said: How can I forget? I belong to a barbarian race!

Instead of getting angry, Old Master nodded as he watched his son reluctantly put on the queue. Second Master turned to leave, but his father called him back and told him he had something to say. Second Master told him to say it quickly, because he had things to do.

That did not please Old Master.

He said: Your mother and I have arranged for you to get married next month.

Old Master brushed some dust off his pants and returned to his room to stew a potion, leaving Second Master standing on the steps of the main room like a wooden statue, his eyes glazed over. He was mumbling to himself in a voice that wasn't much louder than the buzz of a mosquito.

He said: I wrote to say I wanted out of the marriage, and they agreed. Why trick me like that? And why force me to go through with it? Ears, what's going on here?

I told him I didn't know a thing about it.

I said: People say she's a real beauty.

But Second Master just bellowed: I'm not getting married! I won't do it!

I ask you, does he sound like a madman or doesn't he?

He staggered off. The fake queue fell off his head and onto his shoulder, but he was oblivious. He looked like a clown wearing a tail. I'd never seen the girl, so I couldn't have told you whether she was a beauty or not, but she couldn't have had the face of a monkey, could she? A twenty-three-year-old man refusing to marry, what could he be thinking?

The servants all said there was something wrong with Second Master.

Some people even said there was something wrong with the whole Cao family.

Talk like that upset me.

I've got athlete's foot.

It's been over forty years since I last had athlete's foot, enough time for two generations to grow up, including yours. I haven't been walking much lately, and I always use my own basin to wash my feet, so how come I've got athlete's foot? My problem is, I talk too much, but if that had anything to do with athlete's foot, it'd be too weird for words. You must have heard that a woman in our nursing home had her period!

I said that can't be, it must have been a tumor.

But they said I was wrong, it was her period.

Our little menstrual sister was eighty-one, and she went around with a smile on her face, as if she'd recaptured her youth. So what happens? The hospital sent an ambulance for her.

There was something wrong with her womb.

No one could say for sure what was growing down there.

I'm going to soak my feet in water with leeks.

They may be a hundred years old, but they're still my feet, and I have to treat them with loving care.

I'm not going to let them itch anymore.

March 5th

No one but Second Master could figure out what the foreigner's name was—Yidulu, or something like that. To this day, I'm still not sure. But Old Master, who was in a carefree mood, chose some Chinese characters that sounded like Yidulu and wrote them on a fan for him. Thrilled by the gift, the foreigner never went anywhere without it, opening it for everyone he met and, with a broad grin, asking them to read it. The character used for his name was Lu— you know, road, not the one that means deer. Road! You know, that thing we step on when we walk out the gate. Later on, someone added the word Big to his name, and everyone in the household, high and low, began calling him Big Road. Hardly anyone called him Mr. Road.

How do you like the food today, Big Road?

Even the cooks called him that. He'd sit there facing a fine meal and shrug his shoulders. Unable to understand exactly what the cook had said, he managed to get the drift, and gave a laughing thumbs-up. But after the laugh, he'd barely touch his food. The Cao family drank goat's milk, but he wanted cow's milk. So we fetched a water buffalo from a nearby village, one that had just had a calf,

and squeezed out some milk for him. He threw it right back up.
But Second Master didn't let minor concerns like that bother him.
All he said was: I was pretty much the same when I first arrived in
France. Give him a little more fruit.

So in addition to the fan, Big Road was seldom seen without a
handful of grapes. He'd walk along, tip his head back, and pop
them into his mouth. It was quite a sight, which even he appreci-
ated. If one of the servants was with him, he'd toss a grape into
the air and catch it in his mouth. That always drew a big laugh.
He was an easygoing guy. Around his hosts he kept quiet, and we
never saw him joke around with Second Master, probably realizing that Second Master wasn't the joking type. Although he was
at least ten years older than Second Master, when they jabbered
away in the foreign tongue, they were so polite to one another you
couldn't tell who was senior to whom. But that all changed when
they were fiddling with the machinery in the sedan shed. Big Road
worked hard, and knew his way around the equipment, while
Second Master was always getting in the way. He mainly stood
around watching the other man work, with a critical look frozen
on his face.

Steward Bing let slip one day that the foreigner's pay was a
hundred fifty ounces of silver a month. Later on he denied that,
saying it wasn't nearly that much. We never did know just how
much he made. But the county magistrate's official salary was no
more than three hundred ounces a year, and my monthly spending allowance was only eighty-five cash. So how could a big-nosed
outsider take in that much for cleaning a bunch of machinery with
a grimy rag? I didn't believe it, and I figured that Steward Bing
had made it up out of spite.

A hundred and fifty ounces is a hell of a lot.

I don't know how much it would be worth today.

In Willow Township you could do just about anything you
wanted to on Eastern Avenue, no problem. But if I'd felt like
having some fun there, it would have cost me two months' spending money, not counting the tea. I barely made enough to stick a
foot in, let fly a fart, then make my exit.

So climbing onto the roof and letting my eyes wander was my only entertainment. That and sitting in Lucky Teahouse letting my ears pick up tidbits. Now? Now I let my mouth take over.

That's the fate of a slave.

I got along okay with Big Road. He used to kid me a lot about my ears. He found out my nickname from Second Master, and every time he saw me, he'd tug on his own ears as a greeting. I'd repay him by putting two fingers on the tip of my nose to kid him about the size of his. To practice his Chinese he'd spit out one word at a time, but no matter how hard I tried, I couldn't figure out what he was saying. It was worse than trying to understand bird talk. Foreigners' tongues and ours just aren't the same. They're different everywhere, bigger, bigger everywhere. And did he love taking a bath! The Cao family bathed in a tall wooden tub that wasn't nearly big enough for him. If he squeezed himself in, there'd be no room left for water. So Steward Bing had some people carry a big clay vat into his room, one that we'd used for stocking fish in the yard, carp that were at least half a foot in length. That tells you how big the vat was. It took fifteen buckets of water to fill the thing. No way to tell how much extra firewood was used to heat enough water for him to take a bath. Not even his hosts bathed as much as he did. As for us slaves and servants, we could go a whole winter without bathing, and in the summer we just ran down to the Black River when we had a few minutes and dove in. It was a mystery to us why keeping clean was such a big deal to Big Road. I guess that's just another difference between foreigners and us Chinese.

Big Road took a bath every single day. He'd close his eyes and squat down in that vat until only his head showed above the steaming surface of the water, as if it were detached from his body. I used to watch him through the skylight. At night it'd be just me and a bunch of cats in heat prowling the compound roofs. And when I got back I'd still see his head floating on top of the water. He'd be thinking his own thoughts, and he seemed to me to be a very lonely man.

Sometimes he and Second Master would play chess out on the veranda of their living quarters—foreign chess on a checkered board with upright chessmen, like wood-carved Buddhist idols.

They'd take the longest time between moves, and you could see that their thoughts started drifting as the game crept along. They didn't talk and they hardly moved.

They were having a hard time finding a place to set up their match factory. Second Master wanted to build it on the north bank of the Black River, beyond the village, but Elder Master wouldn't allow it. He said he'd try to accommodate them in one of the buildings on the family property. So they waited, cleaning the machinery until they got sick of it. What really bothered them was that a Japanese factory was up and running, producing a long, big-headed match with clearly delineated red and white tips. You could light them easily on the sole of your shoe or with your fingernail, and they were cheap. According to Elder Master, our enterprise was bound to lose money, and Second Master probably agreed with him. Which only made things worse. It began to get under Big Road's skin, too, and you can't blame either one of them. They'd spent all that time on the ocean, transporting a bunch of rusty metal, and all for what?

Second Master regularly went into his mother's meditation room.

Probably trying to win her over to his side on the marriage issue.

He'd emerge each and every time looking dejected. A waste of time.

The ceremony was planned for the sixth lunar month, when the summer would be at its height.

My favorite time for prowling the rooftop was on moonless nights when the wind was blowing. I may have been a slave, but when I stood on the rooftop I felt like the master of the house. I could see everything that was going on. I was stepping on their heads, every one of them. A spy sent down by Heaven. My eyes were his eyes. They couldn't get away from me if they sprouted wings!

Guess what Second Master was up to.

He was sprawled on his belly on the brick floor, surrounded by strange-looking bottles, mixing up a batch of stuff for the tips of his matches. Green and blue and red sparks flew, making him look like a blood-sucking devil!

For the first time ever, he scared me.

Over on the other side, Big Road was climbing dripping wet out of his vat.

He was covered with hair!

That corner of the compound was occupied by wild creatures.

I was scared.

How about you, are you scared?

Old Master sent me out to get a green bamboo snake, exactly nine inches long, he said. A snake handler gave me one in a tube of bamboo paper, which I took back to the estate for Old Master. Dates were stewing in his medicine cauldron, probably nine of them, I suspect. He laid the tube on top of the boiling mixture, and when the paper turned soft, the snake fell into the liquid. Old Master then clamped the lid on and held it down, happily swallowing a mouthful of saliva.

He said: This makes a great tonic for the liver.

Now are you scared?

Old Master asked me: What does Guanghan do every day?

I said: Polishes the machinery and reads books.

Then he asked: How about the barbarian, what does he do?

I said: He takes baths.

He asked: Isn't he afraid he'll wash the skin off?

Old Master was smirking as he lifted the lid and removed the snake with a pair of chopsticks. Then, after shaking the soupy liquid off, he started just behind the head and chomped his way to the tail, until only the head and backbone hung from his chopsticks.

While he was eating the snake's organs and skin, he told me to continue keeping an eye on the two men. The snake was delicious, he said. Too bad it was a male, since the nutritional value of females was so much higher. I told him we'd thrown back the females, since they were all under nine inches.

Old Master savored the taste for a long while.

He said: Sooner or later they'll grow to nine inches!

He added: We'll let them wait their turn!

The smell of snake clung to Old Master. His face turned red and
green lights sprang from his eyes, the same green as the bamboo
snake, a soft, tender green. His liver was probably a fuzzy green.
Even then I knew that if he kept on the way he was going, he'd nour-
ish himself right into the ground. But that didn't scare me. Whatever he felt like eating I went out and got for him. I was waiting for
him to eat the last edible thing out there. Waiting for those final
words of his. One day, sooner or later, he'd send me out for that.

He'd say: I'm constipated. Go get me a stick.

I'd ask him: How long?

What are you laughing at?

This is history.

This is modern history, understand?

Oh, no!

I think I'm going to be sick.

Bring me a spittoon!

And hurry!

March 6th

When word arrived that someone from the bride's family was coming, Second Master went into hiding. Instead of walking through
the main compound, he slipped out through the back gate by his
left-corner quarters, a hunting rifle slung over his shoulder. Big
Road was in the sedan shed, where he took apart a machine that
was half as tall as he, and just left it that way for a couple of days,
content to unhurriedly count ball bearings and whistle loudly
enough for people outside the gate to hear. When the guests en-

tered the compound, they looked around, trying to determine the source of that greasy smell, and wondering where in the world the sound was coming from.

The visitor was the bride's elder brother, a tall man of twenty-five or twenty-six, with a date-colored face and piercing eyes. He brought along a geomancer, who first went to the buildings in the left-hand corner to check the *fengshui*. Then, in the presence of Old Master and Elder Master, he drew some divination lots. Two things were determined. First, the setup of the wedding chamber was all wrong. Either a bridge would have to be built over the pond or a wall erected between the living room and the bedroom. If not, a clash in *fengshui* was inevitable. Second, the date was fixed for the sixth day of the sixth month, and couldn't be changed.

Second Master never showed his face.

Old Master asked me: Isn't he home yet?

I said: I don't know.

He said: Go get him.

The guest said: No need for that. We'll see him sooner or later.

Just before the guest left, Elder Master found a photograph for him. It was one I'd seen before, one he'd taken abroad. Second Master was lying on a lawn, propping his head in his hands and gazing at something. The guest was very interested in the machinery by the gate. When he climbed into his sedan chair, he asked me: This Master Guanghan, does he always go around with a worried look on his face?

I said: He's a good man. You'll see that when you meet him.

The guest's name was Zheng Yusong.

His sister's name was Zheng Yunan.

At the time, all I knew was that he was from Mulberry Township and belonged to a renowned and very rich family from north of the Green River. I had no idea he was also a leader in the secret Blue Kerchief Society. By the time I found that out, the Blue Kerchiefs had become an organization powerful enough to rock heaven and earth.

But I saw right away that he was someone to reckon with, that there was nothing ordinary about him. And I assumed that his sister would be a lot like him, certainly more than Second Master could handle. Boy, was I wrong. Everyone said she was a true beauty, and everyone was right. Nevertheless—how shall I put it? About all I can say is, luck was not with Second Master.

At the moment I can't recall what she looked like.

I don't dare even try.

I feel terrible.

There are some topics that are off-limits with old folks, if you want to avoid causing pain. You breathe, you talk, but you're out of the picture altogether. Whatever you once had, it's gone and won't ever come back.

He returned after dark, slipping into the corner compound through the back gate, looking sheepish and more than a little stupid. Big Road and I spotted him across the pond.

His fake queue hung from the barrel of his rifle.

He said: There are snakes all over the place. Everywhere you look.

Was that really worth making such a fuss over?

The mountains around Elm Township were known for that.

But he was so frightened, even his voice had changed, as if someone had tried to strangle him. We heard the sound of ripples on the pond, probably caused by a water snake. I couldn't see one, but the sound was unmistakable. I didn't say anything. I just held up my lantern to lead Big Road onto the veranda.

Big Road walked over to Second Master with his chessboard.

They sat down at a stone table in a little pavilion.

They spoke to each other in that foreign tongue.

I tried to guess what they were talking about.

Big Road was talking about the machinery.

The machines are in great shape!

Second Master was talking about snakes.

As if it were a snake's head, his finger rose and fell in the light from the lantern. Big Road fell silent. Second Master's mouth was like a black hole, and I imagined a pink snake slithering out of it.

Second Master said: Ears, get me something to eat.

When I returned, he was standing on the veranda. By then his whole body was a snake, and he was moving around the stone table for Big Road's benefit. Big Road had scrunched his neck down between his shoulders and was sucking in the cold air with a hissing sound.

Second Master was in the coils of a snake spirit.

Too bad I couldn't understand what he was saying.

He didn't ask a single question about the visitor.

What was he hiding from?

One day toward the end of the fifth month, Old Master Cao was tearing up some elm bark and dumping it into his cauldron when he suddenly gasped. I thought he'd been scalded by the boiling mixture and ran over to help.

He said: Air out the books!

I asked: Air out what books?

He said: The sixth day of the sixth month is the day we air out the books.

This was an age-old family tradition, one that had been carried on for years and years in Elm Township. It wasn't a big occasion, and certainly not a holiday the locals looked forward to, which meant that people tended to forget it. But now it was going to clash with Second Master's wedding day.

Elder Master had just returned from feeding the needy in the county seat, where he'd made a number of purchases for the impending wedding. He'd barely had time to catch his breath before getting back into his sedan chair for the trip to Mulberry Township to arrange for the bride's arrival on the wedding day. Showing no sign of displeasure, he opened the cap of his little wine gourd and poured some of its contents down his throat, then smiled confidently.

He said to his father: Don't you worry about a thing. Go ahead and air out your books. I'll make sure he gets married. There's no reason why the two events can't be carried out as planned.

He returned from Mulberry Township with a new wedding
date: the eighth day of the sixth month. He also brought back a
photograph of the bride, apparently taken during a family visit
to the provincial capital. It was given as a courtesy in exchange
for the photo of Second Master. Up till then, Old Master and his
wife had only heard from the matchmaker what the girl looked
like; now they could see for themselves. Old Master himself took
it to his wife's meditation room, where the sound of the wooden
clapper being struck stopped for a long while. It started up again
as soon as he emerged from the room, a tranquil sound—*tap tap
tap*—matched by the tranquil footsteps of Old Master down the
hallway. He and Elder Master stood on the steps of the main corridor, and I made a point of walking past them with a pot of tea,
hoping to catch a glimpse of the photograph from behind the Old
Master. But he'd already handed it to Elder Master.

Old Master said: See how big her feet are—they've tricked us!

Elder Master replied: The bigger the better. That'll give Guanghan
less to complain about.

Old Master said: Your mother thinks she has a frivolous look.
What do you think?

Elder Master replied: That's how these modern girls are.

Old Master sighed, but didn't say anything more. Deep down
he was satisfied. That I knew. Whenever I brought him something
unusual to eat, I could tell it had passed muster if he sighed softly
like that. It was as if someone had touched him under his arm, and
he'd pretended it hurt rather than tickled.

Second Master and Big Road were in the corner compound playing chess. I brought some tea, then stood around waiting. Before
long, Elder Master came in with the photograph.

Second Master was clearly nervous.

I was more nervous than he.

I couldn't tell you why.

He barely glanced at the photo before tossing it onto the stone
table. His face was pale, as if someone were trying to throttle him.
I felt bad for him. I assumed he must have been bowled over by

the photo of an intimidating, even ferocious, woman, more than he could handle.

Sensing an ominous change in the atmosphere, Big Road started to get to his feet, but was held back by Elder Master and Second Master, who said, Don't worry, it's all right. Big Road wanted to look at the photograph, but was too embarrassed to pick it up, so, in a joking manner, he cocked his big head to get a look at it.

She's very pretty, he said in Chinese.

He laughed, but no one laughed with him. Embarrassed, he got to his feet again, and this time no one stopped him. He turned and walked to his room, giving my ear a hard pinch as he passed. He meant it as a joke, but his big nose was so red I actually felt sorry for him.

Elder Master looked at Second Master.

Second Master stared at the chessmen.

Elder Master said: No matter what you say, she studied at the girls' school in the provincial capital, and her family's at least the equal of ours. So will you tell me exactly what's bothering you?

Second Master replied: I don't want to get married.

Elder Master said: This was settled a long time ago. She's nineteen now and has been waiting for you since she was fifteen! Besides, the wedding's only ten days off, so what you want doesn't make any difference. Are you dead-set on causing two families to lose face?

Second Master asked: What am I supposed to do? I told you I wanted out of the marriage a long time ago. But you wouldn't let me, so why ask me about it now, then show me something like that? I'll do whatever you say. I don't care whom I marry.

Elder Master said: What kind of talk is that? You need a reason to get out of a marriage. If you can't find something that makes her a bad match, then don't pull a long face on me. Father and Mother have doted on you, so why break their hearts?

Second Master replied: Why did they have to be like that? I'm not worth it.

He reached out to clear the table of the chessmen, but they kept
falling over, and when Elder Master tried to help him, he turned
on his heel and went to his room.

Elder Master sat on the veranda, alone with his thoughts, for a
long time.

I was hiding in a corner nearby, trying hard not to cry.

I couldn't figure out what was going on.

All I knew is that everyone was unhappy, and it rubbed off on
me. I desperately wanted to look at that photograph, and was already
starting to feel sorry for the girl in it. Though I'd never laid eyes on
her, I couldn't shake the feeling that there was something between
her and me. Just what that was, to this day I couldn't tell you.

For a sixteen-year-old, feeling sorry for others is all a sham.

The only person you really feel sorry for is yourself.

All of a sudden, I felt like someone with no family at all.

I couldn't make up my mind what to do that day, so I just stood
there in a daze. After a while, I swept the compound, cleared the
pond surface of floating weeds, then went out and swept the main
compound. After that, I went over to the kitchen to help chop firewood, and didn't stop until the stars came out. Exhausting myself
like that just increased my self-pity. But that turned into something
wonderful.

Should I try feeling sorry for myself now?

I still have no family, but my heart has grown old!

It's hard as a stone.

But I miss her now.

She turned to mud a long time ago.

Where could I go to find that mud?

Don't mind me.

An old man's tears aren't worth anything.

They seep out of a stone.

Even I can feel the cold when I touch them.

Real cold!

Youngster, talking about these events saddens me.

Good boy.

March 7th

We climbed out of bed before daybreak to begin airing out the books. The coral walkway of the main compound was covered by sixteen bamboo mats, leaving almost nowhere to step. The flower garden in the rear was flanked by long, rectangular buildings with high windows: a storage room for odds and ends on the left, another for books on the right. We tiptoed down the narrow space between the main compound and the book storage building, carried Old Master's precious books outside, and laid them on the bamboo mats. All those books, whatever they were, boxes and boxes of them bound in blue cloth and blue satin, gave off the sweet smell of mildewed paper and dirt. Old Master stood next to the gate to the garden, firing off one command after another: Not so fast, Slow down, What's your hurry? You'd have thought he was drunk, the way he was ordering people around.

When the sun made its appearance, sacred memorial tablets were set out, leaned against the corridor wall. The front row consisted of those for the great masters: Master Confucius, Master Yan, Master Zisi, Master Zeng, and Master Mencius. To the left were Master Min, Master Ran, Master Duanmu, Master Zhong, Master Bu, and Master You. To the right, another Master Ran, Master Zai, Master Yan, Master Zhuansun, and Master Zhu. Master Master Master Master! It wasn't until years later that I figured out who all those Masters were. I know it sounds disrespectful, but a bunch of us young servants gave our own names to those tablets: Master Old, Master Son, Master Grandson, Master Blind, Master Deaf,

Master Cripple, Master Peach, Master Plum, Master Eggplant . . .
more Masters than I could count. The reason for our blasphemy
was simple: those deities had nothing at all to do with us, and not
a single page in all those books spoke for us!

Even Old Mistress made an appearance.

She emerged from her meditation with an armful of incense,
which she placed in the censers in front of the tablets, one stick at
a time. As she kowtowed and paid her respects, I saw that her pale,
round face was all sweaty. Old Master performed the rites along
with her, muttering something the whole time, though I couldn't
tell you what he was saying, since it was all gibberish to me. The
mistress's pale plumpness was a stark contrast to the Master's dark
gauntness: one looked like an iron pestle, the other like bean curd,
and the hard, ugly one was ready to mash the soft, pretty one. We
honestly didn't know how Old Mistress could stay so young by
spending all day in her meditation room, or how Old Master could
be so listless all the time after taking nourishment the day long.
She courteously paid him her respects before floating back to her
meditation room like a fluffy cloud. Old Master breathed a sigh,
as if shedding a heavy burden; then there was no more muttering
as he stepped over to where the books lay and began flipping
through them.

For a long time he stood directly under the sun holding one
particular book.

He knelt down on a mat and began to chant, as if reading poetry.

He said: Wonderful! Truly wonderful!

There were tears in his eyes. Like a fish tossed onto a ridge in
the field, he seemed on the verge of breathing his last. We watched
him from the shade of the winding corridor, conscious of both the
seriousness and the humor of the situation. As the sun's rays grew
more and more blinding, the words on the pages of the books were
transformed into nests of black ants, forced by the blazing heat
toward the edges. But, unable to move, they died in clusters on the
thin, yellowing pages. Sometime before noon, Old Master got up
to go back to his room, walking on rubbery legs. If he'd stayed out
any longer, he'd have collapsed from heat stroke.

He said: Ears, give me a hand.

He added: Too much heat. I've had too much heat!

He was as red as a fried cake right out of the pan. Hot and soft. When he reached the doorway he turned and looked back, then pointed to the sky. He said: Pigeons. Careful of the pigeons. Watch out for their droppings!

The pigeons were far off in the distance. Close up, only hornets.

I picked up a long bamboo pole and sat on the compound steps, directly opposite the Confucius tablet. I could reach out and touch it with my pole. But I was too lazy to do that. In the hot midday sun I fell asleep.

Somebody was walking back and forth among the books.

Then whoever it was stopped and stood still.

I don't know how long I'd been in a daze, but I'd let go of the pole, and, sure enough, it was resting against a tablet; but Mencius, not Confucius. That snapped me awake. And the man standing under the eaves of the winding corridor flipping through a book was also shocked. It was Big Road. He flashed a smile, quietly put the book back, and, looking flustered, slipped inside.

Why was he acting so strange?

I knew of no restrictions against flipping through books.

I righted the Mencius tablet.

It was made of a piece of black wood that had seen better days.

Then I walked over to where Big Road had been standing and flipped through some books. I stood there for a long time. And while I was there, I sensed that my body was covered with seeing eyes. Everyone in the family was napping. Even the slaves, by then exhausted, were resting. There was no one to watch me. Finally, I thought I'd found the book Big Road had been looking at. It was one of a set, and looked pretty much like all the others. Even though I couldn't read very well, I could see that the set next to it was the *Confucian Analects*. Remembering its place among the others, I put the book back where it belonged and didn't touch it again, even as the sun went down behind the hills. When I saw a servant pick it up with its neighbors and lug them all back to the storage room, I picked up a bunch of books and followed him,

to watch him as he placed it on a wooden shelf. I fixed the exact
spot in my mind.

I promised myself I'd come back often.

You deserve to know what kind of book it was. Now Big Road must have just picked up the nearest book when he walked out of the corridor, and the only reason I can think of for why it happened to be that particular one was that there was some sort of divine intervention—Heaven was up to a little mischief. Old Master had so many books—a whole sea of them—that even he couldn't have known where this one was stored, all mixed in with the sacred classics.

It was an erotic picture book.

It showed 360 different positions.

This was an earthshaking event in my life. It was the first book I'd ever been drawn to. Before that, I'd thought that books and I were worlds apart, but after that, I knew that we slaves could find friends in books.

The men and women in the pictures were all my friends.

I envied them, envied them for a long time.

That day I couldn't stop thinking about Second Master's wedding.

In two more days, the world would be a different place. A naked woman would be flitting around the wedding chamber, which was just on the other side of the pond, where there was also a wisteria trellis and a man-made hill, plus the dragon wall the geomancer from Mulberry Township had ordered built between me and the wedding chamber. But I had the feeling I was everywhere at once, and that everything was right in the palm of my hand.

On the sixth night of the month I had one hell of a dream.

I was bouncing along on a horse galloping like the wind.

The horse was running without a saddle.

It was usually a horse.

Sometimes it was a mule.

It was our mutual friend. It carried all us sixteen-year-old boys, generation after generation of us, flying like the wind until we didn't need it anymore.

Now I dream mostly about centipedes.

The only sensation I have is a tightening of the scalp.

No more tingly arousals.

No more.

Another earthshaking discovery occurred, this time on the rooftop. I was walking along the ridge on my way to the compound wall to get a look at the Black River. When you observe the river from a rooftop, you can see stars reflected in the water. I saw a green light coming from Second Master's room. He was experimenting with phosphorus and sulfur again. I sidled over to the skylight, where the pungent smell of smoke hit me full in the face. The room was set up as a wedding chamber, with several thick-wicked oil lamps. Second Master was standing in the doorway between the bedroom and a sitting room, a line of ceramic bowls filled with chemicals arrayed on the floor in front of him. He was wearing a white satin nightshirt and holding a smoldering stick of incense in his hand.

A rope tied to the top of the doorway ended in a noose around his neck. What a shock that gave me, though I wasn't sure right away what was going on. His body drew the rope taut as he leaned forward to touch the bowls with his stick of incense, but he was about half a foot short. The rope was stretched to its limit; his pale face was hideous. His bent knees kept getting closer and closer to the floor. He was strangling himself! I was just about to cry out when the incense stick touched one of the bowls. Red flames shot in all directions. Second Master's purple face twitched. He was going to die!

Suddenly his knees straightened and he stood up, shaking, a look of insane pleasure on his face. My shout wouldn't come. He repeated the process, strangling himself till tears filled his eyes, a look of obstinacy and despair on his face. I had no idea what he was doing. All I knew was, these suicidal actions were not aimed at committing suicide. No, he was searching for something far more bizarre and frightening.

The last bowl took just about everything out of him, but it sizzled and gave off yellow sparks, and drew a gasp from him. Then he undid the rope and stood in the doorway, heaving but unable to vomit. So he just stood there gasping for air and letting his tears flow.

Was he laughing, or crying? I couldn't tell for sure. My legs were rubbery as I slid down the roof, and I damn near fell over the edge. All this happened on the night of the seventh day. The next day was when this demonic Second Master was supposed to get married.

Big Road was soaking in his bathtub.

Just like every other time, he was asleep, and his eyebrows were twitching.

I knew his head was filled with Chinese dirty pictures.

The bound-foot women in the pictures all had big asses.

Big Road heaved himself out of the water.

I slipped away to my own room and went to bed.

The next morning, the smell of sulfur hung in the air.

Second Master had dressed in his wedding clothes without a fuss.

He'd died and come back.

Nothing mattered anymore.

Spinach at every meal. That's what they give us—spinach. They say greens are good for us. We've all got one foot in the grave, so who cares about nutrition? We want variety! We don't have much time left, and we'd like to taste a bit of everything, whether we've had it before or not. Taste is more important to us than nutrition. But all they ever give us is stewed spinach! That's abnormal. Our old faces are getting greener every day, and those people couldn't be happier. When I'm outside, I don't dare even look at a tree. One sighting of anything green, and I lose my appetite. It's terrible.

I'd like to eat some interesting meat.

Frog, say, or snail.

That attitude of theirs, you'd think I was asking to eat human flesh.

And not just human flesh, but a woman.

I tell you, it's abnormal.

Abnormal—I like the sound of that word.

March 8th

The bridal palanquin hadn't arrived, and I'd already welcomed fifty-three sedan chairs. Tables piled high with food and drink had been set up in the sedan chair shed to entertain the sedan bearers, so there was no room for the chairs themselves, and everything, including the machinery, was moved outside, up against the wall.

Sedan chairs filled every inch of space in front of the gate tower at the compound entrance, as if thrown together to make a row of little buildings. And more were coming all the time. I had no choice but to park these out on the cobblestone street. I personally greeted every man and woman who stepped out of the sedan chairs, kneeling in the dirt in front of people I'd never seen before.

I was the official greeter for the Cao family, which meant I represented the family prestige, its *face*, if you know what I mean. I knew I mustn't bring shame to the master, and felt I had to show my gratitude for the honor he'd given me. I greeted the guests in a clear, high-pitched voice, looking rather splendid in my three-quarter boots, my queue adorned with a red ribbon. I hopped around bursting with pride.

Since there was nothing for Big Road to do, he wandered among the parked sedan chairs, fascinated by the fancy embroidery on the curtains and canopies. A bunch of kids followed him around as he stuck his head inside the chairs to inspect their interiors.

I signaled him to go back inside and join the party.

But he shook his head. He wasn't interested. Instead, he lifted a little boy onto his shoulders and continued his excursion among

the laughing, dirty-faced little boy's head floating above the white
felt and woven bamboo canopies of the sedan chairs.

The guests all smiled at me; the bearers did as I said. They went
where I told them to go. They peppered me with Elder Brother this
and Elder Brother that. We're putting you to a lot of trouble, Elder
Brother, or You're doing a terrific job, Elder Brother. I was the center of attention for the first time in my life, all because of the anticipated appearance of a woman from outside. Her arrival was
giving me the opportunity to show what a slave could do. I wished
she'd hurry up and get here, so I could get down on my knees in
the dirt, crawl up to her palanquin, and let her step regally down
on my back before touching the ground.

That was something I'd dreamed of doing.

Among the guests was the priest from the Acacia Township
Catholic church. He arrived on the back of his mule, accompanied
by five porters with shoulder poles carrying bamboo baskets to be
filled with hog bristles. He looked a lot like his mule: long legs, a
long face, a large nose—but not as large as Big Road's—and a
deeply wrinkled forehead. He handed me the reins and said in stiff
but proper Chinese: I submit my friend to your care. Make sure he
gets enough to eat.

I said: We have plenty of black beans.

Just then Big Road emerged from the space between a couple
of sedan chairs. The two men froze when they saw each other.

Where did this fellow come from? the priest asked.

He stopped speaking in Chinese, and Big Road answered him
so loudly his nose turned red from excitement. All the locals who
walked by stared wide-eyed at the two of them. They were both
French. Big Road had stumbled across one of his countrymen.

A black cloud floated over from Jade Mountain, and when it was
directly above Elm Township, it threw the people below into an
uproar. But it quickly broke up, and the panic ended. The toots and
drumbeats of a wedding procession drifted up from the mountain
road leading from Willow Township. My heart leaped into my
throat. The bright red canopy of the bridal palanquin drifted in and

out of view in the spaces opened up by the bobbing heads of men in the procession. I felt a wetness on my nose and ears, then on the backs of my hands. Steward Bing called out from the gate tower: Ears! Go get rain covers! Bring rain covers for the sedan chairs!

I saw Second Master, perched high on his horse, his head weaving back and forth behind the canopy of the bridal palanquin like a gigantic beetle.

Raindrops splattered noisily on the ground.

There went my chance for those feet to step on my body!

I ran to the storeroom out back. Banquet tables in the front and main compounds were being moved over to the winding corridor, creating mass confusion with people and furniture suddenly crammed into a tight space and assailed by the sounds of smashed crockery. As I passed through the main compound, I spotted the dark face of Old Master and the white face of his wife as they took cover on the veranda. I couldn't bear to look at them. Rain was beating down on the roof tiles, and the stone path was wet and slippery.

The storeroom was so dark I couldn't find the tung-oil rain cloths I was looking for. I raised a cloud of dust digging frantically through all the junk, while outside I heard explosions from blunderbusses, fired by the family's retainers. Too late! The woman from Mulberry Township was stepping down out of her palanquin.

Just then Big Road and several of the servants ran into the storeroom, also in search of rain cloths, which we found at last under a pile of bamboo curtains. Big Road looked at me and said: Lust! I knew he meant to say rust, because he was concerned that the machines would get rusty in all that water. As he turned to rush back outside, he got tangled up in the bamboo curtains and nearly fell. After starting out so well, everything was turning bad in a hurry. It pained me to see Big Road struggle to keep his balance. Another burst of gunfire, this time a bit ragged. The bride was entering the house! Carrying piles of rain cloths, we ran out to the main compound, arriving just as the bridal procession had crossed the front and main compounds and was about to enter the house. The rain was really coming down, and servants were trying their best to keep people dry with their umbrellas, but with little success. The bride's red wedding dress and headdress were soaked, as were Second Master's shoes and shoulders. Beads of water clung to his pale face. Puddles quickly formed, and since the bride's veil kept her from seeing the ground, servants steered her around them as best they could. Her docile, confused behavior made her look clumsy—quite wretched, actually. When her attendants stepped aside for her to enter the house, we slipped out through the veranda, water from the eaves splashing down on our heads and running down our backs. As a result, we missed the chance to watch the bride pay her respects to the ancestors' spirit tablets. But I was no longer interested in the activities, not remotely. I took all this interference with the rituals very personally, and was devastated by the loss of face I'd caused everyone. As far as I was concerned, it was all my fault. The image of the bride's hesitant steps on the ground was seared into my heart. Her red satin headdress, which should have been her crowning glory, was droopy and ugly. The poor thing. Heaven really let us down that time, damn it!

I was running around covering sedan chairs and anchoring the rain cloths with bricks. Those down below were harder to manage, and I recruited a bunch of local kids to scrounge up enough bricks to elevate them off the ground. The lush green Jade Mountain behind Elm Township was shrouded in white. Most of the ground water gathered in the foothills and spilled into the township's winding streets, which were transformed into a river, its murky yellow water carrying dead twigs and branches and small rocks along. One inadequately anchored sedan chair, with a white felt canopy, was swept away by the rushing water, like a little boat. I ran after it, shouting at the top of my lungs, Damn you, where the fuck do you think you're going?

I was soaked to the skin, and mud had seeped into my boots.

I saw Big Road over by the gate tower. He, too, looked like a chicken in the soup, as he climbed around the machine, feverishly trying to cover every inch of it with rain cloths. Second Master walked up, under the protection of an umbrella held by Steward Bing.

He said: Who told you people to move the machinery outside?

Steward Bing replied: We had to set up banquet tables in the sedan shed.

Second Master said: If there was no room in the shed, you could have moved the machinery into my quarters. Why didn't you do that?

Anger bordering on hysteria had turned his voice loud and shrill. People inside the compound and out turned to see what was going on. When he went over to help out, Big Road calmly said something to him, after which he lowered his head and anchored a corner of oil cloth with a piece of wood. Elder Master led a group of servants into the compound, where he sized up the situation, then coaxed and dragged Second Master back inside the house.

Big Road kept attending to his machines until he spotted me. He made a face, then grinned and grabbed his ear. I didn't laugh—I couldn't.

Eventually, I was all alone at the gate tower. Everyone else was enjoying the feast, including the sedan bearers, who were stuffing themselves with meaty dumplings and drinking rice wine on the veranda. I dined on the rainwater running down my face. As I kept a watch over the empty sedan chairs, my thoughts were on the favor the Master had bestowed upon me, on my devotion to the family that had taken me in, and on the disastrous events of the day, which I'd been unable to control. My nose began to ache. The bridal palanquin, which was parked beside the gate tower, was larger than all the others, and the rain cloth couldn't quite cover it. As I was adjusting the canopy, a fragrance—sweet and soft—reached out like a hand to caress me. Since there was no one around, I pulled back the curtain to look inside. I saw a semicircular indentation on the cushion, where someone had sat, and smudges on the felt carpet where shoes had rested. I reached out to feel both the cushion and the carpet. They were cool to the touch. I imagined how terrible she must have felt about getting wet when she stepped down from the bridal palanquin.

Someone called me to come and eat. I didn't go, said I wasn't hungry. And I wasn't, I was too upset. It may sound crazy, but I felt I had to punish myself by standing out in the rain and getting sopping wet. Only that might make me feel a little better.

I'll never forget my strange feelings that day.

Guests started leaving just before dark. By then the rain had let up some, and I could hear the roar of water rushing down the Black River. I bowed—low and long—to every chair as it left, not straightening up until I saw it turn into the street. Then I rushed back to take care of the next one. The gratuities they tossed landed in the mud in front of and behind me. I thanked them, of course, but I didn't pick the coins up out of the mud. In a high-pitched voice I said: Have a safe journey, sir! Have a safe journey, sir! I must have looked like a drowned rat, but I wanted them to see just who had raised me. I may have been a slave, but I had my dignity! When the bride's elder brother climbed into his sedan chair, he gave me a long look before tossing down not a few coins, but a tiny silver ingot. Gritting my teeth, I forced myself not to pick it up. When one of the bearers thought no one was looking, he scooped it out of the mud for himself. Without so much as blinking, I let my mouth show what I was made of. I said: Have a safe journey, sir. May you ride on the clouds! As his chair was whisked through the gate, the bride's brother left behind a dazzling comment:

He said: That took balls.

I brought the mule over for the old priest, who mounted it with ease. It was still raining. The mule was blanketed with a rain cloth, while the priest carried an umbrella. The five porters fell in behind him with their heavy loads of hog bristles. Big Road walked with him a short ways, talking very seriously. Elder Master ran up and called out to the old priest: Keep that load of goods for me. You'll get a fair price. I'll come over in a few days to examine it.

The departing priest said he understood.

Big Road tried to drag me back to the compound to get something to eat, but I refused. Then he held his umbrella out to me. I wouldn't take it. His eyes widened, like those of an owl. A few minutes later, he ran up to me with some meaty buns.

Five or six small sedan chairs still hadn't left.

Their owners were standing on the steps of the gate tower.

When I saw the buns in Big Road's hands, I didn't know what to do, and burst into tears. I cried so hard I could barely breathe.

Someone said: That boy's been on the move all day long. He must be exhausted.

All the time I was crying, I was thinking only about that poor bride.

She was so tall, and looked so miserable in that sopping head-dress.

And I was such an idiot, I couldn't do a thing to help her.

You see, it was the eighth day of the sixth lunar month. She was somebody else's wife now, but I was more concerned about her than anyone. There's nothing wrong in a man falling in love with a beautiful woman at first sight. But what was wrong with me? I hadn't even had a glimpse of her face, and already I pictured her as a woman who was as dazzling as her elder brother. In my mind, she was someone with a good heart.

I fell in love with her before anyone else did!

At least before anyone I knew.

That day I had no idea what I was crying for.

But now I know. I was crying over suffering that never ends.

My tears came before anyone else's, too.

What good does it do to cry over the decrees of fate?

Have a safe journey!

Hear that? Those are the words of a dog-slave.

Safety plays no role anywhere on this earth.

Seeking out safety only brings disaster.

And that goes especially for anyone who tries to make things hard on himself.

Not only do people make things hard on themselves.

They even go looking for death.

Thunder rumbled that night. It rained off and on and lightning flashed in the sky, lighting up my little room. My furnishings consisted of a bamboo cot and a bamboo stool, plus two trunks under the window. They held my winter clothing and all my personal belongings. Drenched by the rain, I was burning up with brain-numbing fever. And when the flash of lightning entered my cold little room, there was a void in my heart, a powerful loneliness.

I heard footsteps out on the veranda, a shuffling that moved back and forth outside my door. It was the sound a skittish horse makes when it paces the stable and no one can force it to stop. For the longest time I couldn't be sure it was Second Master. The fever was affecting my mind. I thought it might be me pacing out there, looking for a mother and father I'd never known. I was walking in some distant place I didn't recognize. And I fell asleep walking.

When I woke up, my mouth was full of fever blisters.

Then I was reminded of the bridal chamber on the other side of the pond. I knew I hadn't moved from the bed, and that it was somebody else who'd spent half the night walking. Second Master's dilemma began that very first night. Before the sun was up, I sprawled up against the window and looked out that way. I couldn't see a thing—the veranda that followed the contour of the pond was deserted—except for red candlelight behind the wisteria trellis that flickered lazily. It had stayed lit all night long, and was as red now as it had been last night. I wondered how many candles had been lit. How horrible it must have been to stare at one candle after another as it burned down, then use it to light a fresh one. The sun came out, and the candle stayed lit, although its light turned white and virtually disappeared. The sound of Old Mistress beating her wooden clapper came from far off. Big Road was whistling as he walked beneath my window, opened the gate in the corner compound, and took the path alongside the main compound on his way to the front gate. He took a stroll out beyond town every day, a thick foreign cigarette dangling from his lips. He was always looking right and left, as if on the lookout for something new.

I was sick, but that didn't keep me from getting out of bed to do what was expected of me. The steward had already told me that the new bride had brought her own maid with her, so I was no longer responsible for chores in Second Master's quarters. Besides taking care of the corner compound, I was to do the bidding of the foreigner. To everyone else, this was considered a tough assignment, but not to me. Except for the fact that I couldn't understand a word he said, and felt a little awkward reporting his activities to the Old Master, it was no trouble at all. I was so sick that day I wobbled when I walked. Since Big Road was late coming home, I went into town to look for him, and found him on the bank of the Black River net-fishing with a bunch of farmers. The river had risen until its yellow water reached the top of the banks. I could see foot-long fish flopping in the water. That always happened when the river flooded, to the delight even of the folks in Elm Township, let alone this big-nosed alien. His pant legs were rolled up, his jacket was spotted with mud, and he was jumping around shouting like a little boy.

Splish! he called out.

What he meant was, fish.

Eventually, he headed over to the corner compound carrying two live fish, with me right behind him carrying a live fish of my own in one hand and his shoes in the other. Those big pale feet of his slapped noisily on the paving stones. We had no idea what was waiting for us. At first we were startled; then we just stood there dumbstruck.

It was as if someone had plunged a knife straight into my heart.

But it didn't hurt. I don't know if the same could be said for the foreigner, but he had a pained look on his face, and all he could do was gurgle. One of his fish fell to the ground, where it flopped around, bouncing waist-high at least once, until it was covered with dirt.

Neither of us paid the slightest attention to it.

I didn't hurt anywhere, but every drop of energy simply drained from my body.

She was gorgeous!

Who? you ask.

Who do you think?

We'd damn near run smack into Young Mistress there in the corner compound. No, not Young Mistress, a goddess. We encountered a goddess there in the corner compound. She was waiting for us. She must have heard the sound of his footsteps, and moved over to the steps beside the gate. But we sure weren't ready for her. When we saw that gorgeous woman standing there smiling at us, we didn't know what to do. I can't say what was running through Big Road's mind, but mine pretty much shut down. How could she smile like that? With all the bad things that had happened since her arrival, how could she still manage a smile? And such a pretty smile at that.

That's what made Zheng Yunan different from other people.

In my life I've never seen another woman like her.

She said: My, what big fish!

Her teeth were sparkling white. The fish were as big as little babies, and I assumed she'd be frightened by them. But she bent down, picked up the one flopping around on the ground, and, following our lead, tossed it into the pond.

She laughed gloriously!

I can't hear laughter like that anymore. I'm not deaf, and I'm not intimidated by young people. They often have little parties here at the nursing home, where they invite nice little boys and girls over. They laugh, of course. The laughter of those sweet little girls is like the tinkling of bells. But it means nothing to me. That's because I can't hear joyous laughter like that anymore. I'm not saying you youngsters don't know how to laugh. The world is filled with happy people. What I'm saying is, I can no longer hear the sort of laughter that lifts me off the ground and holds me up in the air.

That's just me.

I'm not as light and carefree as I was at sixteen.

She said: My, what big fish!

And I was floating on a cloud.

The big-nosed fellow? you ask.

His soul took flight, and wherever it went, it never returned to France.

That was his fate.

March 9th

Old Master summoned me to ask about goings-on in the corner compound. What had I seen, what had I heard, had I discovered anything strange or incomprehensible? I said I hadn't seen anything, that the red candle of joy had stayed lit the whole night in the bridal chamber, and that I hadn't heard anything, except for the footsteps of someone walking back and forth on the veranda. I said it might have been Second Master. That was all there was to report.

Old Master asked: Why was Second Master out walking?

What I felt like saying was, How should I know?

What I said was, Maybe he was afraid.

Old Master asked me what he could be afraid of.

I said: I don't know.

Troubled by the news, Old Master stirred the mix in his medicine cauldron. I detected the smell of artemesia, faintly. But I knew that lizards give off a similar odor when they're cooking. He sighed, sucked on his chopsticks, then licked his lips loudly.

He's worthless! he sighed.

I nearly blurted out how Second Master had almost strangled himself, but clenched my teeth and held it back. I was burning up and could barely open my eyes. Old Master asked me what was wrong.

He said my face was so red it looked like a monkey's ass.

I reached up and rubbed that ass. It burned my hand.

Old Master asked: Do you have a headache?

I said it was nothing, then turned and went outside, where I stumbled into my little room, fetched a broom, and began sweeping the compound. Second Master was on his way out with a wrench, his face as white as a sheet, dark rings around his eyes. The eyes themselves were somewhat glazed, but not as badly as when he'd tried to strangle himself. When he saw me, he seemed calm and steady.

He asked: What's wrong with you?

Nothing, I said.

He asked: Do you have a headache?

I said: No, my head's fine.

He continued on his way with the wrench, and I went back to my sweeping, starting with the area in front of my and Big Road's quarters. I felt like I was sweeping cotton, all fluffy and wadded up. When I reached the pond, I looked over at the wisteria trellis, and there stood my goddess, accompanied by her short maidservant. Together they walked up to the pond and waved to me. I didn't know why they looked so worried, and I couldn't make sense out of anything they said.

Then I passed out.

I slept for two days straight, drifting in and out of consciousness. Lots of people came to my little room. I could hear their voices coming from far away, even though I couldn't make out who was speaking. Afterward, I learned that Young Mistress had come by once and left a plate of pear slices on one of my trunks, then stood there for a few minutes before leaving. I wasn't aware of it at all. If I'd known she'd brought the pears over, I wouldn't have eaten a single slice. I'd have put them away, then taken them out to look at when no one was around. That's how I would do things later on.

During those two days, events must have occurred in the corner compound without my knowledge. On my first venture outside after falling ill, I saw Big Road and Second Master playing chess on the veranda. Another uncombed head was bent over the chessboard; it was the intrigued young bride. They all looked up at the same time.

Young Mistress smiled.

Then Big Road smiled.

Second Master was the last to smile, and the first to stop smiling. Even that was a rarity, since I almost never saw him smile. He looked pretty good that day, rather healthy.

Young Mistress's little maid was smiling, just like the others.

I didn't know what was going on. I reached up to feel my face and head, then looked down at my clothes. I didn't see what was so funny. I was embarrassed; their smiles reminded me that I was, after all, a slave. Big Road waved me over, but I was having none of that. I slinked back to my little room.

Not until I saw Steward Bing did I learn that I'd soiled myself in my sleep. My blood ran cold when I heard that. He said: I'm the one who told them to clean your ass. You little imp, you grew into a man in the blink of an eye! I felt as if I'd fallen into a well.

Young Mistress's personal maidservant was called Wuling—Five Bells.

She and I became friends after a while, and there wasn't anything we didn't talk about. She said she was the one who'd washed my clothes for me. Did they stink? I asked her. She said they didn't, and that my inner heat level was so high that my feces were white. She was a good girl, just not terribly bright, and if I didn't change the subject, she'd talk about nothing but that embarrassing incident that had me wanting to jump down a well.

She also told me some stuff about the bridal chamber.

I started by mentioning the wedding itself, the red candles, the thunder and lightning and the footsteps outside my door. Then she told me things. She said her mistress liked to wear pastel greens, and that red made her uncomfortable. On and on she prattled, until she finally got around to the stuff I wanted to hear about.

Second Master couldn't have imagined what kind of woman Young Mistress was, and when he removed her headdress, he turned red as a beet. They engaged in polite small talk until they were both sleepy and decided to go to bed. Sweat beaded on his forehead and his arms trembled while he watched her undress. When she asked him what was wrong, he said, Nothing. She suggested that he go outside for some fresh air, since it was so stuffy in the room. And that's what he did. But when he didn't come back, she went to bed alone and slept like a baby.

Wuling related all this matter-of-factly, and I wasn't inclined to believe it. But it's what she said, and she wasn't bright enough to shine at the art of lying. So I had to take what she said at face value. But I also worried that there were things she simply didn't understand. Then again, the same could be said about me. All I knew I'd seen in those Spring Palace pictures, plus what I'd seen of animals I'd taken care of, big and small, belonging to the Cao family.

Chickens.

Pigs.

And horses.

The horses were the most beautiful.

Except for people.

I asked Wuling: Have they slept together?

She said: Yes.

I asked: How?

She said: Head to head.

I asked: What did they do?

They talked, she replied. I couldn't hear much in the next room, but the mistress loves to laugh, and she doesn't let anything bother her. Your Second Master is an odd bird. He won't say anything unless you ask him a question. So when the mistress fell asleep, he rolled over with a sigh and suffered his way through the rest of the night. I got up to give him some water, and he chewed me out for meddling, then glared at me with those dead eyes of his. He'd had a chip on his shoulder since the day he was married, and I disliked him from the first. Our mistress was unlucky when she married him. She's the finest person you'll find anywhere under the sun!

You hear that? Another wretched slave!

Wuling was so short she appeared to be about twelve or thirteen. She had a dark complexion and eyes filled with kindness. She didn't look like a fussy person. The truth is, she was a few years older than me, and even though she clammed up around strangers, once she knew you, it was impossible to get her to shut up. She called me Elder Brother—Elder Brother Ears. I saw hope in her eyes whenever she looked at me, almost as if she wanted me to soil myself again so she could wash my clothes as a way to show how much she cared for me.

But to me she was just a tool.

One I could use to get closer to Young Mistress.

Like, for example, you want to see what's going on behind the curtain, but your arm's not long enough, so you find a stick, and use it to pick up a corner. Then when you've seen enough, you throw the stick away or you put it somewhere you can get to easily the next time you feel like looking. Wuling was my stick. But she didn't realize it. The way she saw it, I was a good listener. She might even have thought I was a bucket she could just keep pouring stuff into. Either way, I didn't care. She was my stick, and there was no way I could stop her from getting a little carried away. As long as she kept talking, she'd remain under my control.

Now I'm the stick in your hand.

And you, you're probably my bucket.

You have to listen to me.

But have you given any thought to one thing?

What if I soil myself?

The past is being excreted.

The exhalations of an old mouth stink up the sky.

It's not modesty.

If you can put up with it, that's fine with me.

I can't stand my own odors.

But I'm not happy unless I'm spitting stuff out.

Whose idea was it for me to become a respected senior citizen?

One foggy morning, I was sweeping the area outside the corner compound gate when Wuling came out carrying a little box of food. One look at her face, and I knew there was something she wanted to tell me. I took a look around the area to put her mind at ease.

She said: Elder Brother Ears, I heard it.

I asked: What did you hear?

She said: I heard them together.

I asked: What did you hear when they were together?

My mistress screamed, she said.

She'd scream if a bedbug bit her, I said. So what?

She said: Second Master screamed too.

Little scaredy-cats scream too, I argued.

She mumbled something as her face turned red as a lantern.

I said: Don't breathe a word of this to anybody.

She didn't quite get my drift.

So I said: If you go blabbing this, I'll strangle you!

I was smiling the whole time.

And her face was ghostly white.

Later events would prove that Wuling's ears hadn't betrayed her. Steward Bing's wife, Mrs. Bing, walked out of Second Master's quarters carrying a black lacquer tray with a piece of white silk. She took it into Old Master's study, then to the meditation room. Soon afterward, she reemerged, empty-handed, and the servants began spreading the word.

They said: Finally, there were a few drops of red!

The way they said it mocked Second Master.

The piece of silk stayed in the meditation room. At the time, the Old Mistress was fasting, existing only on well water drawn at midnight. The person who brought her the water saw the piece of white silk hanging from the hand of the Guanyin Bodhisattva and noticed a red stain in the shape of a rose. Everyone said the old lady was protecting her son so he could grow into a man worthy of the name. And everyone said that without the old lady's protection the bride would have nothing to do in the Cao home.

See how vicious the tongues of servants can be!

I told Steward Bing there were rats in the book storage, and that we should put out some poison. He told me not to worry about it. But a few days later I went back to him and said: There are some really big rats in there, and they scurry around anytime somebody sets foot in the door. He gave me the key and some poison, and said: Wash your hands after you put this out, and don't touch your mouth.

That's where I found that book, in the storage room.
I was the biggest rat in there.
There were a few drops of red!
After thinking about that comment, I settled upon a position.
Second Master didn't drink his mother's milk any longer.
Second Master didn't try to hang himself anymore.
Second Master had managed to take care of business.
I wondered, Is that how Second Master did it?
Or did he do it this way?
The first time, I was thinking of a cart with two handles.
And the second, I was thinking of a horse.
Those pictures burned themselves into my eyes like hot peppers.
Young fellow, I'm a dirty old man.
Everything I've said so far is proof.
And you?
What kind of person are you?

March 10th

If you've seen blue eyes, then you know what those blue eyeballs looked like. But have you ever seen blue eyes just a few inches away from you? You've probably seen someone sleep with his eyes open, but I'll bet you've never seen anyone with blue eyes sleep with his eyes open. I've seen them all. Big Road slept with his eyes open. Not completely, just halfway, but it was enough to scare the hell out of me. I watched him several times, until my curiosity got the better of me, and I went up to get a closer look, wondering what I'd find in there.

Old folks say you can see the image of someone a person likes in his eyes, and you can't remove it, not even if you scrape it off. Gouging out the eyes is the only way. I had no interest in gouging out Big Road's eyes, but I wanted to see whom I'd find in there. I looked and I looked, but all I ever saw were some squiggly designs on his eyeballs, like you see on clams or mussels.

What I expected to see was the image of Young Mistress! Say what you like, but there was something wrong with Big Road's eyes, and that was because he spent too much time looking at Young Mistress.

Others couldn't tell, but I could, since my eyes and his were guilty of the same thing. His were blue, like deep pools that longed to draw Young Mistress into them.

When Big Road was playing chess with Second Master, Young Mistress sat between them. Wuling and I sat on the lawn near the veranda, talking. I'd chosen a spot where I could gaze at Young Mistress's face. By simply raising my eyes a little, I could see the top of her head as she bent over the chessboard. Beneath that were her straight nose and red mouth. Whenever those red lips parted, the tiny pearls that were her teeth showed. Wuling was saying something, but I wasn't sure what. All I knew was that my neck, my wrists, and my chest prickled and ached. I was caught up in a daydream in which those teeth were biting me all over.

Young Mistress was staring down at the chessmen.

Her husband was staring down at the chessmen.

And Big Road?

Naturally, he was staring too.

But I knew where his gaze had wandered.

His eyes were on the back of her hand.

And on her pale, long neck, which rose above her collar.

And on the hair at her temple.

And on her earlobes.

And on the fine hairs of her upper lip.

And on her chin.

And on her bodice, where her breasts jutted out.

His eyes were undressing her.

He couldn't fool me.

He wanted to gobble her up!

Your move, Second Master said.

Big Road buried his face in his hands and moaned softly, as if he'd been backed into a corner. But when he took his hands away, he smiled like a little lamb. No idea why. Normally he had a booming laugh, but in the presence of Young Mistress he was more reserved about when and how he laughed, seemingly afraid to startle her. I knew it was all an act. Because when he looked at her out of the corner of his eye, he had the hungry look of a wolf!

They left the veranda to go for a stroll.

Wuling had her back to them.

She asked me: What are you looking at?

I told her I wasn't looking at anything.

The truth is, I was looking at Young Mistress's back. So was Big Road. His gaze traveled from the bun at the back of her head all the way down to her large feet. He couldn't fool me. He kept up a conversation with Second Master, in their foreign tongue, but his eyes were fixed on Young Mistress like suction cups. She was wearing a pastel green dress, tapered at the waist, and billowing out below, as if encircled by a cloud.

Wuling asked me: What are you staring so greedily at?

I said it was nothing, just a little grasshopper.

Wuling got down on all fours to search in the grass, her little rump sticking up in the air. It didn't do a thing for me. I looked over the horizontal line of her back to the pond, where Young Mistress was leaning on Second Master while she took off one of her satin shoes to remove a pebble, which she tossed away. That wanton act floored me.

Her foot was encased in a white cotton stocking.

She swayed slightly as she put her shoe back on. Big Road nearly reached out to steady her, but drew his hand back at the last minute. Wuling was still looking for that grasshopper, the two little half-moons of her rear end sticking up in front of me. Like an idiot, I reached out and spanked her, to her shock and amazement.

She was blushing bright red when she turned to look at me; her nose was dotted with perspiration.

She said: What's wrong with you?

Your mistress took off her shoe in front of a man! I answered.

She said: We Zhengs worry less about such things than you Caos do.

I said: If you don't worry so much about things like that, how about taking off your pants for me? Wuling really was a dim light. She actually sat there thinking it over before she realized it was a joke, then spat at me and ran off.

That's how things were back then. A woman's foot was so cherished that taking off her shoe was about the same as taking off her pants. I'd never seen anyone as casual about such things as Young Mistress. Thinking back on it later, I decided it wasn't her fault. She'd been educated in a girls' school, had studied foreign ways, was good at the classics and arithmetic, could write poetry, even knew something about foreign languages and could tell you where different countries were located. The problem was, a woman like that was all wrong for Second Master. What difference did it make if she took off her shoe in front of another man? And what difference did it make if she laughed openly whenever she felt like it?

I'm relating this incident not to show that she was ill-mannered, but so you'll know that in my eyes a woman's foot was precious. Even encased in a stocking, it was still a woman's foot, and not just anybody's foot, but hers! Seeing that foot was about the same as having a view of her private parts. I loved her foot, even though it was sort of big, just as I loved the sound of her laughter. Women weren't supposed to laugh out loud. That could only bring trouble, since people would call them loose. But loose or not, I loved the sound. Second Master loved it too, I suppose. Big Road did, that I know. Because every time she laughed, his eyes lit up, as if every fiber of his body were quivering joyously. I quivered too. I felt as if I were being lifted into the air, higher and higher, into some demonic realm!

It wasn't often I saw one of her feet.

And it wasn't often I heard her laugh.

Steward Bing's wife once brought word to Second Master Guanghan from his mother that she wished that Young Mistress wouldn't laugh so loud while she was meditating. Well, when Young Mistress learned of her mother-in-law's wishes, she continued to laugh, but managed to do so without making a sound.

Young Mistress was a remarkably obliging person.

Her noiseless laughter was, if anything, even more memorable.

She said to me: Ears, don't you get tired running around doing chores all day long? Why not go inside and rest a while? Let other people do some of your chores, instead of wearing yourself out like this. Get some rest.

I said: That would be idleness. That's how it is with a slave.

You're so young, she said, yet you work so hard.

I'm not as young as you think, I protested. I'm sixteen. The family's affairs are my affairs. The more I do for them, the better. If I don't do something, I don't feel right.

She said: Then I'll let you do something for me. Go to my quarters. Have Wuling give you some betel nuts she keeps in her little box. Hold them in your mouth and suck on them. They'll cool you down. But when you're sucking on betel nuts you mustn't do anything else. Just lie down and don't get up until they're all gone. Do you hear me?

She was smiling the whole time, gently, the corners of her mouth and eyes slightly arched. But there was no sound, just a quiet smile. I could barely endure her concern for me, but I did as she said. As I lay on my cot, I stared at a cobweb in the corner and cried. The betel nuts lay on my tongue, like tiny living objects. I didn't move, but they skittered around on their own.

Sucking on those betel nuts was like sucking on Young Mistress's toes.

I curled my tongue back so they'd melt.

The power of feet.

What does a woman's foot mean these days? Look at the girl in that calendar up there. Take away those two little pieces of cloth

covering her tits and the one around her crotch, and she won't be   63
wearing a thing. See how puffy her feet are, and those thick toe-
nails—those aren't feet, they're hooves, a mare's hooves. Take those
strips of cloth off her—if she isn't a mare waiting to be mounted, I
don't know what is.

The Senior Citizens Benefits Foundation sent those calendars
over. No one knows what those people had in mind. Maybe they
think we're not old enough or we're too old, and they either want to
seduce us or shame us by hanging some buck naked girl's picture
up there. However you look at it, it's demeaning. If they're worried
that we're not dying off fast enough, they'd do better to send us some
living bare-assed girls. And if they're worried that we're getting
bored with life, they should swap these calendars for some fly-
swatters. I'd rather swat flies than waste a lot of gray matter on
those girls. We've already done all the things we were supposed to
do, so the sooner these giggly little sluts get lost, the better. They
should be out looking for someone who can get their juices flowing.
We sure can't do it. Bo-ring! No matter how good they look, they
mean nothing to us, sort of like horsemeat or rabbit.

I'm not saying they're not attractive, that's not it.

They're attractive, all right; just look at those legs.

What I'm saying is, there are two kinds of people who should
never look at calendars like that. The very old and the very young.
They need wholesome stuff. The Senior Citizens Benefits Foundation is going about it all wrong, and they're doing more harm than
good. They should give us other things to look at. You can get calendars with porcelain vases, or fish, even monkeys. But you see
what they're doing to us?

They bring girls to people who are dying.

That isn't what I want.

Besides, I have no use for them.

In my mind there's a single foot.

That's enough for me.

My heart is weary. Whenever it seems to want to stop beating,
that foot comes over and steps on it, and really gets it pumping
again. I'm not about to die anytime soon!

Yunan!
Bring your foot over here!
Step here!
Now here!
And here!
Young fellow.
What was I saying just now?
A foot?
Whose foot?

March 11th

After I'd gotten over that attack of fever, I couldn't get up the cour-age to climb onto the roof for a long time. My legs were too rub-bery. The rooftops on the Cao family buildings were very high, and peaked at a steep angle, and I dreaded to think what might hap-pen if I fell off. But while I was afraid to actually climb onto the roof, mentally I was up there as soon as night fell, desperate to know what went on in those rooms. I wanted to watch, watch all the people, see what was going on. To get a good look at the antics of all those men and women, young and old, after the lamps were lit. And I wanted to hear the sounds, all those strange, jumbled noises.

Not having the courage to climb up there made me lonesome.

Eventually my legs grew steadier and my health improved. So one moonless night I climbed up over the wall, like a lizard. I didn't dare venture to where I really wanted to go—Second Master's room. Instead I stepped from the left-corner compound wall over

Then I turned and went back, stopping at every place where there was a lit lantern and a skylight. I didn't want to miss a spot anywhere in the Cao estate.

Like a tomcat, I went where I wanted to go, saw what I wanted to see.

And what did I want to see?

I went over to the female servants' quarters. Their lights were off, but because it was so hot, they'd left the skylight open. I heard their snores, I heard them licking their lips, and I heard them relieving themselves in an earthenware chamber pot.

Hot, sweaty air hit me square in the face.

My nose felt like it was stuck up inside a woman's armpit.

In the night watchman's shack, some of the servants were shooting dice, but the lantern wick was turned down so low I couldn't make out any of the faces. They were afraid Steward Bing might catch them gambling, so instead of cash, they used bullets for chips. The brass casings on the brick floor glimmered in the faint light, like fireflies. The men huddled together over the rolling dice to keep the sound down. I'd known their secret for a long time, but I never could make up my mind whether I should report them or not. And if so, when?

They'd never done anything to me.

They knew I was old man Cao's spy.

If I didn't report them, I'd be letting Master Cao down somehow. But what I didn't see I didn't have to worry about, so I quickly crawled past above their heads.

Steward Bing was working on his abacus.

His wife was wrapping her bound feet with a cloth.

The old couple didn't have anything else to do.

In the kitchen area, the miller was turning a millstone, making bean curd. Every time he made a complete revolution, he spat into the center hole and gnashed his teeth in anger, though I didn't know where that anger was directed. Did he think they worked him too hard? Paid him too little?

I watched him for quite a while.

I was waiting for him to climb up and piss into the millstone hole.

But all he did was spit.

I had no interest in jumping down and nabbing him.

Let him spit!

I climbed onto the wall of the right-hand compound. It was bigger than the left-hand compound, but had no pond or man-made hill. All it had were a few dozen pomegranate trees that filled the compound with lush greenery. Elder Master Guangman had a wife and a concubine, who, combined, had presented him with seven daughters but no sons. The women and girls in that family were seldom seen outside the compound, since they had their own cook and their own servants. The gate between the main compound and the right-hand compound was always locked, because the people there annoyed Old Master. In order for Guangman to come to the main compound to take care of things, he had to exit his compound through the rear gate, go down public streets, and reenter the family property through the gate tower. We were forced to do the same thing, in reverse, if we had something to say to him. And the minute we walked through his gate, we'd invariably see his obviously pregnant wife and equally pregnant concubine. His concubine was a farmer's daughter, and when she called to her daughters, she seldom called them by name; it would be: Little Cunt this and Little Cunt that. His wife's father, on the other hand, had been an official, a subprefect who'd been removed from his post. But that hadn't led to any greater refinement in her speech. I'd be in the main compound, and I'd hear her on the other side of the wall, laughing and saying Cunt this and Cunt that; she and her husband's concubine would be having a grand old time. According to the servants, the one man and two women in this compound often slept in the same bed, but most of the time it would be just the two women, since Elder Master would be pacing the floor in his study, just thinking, or looking over the books, or counting money. Elder Master Guangman was very attentive to family business, and didn't seem concerned over the parade of daughters, possibly assuming that sooner or later a son would emerge, if not from the belly of his wife, then from that of his concubine. As long as those two bellies kept jutting out, there was hope. All he had to do during this time was find the time to keep their bellies filled.

But finding the time was not easy.

The lamp in his study was turned down, but I heard the sound of money being counted—gold coins jangling against one another. He was in the room counting, I was on the roof doing the same. I counted up to a thousand, and he was still going strong. So I counted to a thousand again, and that was as far as I could go. I could imagine a stack of gold coins all the way to the ceiling, about to spill out through the skylight. No, there couldn't have been that much money down there. He was probably counting it over and over because he liked the sound it made. He could keep it up till dawn.

His wife and concubine were in the bedroom giggling.

Giggling like a couple of little girls.

Were they tickling each other?

Their husband's hands had grown onto their hands.

Giggling.

The coins kept jangling against one another.

Having no son was retribution against Elder Master.

Money was his son.

Old Master Cao's room was dark too, except for rays of light from the brazier in the corner. The stench of a toad cooking in the pot rose to the ceiling.

The meditation room was lit up, not by a lantern, but by a thin candle. The weak light fell on a room full of Buddhist icons, on the table and on all four walls—clay, brass, and wood, the tallest of them life-sized. I couldn't see Old Mistress, but I could hear her beating the wooden clapper with a steady, conscientious rhythm.

She hadn't eaten a thing for days.

But she'd live.

I crawled back to the left-hand compound, quiet as a cat, and happy as could be. I knew that Big Road would be in his bathtub, so I made my way over to take a look at his head floating on top of the water. See if you can guess what I saw. Go ahead, try. A foreigner who'd come all the way to China to help a Chinese fellow named Cao set up a little match factory. No factory yet, and he was already finding life unbearable.

Big Road was standing in his tub, the water covering his thighs. He was facing the wall, his rear end opposite a chair he'd moved up next to the tub. The wick of a tin lantern on the chair cast his shadow on the wall.

He was doing what bachelors do a lot.

I watched him, from start to finish.

I couldn't see his blue eyes, so there was no way to tell whose image showed in his eyeballs. Sprawled there on the bricks around the skylight, I was worried about sliding off the roof. Then I worried about Big Road, afraid he might tip the tub over, dumping both him and the water unceremoniously to the floor.

Second Master's room was dark and silent. Nothing going on there, I was sure of that. But I tiptoed over anyway. The skylight glass was slick to the touch. I couldn't see a thing, so I closed my eyes and imagined Young Mistress lying on the far edge of the big carved bed, raising her soft white feet in the direction of someone walking toward her like a hungry wolf.

The wolf was the sopping wet, naked Big Road.

From my hiding place inside Big Road's body, I reached out and grabbed those two inviting feet. They were soft and slippery. When I tugged on them, I heard a shout.

Big Road rocked the bathtub, tipping it over.

I fantasized overturning the room.

I felt I was no longer human.

I was a dirty swine. When a boy reaches the age of sixteen, he becomes a dirty swine. You live your life, day in and day out, but there'll always be a few minutes when your mind is clouded and you have no idea what you've become. As long as you can bear the pressure, what you really want to do is take a knife and spill all the blood in your body.

Spill it, that's the only solution.

You understand what I'm getting at?

Look at you, you're smiling.

I can tell you understand.

You've done it.

Who hasn't?

Why wouldn't someone do it?

It's something Heaven arranged just for us men.

I'll never forget the sight of Big Road standing there in his bathtub.

When he was finished, he began whistling.

I've already told you, boys and girls are always coming over here for a little entertainment. They play the piano, read poems, sing some songs, and dance. They do what they can to console us old bastards. But consoling isn't what we need. We have a good life here, and it's those wet-behind-the-ears kids who cause all the trouble. You probably know that this place has public toilets. Well, after the little bastards sang their songs, dusted themselves, and went home one time, guess what they left behind. I don't know about the women's toilet, but the wall of one of the men's sported a new decoration.

A boy had drawn a picture of a cunt.

He drew it for himself, then left it for us.

We stopped using that stall.

That wasn't something we wanted to look at. It was like some scary insect, with fangs and claws, which had crawled up the wall and was waiting there motionless. Finally, one of the health workers painted over it. From then on, whenever the teenage kids came by, a health worker stood under the window screen outside the toilet shouting: Flush the toilet! Flush the toilet! Flush the toilet! She was a middle-aged woman, and when the boys emerged from the toilet, they gave her a strange look. How could they have known that she was beating the grass to frighten away the snakes, alerting the enemy?

That painted-over spot is still there. Go see for yourself.

Eight out of ten toilets are just like that.

Heaven knew what he was doing.

The damned thing forced you to do it. You couldn't help yourself.

The little bastards had to sneak around to do it, the poor little wretches.

The health worker was a busybody.

She said: How disgusting!

Is it disgusting?

Was it disgusting for me to be prowling around the rooftops? I can't recall if I felt it was or wasn't.

All I remember is how good it felt, and that it tired me out. I climbed down off the wall and went back to my room, feeling like a pigeon that had been flying for the longest time and was heading back to the nest with droopy wings.

I wasn't disgusting at all.

March 12th

I forget what day it was when the mournful news from the Imperial Court came to us from the lower reaches of the Green River. We were told that the Emperor and the Empress were both dead, and that a three-year-old Manchu child was now on the throne. Elder Master returned to Elm Township with a shipment of goods and reported to Old Master that the situation was turning ugly, that somewhere along the Green River someone could create a real uproar. He urged Old Master to hire more servants just in case. Old Master said: Do as you see fit.

Calling upon the connections of his father-in-law, the former subprefect, Elder Master secured a permit from the Chamber of Commerce to build a factory. Then, thanks to his uncle, he received permission from the governor's office to buy fifteen hundred kilograms of sulfur. He also bought a consignment of machine oil. Everything Second Master asked him to buy, he bought. He knew that anything his young brother was involved in would lose money, but his parents wanted him to at least go through the motions, and so he did. He reported to his father that no matter how much sulfur they went through, they'd never use it all, and if they stored the excess, it would appreciate in value over time. Old Master told him to do as he saw fit.

Elder Master then asked his father if it would be all right to remodel the old granary on the banks of the Black River for Guanghan's match factory. Old Master told him to do as he saw fit.

Old Master was growing impatient.

I was there that day, and with my own eyes saw Old Master dismiss Elder Master with an impatient wave of the hand. I was standing next to the brazier, holding a packet made of fan paper. Inside were three live butterflies with yellow wings and blue spots. In flight they were as big as a rice bowl. I didn't know if he expected me to open it right away. Old Master was in bed, his eyes closed, curled up like a chrysalis. I knew what was wrong. He was caught up in the fear of death again.

He said: Ears, I'm going to die.

I replied: You're not going to die.

He asked: What's the use?

What's the use of what? I asked.

He asked: What's the use of living?

Enjoyment, I said.

He asked: What's the use of enjoyment?

I had no answer. But he kept the questions coming.

What's the use of rank and privilege?

What's the use of riches?

What's the use of a beautiful wife and a fetching concubine?

What's the use of filial sons and worthy grandsons?

What's the use of poetry and lyrics?

What's the use of eating, drinking, shitting, and pissing?

He answered all his own questions.

He was frothing at the mouth from all that muttering.

He said: Ears, I'm going to die.

I said: You're not going to die, Master.

I removed the lid of the pot on the brazier, opened a corner of the packet, and dumped the butterflies into the boiling mixture. The second they touched the water, they dissolved, fell apart, all but one, that is, which spread its scorched wings and fluttered in the air, like a yellow porcelain bowl being tossed back and forth. As Old Master watched the butterfly flit around the rafters and above the window frame, his nose scrunched up and tears slipped down his cheeks.

His fear of death knew no bounds.

I've never seen anyone that afraid of dying.

People can't live without being useful in some way.

Even if he's useless, he has nothing to fear.

He can eat butterflies, can't he?

And drink butterfly soup.

What's the use in living?

I just told you.

The old granary was located on the stone steps of the Black River's northern bank, less than half a mile from Elm Township. It had been inundated by floodwaters once during the Tongzhi reign of the late Qing, and after the waters receded, had been converted into a rent-collection station. Then, during the Guangxu reign, floodwaters carried away a section of the wall, and the Cao family stopped using it to store grain. It now served only to store building rocks and lumber, a storehouse for nonperishable items.

The lock on the old granary's gate was nearly rusted through.

Moss covered the rock piles inside.

Edible fungi covered the lumber.

Mushrooms flourished inside and out.

Second Master walked in with Big Road, sending a bunch of green snakes scurrying up onto the walls, as if climbing a trellis. Second Master said to me: Go in and beat the grass with a stick.

I did as he said, but only scared up a few grasshoppers.

Individual storerooms lined three sides of the granary. There were no front walls or doors, sort of like stalls for sedan chairs, but

deeper and taller. Second Master frowned and turned to Big Road,
then gestured and said something I couldn't understand. Whistling
to himself, Big Road paced off the length and breadth of the storerooms. With his long legs, one pace equaled two of mine. He kept
looking up, as if afraid a tile or one of the rafters might come crashing down on his head. Not altogether satisfied with the results, he
was, nonetheless, happy, now that he was finally about to get something done after being idle all that time.

By then he'd learned quite a bit of Chinese.

Some of it from me.

I miss home!

He frequently blurted out stuff like that when he was playing
chess, then laughed loudly. Second Master and Young Mistress
would look at him and try to smile. Once construction of the match
factory was under way, he could begin counting the days till he
could return home.

He worked like a trained bear in the employ of the Cao family.

Over the granary door Second Master hung a white signboard
with calligraphed characters as big as a man's head. Hardly anybody in Elm Township could figure out what it said. The words
themselves were recognizable, but the meaning escaped them. And
it remained unclear until Second Master hired a dozen or so pen-
niless vagrants, and the residents of Elm Township got a glimpse
of what he had in mind. People said that Second Master wasn't
quite right in the head; apparently they were right.

I can still tell you exactly what the signboard said.

Elm Township Match Commune

Commune: *gongshe*. What did he mean by that? *Gongshe* sounded
the same as male quarters.

All the workers in the granary were men, so when Young Mistress led servants over with food for the hired help, local gossips
said, A female's loose in the male quarters!

Even the stupidest person in Elm Township knew that the commune was in the business of manufacturing wooden matches, not
supplying a breeding service! But still they couldn't figure out what
the word commune meant. I personally saw some elderly peasants

stop Second Master on the street to ask him what it meant. He blushed as he said: Commune means family.

With that he walked off, the creases in his brow showing his own dissatisfaction over his response. And the simpleminded peasants? They were more confused than ever.

The commune evolved into a strange place.

An inauspicious place.

But by the time people comprehended that fact, it was too late. It was all over!

The other day some big shot dropped by the nursing home with a congratulatory silk banner. Go ahead, we said, put it up. But no, he needed a group of children playing horns and beating drums to liven things up. Once the banner was up, he took off, but we'll stay here till our dying day. Meanwhile all those toots and drumbeats still pound on our eardrums and make us feel like we're listening to our own funeral processions!

By hanging up that banner, he turned the nursing home into an inauspicious place.

Take my words to heart, young fellow.

Don't put up signs for you or anybody else without giving it plenty of thought.

Don't put them up even if you understand what's written on them.

They only bring bad luck.

March 13th

Big Road poured oil into a machine lying on the ground, then stomped down on a pedal, sending the thing roaring to life. The only ventilation in the old granary came from the front door, an arrangement that greatly amplified the sound of machinery and set the aging rafters and newly installed doors and windows rattling. Second Master announced loudly to the commune workers: That thing's more powerful than all of us here, as powerful as fifteen horses! As his enthusiasm rose, the machine suddenly turned mute.

He turned mute right along with it.

Big Road fiddled with the machine for a while, until it shuddered and roared to life again. Second Master smiled. He was much more talkative than usual. He said: Link this to the other machines with a leather conveyor belt, and a piece of wood as thick as a bucket will be turned into matchsticks. He added: It's an old machine nobody in the West uses anymore, and the only reason it seems strange here is that Elm Township is so backward. He said: We've got no choice. People are living objects, machines aren't. So we all have to pitch in and work together to open up a new universe for our commune.

There was more he wanted to say, but the machine turned mute again. This time the failure hit him especially hard. His face reddened, then turned ghostly white, as he stood impotent in front of the commune workers and curious observers, humiliated. He waited for the machine to come to life again, but the damned thing refused to cooperate, and just sat there. Not knowing how to smooth things over or explain them away, all he could do was cast a traumatized look at Big Road, then at the machine, and finally at his own greasy hands.

Young Mistress stepped out of the shade behind the crowd just then and walked up with two teacups. Wuling brought up the rear carrying a teapot. Young Mistress came up to her husband, poured a cup of tea, and held it up to his lips. His face twitched briefly, as if he wanted to say something, but nothing emerged. She smiled for all of Elm Township to see—a smile, not a laugh.

Don't worry, she said, calm down.

Then she said: Come rest in the shade. Stay out of the sun.

Tipping the teacup, she held it until he drank it all down. He exhaled, but that's all; he didn't move. Then Young Mistress poured another cup of tea and carried it over to Big Road. Mr. Road, she said, rest a while.

She said it half in Chinese and half in the foreign tongue.

The language taught in the girls' school was English, which Big Road understood much better than Chinese. But he didn't speak it all that well. Back then I thought all foreign languages were about the same, and couldn't understand why he could talk so easily with Second Master but was so halting in his conversations with Young Mistress. Later on I found out he wasn't speaking to Young Mistress in his native tongue. Not only that, she only knew a few words in English, which she pronounced rather badly. But when she was speaking in that foreign language, the residents of Elm Township watched and listened in stupefaction. Behind her back, while they still remarked that the second daughter-in-law of the Cao family had big feet, they agreed that she was a remarkable woman.

She raised the teacup to Big Road's lips.

Stripped to the waist, he was all sweaty and greasy. Since he hadn't anticipated major problems with the machinery, he was also anxious and disheartened. He didn't feel like drinking anything, and kept thumping himself on the forehead. But Young Mistress held the cup out and wasn't about to leave. So he straightened up, spread his greasy arms, and leaned over toward the cup. But then he froze. He signaled me to come over, which I did, and then I quickly took the cup from Young Mistress's hands, spilling a few drops of the hot liquid on my fingers. That didn't faze me, because our hands touched as I was taking the cup from her. It's impossible to describe what that felt like, but my hand and arm seemed to weigh a ton, as if they'd swelled to twice their normal size.

Young Mistress's hand was lethal to me.

Her smile too was lethal.

I felt that if I looked at her a second longer, I'd die.

I was thirsty too.

But no one offered me anything to drink.

So there I was, holding the cup for Big Road, instead of Young Mistress. The water dribbled down his chin onto his hairy chest. Did I mention that he was powerfully built? When he bent over the machine, the muscles of his back rippled. I handed the teacup back to Young Mistress, making sure our hands touched again. She wasn't looking at me; no, her eyes were fixed hungrily on Big Road's back. So I sneaked inside his body, making his back mine, and flexed it in her direction so she could see what I was made of. And while I was caught up in my daydream, Young Mistress's green blouse and skirt floated back to the shade. I heard Wuling's voice beside me: Do you want some water?

She was holding a cup out for me.

I said: No.

Even after the sun had slipped behind the mountain, the machine was still broken. Elm Township's onlookers drifted off and so did the commune workers. Second Master lit a lantern and said to Young Mistress: You two go on home.

Then he held the lantern above the head of Big Road, whose greasy body made him look like a dark, shiny eel as he climbed all over the machine. He didn't say a word. Nor did Second Master. The two men acted as if they were being abused by the machine, and were hanging around like avenging ghosts, just waiting to get even. But the machine refused to come to life, in spite of all the thumps and pinches it suffered.

Young Mistress asked: Can't you do this tomorrow?

Go on home, Second Master said.

Young Mistress asked: What about you?

Second Master said: It's getting dark. Ears, walk them home.

He was a very unimaginative man, and once a thought entered his head, nothing anyone said or did could dislodge it. Young Mistress laughed softly as she turned to leave. But first she said something in the direction of the lantern, and Big Road responded by looking up and waving his wrench in the air. He was such a sorry sight, with only his eyes and his teeth showing white on a face covered with grease.

Since the ground was uneven and we had no lantern, we walked off very slowly. As she was negotiating the stone steps, Young Mistress rested her hand on my shoulder until she was on the road. My heart was racing out of a fear that she might somehow detect the impure thoughts in my head. I wanted to take her hand, I wanted to carry her on my back, I wanted to lead her over to a hole in the ground, where she'd step on air and tumble down on top of me.

She said: Ears, Mr. Road is a very courteous man. He won't tell anyone if he needs something, so it's up to you to speak for him.

I replied: He doesn't need anything. We serve him better than we serve the Old Master. He wants for nothing.

She said: It was no easy matter for him to come all the way to Elm Township, so it isn't possible to serve him too well. Has he gotten used to eating rice with his meals?

I said: That didn't take him long. He eats more than anyone.

Big as he is, she said, I'd be surprised if he didn't.

Wuling said: Are you being critical? It's not your rice he's eating.

Why should I be critical? I replied. I was just telling Young Mistress that he's well taken care of, and that the Cao family has done right by him.

Wuling said: Just look at you! Why are you getting so defensive?

Young Mistress giggled and asked no more questions. We'd nearly reached the town's main street when we heard the machine back at the old granary roar to life, loud and crisp, drowning out all the other night sounds. With a sigh, Young Mistress sat on a boulder at the intersection, and I realized that something had been

occupying her mind the whole time we were walking. We'll wait
for them, she said. Listen, you two, hear the sound echoing off the
mountains?

The Elm Township valley was filled with the chugs of a motor.

Young Mistress looked off in that direction, her face suffused
with moonlight, lips and nose glowing. Neither she nor Wuling
knew what I was looking at, since I hid in the shadows, lost in the
sight of Young Mistress's foot on the moonlit stone path. It peeked
out from beneath her skirt, like a little rabbit, or a weasel, or a
nameless little bird with its wings tied to its sides.

Wuling cried: That noise shakes up my insides!

Young Mistress said: This time it'll stay fixed.

But the machine stopped again, returning the valley to an
eerie silence. Hardly daring to breathe, we stayed with Young
Mistress as she sat there at the entrance to town. Before long, we
spotted the light from a lantern, followed by the sound of Big
Road whistling.

Young Mistress said: Mr. Road's mouth is like a flute.

She was in obvious high spirits. Wuling's spirits rose right along
with her, even if she didn't know why. Big Road and Second Master must have been in high spirits too. The only one who wasn't
was me. My general sadness was compounded by losing the opportunity to keep Young Mistress company, and the chance to
secretly enjoy the bewitching odor of her hair.

I hated those two men walking up the path.

I knew that made no sense.

But I hated them anyway.

Something like that makes no sense at all.

Now she's right here in front of me.

I can reach out and touch her.

I can smell the fragrance of her body.

Can you?

March 14th

Second Master took some men up to Jade Mountain, where they cut down pine and China fir trees and pushed them into the Black River to float them downstream. Commune workers walked along the banks following the felled trees, breaking up logjams with their hooked poles and keeping the trees out in the deep water. Below the stone steps of the old granary, the floating logs filled half an acre of the river bend, where Big Road and a carpenter built a pulley, enclosed by sheet metal, then set up a block and tackle. That way, two men could move a log from the water all the way up to the compound through a large opening in the wall. The parallel greased skids looked like a pair of boas slithering down to drink from the river. That's when residents of Elm Township discovered that the foreign devil, who had seemed to be a greedy parasite on the Cao family, was in fact a very smart, very capable man.

Second Master dug some bolts of bark-colored fabric out of the storeroom, and had a set of clothes made for each worker. He called them overalls. Even he and Big Road wore them at work. Strange-looking things, neither local nor foreign, they were sort of like sacks with holes cut in the top for the head, and no buttons or sleeves. But they were neat and uniform. Me, I didn't get a set. As a slave, I couldn't be a commune worker. My duties were limited to bringing tea for Second Master and Big Road, fetching water, passing messages, fanning the men, and supplying them with towels.

If I felt like it, I could also give them a hand when they were working.

I loved the work, but had no use for the men Second Master hired. All the hardworking peasants already had part-time jobs at the slaughterhouse, the fan factory, or the paper mill, leaving only the dregs behind. Elder Master told Second Master right off that he could have his pick of workers from the fan factory and paper mill, but Second Master said no, preferring to hire his employees off the street or from neighboring villages. What kind of men do you think he chose?

Man Mountain had scabies. A yellow liquid oozed from spots all over his body.

Double Egg's parents were both paralytics.

Black Ox had sired six kids.

Sky Water was a drunk.

Old Barren was one step this side of being an idiot.

And Short Watch was so loaded down with debts he could hang himself at any time.

Not one of the dozen or more men was a regular guy. And Second Master called each of them a commune worker. He'd said the commune was family, which meant that this motley assortment of individuals comprised the sons of the family. And what was he?

Apparently, he saw himself as the patriarch.

Big Road was a nanny he'd brought into the family.

Me?

I was the family watchdog.

Second Master said to his sons: All people are born equal, and should love one another. From today on, we do the same work, eat the same food, and earn the same wages. Stop calling me Second Master. You may use my name. We're family, and our future is in our own hands. Relying on Heaven is a waste of time. So is relying upon the Emperor. Self-reliance is what's needed. As long as you love your work and the people around you, you'll be happy, easily the equal of anyone in the world.

No one believed a word of his deranged comments. The workers nodded politely, but their expression was of men keeping a wary eye on a madman or an idiot. The family had spent all that money to send him to school overseas, but instead of learning anything useful, he'd come back with nothing but weird ideas. Everyone in Elm Township said that Old Master hadn't gotten his money's worth.

But the commune workers were an obedient lot.

What they wanted was to get as much out of the Cao family as possible. Their wages were on a par with workers at the paper mill and the fan factory, but they also got a free lunch, free work clothes, and other perks. Who but an idiot wouldn't be obedient? Their enthusiasm invigorated Second Master. The perennial frown on his face eased a bit, and once in a while I even thought I saw him smile. Young Mistress, Yunan, could never compete with the commune, which consoled his inscrutable heart.

He must have been possessed in France!

Well, what do you think was wrong with him?

Utopian?

I know what that means.

I think he was a little like the Communist Party.

Right, but even more muddleheaded.

Right, right, weaker even than the Communist Party.

He never knew how to get tough. He was a softie the day he was born. If he'd been tough, he'd have gone out into the world to make a name for himself. Why cower in Elm Township? If he'd been a real man, instead of closing himself up in the compound to make matches, he'd have gone off and joined a bandit gang.

Back then, any man worth his salt was off fighting for the Emperor. What was he thinking when he decided to settle down and make matches? Saving a few poor people and helping out some of the scum of the earth, was it worth it? No, he did it for himself, did it so he could shed the stones that had formed in his heart. He was no different from his prayer-intoning mother and potion-taking father.

Day in and day out he worried, worried about everything under the sun.

And he was so incompetent even his chopsticks wound up in his nose.

No wonder he liked hanging around with bums.

He was one of them.

But he had a good heart.

There was something about the look in the foreigner's eyes that bothered me.

There was something wrong with the look in Young Mistress's eyes too.

But for Second Master it was commune commune commune.

Youngster, this old bastard's going to give you some good advice.

Never feel sorry for cuckolds. Those assholes.

They get what they deserve!

The paper mill was downriver. If you stood on the threshold of the old granary, you could see the drying sheds beyond the woods. There was also a waterwheel, which they used to make pulp. Cut bamboo covered the surface of the river. The fans and stationery made from this paper were famous beyond the borders of Elm Township, since it was rugged enough for examination papers and Yamen official proclamations, and when it was dyed red, it was good enough to wrap small tribute items.

Second Master chose this paper for his matchboxes, because it stood up so well.

The slaughterhouse was farther away from town, downriver from the paper mill, a good five or six bends in the river. But you could still hear the squeal of pigs being slaughtered, and by climbing onto the granary roof you could see that the water of the Black River was red at that spot. The butchers owned lots of knives. Those for slaughtering pigs were different from those for slaughtering goats, and those for slaughtering chickens were different from those for slaughtering geese. The knives used for killing an old ox or an old horse were like little chopping boards, small but heavy.

The biggest knife in Elm Township was for cutting straw. As a groom, I'd used it to cut hay for the horses. That was easy. But sharpening the blade was hard work, and I could usually only manage a couple of swipes with the stone before I had to stop, tired, hot, and sweaty.

But once we had match-making equipment, the straw cutter was no longer the heaviest knife in Elm Township. The knives that sliced the rotating logs were both wider and thicker; but they had to be sharpened often. Big Road had a honing rack, which was off-limits to everyone but him. Instead of water, he used oil on the stone, which was also different from those normally used in Elm Township: it was flat rather than crescent-shaped, and black, like a block of sandalwood. When Big Road mounted the rack and moved the stone back and forth, his back muscles danced and popped. You'd have thought a live animal was loose under his skin. But everyone else was working too hard to notice. I was the only male who couldn't keep his eyes off his bare back. I made a habit of looking at him because I discovered that Young Mistress was doing the same thing. I wanted to know what caught her attention, see what the attraction was.

There was sweat.

The valley of his backbone was deep.

No bones were visible.

The muscles were divided into strips, patches, and knots.

They all danced and leaped.

And what else?

Young Mistress sat in a bamboo chair in the shade, reading a book and raising her head every few lines to watch the men working. Once in a while she'd put down the book and stroll around the yard, accompanied by Wuling, who held a parasol for her. She tried to help strip or pick up bark, but the commune workers wouldn't stand for it, even got down on their knees in front of her. Wuling gently tugged her away, so she smiled and walked up to Second Master, who was working one end of a two-man saw. He was very clumsy, and his overalls were soaked through. Young Mistress mopped his sweaty face with her handkerchief, including even the base of his ears and his chin. Wanting to keep working, and embarrassed by all the attention, Second Master tried to get her to move back. Be careful, he said, I don't want to bang into you.

His fake queue hung from one of the granary posts. His real hair, cut short, was covered with sawdust. Except for his pallid face,

skinny arms, and the fact that he was clumsy, he didn't look all
that different from the workers he'd hired. To all appearances, he
was kind of pitiful, actually. A prince who'd come to grief.

Young Mistress turned and went back to her chair, picked up
her book, and started reading again. During her stroll around the
area, in which she'd done a little of this and a little of that, taken a
look here and a look there, not once had she so much as glanced at
Big Road, who was huffing and puffing as he sharpened the blades.
She stayed as far away from that hairy bear's back as possible,
covering her face with the book. But I was pretty sure she had
trouble keeping her eyes off him, because when I sneaked past her
chair and glanced at her out of the corner of my eye, I saw her gaze
spill over the top of the book and settle on the foreigner's back.

I had no proof.

But I'd be willing to bet on it.

Young Mistress wasn't a woman who found men disgusting.

But she was not a lustful woman either.

Are you a sex fiend? Youngster, when you're out walking on a
summer day, what besides women's skirts do you look at? You look
at their legs and at all the mosquito bites on them. No matter what
you look at, you're right. Nothing's wrong with you. So long as
you don't lie on your belly to look at women's spit on the ground,
there's no problem.

You're not a sex fiend.

I am.

I've gotten down on my belly to sniff Young Mistress's footprints.

Believe it or not.

March 15th

When Big Road lost his temper, his anger surfaced in a very strange way. He didn't throw anything, he didn't scream, and he didn't fume. He just talked faster than usual, shrugged his shoulders over and over, and gnawed on his cigar, as if chewing raw vegetables, until there was nothing left. At first, you couldn't tell he was angry, and everyone just thought he was having trouble with the heat.

The machine broke down—it stopped shaving wood. Big Road gripped a log with a pair of pincers so it would turn on the belt, then he lowered the blade by hand. The wood was supposed to come off in fine, thin sheets, but now it flew off in pieces, most of them not thin at all, and some chunks sailed up into the rafters and sent dust raining down. He tried several times, but couldn't get it to work.

When he turned off the machine, his lips were trembling. Second Master walked over and said something to Big Road, who chewed on his cigar, tossed his head back, and spit a chunk of tobacco a good five feet in the air. A moment later, he spit out another chunk. By then, Second Master had stopped talking and just listened.

Big Road's speech was faster than normal, his shoulders pumped up and down, and he kept raising three fingers. I didn't know what that meant. Finally, he chewed up the end of his cigar, and was about to spit it out when Young Mistress and Wuling walked up, followed by servants carrying lunch.

Caught by surprise, Big Road walked to the breach in the wall without a word to anyone and followed the skids down to the log-

jam at the river bend. He strode deftly partway across like a log-
roller, before diving into the water and swimming to the opposite
bank.

What was that all about? Young Mistress asked Second Master.

Second Master replied: He refuses to accept that the machine is
broken.

Young Mistress asked: What did he say?

Second Master replied: He said the wood's no good.

Young Mistress asked: Did you say it was his fault?

Second Master replied: No. He blamed himself. I think he's
getting all worked up. He was supposed to return home in three
months, and now it doesn't look like he'll make it.

Everyone crowded around the breach in the wall to watch Big
Road's head bob on the surface. The three fingers waving back
and forth meant three months. So there's this guy going around
whistling all day long, happy as can be, and now, apparently, he
misses his home. And that look in Young Mistress's eyes, it was
sympathy.

She said: Don't pressure him. Take it slow.

Second Master replied: If I'd known he wasn't any better prepared than this, I'd never have taken him on. He keeps complaining that the machinery's no good. Well, it's old, and he knew that.
Now I'd like to see what he can do.

Second Master's face darkened. It was resentment, I could tell
that. Young Mistress cocked her head and looked at his chin without saying a word. The workers sensed that something was very
wrong. If the machine had to be scrapped, not producing any
matches would be the least of their worries—their rice bowls would
be smashed! So they picked up rags and began wiping down the
machine diligently, forgetting about lunch. Maybe they were waiting for Big Road to climb up onto the opposite bank, which infuri-
ated Second Master.

He said: What good does wiping it down do? You've got your
jobs, and taking care of the machinery isn't one of them!

See what I mean! All that talk about how commune workers are
equal. But when the chips are down, out the window that goes.

The master's still the master, whether he eats with the slaves or not, or does the same work. The blood of a master flows through his veins.

I never learned anything about Big Road's background, except that he was related to Second Master's overseas landlord. Some sort of nephew, I think. I don't know if he left a job to come to Elm Township or if he was out of work at the time. Did he have a wife? Children? I couldn't say. But I know he left an aging mother back home in France, because he wrote a letter to her. I saw it with my own eyes. He pointed to the envelope and said in Chinese: Mama! He pronounced the word just right. Whatever sort of life he'd lived over there, I concluded by watching the way he threw himself into his work that he hadn't come from a privileged class.

I'll bet he was a slave!

He belched when he ate.

He swam in the river with his pants on.

He slept with his eyes open.

He stole glances at Young Mistress's waist and hips when she wasn't looking.

He stood in his bathtub and masturbated.

He was low-class!

Which meant that he and I weren't all that different. So when I realized he'd jumped into the river not to escape the heat, but because something was gnawing at his guts, because he missed his home, because he was so lonely, the distance between us narrowed. There was only one thing about him that disturbed me. He was just too big and strong. When I stood beside him, I looked like a newborn chick. So whenever Young Mistress was nearby, I made a point of standing away from him. And on those occasions when I had no choice in the matter, I stood on a log or on the steps whenever possible. Since we were both slaves, why should I be lower than him?

Big Road showed no interest in coming out of the water, so I walked up to the edge of the river and pointed to a spot near him. Snake! I shouted. Snake!

That was a word he understood.

In the grip of panic, he swam for dry land.

With smug satisfaction, I looked back toward the breach in the wall, figuring I'd be rewarded with one of Young Mistress's smiles. But what I saw was a face white with fear. I had no choice but to pick up a stick and run along the bank trying to hit a snake that didn't exist, yelling even louder than a moment before. Take that, you blind bastard! I'll kill you, just wait and see! I kept it up until even I started to believe there was a snake in the river, that the river was full of big green boas.

It didn't make any difference that I knew it was a piece of bamboo.

Just the thought of it was frightening.

Her face was white as a bleached bone.

I didn't know what she was afraid of.

I really didn't know.

That evening I prepared a mugwort braid to keep mosquitoes away from Big Road. He was writing a letter under a lamp and asked me to wait a moment. So I sat on the steps and gazed at the lamplight across the pond. Second Master and Young Mistress were on the veranda playing chess. She was sitting in the chair usually occupied by Big Road. Wuling had commented on the fact that even she now knew how to play that strange variety of chess.

When he finished his letter, Big Road came outside waving the envelope in his hand. Mama! he said. Mama! I echoed him, to make him think I was happy for him. But how could I be happy, since I didn't have a mama? I lit the mugwort in his room and carried it all around the room. The smoke gagged me, and I started coughing so hard that tears flowed.

When I bent down to fumigate the area under his bed, I spotted his leather shoes, looking lonely down there, and big as boats. I was struck by thoughts of what his mother might be doing in that faraway place. Was she crying because she missed her son? The thought saddened me, and I couldn't help feeling sorry for Big Road, who was worrying and working himself to exhaustion over some broken-down machines. I cleaned his shoes with my sleeve.

Worried that the bathtub was a breeding place for mosquitoes, I stuck the mugwort inside to fumigate it. It had been scrubbed clean, as had the wall behind it. In recent days Big Road had gotten into the habit of bathing in the Black River, leaving the tub to sit there unused.

They called to me from the other side of the pond.

I walked over with the burning mugwort.

The moon was big and bright.

Tears kept flowing from my burning eyes. I moved from feeling sorry for Big Road to feeling sorry for myself as I stood in the moonlight. Young Mistress was still on the veranda, and I felt like walking up and talking to her. Me, busy from sunup to sundown, doing what? The burning mugwort was starting to make me sick. If I wasn't a mosquito, what was I?

Second Master said: Ears, didn't you hear me calling you?

I answered: I'm coming. What do you need?

He said: You don't need to go to the granary tomorrow. I want you to take Mr. Road's letter over to the church at Acacia Township and ask Father Ma to put it in the church post. You hear me?

I said: Yes, sir.

He said: It's time for you to go to bed.

I replied: Um-hm.

They were sitting there with Young Mistress, moving chess pieces back and forth on the board. The only thought in my head was to stand beside Young Mistress and talk with her. One sentence would have been enough. What I wanted to say was: There are mosquitoes out tonight. Will you permit me to fan you to keep them away?

I don't know what she'd have said to that. But a smile would have pleased me no end.

I tossed the mugwort into the pond, where it sizzled and went out. Then I went back to my little room, lay down in bed, and listened to my own heavy breathing. I was reminded of Old Master Cao's comment: What's the use of living? What's the use?

In the middle of the night, when I was fast asleep, Big Road came knocking at my door. I let him in and lit the lamp. He looked worn out. After he sat down in my bamboo chair, by means of hand gestures I was able to understand more or less what he wanted to say. He said he couldn't sleep, and had decided to go to the church himself. He wanted me to lead the way, to which I enthusiastically nodded my willingness. That made him happy. And still he sat there, unwilling to leave, yet unable to find the words to say what he wanted. His face grew red from frustration. There was so much he wanted to unburden himself of, but he couldn't. It wouldn't feel right telling me what was on his mind, but not telling me was even worse. He puffed away on his cigar, frowning and shaking his head, then smiling weakly, until he could sit there no longer. He stood up and made the sign for a rising sun.

I said: I know.

Thank you, Ears! he responded.

He stumbled as he walked out the door, but caught himself before falling. The compound quickly returned to stillness. Then the sound of the night watchman drifted over from the street—*bong bong*—and I felt my eyelids getting heavy. I knew what was bothering him. He felt empty inside. He didn't miss his home, he was afraid. He couldn't fight anymore.

He wanted to run away.

He didn't want to cause any trouble.

Was there any question what was happening?

He was in love!

What could he do?

The man had fallen in love.

Fate had decreed that there was no escape.

He was done for!

March 16th

Acacia was a small township less than half a mile east of Willow Township. The church, which was in the middle of town, was taller than all the other buildings, its steeple stabbing the sky above. It was built of dark green bricks, had stained-glass windows, and was reached by a cobblestone road. When we got there, the street was nearly deserted, except for a few dogs on the loose.

I squatted on my heels in the shade of a tree across from the church to wait for Big Road. He had joined the congregation listening to a sermon by Father Ma, who spoke softly and slowly. It was little more than a hum, mysterious and slightly eerie, which drifted lazily out onto the street.

When he stopped, a dozen or so people began to sing.

The rest of the congregation gradually joined in.

A hen that had just laid an egg flapped up onto the church's bamboo fence, cackled a time or two, then jumped down and ran out into the middle of the street.

The parishioners filed out of the church and headed off in all directions. They looked like people who had just dined on food unavailable to others. Smug but not wanting to let on what they were up to, they strolled along cautiously until they were out of sight and could have a good laugh.

Big Road was not among those who filed out of the church. So I went looking for him, and found him sitting motionless in a pew at the rear, his eyes shut. The church, which was dimly lit, smelled of sweat and chicken droppings.

I went back outside to wait for him to come out of whatever
trance he was in.

When Father Ma finally walked out with Big Road, they stood
in the roadway and chatted awhile. Big Road was holding a jar in
his hand, probably something Father Ma had gotten from behind
the church. The jar had a funny smell, like pickled bean curd.

It was cheese.

On the road home, Big Road sampled the cheese and asked if
I'd like to try some.

I said no.

On the outskirts of Willow Township, we spotted the corpse of
a famine victim on the ridge of a field next to the road. We hadn't
seen it on the way over, but maybe we'd mistaken it for a log or
something. It sure didn't look human, wasn't much more than skin
and bones partially covered by a few tattered pieces of cloth. The
skin was dark brown, the color of tung oil, and white teeth were
bared in the gaping mouth.

Big Road, who'd been enjoying his cheese up till now, suddenly
stopped eating. At the entrance to Willow Township, a cluster of
famine victims who'd had their eye on us from the moment we
came into view quickly surrounded us, begging for something to
eat. Big Road, caught unawares, simply stood there as the jar of
cheese was ripped out of his hand. It neither upset nor shocked
him—he just stood there watching them fight over the jar. Inevitably, it fell to the ground, breaking open and emptying its contents into the dirt, where it was trampled by many feet. The starving
people fell to the ground and crammed the dirt and cheese into
their mouths, some actually licking the ground. Now Big Road
was scared, and he quickly backed off. I was scared too. I knew
it wouldn't take much for those hungry demons to turn to us as
a source of food!

We hurried over to Eastern Avenue and headed toward the pier.
The narrow street was lined with two-story frame houses, leaving
only a sliver of sky overhead, and very little sunlight. Women with
gaunt faces sat under the eaves. They were prostitutes. In twos and
threes they approached us, giggling as seductively as possible. Big

Road slowed down to look at them. One of the brazen women grabbed my sleeve and said: Little brother, bring the foreigner inside for a cup of tea, fresh tea; we'll make it nice and special.

I said: I don't have any money.

Maybe you don't, she said, but he does.

I said: He doesn't have any either.

She replied: We'll give the two of you a cut rate. Have the foreigner pay for himself, and yours is free. What do you say? Little brother, what's there to be afraid of, as long as you're in the company of the god of wealth? Yours is absolutely free.

I said: But I don't know how.

That was the truth, but the prostitutes laughed anyway. When Big Road stopped to look at me, wondering what they were laughing at, they swarmed around him like flies. One hand removed the cigar from his mouth, another separated him from his hat. Showing no signs of anxiety, he smiled and looked each of the whores over carefully. I couldn't tell what he was thinking. The girl who'd come up to me took my hand and laid it on her breast. It felt as soft as a handful of river mud. She wouldn't let me pull it back, so I just rested it there, as my heart raced wildly. There are some things you can think about without any trouble, but when you actually do them, it's like cutting off your own flesh.

She asked: How's that?

I replied: I don't have any money.

I watched the others drag Big Road over to the doorway of a little shack. Still no anxiety, as he looked them over, one after the other. There was a dreamy, glazed look in his blue eyes, and I could see he couldn't hold out much longer.

I said: Big Road, let's go!

He turned to look at me. There was no life in those eyes.

Let's go home, I said again. Home!

One of the prostitutes, a tall woman, was stroking his beard. It was White Horse. Pressed up against her, he gazed into the sky, then turned and looked behind him, as if searching for something. His face was red and his hair was mussed, thanks to them.

We have some important business, I said. We'll come back some other day.

One of the whores said: What could be more important than this? You're old enough to understand that, aren't you?

She reached down between my legs.

She grabbed me!

The other whores laughed.

So did Big Road.

I cried: Fuck your old lady!

The whores stopped laughing.

I said it again: Fuck your old lady!

The whore let go of me.

They didn't know what that was all about, and neither did I. All I knew is, I'd salvaged some dignity. I turned and left—what Big Road did was his business—and ran straight to Lucky Teahouse, where I ordered a cup of Emerald Conch tea. But before I took my first sip, Big Road came running anxiously out of Eastern Avenue, followed by the sound of women's shouts. I ran to the entrance of the teahouse. Your hat! I shouted to him. Where's your hat?

He turned around, dazed for a moment, before figuring out what was wrong. White Horse ran up to him, hat in hand, and in front of a crowd of people on the pier stroked his beard and tugged him. He put up with it for a few minutes, before reaching out and grabbing her by the throat. Like everyone else I thought he was just having some fun with her, until I heard her shriek, and realized he was squeezing too hard. Tall as she was, the whore was on her tiptoes, her chin sticking way out. He damn near picked her up off the ground. Then he let go, took some coins out of his pocket, and held them out to her. But she was too frightened to take them, so he bent down and laid them at her feet. Then he came into the teahouse and had tea with me as we gazed out at boats on the Green River without exchanging a word. Lucky was reporting snippets of news he'd picked up from here and there. One item was very serious. He said that the Blue Kerchiefs had sunk four grain transports belonging to the gendarmerie, and that people were already being arrested in the prefecture capital. The peaceful days were over.

How's your Master Cao? he asked.

I replied: The old gentleman's doing fine.

He said: Everybody says this foreign friend of yours is a very competent man. Is that true?

I replied: Come over to Elm Township when you've got the time and see his work for yourself.

He asked: When are we going to be able to use some of your matches?

A few days at most, I answered.

I was just boasting, of course. We hadn't seen a sliver of wood shaped like a match yet, and it was going to be a lot longer than a few days before we did. But I didn't want outsiders laughing at the Cao family. What did I care if they were arresting people in the prefecture capital? What was important was for our Elm Township commune to start cranking out matches as soon as possible. If no matches were produced, no one would find peace of mind.

And if no one enjoyed peace of mind, there'd be trouble for sure.

And once trouble erupted, there'd be no turning back.

Old Master Cao was on the road to recovery. Just how that death switch in his brain was turned off, nobody knew. His mood improved, and he returned to his desk and his fan calligraphy. Sooner or later the switch would be turned back on for the last time. Things weren't too bad when his mood soured, but when he was in a good mood for too long, that dread of his set in. The fear that he'd see through his own game.

He said: Ears, burn some horsetail ashes for me.

I did as he said.

His little cauldron bubbled on and on.

The room filled up with the smell of burning hair.

He drank his stinking soup with gusto.

The old man was getting more and more like a child.

He asked me what I'd seen and what I'd heard, whether any-thing interesting was happening out there. I told him about the Blue Kerchief rebellion.

He said: They've got a death wish.

I responded: They can raise all the hell they want, and they'll still be bedbugs between the Emperor's fingernails. I can let you go if I want, he'll say, or I can pop you just like that.

I also told him about the match commune.

He said: He's still playing his games. One day he'll tire of them.

He spoke calmly. To him all these things meant nothing. When he was in a good mood, he was completely open-minded. It was as if he'd died and been reborn, and nothing else mattered. I liked it better when he was afraid of dying.

Then all I had to do was show some sympathy.

March 17th

Troubles with the machinery continued. No usable shavings were being produced. Big Road blamed it on the wood, Second Master blamed it on the machine. At first they argued with the machine between them, but before long they stopped talking altogether. Big Road took the machine apart and cleaned every part. No one else was permitted to help. That included me. When Young Mistress volunteered to help, he started to say something, but decided against it. Her arms, which were as soft and fair as lotus roots, were quickly smeared with grease, but that didn't keep her from throwing herself into the work. Yet that only seemed to make matters worse. The thing still wouldn't function. Once he had it reassembled, it sputtered back to life, but sent ragged wood chips flying again. So he broke it down a second time, methodically and unhurriedly. When he looked at Young Mistress, his eyes sent an unambiguous message: there was nothing he could do but consider himself one of the machine's parts.

Young Mistress cleaned the parts with the care she showed in her embroidery. Unlike the men, who scowled and fumed, while she worked she remembered to have Wuling keep everyone supplied with water and for me to keep fanning Mr. Road and Second Master. I could see that her concerns lay not with the machine, but with her husband.

Second Master was on the verge of breaking down.

After giving the workers the rest of the day off, he wandered around the woodpiles like a lost spirit. Before Big Road tried to start the machine, Second Master's face paled and he walked out of the yard in front of everyone. Once the machine had stopped, it was a long time before he showed his face again, and then he looked like someone who'd just climbed out of his coffin.

By now he was muttering to himself.

Everyone was afraid to talk to him.

Young Mistress said: Ears, I know you can wiggle your ears. Do it for us. Guanghan, watch Ears.

I knew what she was up to. So I wiggled my ears as hard as I could, then did it again, one at a time. Young Mistress laughed delightedly. So did Wuling. Big Road didn't so much as look up. By the time Second Master looked at my ears, they'd long stopped moving. But he stared anyway, and said: That's something I never imagined.

He said: I never imagined it, not at all.

He was talking about something altogether different.

Young Mistress stopped laughing.

Even making my ears dance couldn't get her laughing again.

Laughter wasn't what she had in mind.

Second Master walked around in a daze, his neck scrunched down between his shoulders, as if expecting the sky to fall. Out on the road, he often jumped to one side, as if to avoid stepping on an ant, or to dodge an invisible fist. Although her face didn't show it, I could see in Young Mistress's eyes that she was worried. Worried and a little scared. Scared, I guess, that something unexpected was about to happen.

One day, inevitably, Second Master simply vanished.

He left their quarters before sunup, apparently for a stroll around the compound that would last late into the morning and maybe end in a trip to the old granary. But when Big Road and I went to work that morning, we didn't see him. We assumed he'd gone up into the foothills. When Young Mistress showed up with the noon meal, and we learned that he hadn't come home, we knew this meant bad news, really bad. So we sent the commune workers out looking for him, but they returned empty-handed. Then we asked the servant who kept an eye on the road if Second Master had gone to Willow Township. He said no. When darkness fell, Young Mistress had no choice but to have Steward Bing break the news to Old Master Cao.

Elder Master had gone into town to check on some of the family businesses, so he wasn't around.

I assumed that Old Master would jump to his feet when he heard the news, and either wail or give everyone an earful. But no. He sat in an armchair in the main room, looking exhausted, too tired to talk. His face was lit up by an oil lamp on the tea table beside him, but I couldn't tell if he looked worried or sad.

He said: He's beyond saving. I'd hoped that getting married might make him more responsible.

He continued: He was always one to hide, even as a little boy. And the harder you looked for him, the less willing he was to come out of hiding. It was best to ignore him. Go look for him if you want, but don't say anything to his mother.

The words were no sooner out of his mouth than Old Mistress, who had gotten wind of it, arrived.

Young Mistress greeted her respectfully.

Old Mistress made no reply. Her fast had ended, but now she'd taken a vow of silence for forty-nine days. That was nothing new to us. She did it once a year. Steward Bing gave me a sign with his lips, and I quickly put a cushion on the floor in front of Young Mistress, who paused momentarily before kneeling in front of Old Mistress.

Old Mistress was crying.

Young Mistress said: It's all my fault. I should have gone with him.

Old Mistress pointed to Young Mistress's face.

Young Mistress stared at the finger.

Then the piece of jade in Old Mistress's mouth fell to the floor. It was the same piece she held in her mouth every time she stopped speaking. It was rounded, green, sort of like a bird's egg. When it hit the floor it bounced quite a distance away. I ran after it, but was called to a halt by Old Mistress.

She said: Don't move.

Then she said: He won't be back, so there's no reason for *you* to come back.

Her tongue was stiff; tears were streaming down her face. Young Mistress nodded, stood up, bowed to Old Master and Old Mistress, then turned and walked out. Old Mistress's maidservant retrieved the stone and wiped it clean. Then Old Mistress opened her mouth to permit the maidservant to carefully lay it on her tongue. Old Mistress's tears never stopped flowing, possibly out of remorse for speaking.

Old Master sat there the whole time, utterly serene.

He knew that nothing serious would befall his son. No one knows a son better than his own father. Whether it was running away or jumping into the river, Old Master knew that Second Master Guanghan didn't have the guts. If he did, he wouldn't have been Old Master's son.

That night, Steward Bing led half the town's peasants up the mountain to look for Second Master. Big Road and Young Mistress went with them, while I went to Willow Township. As they scoured Jade Mountain, I watched the valley fill up with torchlights. The people called out to Second Master, soft one minute, loud the next, as if calling his soul back. I heard Young Mistress's voice— Guanghan, Guanghan—calling until she was hoarse.

Second Master would have been able to hear her even if he was no longer in the land of the living.

Lucky said he hadn't seen Second Master. I was concerned he'd had boarded a passenger ship heading downriver, but Lucky said: The gendarmerie has sealed off the river, so he couldn't have boarded a ship. And why would he head downriver anyway, unless he killed or robbed somebody? If it was me, after spending all that money to buy machinery and hire workers, and I couldn't produce a single match, I'd throw myself into the Black River and end it all. Why go on living then?

As I hurried back to Elm Township in the dark, I saw rocks sticking up out of the Black River, white in the pale moonlight, and couldn't help feeling that one of them might move at any moment and turn into Second Master's bloated, water-soaked body.

Just about everybody assumed he was dead.

And for one simple reason.

The aura of bad luck around him was too strong.

I arrived back in Elm Township at daybreak. I don't know when Young Mistress had returned from the mountains, but as I entered the corner compound, she was sitting on the veranda, alongside Wuling, who was fast asleep. I walked up and told her what I'd learned in Willow Township. She asked about a welt on my forehead, which I said I'd gotten from a fall on the road. I was afraid I'd burst into tears if she asked another question like that. Fortunately she changed the subject.

She said: Ears, no matter what I ask you, I want you to tell me the truth.

I'd never seen such a dark look on her face before, gray and cloudy.

She asked: Was Second Master in the habit of acting strange before we were married? I want you to tell me about all his eccentricities.

I said: Second Master is not a sick man!

I knew that was the wrong thing to say the minute it left my mouth. Young Mistress's eyes narrowed and were hidden by her eyelashes.

She said: I didn't ask you if he was a sick man or not. I asked you about his eccentricities. Now will you tell me?

I didn't want to.

She looked at me, and I was putty in her hands.

I looked over at Wuling.

Young Mistress sent Wuling away, and I started telling her about Second Master's eccentricities, including his chemistry experiments and the ugly incident in which he nearly strangled himself. I'd never breathed a word about any of this, even to Old Master. Tears fell from her eyes as she listened.

I emptied my heart to her.

I said: Second Master is a good man.

She said: I know.

She attempted a smile, but her tears kept flowing.

He didn't want to get married, did he? she asked.

I said: That's not it. He was afraid!

She asked: Afraid of what?

I said: I don't know.

Young Mistress covered her mouth and began to sob.

I've done plenty of stupid things in my life, although some didn't seem so stupid after I thought about them. But I've never been able to feel that way about what I did that day. And not just stupid. There were things hidden in what I said that even I never understood. They had nothing to do with sowing discord, and even less to do with taking advantage of someone who was so vulnerable.

I was a slave.

I couldn't have told you what I'd hoped to do, but even as I stood there watching Young Mistress cry her eyes out, I didn't have the good sense to shut up. I told her everything. What must I have become in her eyes? Was I thinking that Second Master hadn't done enough weird things?

Maybe I was talking about Second Master as if he were already dead.

Does that make sense?

I'm even stupider than I thought!

March 18th

Second Master returned at lunchtime on the third day. That morning, Big Road had told me to summon the commune workers to the old granary and have them drag all the floating logs up onto the riverbank. Then a white poplar, about the thickness of a human thigh, floated down from the upper reaches of the Black River, followed by another, and another, until there were five altogether. Big Road stood on the bank and watched their progress for a while, then jumped into the air, pointed at the newly arrived trees, and shouted: Cao! Cao!

At lunchtime, while people were telling Young Mistress about the poplars, Second Master walked in through the breach in the wall with faltering steps. He was dirty and obviously tired, and blinking like a man who'd been badly shaken. Without a glance at anyone, he muttered something to Big Road before collapsing on the spot, his head banging loudly against one of the skids.

We picked him up and carried him into the shade. Young Mistress cradled his head in her arms the whole time. In appearance, there was little to set him apart from the famine victims of Willow Township: his cheeks were sunken, his lips chapped and blistered.

Big Road whistled into Second Master's face.

Everyone breathed a sigh of relief.

The look on Young Mistress's face gave nothing away as she rubbed Second Master's face, as if to reassure herself that he was still alive. Big Road turned and walked behind the machinery, where he lit a cigar and stood there looking at Second Master, cradled in the arms of Young Mistress.

Big Road! I shouted.

That gave him a start.

On the back? I asked.

On the back!

He understood me, with the help of hand gestures, and as I bent down, the others helped Young Mistress pick Second Master up and lay him across my back. Since I was still bothered by a sense of betrayal, carrying him to his room made me feel a little better.

Second Master slept all that day and night, during which time Big Road put the men to work producing white matchsticks, then soaking them in treated water and laying them out in the drying room, turning them into countless slivers of ivory. I carried a handful of them over to the corner compound and told Wuling to lay them next to Second Master's pillow. Afterward I asked her what he said when he saw them.

Not a word, she said. He just snapped them into small pieces, then stared at them like an idiot. Young Mistress stood nearby weeping. Wuling said that Young Mistress felt terrible for Second Master.

Was all this my fault?

A talkative slave is not a good slave.

Water, once spilled, can never be retrieved.

Just think. Snapping a bunch of matchsticks—what's the big deal? A little childish temper, that's all. But if you knew the background, you could see that something was very wrong. Second Master's downfall was caused by fate. But changing the way Young Mistress looked at things was my doing. Nothing he did escaped her attention, not even the slightest movement of his finger. Which of them had I let down? Both of them, that's who!

I still feel that way, even now.

But I learned one important lesson, and that is, if someone you're devoted to tries to get you to tell the truth, if you think it's a bad idea, then lie. Sometimes telling lies is the only right thing to do. How do you feel about that?

Take the time to master the art of bending the truth.

Once the gendarmerie sealed off the Black River piers, water traffic came to a halt. Elder Master, who was off settling accounts, found his way home blocked. His concubine, unable to wait for his return, went into labor and delivered his child. We heard the baby's cry on the other side of the wall, and I said: Another little damsel! Steward Bing whirled and slapped me. That shut me up.

But I was right, it was a girl. For some time afterward, Steward Bing kept looking at me out of the corner of his eye, as if suspecting that the girl had somehow emerged from my mouth, and not from the woman who'd carried her. The gate to the right-hand compound was unlocked so the child could be taken in and shown to Old Master and Old Mistress. Then it was locked again. Old Master, in a rare gesture of goodwill, gave the baby a name, but the locked gate was proof of his overall unhappiness. Normally, he didn't concern himself with other people's affairs, but eight granddaughters in a row seemed a bit much, even to him.

Sometimes you can't help but wonder if Heaven has it in for you.

And if it does, that means you have a guilty conscience.

If you don't, it's time to ponder whether you were guilty of some offense in a previous life. And it's not enough for you to ponder the matter—others will help you in this regard, until you feel you've done everyone wrong. It was an issue the Cao family servants and tenant farmers loved to ponder. I did my share too. But, unlike the others, I never celebrated a setback in the Caos' fortunes. What caused me the most pain was the look on Elder Master's face when he finally made it back home, travel-worn and weary. He knew something was wrong, but for the benefit of others he brushed it off with some light humor. He said: Fortunately, I was very careful out there, with my head tucked all the way down in the crotch of my pants. Otherwise, I'd never have been able to lay eyes on my youngest daughter! His raucous laugh was infectious. Although they were born of the same parents, Elder Master and Second Master couldn't have been more different, which we slaves found utterly baffling.

When he learned that his younger brother had actually produced some matches, Elder Master treated all members of the commune to a banquet, at which several of them got roaring drunk. Second Master sat there striking matches, one after the other. Look! he said. Look at that, Guangman! I am looking, Elder Master said. You don't have to keep lighting them, I can see you've done a great job!

Big Road laughed giddily, then threw up.

He wasn't used to drinking rice wine.

When Elder Master told everyone about a jailbreak by the Blue Kerchiefs, Young Mistress was all ears. Was anyone killed? she asked. Lots of people! Elder Master said. Including six members of the Blue Kerchief Society; their heads are hanging from a gendarmerie ship.

Hanging how? someone asked.

Elder Master said: What do you mean, how? From a pole.

No one at the banquet said another word. Meanwhile, Second Master, who was now drunk, kept striking matches. Since different chemicals made up the heads, some of the matches glowed green, others blue, and all of them put a ghostly cast on the faces around the table. Except for Young Mistress, who was lovelier than ever in the glare of the matches. Big Road looked at her and smiled giddily.

Then he promptly threw up again.

He said to me: I want to go home.

He threw up all over me.

Elder Master wasn't drunk, but he was as thick of tongue as if a wasp had stung it. He said to Second Master: It's all up to you now. Figure out a way to coax a son out of her!

He may not have been drunk, but he talked as if he were.

Second Master said: How about a name for our matches?

Elder Master replied: How about Oolong—Black Dragon? That's the name I chose for my son, the one who still hasn't appeared.

There's no sense in wasting it, so you can have it. Put it to good use by making more matches. They'll be the sons of the Cao family!

In that drunken atmosphere, a name was chosen.

Oolong—isn't that the name of a tea?

Once everyone sobered up and realized they hadn't chosen a very good name, they couldn't muster up the will to change it.

That night, someone was striking matches in Second Master's quarters, slowly, methodically, one after the other. I figured it was probably Young Mistress, not Second Master, but I couldn't say why I thought it was her. So I climbed onto the roof, determined to see what was up. The main room was empty. The glare came from the bedroom. I couldn't see anything but an embroidered shoe that had been tossed to the floor, lonely and a long way from the bed. The glare from the matches swayed as they burned slowly.

Then it was pitch black down there.

That shoe had now moved to my heart.

I looked closely at that which I could not see.

Even in my dreams.

The shoe began to stir.

March 19th

Big Road wanted to leave, but the Cao family wouldn't let him. The quality of the matches was uneven, one good batch followed by a bad one. The poor-quality matches would invariably snap in two before they'd ignite. Either that, or the ignited match heads would spray all over the place and set clothes on fire. Second Master said: We can't let him go. If he does, all his good work will be wasted. Elder Master said: That's easy, we'll just give him more money.

But money didn't mean that much to Big Road. He wanted to go home so badly that after a while he even stopped eating the rice he liked so much. He was waiting for a letter. I went with him a second time to the church in Acacia Township, where the postman said there was no mail for him. The news made him weak-kneed, and he sat for the longest time in the otherwise deserted church. Father Ma, who was a pretty decent fellow, gave him another jar of cheese, but even though this time he managed to keep it out of the hands of famine victims, when he returned home to Elm Township, he suffered a bout of diarrhea so severe he was laid up in bed for several days. The machinery in the old granary was up and running the whole time. When I took him his meals, he just shook his head and sighed. The same! he said. The same! You, him, me, the same!

What he meant was, the machinery ran with or without him.

I said: You are this! and showed him my thumb. He just shook his head.

We are this! I raised my littlest finger. He smiled.

The same old thing was bothering him.

He was fond of Young Mistress, yet afraid of being too fond of her.

He couldn't bear the torment.

The Caos had brought him over from far away, put him to use, fed him and kept him warm in the winter and cool in the summer, but not a single one of them had ever taken into consideration his needs. Anyone who had any interest in treating him as a human being would have taken him to Willow Township's Eastern Avenue. But when I did, he couldn't make up his mind. Did he think they were unclean, cheap, or what? If the idea had actually occurred to him, I knew, nothing I did would make a bit of difference. The next time I took him to Eastern Avenue, he kept his eyes straight ahead, totally disinterested.

He preferred to stand in his bathtub alone.

Is this what's called exercising self-control to protect oneself from immorality?

That says something about Big Road's integrity.
How could he not miss his home?
Yes, I keep bringing this up, so what?
Everything has its cause.
The cause?
We need to look for it.
It's hard!
Harder than rubbing your own ass to locate a tail.
It's not that it isn't there.
It's just changed into something else.
And moved elsewhere.

One night, Second Master finally showed his true moral character, either because he was incredibly happy or because he was depressed. I was tossing and turning in bed when I heard somebody cry out, a woman. It wasn't all that loud, more like what you'd hear if someone nearly steps on a centipede, or if you're searching for crickets under rocks and a scorpion takes your breath away. The next morning I asked Wuling: What were you shouting at last night?

She blushed and stammered something unintelligible.

I said: Did somebody try to sneak under your covers?

She said: Damn you!

If you don't tell me, I said, I'll pretend I'm a ghost and come in the night to scare the hell out of you! Now, tell me, what were you shouting at?

She said: It wasn't me. It was Young Mistress.

I asked: What was wrong with her?

She said: I'll tell you, but nobody else must know.

According to Wuling, when she heard the shout, she ran into Young Mistress's room, but couldn't see what was happening. She was told to get out, which she did. In the sitting room, she saw some bowls on the floor and a satin sash hanging on the wooden divider. She said the sash looked like a hangman's noose, the bowls looked like sacrificial vessels, and she wondered which of the two people was thinking about suicide.

I said: You were seeing things.

Like hell I was! she protested. When I went in there, the noose was still swaying! I didn't close my eyes the rest of the night, not with it swaying like that. I was too scared!

I insisted: I tell you, you were seeing things.

I don't think so, she said.

I said: Then no more wild talk about things you *didn't* see. It's okay if you tell me, but I'll throttle you if you breathe a word of this to anyone else.

I made a choking gesture with my hands. Wuling was so gullible, it didn't take much to frighten her. It wasn't the threat of choking that scared her as much as it was the fear of saying something wrong, of screwing up. From the fearful look on her face, you might have thought she'd hung the noose up there herself.

Which is how it should have been!

That day, Second Master busied himself with chores at the match commune, like any other day. He was working on the chemical-mixing machine, moving the handle back and forth and directing people to do this or that. He didn't miss a beat. Not until Young Mistress came over with the noon meal did he seem spent, burned out, too tired to even look up. There was something different about Young Mistress too. She wouldn't look at anyone—not Big Road, not Second Master, not even me. When everyone else was eating, she picked up a rake and began raking up the pieces of bark strewn across the compound. Wuling followed her with another rake. Her strange behavior caught the attention of the people as they ate. Normally at this time she'd be in a wicker chair reading a book in the shade. I walked up to her and said: Why not let them do that while you rest. I cleaned off your chair for you.

She just said: Ears, don't you have things to do?

There was something in her eyes that saddened me. She could see that I knew what was what, and was incapable of putting on an act in front of me. On the surface, she was as beautiful and elegant as always, but she was in torment deep down. A twenty-year-old woman, no matter how worldly, no matter how strong, could not conceivably bear up under this sort of bizarre treatment by her

husband. Having graduated from a girls' school, filled with pride
and self-confidence, and then being married to a man who had
studied abroad, she could be forgiven if she fancied herself a near
immortal. But confronted by so many bizarre developments, her
dreams, however lovely they might have been, were doomed to
be shattered.

During the early days of her marriage, we saw a smile on her
face just about every day. It was the smile of an artless young
maiden. Second Master wiped that smile from her face. He had
crossed the river grasping a straw, thinking it was wood, and when
he realized it was only straw, he sank beneath the surface. Marriage couldn't save him. No woman could. His fate was in the
hands of Heaven, who watched him lose face for the entire Cao
family, and show how debased a fine family's son could become.

He still had the gall to patiently mix chemicals for his matches.

He still had the gall to say to me: Get a chair for Mr. Road!

He still had the gall to greet his father and mother each morning.

He still had the gall to summon Big Road for a game of chess.

Most important of all:

He still had the gall to share a bed with Young Mistress!

Why hadn't he gone ahead and hanged himself?

But why was I getting so exercised? His gall had nothing to do
with me. Who could shame him into leaving Young Mistress's bed?
Me? Was I the equal of a single mosquito inside her bed net?

The visit of Young Mistress's elder brother to Elm Township
returned the smile to her face. He asked her: How's everything?

She said: Fine. Why wouldn't it be?

He asked: Isn't it oppressive here in the valley?

She replied: Oppressive? Here in Elm Township, there's none
of the chaos you see everywhere else.

He said: Your man doesn't beat you with a broom, does he?

She said: Of course he does. A lot harder than you beat your
wife, so hard I run to the ends of the earth!

She roared with laughter. Everyone else laughed too. This all
took place on the veranda, where people had gathered to talk with
Zheng Yusong, Young Mistress's brother. Second Master and Big

Road were there. She laughed with such obvious joy she looked like a budding flower. But I knew it was all an act. She didn't want her husband's family to know the pain in her heart, or her own family, for that matter. Too bad her brother had to leave and take her smile with him. I'll bet she couldn't have laughed if she'd wanted to after that.

If I'd been her brother, how could I not have been happy for her? She really put on an act.

It's not something every woman could do.

She kept things bottled up inside her.

How I admired her.

March 20th

During Zheng Yusong's visit to Elm Township, in addition to visiting his sister, he bought several hundred pounds of cured pork at the slaughterhouse and two hundred fans from the fan factory. The porters he brought with him, broad-shouldered and thick-waisted, walked with a bounce in their step. At the match commune, he asked his new brother-in-law what the word commune on the signboard meant. Second Master sputtered an answer. Wonderful! Zheng Yusong said. What a terrific name! When I get some people together and set up my own business someday, I'm going to use it. It has style, and power!

He was the first person to approve of the word commune. Later, after I'd learned that he was the leader of the Blue Kerchiefs, that no longer seemed so strange.

During the banquet that day, Zheng Yusong also tried to buy some sulfur from Elder Master, a discussion that didn't turn out well. Elder Master said he'd be happy to give him gold or silver, but that sulfur was out of the question, since its unauthorized sale was illegal.

Zheng Yusong said: All right, I won't buy and you won't sell. Just pretend I'm a beggar, and give me a little, how's that?

Elder Master asked him: What do you want it for?

Zheng Yusong said: My father's going to be seventy in a few days, and I'd like to make some fireworks for him.

Elder Master asked him: Will five pounds be enough?

Zheng Yusong said: That's up to you. But I was sort of hoping for a hundred.

Elder Master said: Why don't you just take my head with you instead.

The two men laughed lightheartedly as they walked down the steps. Wuling turned and mumbled something about what misers the Caos were. You don't know shit! I said. The sale of sulfur is regulated by the governor. If we give it all away, what'll we use?

She said: Owning a huge supply like that, and he'll only give five pounds?

I said: That's enough for dozens of big crackers. That's plenty.

I said all the right things, but deep down I agreed that Elder Master was being pretty miserly. An angry look appeared on Second Master's face, and I wondered what he was thinking. As Zheng Yusong was walking out, Elder Master said: If someone checks up on the sulfur, and you own up to the transaction, I'll say you stole it.

Zheng Yusong said: Why would I do that? I'll say it was part of a gold mine sold to me by Cao Guangman of Elm Township, and they won't be able to lay a hand on me.

They had a good laugh over that, but beneath the surface there was resentment. The Cao brothers had a hushed conversation on the path. I overheard Elder Master say: Have you lost your mind? Do you have any idea what he's up to? Can you speak for him?

Young Mistress walked softly past them.

I wasn't sure what they were talking about.

Big Road was whistling somewhere off in the distance.

If not for the fact that he missed home, he'd have counted as Elm Township's happiest person.

And who would have been Elm Township's saddest?

Old Master Cao?

Old Mistress?

Second Master?

Yunan?

No matter how you looked at it, there was only one candidate.

Me!

It was me!

Don't ask me why.

Don't ask.

Sadness is a factor in longevity.

Didn't I just say, don't ask?

I accompanied Second Master and Young Mistress to Willow Township. They were going to Mulberry Township, where he was to deliver birthday greetings to his father-in-law. When we arrived at the Willow Township pier, we saw bloody heads hanging from flagpoles. Soldiers from the local gendarmerie were standing watch at the base of each flagpole, but, having grown weary of their assignment, they were resting on their haunches and smoking. A notice had been pasted on the wall of Lucky Teahouse. Passengers waiting for their ships were crowded around the notice as one of them read it aloud. The Blue Kerchief Society again. They'd hijacked a government ship on the Green River, were caught, and were beheaded.

I had seen those heads right off, and was about to tell the bearers to go on into town before stopping. But the crowd made it necessary for them to put the sedan chair down there on the pier, and when Second Master and Young Mistress climbed out, they couldn't miss those things directly overhead. She turned her back to them, but he scowled and made a sweep of the area, looking into the face of each of the heads. None were familiar. Having forgotten all about Young Mistress, he took another turn around the area,

They continued on their journey to Mulberry Township. The
sedan chair was laden with gifts for Young Mistress's family, including a hundred boxes of Black Dragon matches. When they
boarded the ferry, Young Mistress sneaked a quick glance at the
flagpoles. I knew she couldn't stand the sight of blood. I still recall
the time I accompanied her to the slaughterhouse, and how her
enthusiasm vanished as soon as she saw the pigs' blood coating
the Black River.

There's nothing good to be said about blood.

People don't grow heads just to have them hung from a flagpole.

Though, of course, there was a reason for hanging them up like
that.

Once I'd seen the ferryboat halfway across the river, I went over
to Lucky Teahouse for a cup of tea. There weren't many customers that day, probably owing to the proximity of the heads, and
Lucky voiced his displeasure: Of all the places they could have
hung those things, why right outside my window? Are we looking at them, or are they looking at us? Look at that son of a bitch
over there. All he's got is a head, so what's he got to smile about?

One of the patrons said: Kill 'em, I say! Kill 'em all, that'd be
something new!

Lucky asked the man: What the hell do you mean by that?

The patron said: Putting a three-year-old whelp on the throne
to govern us just proves their days are numbered. So what does
killing a few people accomplish?

Lucky said: Fuck you! I don't want to hear talk like that in here.
If you're itching to say something, talk about visiting brothels and
whoring around, if you want. They can turn a three-year-old child
into your ancestor, into your granddad, if they want, and what can
you do about it?

The patron said: All right, I'm going. I'll cut off my head and
hang it up there for you.

Lucky said: You'd be getting off too easy. Be careful they don't
throw you into a pot and boil you!

A crow flying above the flagpoles flapped its wings in preparation for landing atop one of the heads, but the sentries and onlookers scared it away with their shouts. When it finally flew off, the people below laughed heartily.

The heads had been lopped off recently—the drops of blood at the base of each flagpole proved that. The victims appeared to have been young men, but they were aging fast. By the time I left Lucky Teahouse, they were old men with sunken mouths.

They hung at the ends of blue kerchiefs.

That was the society's identifying mark.

Normally they tied them around their waists as sashes.

During an uprising, they tied them around their heads.

When those heads were lopped off, that's what they hung them by.

Four days later, I returned to the pier to meet Second Master. Young Mistress returned alone, saying he'd gone to the government seat with Zheng Yusong to make arrangements for the sale of matches. She walked down the pier with her head lowered, followed by the greedy stares of the sentries.

The soldier in charge said: Stop right there, you lousy cunt!

Young Mistress didn't stop, but I did.

The soldier said: I didn't say anything.

I looked at him, and my knees were knocking.

The soldier said: That head hanging up there said it. You tell that woman that tonight she's to await a visit by eight ghosts.

When he saw that no one was laughing, he yawned, turned, and walked off. The heads were now round black things, sort of like rotten pumpkins, or wasps' nests.

Tragic!

I mean unbelievably tragic!

No one paid attention to crows perching on them anymore.

You could hear them pecking away.

Ke-chunk!

The pumpkins split open.

From that day on, the Emperor was my mortal enemy.

Part Two
March–April 1992

March 21st

There was something new in Second Master's eyes when he returned from his travels. Up till then, his eyes were either cold or weak. There was always something to sadden him. But one trip with a gritty type like Zheng Yusong, and his eyes turned hard. We had no idea what had happened to him out there. He seemed shorter than before, as if a chunk of iron were pressing down on him; his shoulders slumped when he walked. These changes made the hard look in his eyes even more threatening.

His leather shoes were covered with mud.

One was missing its sole.

The other had a hole in the toe.

He stepped down from the sedan chair and stumbled in through the gate. The Cao servants said he was dirty from head to toe, absolutely filthy. To look at him, you'd have thought he was one of those poor scholars of old, or a beggar. For most people, it was only natural that Second Master would turn out to be a failure. But I thought he came back a better person. There was something new in his eyes.

He said: Ears, call Steward Bing for me.

Steward Bing's sick, I replied. He's in bed.

He demanded: I told you to call him for me. The wages haven't been paid for several days, and I can't put it off any longer. You tell him what I said. I'll wait for his answer.

He was stooped over; his eyes were as hard as nails. He looked like a man who was planning something. And he was pumping himself up in order to do whatever it was he had in mind.

He was putting himself to a whole lot of trouble.

One night after that, the people who lived in the left-hand compound were sitting on the veranda playing chess as usual. After putting away their chess pieces, Second Master and Big Road had a heated conversation about something.

Young Mistress sat off to the side watching them.

I couldn't understand what they were saying, but I knew what Big Road had in mind, and I knew what Second Master was saying as well. Big Road wanted to leave. Second Master wanted to keep him around. And the longer it went on, the louder their voices grew.

I wondered if they were about to start swearing at each other.

Second Master said something in the foreign language three times.

Big Road shouted.

Young Mistress said: Take it easy, Guanghan.

They sat there woodenly, not saying another word. Then Second Master got up and went inside. He returned with a hardwood box about the size of a traditional Chinese book. Taking several gold ingots out of the box, he laid them on the table, to the astonishment of the other two people, then slid them over to Big Road. He spoke to him in a soft voice. Big Road covered his eyes with his hands, shaking his head and heaving a sigh. But he didn't say a word.

Big Road got up and walked off the veranda.

He never so much as touched the gold ingots.

Second Master glared hard at the shade over the oil lamp. Next to him, Second Mistress's eyes were soft and gentle. She was clearly on her guard, even a little frightened, as if worried that Second Master might do something strange and terrifying. I was frightened too, afraid that Second Master might go mad. I had reason to be afraid. The hard look in his eyes—like a sharp-edged date pit—was proof that something was wrong.

Big Road called out to me from the pond, saying he wanted to take a bath.

He said: Ears! Boil some water!

Boil some water! He pronounced the words perfectly, with no trace of an accent. Boil some water! And not just correct, but with authority, as if I'd done something wrong, and the only way he'd feel better was by taking his anger out on me.

I said: Yes, right away!

The porter brought over some water and boiled it. Then I led him over with my lantern. After I filled the tub with the boiling water, and before I had a chance to add a bucketful of cold water, Big Road stripped down to his shorts and waited with an impatient frown on his face. By the time the last bucket of cold water arrived, he'd already climbed into the tub.

His head was suspended atop the water amid a cloud of steam.

I put the bucket of cold water down next to the tub, but before I walked off, he picked it up and poured the water over his head, nearly drowning the lantern with the splash. I wondered what it felt like to add cold water on top of hot. His chin was shuddering in the steamy air and his voice quivered.

He said: One year!

I didn't quite make that out at first.

He repeated himself: One year! Me, one year!

He stuck one finger out of the water.

Second Master wanted to keep him on another year.

I said: That's great!

Not caring if it made him happy or not, I gave him a big thumbs-up, then ran out of the room. I saw how bad he felt. I felt bad too. But sadness varies from person to person. Your toe hurts, the other guy's tongue hurts. Ask somebody else, and he'll say his balls hurt. Everybody's different, and that's a fact.

The gold ingots crashed to the ground, like the peal of bells. My heart crashed too. They were worth more than all the money I could make in my lifetime. I was a house slave. Money didn't mean that much to me. I couldn't use that much money even if I had it. But when those shiny ingots clattered to the ground, my heart crashed painfully.

I realized just how little I was worth.

I also realized that there was something wrong with the look in my eyes.

That realization hardened me inside and out.

Second Master concerned himself only with mixing chemicals, stirring the mixture, and dipping the match heads in them.

Big Road was in charge of the machines. I was in charge of the drying room. Young Mistress was in charge of gluing the matchboxes. Her job consisted of taking workers to peasant homes in Willow Township with wood chips, bamboo paper, and glue, then teaching the wives of poor families how to make the boxes so they could earn a little extra money for their families. She went in and out of the granary, usually with her sleeves rolled up to reveal arms coated with glue and phosphate; her clothing too. Her labor escaped Second Master's attention. He wasn't watching. He was too absorbed in his own activities.

What he was concentrating on was the sedan chair shed.

That and the stable.

People had told me, but I didn't believe what I heard. So I followed Second Master into the shed, stealthily, where I saw him sniff the wall, then chip off a piece and put it on his tongue. My spine nearly froze. I slipped away in a hurry.

I could get by without telling Old Master.

But I couldn't try to deceive Young Mistress.

I told her.

She wasn't the least bit surprised.

She said: He'll be fine in a few days, so let's leave him alone.

When Second Master tired of staying in the sedan chair shed and the stable, he started running over to the peasants' charcoal kilns. He always returned covered with soot, his face as black as the bottom of a frying pan, only his mouth and eyes showing through. He'd walk all the way through town like that, oblivious to the mocking stares of townspeople. But we weren't. His strange behavior and the townspeople's stares depressed us. We were unhappy with Second Master. We felt he shouldn't be that way,

that his eccentricities were a slap in Young Mistress's face. But there
wasn't a thing we could do about it.

Not a single thing!

All we could do was stand by and watch him lose face for the
Cao family.

Steward Bing said: He's eating earth!

Steward Bing was trembling all over.

He said: The damn guy's eating earth.

It didn't concern me as much as it did him.

Why was it such a big deal?

All I could think of was, Now there's something Old Master has
never eaten.

I wondered when he would.

I felt my way into the sedan chair shed, peeled off a strip, and
put it on my tongue.

It was puckery.

And bitter.

Terribly bitter!

My tongue swelled up.

I got a splinter in my finger and couldn't get it out. When Wuling
came out with an empty meal box and walked toward the gate, I
called her over to help me. She came into my room, where we
huddled under the window to stare at my injured finger. She had
a needle in her hand, but lacked the nerve to use it. She didn't
look so good, and didn't feel like talking. There was sleep in her
eyes.

What's the matter? I asked her. Caterpillar crawling up your
back?

No, she said. I'm just sleepy.

I asked: How come?

Without replying, she attended to my finger. I kept teasing her,
but was surprised to see her eyes redden and tears gather. When I
asked her why she was crying, she wouldn't tell me, so I stopped
asking. Then, amid sobs, she started talking. She said Second
Master was getting worse all the time. He'd found a whip some-

where, and had asked Young Mistress to use it on him. He cried and shouted that he didn't deserve to live, that he was useless and unworthy of Young Mistress's affection.

I could see that Wuling was telling the truth.

The image of a whip reminded me of a snake, and my heart skipped a beat.

I couldn't begin to imagine how that had frightened Young Mistress.

I felt so sorry for her.

Seeing Wuling cry like that saddened me.

How could things have turned out so weird?

I didn't know whom to loathe.

I asked Wuling: Did Young Mistress whip him?

Wuling said: I don't know.

I asked her what Young Mistress said.

Wuling said: I don't know. I didn't hear a thing.

I didn't know whom to loathe.

So I loathed Wuling for telling me. And I loathed myself for knowing things like that. I loathed myself for not clapping my hand over Wuling's mouth. But she started crying again, washing the sleep from the corners of her eyes.

She said: When I couldn't hear anything, I thought Young Mistress had died!

She kept working on the splinter as she wept. She hurt me.

She said: When I woke up this morning and saw Young Mistress, I wished I could have died for her.

Wuling's needle drew blood. I sucked in a mouthful of cold air. So did she. Then the silly little girl stuck my finger in her mouth. Her tongue was so soft. That was the first time in my life I'd felt a woman's tongue and teeth. Her upper palate was rough to the touch, and scratchy, with lots of little bumps, like the skin of a bitter gourd. Her lips pressed down over my finger to hold it steady as she sucked out the blood. She loosened her hold a bit when I pushed down on her tongue.

I looked out the window and spotted Young Mistress.

She didn't see Wuling or me.

The morning dew had burned off, but a layer of mist hanging above the compound seemed to suspend her in air as she negotiated the curves of the veranda. Her body showed up long and straight; her pastel green dress made her face look like a lotus flower. Lotus flowers are supposed to be fresh and spotless, but she had a withered look. The distress wasn't on her face, it was in her eyes. When I looked at those eyes, I could see she was crying. Then I studied her face, with her neat, regular features, and saw the depth of her endurance. But that face gave me the feeling that there would be something in her future she could not endure. On that day, tears would be her only option.

I couldn't help but think about the smile that normally adorned her face.

What a wonderful smile!

The forced look of serenity on her face now allowed for no smile.

The look made Wuling cry.

I didn't cry.

But tears filled my depraved heart.

Second Master wanted her to whip him!

A man who didn't act like a man.

My finger was swirling around in Wuling's mouth, touching her tongue and her teeth, brushing up against her lips and the inside of her cheeks. I said to her: Let me take it out.

Wuling's saliva smelled bad.

Her tears were on my fingers.

I said: Don't tell anybody about the whip.

She nodded vigorously.

My nose ached so badly I couldn't stand it.

How could it not ache?

What could we do about the fact that the person we liked had such rotten luck?

Absolutely nothing.

But, my young friend.

It was unbearable.
An aching nose was all I had.
That's one of the factors in longevity.
Try it.

March 22nd

A cement mason built a compound for Second Master alongside the
west wall of the old granary. It was a big one, covering the entire
stone platform. It had only two rooms, with a built-in brick platform
that served as a bed and a stove for the oversized wok. The opening
of the stove was shielded by a head-high brick wall, which kept
the flames from coming into the rest of the room. The compound
had two gates. One opened onto the path to Jade Mountain that
ran along the bottom of the stone steps. The west wall of the granary
was breached to create the second gate, which led straight to the
commune's chemical-mixing room. The room was filled with clay
crocks and glass. The smell was strong enough to bowl you over.

Once the construction was completed, Second Master called out
two commune members. One was Old Barren, who was just short
of retarded and went around drooling until his lapels were all sticky.
The other was a man they called Hole in the Ground, a very competent mute who was stubborn as a mule. One look at these two and
you knew they weren't destined for interesting or enjoyable work.

They lugged loads of charcoal into the compound, crushed it
with a stone mortar, sifted it with a sieve, dried it on the brick bed,
then raked it out. It was as fine as flour.

Then they shoveled dirt from the sedan chair shed and the stable and carried it over to the compound, where they dumped it into water-filled pots and boiled it. After that they dumped the gooey mixture on the stone terrace, where it crystallized into a white powder that looked like salt.

It was saltpeter.

They then crushed the saltpeter into powder.

Their last job was to crush large chunks of sulfur into powder.

Although the workers at the match commune didn't pay any attention to this seemingly meaningless work, I did. But not for a minute did I imagine that Second Master was making anything but match heads. He had deceived everyone associated with the match commune!

And me?

I was happy for him, still.

I knew that when he tasted the lumps of earth, he wasn't actually eating the stuff; he was looking for saltpeter residue. There was nothing abnormal about him in this regard. Which is what I told Steward Bing. I was happy for the man. So was Steward Bing, who'd seen a lot of this world, and yet was deceived along with everyone else. He said to Elder Master: The chemicals for match heads don't come cheap, and they'd save a lot of money by finding a way to make their own.

So Elder Master was deceived along with everyone else.

Elder Master said: There's nothing anyone can do if he's determined to fool around. Lucky for us, he's now as worried as the rest of us about expenses. There's nothing wrong with that.

Everyone was sure there was nothing wrong with what Second Master was up to.

If they'd only known!

Saltpeter.

Sulfur.

Charcoal.

Second Master was making gunpowder!

He was hanging his head on his own belt.

And everyone was deceived.

No one could know that he was courting death.

Old Master summoned me to ask if I'd seen or heard anything, or if anything had happened that he should know about. I told him they'd butchered a castrated hog in the slaughterhouse, and when they opened it up, they discovered a three-legged, one-eyed piglet. Its heart was still beating when they first removed it.

Old Master asked me: Did you see it with your own eyes?

I said: No, but the slaughterhouse people said it was a bad sign, and they buried both animals in the riverbank.

Old Master cocked his head and meditated for a while. His face was sort of puffy, the ridges of his ears and his nose were shiny, the bags under his eyes were full as dumplings. He was always dumping talcum powder into his cauldron, and he probably took in too much of the stuff.

They got it all wrong, Old Master said. It wasn't a castrated hog, it was a sow.

What else have you heard? he asked.

I said: There's talk about some strange new disease in town.

He asked: Is it a swelling of the bones?

Yes, I said. They say people's joints are swelling up like grapes.

He said: I've heard that. The water there's no good.

Old Master's comment left no room for doubt as he reached down and massaged his knees.

We've got better water here, he said.

Then he clammed up. After massaging his knees, he massaged his elbows and ankles, then his wrists, his shoulder blades, his skull, and finally his ribs, one after the other. Having run out of body parts to massage, he took one hand in the other and sucked on it, as if it had been scalded.

I kept quiet and waited for him to calm down.

I could tell there was something the old fellow wanted to say to me, and experience told me he wanted me to get him something new to ingest. But for some reason, he couldn't say it. Now was not the time for me to ask anything. All I could do was wait patiently until he'd made up his mind to tell me, in detail, what he wanted. There were times when even he found things hard to say. That always saved me trouble.

I was hoping it was something he hadn't tried before.

At the same time, I was afraid it would be hard to find.

My mind was heading in two different directions, and the battle was on!

One voice said: No more, you've tried enough!

The other said: Go on, try it, whatever it is!

The first voice said: You'll kill yourself one of these days!

The second voice said: Go on, eat shit, if that's what you want!

I saw that Old Master Cao had made up his mind.

My heart was about to leap into my throat.

But what he said didn't frighten me.

It made me blush.

He wanted to consume blood.

Menstrual blood.

He said: It has to be clean. From a virgin.

He said: Go on, get it. But be careful.

Old Master blushed too.

The color of blood.

Steam gurgled up from his little cauldron.

I had the feeling it was his phlegm stewing inside.

Either that or his snot.

There weren't many things left that he hadn't tried.

He said: Ears, be careful!

The time for the really important eating was nearing.

He was warning himself!

Be careful!

Here comes the blood.

Ai!

Ai!

I was thinking about the girls in town, the way they walked with mincing steps, their legs rubbing against one another. But that wouldn't do. Old Master said to be careful, and that's what I planned to do. Dealing in some crotch humor with them would be easy, but reaching in and snatching that thing they wear presented a real problem. Then I thought of Wuling. She was my best chance.

I said: Wuling, I'd like to borrow something.

She asked: What is it?

I said: Something on you.

She asked: What could that be? A needle? A thimble?

I said: Something between your legs.

Obviously misunderstanding, she spat at me and ran off. And, to my surprise, I found I couldn't say the words. On the path to the granary, I shouted for her to stop. Bushes and waist-high artemisia grew on the northern side of the path. I told her to follow me in, figuring that if she wouldn't, that'd be the end of it. But she did.

I asked her: Can I borrow it?

She said: Sure, Elder Brother Ears. You can have whatever you want.

I still couldn't say it.

Finally I got it out: I'd like to borrow your sanitary pad.

She asked: What do you want it for?

I said: Never you mind.

She said: You mean a menstrual pad.

I said: Yes.

She said: I don't have any, but Young Mistress does.

I said: I don't care whose it is, I just want to borrow one.

Wuling was afraid of me, and probably liked me at the same time. She'd assumed that what I'd wanted to borrow was her body, not something simple like a cloth pad. Naturally, the thought that it was blood I was after never occurred to her. What I'd wanted was blood, but what I wound up with was something Young Mistress wore against her body. Now I didn't know what to do.

That night, I buried my nose in the pad and sniffed deeply.

It had the sweet smell of imported soap.

Gritting my teeth, I banged my nose against the window frame.

Then I staunched the flow of blood with the cloth pad. There was so much blood, it soaked the pad. It was warm, and I was scared. What if I couldn't stop the bleeding? But then the thought that my blood and Young Mistress's blood had flowed onto the same thing brought me a strange sense of well-being. I wasn't disgusted, not even a little bit.

Why should I be?

The next morning, I discovered that my blood had clotted on the cloth pad. It was black, just like the pigs' blood all over the slaughterhouse. I took the thing over to Old Master, who soaked it in a bowl of cold water until the blood dissolved and turned the water purple. His hand shook as he held the bowl.

He said: Good, it's still fresh!

Ears, he said, you can go take a rest.

I heard the sound of the bloody water as it was poured into the cauldron.

It made the blood in my veins boil.

That other blood, it was sticky.

And it smelled like pigs' blood.

I felt terrible.

Youngster.

I don't know what to say.

Can you forgive me?

I bled, and all for nothing.

March 23rd

Wicker baskets filled with matches looked like lanterns, except longer: ten boxes to a bundle, ten bundles to a pack, ten packs to a basket, all lined with oil paper and sealed tight. The matches were so light that porters could carry eight baskets on a pole. Several porters walking side by side blocked the roads.

Every three or four days, teams of porters left the Cao family compound. Beefy, muscular, and strong, they were all Zheng Yusong's men. The striking surfaces on the Black Dragon matchboxes were less affected by the humidity than were the more common big-headed red matches, and since the output was modest, selling them did not present much of a problem. But that didn't mean the Cao family stood to get rich over them. Fortunately, the family had never expected the commune to be profitable from the beginning. But at least it wasn't a drain on the family's resources. Zheng Yusong spent a lot of money to market the matches. He stood willing to share the commune's losses.

People in town assumed that the foreigner held shares in the match commune, and so did the Zheng family. But they were wrong.

Big Road was just a source of labor.

Zheng Yusong was a businessman. But more generous than other businessmen, in that he was freer with his money. And no one was surprised by that. Second Master, after all, was his brother-in-law. He wasn't going overboard, not at all.

He loved his kid sister.

He loved his kid sister, adored her, and yet he had once smashed a teapot in front of her! It was in the autumn, harvest time, and Elder Master was off collecting rents. After sharing a meal with him, Steward Bing took him over to the veranda in the left-hand compound to rest. I'd just returned from Willow Township with some herbal medicine for Old Master, and Steward Bing shoved a teapot in my hand and sent me over to wait on our guest and help him pass the time. Zheng Yusong knew I'd just come back from Willow Township and asked if I'd seen the heads. I told him I'd seen them on previous trips and was surprised to see they were still there. All the flesh had been picked clean, and what good did it do to hang a bunch of white skulls up there?

He said: The Imperial Court is using them to keep the people in terror. How about you, are you afraid?

I said: No. I feel sorry for them every time I see them.

He asked: You feel sorry for whom?

their family members think when they see them? Kill them if you have to, and bury them. But why hang their heads up there like that? It's just cruel, horribly cruel!

He said: You've got a good heart. When my head's hanging up there someday, will you feel sorry for me?

I was too stunned to say anything.

He went on: When that day comes, you won't have to feel sorry for me. If you've got the guts, look up and say something to me, and we'll see if I can hear you. What do you say? Let's make a pact.

He didn't seem to be joking, and I didn't know what to say. But when I opened my mouth to try, he burst out laughing, and I realized he was joking after all. I couldn't think of any reason why anybody would want to hang his head up there, so it had to be a joke.

I'll never forget the sight of him holding his chin up and laughing. He had a big Adam's apple, bigger than most men's, like a real apple.

He was still laughing when Young Mistress came into the compound.

She asked: What are you laughing at?

Her brother said: I'm laughing at you. You're losing weight. How come?

She said: I'm not losing weight. Guanghan will be here in a while.

Her brother said: I'm not going to let Guanghan exploit you like this. Just look at your hands—they're covered with paste. If he can't afford to hire workers, I'll put up the money, how's that?

Zheng Yusong burst out laughing again.

Young Mistress wasn't laughing; she couldn't. I watched her sit at the stone table, her eyes becoming moist, then I moved back a bit. I waited, but she didn't say anything, so I turned and went to my room, where I lay down on my bamboo cot. I was tired. After a while, I heard some noise, but it never occurred to me that they were arguing. I opened my door and walked outside, where I was met by shouts from Zheng Yusong.

He said: This is men's business!

Young Mistress said: You can get anybody you want. But no, it has to be him!

Zheng Yusong said: He's willing to do it. Watching out for him is one thing, but don't start in on me!

Young Mistress said: You didn't even consider whether or not he was up to the task. If you need somebody to do it, you'd be better off with me than with him. Why haven't you asked me?

Zheng Yusong said: I told you, this is men's business! Women have no business getting involved. Maybe you've forgotten the Zheng family practice. Well, I'm here to remind you.

Second Young Mistress said: This is the Cao family!

Starting to lose control, Zheng Yusong said: So what if it's the Cao family, so what?

He smashed a teapot with his fist.

The tea splashed on his and his sister's faces.

It was Young Mistress who spotted me standing near the pond.

They both shut up.

Second Master rushed back from the granary, a hard look in his eyes, his shoulders slumped. He stood by the stone table for a moment, then went inside with Zheng Yusong to discuss something. Young Mistress sat there, her eyes fixed on a spot beneath the eaves of the little pavilion. With a dustpan in one hand and a broom in the other, I went over, as if walking on eggshells, and swept up the pieces of broken teapot. I was in no mood to talk, but I couldn't help myself.

Don't worry, I said. If there's anything you need done, no matter how hard it is, just tell me, and I'll do it.

She said: Go on back to your room after you've swept it up, Ears.

She didn't so much as look at me.

A piece of broken teapot lay under one of her feet.

I got down on my hands and knees.

I said: Lift your foot just a bit, please.

She lifted her foot. Bits of sawdust clung to her shoe; slivers of bark were caught in her cotton stocking. My heart ached as I picked up the broken piece, wishing I could spend the rest of my life on

my hands and knees beside her. Oh, how I wanted to stroke her
foot.

I said: Don't be so sad.

She said: What do you know, Ears?

She was right, I didn't know anything.

I was a slave, so I was supposed to know nothing.

I couldn't stand seeing her so sad, with tears in her eyes.

I felt like jumping into the pond and drowning myself.

Later that day, Second Master saw Zheng Yusong off. I stood by the gate and bowed low when his sedan chair went by. May you have a safe trip, I said. Zheng Yusong lifted a corner of the curtain and gave me a long look. He might have been thinking back to the time he'd tossed a silver ingot to me and I hadn't bent down to pick it up.

He said: Don't forget, youngster. Wherever they hang my head, you come over and say something to see if I can still hear. You won't forget, youngster, will you?

I won't! I promised.

He turned to Second Master and said: That youngster's got balls. You can count on him.

His sedan chair virtually flew onto the road to town. Second Master stood on the steps, giving me a hard stare. Was he thinking about what his brother-in-law had just said? I was standing at the bottom of the steps and stared right back at him. You may be the Second Master, I was thinking, but you're not worth one of Young Mistress's feet. But there was such a scary look in his eyes that I blinked first.

I heard him heave a sigh.

He asked: What's Old Master been taking lately?

I said: Angelica.

He asked: Anything else?

Eggshells, I said.

He looked at me a while longer, then turned and went back inside. The look in his eyes softened a bit before he turned around, reminding me that Second Master was a good man at heart, which I sometimes tended to forget. With his shoulders slumped, he

seemed to be shrinking as he walked, as if something were pressing him down and down and wouldn't stop until he was in the
ground. And that scene reminded me of Zheng Yusong's head.

His head was hanging everywhere, covering the earth.

The sight left me speechless.

Bloody heads had invaded my daydreams.

All the living people in my dreams were submerged in blood.

I asked: Does it hurt?

The head said: No, I'm very comfortable.

The fearless man laughed.

Once Second Master had a new compound, he almost always came
home late, and some nights he didn't come home at all. At first he
had two men stand watch at night, then three, and still he was terrified of the prospect of fire. He had the windows of the chemical
lab sealed, leaving only a palm-sized square of glass in the center.
He followed that up by sealing the lab compound door, except for
a tiny entrance about the size of a man's face, barely wide enough
for an arm to squeeze through. He then had a protective brick wall
built in front of the lab door, as well as several objects the size of
chicken coops in the compound itself; that's where he stored the
gunnysacks filled with charcoal and saltpeter. And still he was
nagged by worries. So he brought over a bunch of vats, some big,
some small, in which he stored his rare items, tightly covering the
big vats with small ones, then covering them.

No one was allowed in his chemical lab. Every morning he walked
out with a wooden bucket filled with chemical paste and dumped
it into a trough, where he stirred it a time or two to test it to his
satisfaction. Then he'd lock the lab door and walk beneath the
match commune signboard, skirt the stone terrace, and enter the
western compound, shutting and bolting the gate behind him. He
could remain there the rest of the day if no one called him out.
There were times when he wouldn't even open the gate for the
servant bringing him meals, who would just leave the tray on the
ground next to the gate. Even when Young Mistress came over to
talk to him, he'd merely open the gate a crack. Be careful, I don't

want a fire, he'd say. His cheek would be twitching nonstop, as if the fire were already blazing, already licking at his pale face.

I often knocked at his gate. I had no choice.

He'd say: Fire! I don't want a fire!

I'd say: Big Road is looking for you.

Or I'd say: Young Mistress is looking for you.

He'd ask me: What for?

I'd say: The mixture is too thick today.

Either that or I'd say: Somebody's here to get something.

He'd come out, lock the door, and follow me, dusting his clothes as he walked, including shoes and socks. His face would be ashen, his neck scrunched down between his shoulders. It scared me to see him like that, as if some calamity were about to come crashing down on him.

I don't know what he was scared of.

I could only think about him strangling himself and lighting the chemicals.

I thought he was up to something weird again.

Old Barren and Hole in the Ground had been sent back to work in the match commune. Somebody asked Old Barren what Second Master did all day long. That borderline idiot said he spent his time mixing chemicals. Said he was trying to make matches that burned black and others that burned purple. No one believed that, but we all knew that whatever Second Master was up to, it had something to do with matches. Big Road had no doubts either, mainly because he wasn't thinking. Nobody but a madman would be experimenting with explosives right next to a match commune.

And Big Road did not think that Second Master was a madman.

At most, he viewed him as an eccentric.

By then he was no longer paying much attention to Second Master. As far as he was concerned, his host could do whatever he damn well pleased. If I'd been asked to pick a madman in the match commune, it wouldn't have been Second Master. I'd have picked that blue-eyed, big-nosed foreigner. Day in and day out, all he saw was Young Mistress. He really had gone off the deep end!

Second Master had a hard look in his eyes.

But he wasn't hard.
He was just stubborn.
He had the eyes of a little lamb.
He looked at people like this.
How would you describe it?
A wolf?
Okay, a wolf.
I was one of the first to see that.
Because I was a wolf too.
I wanted the life of that foreigner.
I admit it.
It was jealousy.
If something's that obvious, there's no need to talk about it, is there?
You're not as smart as you think, youngster.

March 24th

Second Master said he wanted me to accompany him somewhere the following morning, and told me I was to say nothing to anyone. He said it was something very important, but since he kept me in the dark, how could I say anything to anyone? After tossing and turning half the night, I got up and went to see a cook I considered a friend, asking him to make sure he took Big Road his breakfast in the morning. Back in my room, I started thinking, but there was no predicting what Second Master had planned. Then I thought back to Zheng Yusong, how he'd smashed the teapot and how he and Young Mistress had quarreled.

Young Mistress had said to him: If you need somebody to do it, you'd be better off with me than with him.

And Zheng Yusong had shot back: I told you, this is men's business! Women have no business getting involved.

At the time, I was so muddleheaded, all I could think was that Second Master and Zheng Yusong had done something bad when they were off somewhere together. Not until that night did I realize that what they were talking about probably was connected to Second Master's secretive activities in the compound. But even then I couldn't be sure what it was all about, and had no idea what he had in store for me. I wasn't frightened, just curious, and was determined to figure things out. What kept spinning through my head was the bizarre sight of Second Master trying to strangle himself. I could just about guarantee that I was in for more surprises. Far too tense to sleep, I went outside for a stroll. Very quietly I climbed onto the roof.

There wasn't a lit lamp anywhere.

The Cao household was black as ink.

After taking off my shoes, I negotiated the roof tiles barefoot. The clumps of moss on the tiles made it feel as if I were stepping on pigeon droppings. I stood directly over Second Master and Young Mistress's room for a very long time, fantasizing over the scene below. A snakelike whip lay in the middle of the large bed. Second Master was using it to strangle Young Mistress; either that or using it on himself. They were both screaming, but muffling the sound with their comforter. Second Master was sucking Young Mistress's nipple, sucking her swelling breast dry. He was pressing down on top of her until she was little more than a layer of skin spread across the bed. She kept screaming; her screams were as pleasant to hear as her laughter. With a twist of his body, Second Master turned into a snake. Young Mistress's shrill screams tore through the ceiling.

I was having a daydream in the middle of the night there on the rooftop. I stood right over their heads for a long, long time, so long that the tile ridges hurt the soles of my feet. But I couldn't see a thing. And there wasn't a sound. I was standing under the Elm Township sky, a soul beyond the control of anyone and everyone.

All I cared about was my own pleasure.

I couldn't have cared less about what was going on in the world. I knew what to do.

Enveloped in my dreams of Young Mistress's cries, I began to fly.

I was ecstatic!

We were on the road before daybreak. Stars filled the sky, then went out one by one. By the time the sun finally made its appearance, we'd walked all the way to Oxhorn Valley, on the western edge of the basin. The forest was so dense that some light was able to get through, but we couldn't see the sun. We were both carrying packs, front and back. Mine were filled with little sacks of charcoal and saltpeter. He was carrying sulfur powder and an assortment of other items. As we sneaked out of the compound, he said: Don't walk too fast, and make sure you don't let anything bump into your pack. That's all he said to me.

We hadn't even taken a lantern along, so at first we'd had to make our way by starlight. Worried about fire, he walked slowly, as if afraid of sparks from the soles of his shoes. I had a bellyful of questions, but held them back. As I followed him, I vowed that whatever he asked me to do, I'd do it. I was pretty sure he wouldn't ask me to bury him alive or anything like that.

Once the sun came up, I could see that there was something very different about Second Master that morning. To begin with, he didn't look all rumpled. And although he wasn't wearing his fake queue, his slicked-down hair fell all the way to his shoulders, like a curtain. He was wearing the black suit he had worn on the day he returned from abroad—not a wrinkle anywhere. His face was even paler than usual, and cleaner, and there was calmness in his eyes. I don't recall ever seeing him so serene.

He sought out a large rock in Oxhorn Valley, one that was smoother than a door plank, standing in the middle of a dry riverbed. We laid down our packs and ate some dry provisions we'd brought along. For the first time that day he looked me in the eye.

He asked me: What have you been thinking about all day, Ears?

I said: I've been thinking about how best to serve my master.

How was I going to tell him what I'd really been thinking? I couldn't tell anyone, let alone him. I'd just keep my thoughts to myself.

He asked me: What else?

I said: I was thinking about what else I could do.

That was the truth.

He asked me: Why's that?

I said: So I can earn my keep.

Do you think society is fair? he asked.

I said: Yes.

Then he asked: What do you want more than anything?

I said: For the Cao family to be so successful that wherever we go we'll have plenty of face, that we can stand proud!

What makes you proud? he asked.

That stopped me. A good question. What could a slave be proud of? Second Master's cold response to my comment seemed to show his displeasure. He looked serene, but only on the outside. After a moment's silence, he began to reveal what was on his mind.

Are you bewildered? he asked me.

No, I said.

I'm not sure if he even heard me. He was looking at the sun rising above the treetops.

I asked: Are you?

He said: Yes, more than I can say.

What are we going to do? I asked.

He asked me: How old are you?

Seventeen, I answered, by Chinese reckoning.

He said: I'm twenty-three.

That's all he said before starting to remove things from his pack. I tensed. There was something wrong with the way he was talking and acting. All those questions—what was he getting at? He laid a sheet of bamboo paper over the surface of the rock and dumped some charcoal on it, then spread it evenly with a wooden comb. After that he poured the saltpeter on top and spread it even.

He covered that with a layer of sulfur powder, then told me to go over and stand behind a large boulder. But I didn't move, vowing to stay there with him. When he saw what I was up to, he gripped my arm and stood. He was stronger than I imagined. When he started dragging me away, I tried to hold back, but couldn't. His eyes looked like those of a dead man. I couldn't leave him, not now.

I asked: Second Master, what are you going to do?

He said: Ears, you're a mutt.

I asked again: Second Master, what are you going to do?

He said: Just keep your eyes open and your mouth shut. If I call you, come over. If I don't, stay where you are. You hear me?

I stopped fighting him.

He called me a mutt. If that's what I was, then that's what I had to act like. So I took cover behind the boulder and watched him, like an obedient mutt.

After stirring the mixture with his comb, over and over, he scooped it into a small-mouthed, big-bellied porcelain bottle and then, using a twig, inserted something that looked like a lamp wick. When that was done, he sealed the mouth of the bottle, picked up his pack, and came over to where I was standing, his face all sweaty.

With the back of his hand, he mopped his face; his fingers were trembling.

He said: Ears, if anything goes wrong, you go home and tell Guangman to bring some men and bury me. Otherwise, you're to say nothing to anyone about what you see today. Ah, to hell with it! Just forget everything I said. I don't know why I brought you along in the first place. What's the point?

Covering his face with both hands, he wiped it hard.

He said: I wonder what it will sound like.

He muttered something else, then walked somewhat lifelessly over to the rock, where, without a second thought, he lit a match, sending sparks flying. Lurching backward, he stumbled, caught his balance, and started running. Nothing happened. He crouched alongside me, panting like a bellows. The left side of his face was blistered by the sparks, his eyebrows badly singed. A choking sound rose from his throat, sort of like laughing and sort of like sobbing. Now I was seeing the real him, and the lightheartedness of that morning was gone. His taut cheeks were twitching. He was puffing like mad, trying to calm himself; but even the puffs quivered.

He said: Ears, no matter what happens, don't breathe a word to anyone. If Zheng Yusong shows up, bring him here; he'll know what to do. Ears, you're a mutt. Society's fair, you say? Then why are you a mutt?

He was tongue-tied and embarrassed, so he gave me hell, shamed me. I grabbed hold of him and wouldn't let go. He was losing his mind, and I couldn't let him go.

Second Master, I said, let me do it.

All he said was: You still say it's fair? You mutt.

He kicked me in the ankle, and I fell to the ground, writhing in pain. As if in the grip of madness, he took off like a shot. From where I was I couldn't see a thing. But I heard some startled birds fly off. Next I heard the hiss of the burning wick and the sound of running. He was shaking, he was wobbling, he was moving too slowly. He was scared stiff.

In my mind's eye, I could see his ashen face twist and cringe.

I screamed: Second Master! Heaven protect you!

Whoom! It was deafening, it was paralyzing. It was the loudest noise I'd ever heard. I figured Second Master was done for. But, no, he wasn't. When I opened my eyes, he was standing beside the boulder, his teeth bared, like he was crying. I couldn't speak. He couldn't either. The back of his shirt had a foot-long rip, the torn cloth flapping like a banner in the wind. He was shaking like a leaf, but he quickly put together another bomb and exploded it without a hitch. Finally, I understood what Second Master was up to, and with my own eyes I saw him succeed. No matter what he did now or what he said, in my eyes he was a dead man. Everything he did before and after he lit the fuse convinced me that he was a cowardly madman who'd given up on life.

That day he decided to return to the left-hand compound by skirting the old granary. So we hugged the tree line as we headed toward Elm Township, never dreaming there'd be someone bathing in the Black River in the middle of autumn. Big Road rose out of the shallow water, naked as the day he was born, and scared the hell out of us.

Big Road shouted: Ears! Cao!

The words were no sooner out of his mouth than he froze. He'd spotted Second Master's cut face and ripped clothes. Second Master froze too. I couldn't wait to hear what he was going to tell Big Road. But he didn't say a word. Instead, he spun around and walked off.

Big Road asked: Ears, what happened?

I said: I don't know.

You're lying! he said.

I said: I don't know anything.

I spun around and walked off too.

Big Road was screaming something in the foreign language.

I knew he was ranting and cursing.

You can say fuck you in French too.

I didn't know how to say it.

But I knew it when I heard it.

March 25th

I sensed that Big Road knew something was up, and that he could go off the deep end at any time. But he was quiet. That night he lit a lantern on the veranda and set up the chess pieces to wait for Second Master to return.

Steward Bing had described Second Master's injuries to Elder Master, who then told their parents. So Second Master had no choice but to go pay his respects to his father and mother with his face all scarred; Young Mistress went with him. Meanwhile, Big Road sat alone on the veranda, like a piece of cast-off wood. So I sat there with him, replying to his persistent questions with the same answer: Second Master was experimenting with some new chemicals, and they blew up in his face. It was what Second Master told me to say, and what he told his parents. Big Road was so anxious, he didn't know whether to believe me or not. By then he'd smoked all his cigars, so Steward Bing fetched him a pipe that Elder Master no longer used from the storeroom. It had a sandalwood stem with a jade mouthpiece and a copper-nickel-alloy bowl. He smoked it, one pipeful after another, as if he'd been using it all his life. Out of boredom, he dumped the ashes onto the stone table and crushed them with chess pieces. Eventually, Second Master emerged, in the company of Young Mistress. They sat down at the table, where Second Master, hiding half of his face with a handkerchief, explained things to Big Road. I couldn't understand what he said, but Big Road didn't seem satisfied with the explanation, so after knocking out the last pipeful of ashes, he got up and returned to his room. Second Master simply flicked his sleeves and went inside.

Young Mistress sat there alone for a long while, and even though I was concerned that the cold autumn winds might be too much for her, I didn't dare go up to her. So I stayed where I was, off in the corner, watching. All over the compound crickets were chirping. Once autumn turned to winter, they were doomed.

When Second Master left the compound in a sedan chair, five porters, each carrying eight baskets, accompanied him. This time, however, their load was much heavier than before—their poles sagged dramatically under the baskets' weight, and their sandaled feet sunk deeply into the dirt path. Second Master said he was going into town to have his injuries looked at, and that he'd be back in a few days. He said he'd mixed all the chemicals the commune would need. As on his previous trips away from Elm Township, he turned the key for his chemical lab over to Young Mistress.

I walked behind him for a long distance. From where he sat in the sedan chair, he didn't know that I was following. After leaving the township, the procession headed up the path toward Jade Mountain. Unable to hold back any longer, I shouted: Master Guanghan, please take care of yourself!

He stuck his head out, without even having them stop.

He said: Don't forget to guard the granary at night.

He added: And watch out for fires. Now go on back, Ears.

I said: Come back as soon as you can, Second Master.

As the sedan chair climbed higher and higher under the bright sun, it looked like a gathering of gold specks. I heard what sounded like a loud rumble. The sedan chair was still there. So were the porters. But I had an uneasy feeling that Second Master would not be coming back.

Big Road worked during the daytime, but listlessly. At night I brought him his dinner on a tray and laid it out for him. But he just sat on the bed, as if in a trance, and wouldn't eat. He didn't hear me when I spoke to him, so I squatted between the bed and the bathtub with my arms tucked into my sleeves, watching but doing nothing. He sighed, and so did I. He said he felt like drinking, so I brought him a crock of liquor, and a few sips loosened his tongue. Raising his little finger and wagging it at me, he said:

Ears, you're no good!

No good, I said, no good.

You lied to me, he said.

I protested: No I didn't.

He said: They all lie to me.

Nobody lies to you, I said.

He said: Zheng—Yu—nan!

Dragging out the words, he blinked sadly. I didn't know what he had in mind, but I was afraid somebody might hear him calling out Young Mistress's name. What would people think if they overheard him? I pointed to my throat as a sign for him to lower his voice.

She lied to me too, he said.

Although he spoke this softly, the look in his eyes surprised me. Some of the liquor ran down his chin and onto his neck, but he ignored it. He picked up his chopsticks, but they kept falling out of his hand. He was horribly dejected. And getting horribly drunk. I was afraid that if he drank any more, he might go off half-cocked, and so I was glad to see him push the crock away. Whistling, he threw out his arms to indicate an explosion. Then he turned and started to pack his things. His bearlike figure swayed in the flickering lamplight, as if his shoes were too big for him.

I said: Big Road, what are you doing?

He said: I—can't take it any longer.

I asked: What are you going to do?

He said: I want, I don't want to die.

I ran out onto the veranda and told Wuling to summon Young Mistress. I told her Big Road was drunk and was getting ready to leave. She came over right away, bringing with her a subtle fragrance. Although she'd been working hard in the storeroom, she didn't look tired, after changing into clean clothes.

She stood on the steps and spoke to Big Road inside the room.

He was complaining hoarsely about something or other.

Young Mistress said: Come with me, Wuling.

Young Mistress and Wuling went inside. I stayed outside, since Young Mistress hadn't invited me in. Besides, I wouldn't have understood a word even if I had gone inside. Young Mistress didn't want us to understand. It sounded awful when she spoke the foreign tongue, very slowly, but Big Road understood her.

His voice kept getting louder and louder. Suddenly he blurted out: Blow it up! Blow it up! Like a shadow puppet, his outline through the window paper looked threatening, while Young Mistress's outline hardly moved. Then she raised her arm, and the room went silent.

I could tell she was throwing out the liquor remaining in his bowl.

Apparently, she was flinging it at him.

Wuling said: She flung the liquor right in Big Road's face.

I asked Wuling: Why?

Wuling said: I don't know, I couldn't understand a word she said.

That night, while I kept watch in the old granary, I tossed and turned, tormented by thoughts that Big Road must have said something indecent. Either that or he'd decided to rat on Second Master, tell people what he was up to. But my thoughts began shooting off in all directions, and I could see all sorts of conspiracies in the bright moonlight. I started to suspect Young Mistress's actions. So I sneaked back to Elm Township, feeling such a great sense of urgency that I galloped along like a horse. I had a premonition that something bad was about to happen in the left-hand compound. And I knew I had to keep it from happening, at any cost. I got onto the roof by climbing over the wall in the right-hand corner of the compound, then made my way across the rooftops of the Cao household, which was quiet as a graveyard. It wasn't until my feet stepped on the roof tiles of the left-hand corner that I realized what a laughable bastard I was. The compound was deathly still and dark; the pond, lit up by moonbeams, was also deathly still. Everything was just like all other nights. I lay down beside the skylight to keep watch over whomever it was I couldn't get out of my thoughts. Was it Second Master? Or myself? What kind of person was I?

After a while, I got up and sneaked back to the match commune.

Big Road had gone out to work early that morning. He'd gone straight to Second Master's workroom and poured water on everything inside. Once the place was drenched, he'd taken a pickax to the stove, the chimney, and the walls. At the time, I was asleep on a pile of bark in the old granary, and when I heard the crashing thuds, I went over to see what was going on. I ran up to him.

What do you think you're doing? I shouted.

He said: I'm finding a way to live; I want to live! I don't want to die!

I said: You can't wreck Second Master's property. Wait till he comes home.

He just said: Get out of here!

He flung me a good three feet away. I ran back and wrapped my arms around his legs. But that didn't work, since he just dragged

me back and forth as he continued wrecking the place. I started to
cry, but I can't tell you why I cried so easily.

I protested: Second Master isn't here, so don't do that!

Ears, he said, get out of here!

Pretty soon, Young Mistress showed up, but she just stood off a
ways and watched him. She didn't even get someone to come help.
Seeing her not lifting a finger to stop him, I cried even harder. I
knew I looked like a little crybaby, but I couldn't have stopped the
tears even if I'd wanted to.

Young Mistress said: Ears, let him be. He can do what he wants,
it's up to him. What are you crying about, you little baby?

I let go of Big Road's legs.

He scooped up all the sulfur in the corner with a spade and flung
it to the bottom of the steps, sending dirt flying into the air. He was
howling the whole time, like a wild animal, spewing a stream of
foreign words that frightened me every bit as much as the roar of
a lion would have.

I figured that Second Master must already have been blown
to bits.

I hadn't done right by him. I'd really and truly let him down.

But wait a minute.

How had I let him down?

To hell with him.

It was outrageous!

Second Master came home around noon. The trip had been uneventful, and he was in a pretty good mood. Before going over to the match
commune, he got a report on Big Road's cleanup actions from Steward Bing, and apparently took the news calmly. He rushed over to
the compound that had been all torn up only a few days before. He
looked healthy and chipper when he took the key to the chemical-
mixing room from Young Mistress. I didn't witness any of this
myself, because I was away from Elm Township at the time. Old
Master had sent me to the cluttered cemetery on the far bank of the
Black River to catch some toads. After you skin the things and cut
them open, you halve them and dump them into the cauldron while

the water is still cool. The top and bottom halves swim separately, faster and faster as the water heats up, and begin tumbling crazily as the water starts to boil. Then and only then do you clamp the lid on tightly to let them cook. The flesh this time was especially pale, the blood vessels blue as the sky. The toads' claws thrashed around like chopsticks, making loud splashes as they churned in the water. Old Master could hardly contain his joy. I stuck around until he put the lid on, then took the skins and spread them out on the stone steps to bake in the sun. After they were dry, I'd grind them up into powder, which Old Master would take with water.

The sun was setting in the west by the time I went over to the left-hand corner of the compound. I squatted down to smooth out the cobblestone path. First I pried up the loose stones, then I spread some lime on top of the dirt, added water, and reset the stones. Wuling and Young Mistress were the first to return, followed a little later by Big Road. Then came Second Master's familiar footsteps. I was happy he hadn't been blown to bits, happy and slightly uneasy. Gauze covered a good part of the left side of his face, and he was wearing a pair of round, black-rimmed eyeglasses. His lips were unusually red. I stood up and bowed to him.

I said: Good afternoon, Second Master!

He didn't reply as he walked slowly up the path. So I squatted back down to keep working. I sensed that he had stopped, but I paid no attention. I assumed he was watching to see what I'd do with the stone in my hand, so I stuck out my tongue and fitted the stone in just perfectly. He just kept standing there without moving, which puzzled me, and I was sorely tempted to raise my head and look at him. All of a sudden, I felt a heavy blow on my neck—right on the spot that connected my head to my shoulders, just below the ear. Even when I thudded to the ground, it never occurred to me that he would actually hit me. I was lying on my back and trying to get up again when another blow hit me in the nose. This time I saw who it was who hit me, but why in the world would he do it? It must be because of how the yard was all torn up, and I wanted to scream out: Don't hit me, I had nothing to do with it! But I bit down on my lip and didn't let out a peep.

How could I? I had no way of knowing why he'd done it. Maybe he'd gone crazy. He really hit me hard, and I saw a look of delight in his dancing eyes. I didn't try to protect myself, didn't even lower my head. I just let the blood from my nose run down my chin and onto my neck. I counted every hit, and when I was up to eleven, Wuling came out and saw what was happening. She screeched like a pig under the knife, and I heard Young Mistress's voice.

Stop that! she shouted. He had nothing to do with it!

Then she shouted: Ears, get out of here—now!

Why should I? The twelfth punch landed on my nose again, rocking me backward. I regained my balance, but by then hot blood had run down into my throat and had come spraying out of my mouth. A cascade of red that made my knees weak. Just then Big Road came rushing out; he grabbed hold of Second Master's sleeve and pulled him off me.

What's going on here? he shouted.

Second Master stared blankly at his hand, stained with my blood. Then he looked at me. My head looked like a bloody gourd. He rubbed his head with the back of his hand, as if he were trying to think of something that kept eluding him.

Big Road shouted: Hit me! Hit me!

He steered the benumbed Second Master over to the veranda. Knowing that I looked a real mess, I ran to my room, where I dug some cotton wadding out of my tattered quilt and stuffed some up each nostril. Then I cleaned my face and wiped my hands on the front of my jacket. My ears were ringing. The last thing I wanted to do was move, let alone go back outside. Wuling came in to see how I was, and the sight of all that blood on my clothes had her sobbing in no time.

I said: He didn't hit you, so what are you crying about?

What's wrong with Master Guanghan? she asked.

I don't know, I replied. He must be depressed.

She asked: Is he all right? Is he normal? Is he?

I don't want to hear any of your nonsense! I snapped. What I want is for you to get dinner for Big Road. I can't go out like this. And wash my clothes tonight, since I have to wear them tomorrow.

I'd pretty much decided that he'd hit me because he'd assumed I'd been talking about him to Big Road. But I hadn't. The only person who might have been doing that was Young Mistress. If this was worth beating someone for, he should have turned his fists on her. When all was said and done, I'd taken a beating for Young Mistress. Which was just fine with me. And Second Master probably knew exactly what he was doing. He'd given me a beating all for show: beating a person who didn't deserve it to show another person who did. The look in his eyes when he was beating me said it all with one word: mutt!

Mutt!

He'd beaten the right person after all.

I'd gotten what I deserved.

But that day, after swallowing my own blood, I couldn't help thinking that if he'd beaten Young Mistress the way he'd beaten me, I'd have killed him! And not twelve times, as he'd done with me, but just once. He'd have paid with his life. Late that night, I kept asking myself: Would you have the guts? A mutt of a slave like you, would you have the guts?

I answered my own question: You bet I would!

But Second Master, who had turned savage without warning, never laid a finger on Young Mistress. He was the perfect husband in that respect. Wuling said that he stood in the light of the lamp, a whip in his hand, just sighing and crying and calling himself all kinds of strange names: a maggot, a man lower than a pig or a dog. But this time, he didn't ask Young Mistress to use the whip on him. Instead, he put his hand on the lamp glass, raising a blister the size of a hen's egg. Wuling said she could hear his skin sizzle and could smell burning flesh!

A worthless maniac!

What can I say about him.

I want to speak, then stop.

I want to speak, then stop.

I say instead, the weather's cool, it's a nice autumn.

I felt sorry for him.

March 26th

Steward Bing asked what had happened to my nose. How come it's crooked? I said it's nothing, I tripped on the steps and banged it on the doorstep. He said with so many steps in the compound, you have to be more careful. I said, I know, I'll keep my eyes open from now on. I didn't want anyone to know I'd been beaten. If the tenant farmers knew I'd been beaten like a lowly dog, they'd look down on me for sure. So I walked with my head up, as if nothing had happened.

Second Master never mentioned the beating. For him, as well, it was as if nothing had happened. But whenever he looked at me, he seemed to be searching for the marks he'd left on my face and body, or looking for new spots for his hand. I was on my guard— I had to be. He was looking for a clever worker, someone to whom he could teach the intricacies of mixing chemicals, but none of the men he'd hired made the grade. So he wound up choosing me.

I didn't want to go. The way he took leave of his senses when he was mixing up his batches of chemicals made me very nervous. I was afraid I'd get as wrapped up in the process as he was, since I was fond of chemicals. But I was decidedly not fond of explosions. And he was a walking time bomb, ready to go off at any time. I needed to put some distance between us.

So I asked: If I go, who'll take care of Big Road?

He said: He doesn't need anyone to take care of him.

I said: He sweats so much when he works that someone has to wash his towels all the time.

Wuling can do that, he said.

Okay, I said, I'll go.

I followed him to his mixing room, which looked like a haunted crypt. The light was bad to begin with, but before long, I got used to it. He paced back and forth slowly as he spoke to me, pitching his voice high like a little old lady's. First he taught me the difference between talc, glass dust, and gypsum by having me rub them between my fingers. He had me smell rosin, cartilage, manganese powder, and sulfur. He kept his voice low, as if whispering or talking in his sleep or talking behind people's backs.

He said: When they're separate it's no big deal. Mixing them together is a different matter.

He added: They'll do whatever you want them to do. It's all in your hands.

Then he said: Ears, treat yourself as if you were part of all this.

Ears, he said, don't ever sneeze into the mixing bowl.

That's about all there was to mixing the ingredients, but he prattled on and on until my head swam. Later on, when I was alone in the shed, his words emerged from a corner of the wall or from inside a vat and rang in my ears, a drone that actually sounded better than his normal, frigid speech. He became a gentle, calm person when he was mixing his chemicals, like the Second Master I'd known before he went abroad. But I never lost sight of the fact that he could change in an instant, like when he was lighting the mixture of chemicals or during one of those weird moods we all found so baffling.

Second Master began making frequent trips away from Elm Township—for medical treatment, to buy stuff, to see friends, to attend trade shows—until he was a regular visitor at the county and prefecture capitals. Match commune duties were taken over by the foreigner. Elder Master and Steward Bing didn't seem particularly concerned about Second Master's meanderings. Steward Bing suggested he'd grown tired of married life and was keeping a whore out there somewhere. He said that a man doesn't have to be the worldly type to succumb to this sort of temptation. And so what, so long as he doesn't forget his family!

trouble holding on to him?

I said: I don't know. I see them hugging and kissing on the veranda all the time. That's all I know.

That was a lie. I fantasized them kissing, but never actually saw it. What I really saw was something quite different, and in a different place. And worst of all, Second Master wasn't part of it.

It happened in the machine room in the old granary. Big Road was sitting on a bamboo basket behind the shaving machine, Young Mistress was sitting on another basket behind the stripping machine. Only five or six feet separated them, and they were looking into one another's eyes. They were in the grip of a desire to do something they didn't want others to see. They wanted to kiss! But they weren't close enough, and all they could do was look at each other and pucker up. First Big Road puckered up, then it was Young Mistress's turn. Back and forth it went, one after another. He was whistling. She tried to do it, but failed. And that's how it went. The machines were making so much noise, I couldn't actually tell if she made any sound. Finally, she puckered up one last time and held it, whistling a tune nobody could hear.

Her thick, fleshy lips, so soft and red, formed a perfect pink circle, and Big Road just sat there gaping at her, as if he were about to be sucked into that circle. I concluded that Young Mistress was not making any sound, and that it was all part of some sad intrigue. They thought no one knew what they were up to. But I knew. I surrounded them like the dust in the granary, watching their every move, and they didn't realize it. They could not hide the truth from me. I had them right where I wanted them.

I'd lied to Steward Bing when I told him that Second Master and Young Mistress often hugged and kissed on the veranda. What else could I do? So I became an accomplice in their intrigue.

I wanted to watch.

To see without being seen.

I wanted to see how people did that thing I longed for day and night. I wanted to see if the sky would fall or the earth open up. I wanted to see how the goddess who filled my daydreams cried out.

My ears were filled with the cooing calls of doves.

I couldn't take any more of those never-ending daydreams.

And I vowed not to.

At night, Old Barren and I were keeping watch in the granary when that agonizing premonition rose up inside me again, driving me out onto the road back to Elm Township, as if a demon were chasing me. The sky was dark and overcast. Autumn thunder rolled across Jade Mountain, bringing cold winds with it. I had trouble making out the roadway, and in my haste to get home, I stumbled and fell time and time again. It had started raining by the time I slipped into town, and I was barely able to climb up the slippery bark of the elm tree behind the right-hand corner of the compound. The playful laughter of Elder Master and his wife and concubine merged with the sound of the rain. The room was dark as they took turns calling one another cunt and bitch, then burst out laughing when they did whatever it was they were up to. The soles of my bare feet on the cold, hard, dark roof tiles began to itch, and that itch kept moving up, all the way to my backbone and from there straight into my heart. By the time I reached the wall of the left-hand corner, alongside the man-made hill, the rain was coming down in sheets, and trees inside and outside the compound were swaying and howling with the rain and wind.

Lightning split the autumn sky, followed by the crack of thunder. Everything around me leaped into view. My eyes were fixed on the path leading to the main compound, and I thought I saw movement on the narrow path in front of the wall and artificial hill. Peals of thunder rolled through the sky, but I saw no more lightning as I stood on the wall, holding on to a thick branch and not moving. Maybe it had been the shadow of a tree. But maybe not; maybe it was someone rolling around in the rain. He and she were coiled so tightly together that they looked like a huge fish flopping around in shallow water. I felt like I was being lifted up by the wind, light as a feather. Then another bolt of lightning, and I saw it was only the twisted shadow of the old tree on the other side of the wall. Whatever had been rolling around on the watery ground of the narrow path was gone—forever. Were my eyes playing tricks on me? Had those dog-eyes of mine fallen prey to one of my daydreams?

I jumped down onto the path and sprawled in the water to smell what was there. Nothing but leaves, grass, and rocks. Then I felt around; with the rain beating down on the backs of my hands, all I felt were cobblestones, dead leaves, and mud. I was a damned idiot, possessed by a demon, convinced that I could detect the warmth of Young Mistress's body there. I rolled over in the water. At first it was cold, but before long it felt like boiling water.

I called out Young Mistress's name. It echoed like the explosion in Oxhorn Valley! What I'd seen brought feelings of rapture. One of her long legs was sticking up into the sky above Elm Township, through the wind and the rain, swaying like the trunk of a milky white sapling, stripped of its bark.

What exactly had I seen?

Nothing.

A momentary derangement in an autumn rain shower.

How I wished I'd been blind.

The leg wasn't a leg at all.

A flower had grown on the inside of my eyelids.

Close your eyes and give it a try.

Sometime during the day the local basket maker had left a bunch of bamboo baskets by the gate to the old granary. There were fifty or sixty of them, all stacked against the wall. They were so light you could easily pick up five at a time with one hand. When it was time to knock off work, the commune workers went down to the riverbank to remove a felled poplar that was stuck in the pulley. I stayed behind. My face was burning up as I squatted down beside the wall and hid under two stacks of baskets. For a long time I'd been looking for a chance to do that, but had always balked at the thought of actually going through with it. Off on the other side of the wall the men were shouting as they worked the tree loose and sent it down the river with a loud crunch, as if the wall had come crashing down. The tiny holes in the baskets turned the compound into checkerboard fragments, as if I were looking through a sieve. I was afraid that anyone walking into the compound would see me right off and drag me out like a scrawny chicken, then spit in my face as punishment for my disgraceful behavior. But now that I was hidden there, I couldn't stand up.

Finally, all the workers were gone, leaving only the night watchman, who scraped the soles of his shoes on the wooden track as he walked into the compound. Then someone else came in. Whoever it was walked in with a rustle, like clothes brushing against a dry towel. *Pa pa pa.* It was hitting something soft. A thigh? A calf? If you listen closely enough, you can always distinguish sounds. I heard a turtle crawling along the base of the wall, and I also heard the scurrying of ants hidden among the bamboo baskets.

The night watchman was Big Road.

The other person was Young Mistress.

First I heard them.

Then I saw them.

He was digging tobacco out of a pouch with the bowl of his pipe and squinting into the sky. The sun was just setting behind the valley off to the west, and only a sliver of red, like a fiery tongue, was still visible. Young Mistress was facing the gate, sweeping wood shavings off the steps, including some that were wedged in the cracks. They were having a leisurely conversation about trivial matters—exactly what, I couldn't tell. But I think it had something to do with making glue out of skin and bones from the slaughterhouse. Either that or the wages they paid to Old Barren, the hired hand. These were the sorts of things they talked about during the day. During the day they also hid behind the machinery to practice whistling. But now, instead of being five or six feet apart, the distance between them had shortened to less than two feet. Big Road was lying under the machine and reaching out for his wrench. When Young Mistress handed it to him, he grabbed her hand. Instead of trying to pull it back, she looked over at the leather conveyor belt, her face ghostly white, as if she were struggling to make that final commitment to let herself be swept in.

The setting sun turned her pale face red. It also lent a red tinge to the fullness of her body, which seemed almost iridescent. Even her hair, with its bits of wood shavings, had turned red.

What incredible beauty!

What I felt like doing was stealing one of Second Master's bombs and blowing myself up.

How satisfying it would be to blow myself to pieces at a time like this!

Too bad that moment couldn't be frozen in time.

Big Road started to light his pipe, but Young Mistress told him not to. So he dumped the tobacco back into his pouch with a sigh. With her back to him, he took a look around. I thought he might pick up a tool and look for something to do, but instead he fixed his gaze on Young Mistress's back and slowly walked up to her. I couldn't tell if she heard him coming. But whether she did or not, I saw her shoulders hunch inward and her head droop. She kept sweeping the floor.

Big Road grabbed her from behind, one arm around her neck to hold her head up, the other under her arms to press her body to his. She made a feeble attempt to get free, but he lifted her off her feet. Letting her head fall backward, she gazed off at the red horizon, as tears streamed down her cheeks.

I closed my eyes in my hiding place.

I was so aroused my head swam.

I felt terrible.

My heart was like a ceramic bowl that had fallen to the floor and shattered.

I heard the sound of faces touching.

I heard the sound of hungry lips meeting.

I heard the sound of bodies colliding.

And I heard the sound of someone lying down on a bed of bark.

They went into the drying room.

A rack piled with wood plugs thudded to the floor!

The noise kept coming.

It sounded like primitive mountain people stomping their feet.

They were dancing!

They were singing and dancing as if they were the only two people in the world.

I curled up like a singed insect and crawled quietly out of my hiding place. The main gate was shut, and so was the gate in the fence. So, like a dog, I hugged the fence and squeezed out through a crack between the gate and the tracks. But instead of heading back to Elm Township, I went straight to Jade Mountain, like a galloping horse. I tore through the underbrush like a madman, rolling and tumbling in the head-high artemisia. I was looking for a spot on the mountain, while there was still light, where I could compose myself. The red streaks in the sky disappeared and darkness enveloped the mountain as I straggled through the woods, bathed in sweat. Thoughts about the increasingly strange Second Master lightened my mood a bit. But then I pictured him out there on the bank of the Green River secretly mixing his explosive chemicals, and all I felt like doing was cry!

I fantasized that it was me lifting Young Mistress off her feet, and that it was me lighting the fuse on a bomb. There on Jade Mountain I had a really satisfying cry. After I'd cried myself out, I knew for sure that neither one of those had been me. And then the dam burst. I forgot all about Elm Township and the Cao family as my tears flowed again. There was no room in my heart for anything but the sun that set behind the mountain and the woman burning red in the sun's rays.

I dreamed I grabbed her from behind.

Her bones bent until they snapped in two.

She lay crumpled on the ground like a piece of tattered clothing.

Now she has turned into a puddle of mud.

There's no perfume in mud.

And no sound.

Not even a fetid rotting odor.

I can't stop thinking about her.

Especially how beautiful she was as she betrayed her husband.

I'm not worried about her becoming a handful of mud.

I love fried noodles.

I'll never be afraid of the smell of mud, not as long as I live.
I'd like to gobble up handfuls of the stuff.
I'd be eating her!
But where is she?
Won't you please tell me?
Where is she?
I'd like to snap her in two like a piece of firewood.
Who knows, maybe I'd be able to do something else.
I'm okay now.
The pain's gone.
Let's take a break.
Youngster, be very careful when you're committing adultery.
Be sure no one is pointing a dagger at your ass.
Once you're stabbed, it'll be too late to do anything!

March 27th

After the weather cooled off, activity slacked off at the Willow Township pier, and the starving refugees headed south along the Green River for warmer climes. I went to the pharmacy to buy four ounces of young antler flakes for Old Master, taking the long way round by visiting Acacia Township, as usual. Father Ma gave me a letter for Big Road and a sackful of bread. He asked me to remind Big Road that Christmas wasn't far off, and that the idle machinist ought to know what he needed to do.

The priest's unhappiness showed on his long face. But he was nice enough to me, and as I was leaving, he rubbed my head and said: Please give my regards to Mr. Cao, my lovely child, and to all the good people there. I'll ask the Lord to look over you. The heavy stench of body odor wafted out from the priest's robe, and all I could think was, The Lord ought to be looking after you! The church wall was so cracked and crumbling I didn't think it could withstand one more strong wind. Seeing the old priest stand there under that disintegrating wall filled me with foreboding. And all he was concerned about was what someone else ought to be doing. That person should know what he ought to be doing, if anyone did. In fact, he was already doing it, and having a great time!

I went to the teahouse for a cup of tea and the latest gossip from Lucky and his customers. The skulls had disappeared from the flagpole, but the tattered blue sashes and several queues still hung there, swaying in the wind like water reeds. Lucky said that some of the heads had been blown down in a recent windstorm. They'd split open like so many white and yellow teapots when they hit the flagstones, sending bone shards flying all over the pier. He said that human skulls are like walnuts—and not very good walnuts at that, ones that aren't completely formed, shriveled and black and dry. One of his customers disagreed.

The man said: What do you mean, walnuts? I think they're more like gourds!

Don't argue with me, Lucky said. Why don't you just say they're like crusty turds.

The customer said: They're all filled with shit, anyway. Why not?

So shut your goddamned mouth, Lucky said, and keep your shit in it.

Then the conversation turned to events downriver. The word bomb was mentioned more than once. A skiff tied to the northern pier in the prefecture had been blown up. It had a cabin and a sail, but was unmanned. It had been tied up all day, then suddenly exploded that night. The slip next to it had been reserved for the police magistrate, but he had chosen not to moor alongside the pier after sunset, and had kept heading downstream.

Lucky said: Someone planted that skiff there. A Blue Kerchief assassin was hiding in the cabin, but instead of blowing up the magistrate, he blew himself to smithereens!

I asked him: Do you know who it was?

He said: There wasn't a big enough body part left to identify him.

Since the magistrate's boat didn't stop, why'd he blow up the skiff? I asked.

He said: Who can say, when bombs are involved? Thump one of them like you would a watermelon, and if you're not careful, it'll go off. They're a lot riskier than those foreign cannon shells. The local constabulary has received some cannons from the provincial government. Have any of you seen them?

One of the customers replied: They're small, not much bigger than one of those Buddhist drums.

Lucky said: There's nothing wrong with small. If they can fire a shell across the river, even the Blue Kerchiefs can't outrun cannon fire.

I said: But maybe they won't run, and who knows who'll blow up whom?

I dumped out my tea leaves, tossed some coins on the table, and walked out. Lucky was staring at me as if he didn't know who I was. Thoughts of the poor wretch on the skiff saddened me. I couldn't believe that Second Master would ever be that stupid. But whoever he was, his nerves had failed him. He hadn't carried out his mission, and all anyone could do was pity him. My childish outburst in the teahouse invigorated me, as if I'd been a bomb with a short fuse that could blow up in the face of anyone who looked at me cross-eyed!

On the way back to Elm Township, I had the nagging feeling that Second Master might well have been the man on the skiff. Why not? Hiding out belowdecks amid a pile of explosives would be just like him. He couldn't be happy if he wasn't stirring things up. But if it wasn't him, who was it? I'd gone with him to Oxhorn Valley, and couldn't imagine him blown to bits and floating down the Green River, little chunks of food for passing fish. That's not the way he was supposed to end up. But when I thought about Big Road and Young Mistress back at the Cao estate, it occurred to me that it might not be such a bad way to end up, after all. If it'd been me, I'd have preferred to wind up in little pieces over coming back to the left-hand corner of this compound. It was the same old compound, with the same old people, but the atmosphere had changed completely.

Big Road was like a greased machine, or a well-fed horse. I'd never seen him so happy. Whatever he was doing—working, strolling, bathing—he whistled constantly and rewarded everyone he saw with a cocky, happy smile. Only I could see the shame that lay behind those smiles. After knocking off work, he'd stroll down the street, picking up the first child he saw and giving him a ride on his shoulders, surrounded by a whole pack of kids, who laughed, screeched, and kept calling him Big Nose. He'd reach down and grab them by their queues or by the seat of the pants, scaring them out of their wits.

Young Mistress was just the opposite. There was fear in her eyes. Fear of the townspeople. Fear of the commune workers. Fear of the Cao compound gate. Fear of the tail-swishing fish in the pond. Fear of the stone table on the veranda. Fear of the foreigner, whose back was as powerful as a fine horse. She even feared her own shadow. As far as I was concerned, there was nothing anywhere in the world she didn't fear. But when she thought about what had happened, she forgot that there was anyone around, the contented smile on her face revealing what was really in her heart. And what was revealed made her more beautiful than usual, more beautiful than the first day I'd seen her. And that brought me great disappointment, greater disappointment than I felt when any one of my daydreams was shattered. For me, the goddess had ceased to be the goddess I'd once known. She had been soiled!

She'd stopped looking like a goddess when she let Big Road lay her down.

Others couldn't see the fear in her eyes, but I could. And that made *me* afraid. My fear was far greater than hers. I couldn't bear to look at her, and couldn't bear to look at Big Road, as if it were me, not them, who had done that thing. Whenever I had time on my hands, I locked myself up in my little room and stayed there in bed, eyes shut, ears stuffed with cotton. Like the world's greatest sinner, I didn't want to see or hear anything.

in Elm Township. He'd waited so long for a letter from his mother
he couldn't see straight. But by the time I handed him the letter,
his heart had flown off to rest in some distant place. He wasn't
nearly as excited as I'd anticipated. He tore open the envelope and
read the letter with all the excitement of Second Master reading a
letter from an old schoolmate. After reading it twice, he lay down
on his bed and stared at the ceiling, a look of sheer contentment
on his face. I'm not afraid to say that he probably didn't understand a single thing Father Ma asked me to tell him. By then he
was totally immersed in the intoxicating joy of his thoughts.

He carried her into the drying room.

He laid the beauty down on a pile of tree bark.

Hiding behind the closed door of my room, I thought about what
would happen when Second Master came home. It'd be one thing
if he were kept in the dark, but a different thing altogether if he
found out. What if he did find out? What were we expected to do?
I shut my eyes and plugged my ears, and it felt like an explosion
had gone off in my head, blowing the dark, shriveled, dried-out
walnut to pieces.

I couldn't imagine what the skiff looked like after it blew up.

The smell of death seemed to permeate the compound.

In order to help Old Mistress celebrate the arrival of a local deity,
commune workers were given the day off. All of Elm Township
and its tenant farmers were mobilized for the festivities. Both sides
of the road from Jade Mountain all the way to the Cao estate were
packed with people. Musicians banged their drums and tooted
their horns in front of the gate tower, and the valley was filled with
the echoes of woodwinds and cymbals, as if musical instruments
occupied every inch of space. Everyone in the Cao household
dressed in new clothes to await the arrival of the new deity. I was
standing at the foot of the steps of the gate tower. My job, as always, was to direct the visitors' sedan chairs to their parking spots.
There weren't many guests, and some—the lay Buddhists—had
chosen to walk the whole way over Jade Mountain. A sedan chair

with the deity appeared on the mountainside. With a red canopy and red curtains, it resembled the chair that had brought Young Mistress over on her wedding day, and received the same welcome. The tenant farmers—men and women, young and old—were jubilant, their whistles filling the air like those of falconers. When the sedan chair entered town, it stopped in the middle of the street between two rows of attendants who rushed up and lifted the deity's gold-covered icon, commissioned by the Cao family, out of the chair as if it were made of eggshells. Roughly the size of a five- or six-year-old child, it had been carved out of sandalwood. It was seated cross-legged in a lotus platter, its many arms reaching out from both sides, centipede fashion, each palm inlaid with an open eye. All those identical eyes were staring at the jubilant crowd lining the street. Four men—eight strong arms—carried her high over their heads toward the Cao estate, followed by the now empty sedan chair. Bringing up the rear were a dozen or more simply clad monks on foot, their shaved heads floating amid the crowd like gourd ladles.

Old Mistress, in the company of Old Master, came to the gate tower to meet them. Steward Bing told me the new deity was a Thousand-Hand, Thousand-Eye Guanyin Bodhisattva, the Goddess of Mercy, one of the shining stars in the Buddhist firmament. She places her numerous hands and eyes in the service of mankind. In her meditation room, Old Mistress thought only of herself, so why was she bringing this unsettling deity into the house? I figured she was using this Buddha as a crutch, hoping the Bodhisattva would perform good deeds that were beyond her.

Old Mistress and Old Master got down on their knees at the top of the steps in honor of the slowly approaching deity. Old Mistress's face was ghostly white, her skin smooth and glossy; since she never went out into the sun, her appearance had not been ravaged by time. And because of that, the tenant farmers admired her with greater sincerity than even the new deity. Old Master's face was very dark, almost black, with a greenish tinge. Everyone in Elm Township knew that he filled himself with cure-alls and restoratives the year round, and they must have been puzzled over how he could have *restored* himself into this condition. They were surprised, they were sympathetic; some merely gloated. I saw it all from where I stood beneath the steps. What I didn't see was the far end of the deserted street, where a solitary man walked slowly on the cobblestones, a raincoat over his shoulder. Steel taps on his shoes made a wonderful sound on the stones. By the time I spotted him, he was already standing behind the musicians, watching the woodwind players as if in a trance.

Gloomy, melancholy Second Master was back.

He'd been gone slightly more than a week, but in that short time, everything had changed around here. And while he was out there, he'd also changed completely. Downtrodden, he looked exhausted. Obviously, something had gone very wrong. The wound on the left side of his face hadn't completely healed—the long scar was still pink—and now the right side was a mess, covered all over with gauze, even the ear.

I was speechless.

The look of melancholy on his face seemed to say that he already knew everything.

It looked to me like he was just waiting to strike.

I wanted to get the hell out of there.

I wanted to tell Young Mistress he'd come back.

He'd come back for revenge.

But I stayed where I was at the foot of the steps, not moving. There was a smile on my face as I fell to one knee to greet him. After watching the woodwinds for a while, he turned his attention to the drums, and then stepped over the threshold with difficulty.

He said: Ears, what's going on here? The place is a mess.

I said: Old Mistress brought a new deity into the house, the Guanyin Bodhisattva. Do you want to go see it?

He said: No, I'm tired. I need to rest.

I said: Second Master, what happened to your face?

He said: It's nothing. Now no more questions.

Leaving my post, I accompanied him into the compound. We entered through the side gate, not the main gate, and took the path to the corner compound. He didn't seem unhappy with me as I led him slowly up the path, which showed how worn out he was. He was limp as a piece of rope, and his body gave off the smell of mildew. I was reminded of the skiff Lucky spoke about, and considered the prospect that Second Master had been on that skiff but had jumped off just in time and that, confused and disoriented, he had finally found his way home.

We walked up to the gates leading into the corner compound and the main compound. The sound of chanting monks emerged from behind the main gate on our right. But mixed with the monotone of chants, I could tell, was Big Road's laughter. Walking and laughing, he came up to the open area between the two gates. He didn't see us. Turning to the main gate, he made a face at someone inside, followed by a series of strange gestures to mock the Thousand-Hand Buddha. My guess was that the person inside was Young Mistress, and a loud buzzing filled my head. What if the person on the other side of the gate came running out laughing, like Big Road?

That's when Big Road spotted us. The smile on his face hung there for a moment before vanishing. He shot a glance toward the gate, but before he could say anything, Young Mistress came strolling through the gate. She couldn't have known what had startled Big Road, but when she saw Second Master standing there, she froze. People run into each other all the time, so who could have predicted that such a simple occurrence could produce such a strange reaction? Big Road had a guilty look. So did Young Mistress. And those looks made me want to find an ant hole somewhere, crawl in, and not come out until they'd found a way to hide those expressions. Maybe they looked like that because of the melancholy written all over Second Master's face, and they had no inkling as to why he looked that way. So they stood there, looking guilty and afraid, although there was a hint of stubbornness in their eyes as they waited fatalistically for the man they had conspired to deceive to slowly approach them.

Finally realizing that something was amiss, Second Master stopped in his tracks.

The three of them looked at one another. No one spoke.

I heard the monks' chants, and tried to guess what they were saying.

Big Road said: How are you, Cao?

Second Master replied: And how are you?

Young Mistress asked: What's wrong with your face, Guanghan?

Second Master screwed up his mouth and winked mockingly, ignoring the question. He must have been on pins and needles. He sighed and brushed some of the dust off his lapel with trembling fingers. Supporting himself on my arm, he walked ahead on rubbery legs, swaying from side to side as he climbed the steps to the corner compound.

He showed those people his back.

He said to me: I was slightly injured, but don't tell Mother.

Then he said: I'm going to lie down, Ears. Go do your work.

I turned around, not daring to look at the two people standing there stiffly, stupefied. Hunkering down and hunching my head into my shoulders, I walked off, hugging the wall alongside the path, like a rat trying to stay clear of people. Big Road and Young Mistress looked like a pair of rats too. I didn't have to look at them to know that despair and fear had suddenly merged to shatter their hearts. Second Master was now the cat. I heard the beginnings of a cat sharpening its teeth over the sound of the monks' chants, and was terrified by the thought that someone might not be able to hold back a scream.

The screamer was me.

Someone in my daydream grabbed me around the throat.

He said: Out with it, all of it!

Please don't hurt me! I begged.

The blurred figure, whoever it was, was choking me to death.

I knew that death was the only way out. I was pretty sure that Second Master was carrying a bomb on him. He was waiting until everyone was on the veranda playing chess, when he'd light the fuse and blow everything to kingdom come! To make sure it was a surprise, I had to be absolutely tight-lipped.

I knew nothing.

They could go ahead and choke me to death.
I knew he'd become Elm Township's most tragic figure.
But, I knew nothing!
Horrible, just horrible!
Even I'd become an accomplice.

March 28th

The Elm Township valley was protected from the harsh winter wind, caught and softened by the muted green, frosty needles of the pines and China firs on Jade Mountain.

A charcoal pit about half the size of an average room stood alongside the sedan chair shed. Each of the braziers in the house burned a thick pile of charcoal every day, creating a pall of smoke that hung in the air over every inch of the Cao estate. Staying inside on wintry days to warm our hands over one of the braziers was sheer heaven for us slaves.

Second Master stayed closed up in the family home, nursing his wounds. His parents wouldn't allow him to move around, telling him to while away the hours and days in his room. Which is exactly what he did for the first few days. He sat in the living room like a clay statue. Then he moved out to the veranda, where he paced back and forth. No one bothered him, whether he was sitting in a chair or pacing the floor. He was so preoccupied with his thoughts that no one wanted to set him off. After a while, the monotony got to him, and he strolled over to the match commune, half of his face still swathed in gauze. Walking back and forth among the workers, he pressed the gauze tightly with one hand to

keep his face free of sawdust. In a soft voice, Young Mistress urged
him to go back to his room, but he ignored her. Giving her the
briefest glance, he continued his wandering through the old granary, walking on bark, sawdust, and cast-off branches. In the past,
the workers' ears would often ring with his crazed mutterings of
Every man for himself. But not now. He simply patted them on
the back to show that his thoughts and concern were with them.
He kept his mouth shut so tightly that people began to wonder if
his tongue had been injured too. No one could figure out what was
on his mind or what he was planning to do. His behavior had
members of the Cao family, as well as many other people, so concerned they kept a watchful eye on him.

After locking the door of the chemical-mixing shed, I busied
myself stripping bark and making neat piles of the wood strips.
He laid his hand on my shoulder, then gently steered me back to
the mixing shed. I went meekly, as if hypnotized.

Young Mistress said: Ears, help Second Master back to his room.

I said: Yes, ma'am.

But the second I stopped walking, he shoved me from behind,
nearly knocking me over. I'd taken out the key, always the obedient servant, when I suddenly realized that everyone in the commune
was watching me, having seen me stumble when he shoved me.

I said: Second Master, I can't let you go in there. Your injuries
haven't healed yet.

He shoved me so hard I banged my head against the wall.

I said: You can't make matches with your injuries. I have orders
from Elder Master and Steward Bing to keep you from going anywhere. And that's what I'm going to do.

I didn't say a word about Young Mistress and Big Road, wanting to keep them out of this. But he blew up anyway, shoving me
to the ground and kicking me, his teeth clenched in anger. It was a
reenactment of the beating I'd received the last time, and even
though I covered up to protect myself, his shoe found my midsection and nearly kicked the guts right out of my body. I curled up
like a shrimp and wrapped my arms around my head. It felt like
there were ten people kicking me at the same time. He was jump-

ing around and breathing hard, and sounded like he was having the time of his life.

There was noise all around me.

Young Mistress was shouting shrilly.

Guanghan, she screamed, what do you think you're doing?

Second Master said: Get lost! Get away from me!

That shut everybody up.

The last kick caught me in the back of the head. My ears rang as I felt myself begin to float. All the noise around me vanished without a trace.

Get lost?

Who?

Young Mistress?

Big Road?

Me?

Some of those silent people dragged Second Master away. Get lost! he roared. They bundled him out of the granary. Someone was pulling on me to straighten me out. They probed me all over. I didn't move. I was sucking cold air through clenched teeth. I hurt all over. My head was the worst. Waves of heat, like being pierced by red-hot tongs. I didn't want to get up. I wished Second Master would come back and finish the job. I wanted to see if this madman would actually beat me to death. If he didn't, then it would be my turn. A dog can crouch low and get whipped, but it can also jump up and sink its fangs into your neck. Lying there on the cold floor of the commune, one arm wrapped around my head, the other cradled across my midsection, I chomped down on a piece of bark so hard I actually bit right through it.

I thought I was going to die!

I knew it wasn't me he was beating. All those kicks meant for somebody else had landed on my body, that's all. A slave can't take things too seriously. You keep one eye open and one eye closed. Masters aren't like other people. All the same, I knew I couldn't take it anymore. I'd had the best upbringing of any of the Cao slaves and servants of my generation, but I'd taken as much as I could. No more!

Now I was thinking of revenge.
He damn near cracked my skull.
All right, then.
I decided to play the fool.
I'd play the fool in front of them.
That was the only path open to me.
Me, a damned fool!

I didn't really have much choice about it. When other people talked, it took me forever to figure out what they were saying. And when I felt like saying something, I could never find the words, and just stood there with my mouth hanging open. If that's not a fool or an idiot, I don't know what is. Maybe Second Master's kick had done something to my brain. So I just locked myself in my room and stayed in bed. Lots of people came to see how I was, but I couldn't tell you who, and I ignored them all. I just stared at the ceiling, hardly blinking. That's not what I wanted to do, but I really did feel as though Second Master had messed up my brain with his kick. When the tip of his shoe nearly buried itself in my skull, it just shut down. So why force it to work? This way I wouldn't have to show anybody any respect anymore.

Steward Bing's wife brought me over a new jacket.
The old lady's tears had no effect on me at all.
I ignored her.
Steward Bing said: The old master gave Second Master hell.
He also said: You poor thing, Ears.
I ignored him.
Big Road tried every Chinese word he knew, and not one of them drew a response from me. He flashed a kindly smile and whistled a pretty little tune for me; then he just sat there smoking his pipe and waited me out. All for nothing.
I ignored him.
Young Mistress pushed open the door and came in. Big Road got out of the chair so she could sit down. He stepped back, not realizing that she was waiting for him to leave, and just stood there, unwanted. When he finally got the picture, he seemed confused,

and left the room looking embarrassed. To look at the two of them, you'd have thought they were total strangers; either that or mortal enemies. With the eyes of a fool, I observed the two faces I'd seen touching and I felt pretty good inside. Why, you ask? My addled brain couldn't answer that.

I commanded myself silently: Ignore her!

Young Mistress said: Ears, Master Guanghan shouldn't have done that to you. But don't hate him for it. He's terribly moody these days, and he knows it. I'm here to apologize for him. Open up your heart and forgive him. We need to make allowances for him. Ears, you know Master Guanghan—he is what he is, and there's nothing anyone can do about it. We just need to be more careful around him. Do you understand what I'm saying, Ears? Tell me, where do you hurt?

I didn't tell her.

I didn't even look at her.

She got up and left.

I lay in bed, my head feeling like an empty jar. Nothing went in, and nothing came out. My nose ached the whole time Young Mistress had stood beside me, but I hadn't shed a single tear. She'd said to be more careful around him, but what had I done? Why should I be more careful? He's the one who should be more careful. Very careful, in fact! And she wanted me to make allowances for him. That's what a slave does—make allowances. What did she expect, that I'd turn around and give him what he gave me? Could I just up and kill him? If I had the heart and the guts to do that, I wouldn't be me. There wasn't a thing I could do, except play the fool.

I eventually realized that fools are the lucky ones.

They are the only ones who hear things not meant for their ears.

And fools have the best daydreams.

The next day was a repeat of the first. No eating, no drinking, no going to the toilet, just lying there staring at the ceiling. Wuling was sent over to look after me. Sobbing the whole time, she kept sniffing the air, waiting expectantly for me to shit my pants, giving her the excuse she needed to pull down my pants. But I was in no mood to humiliate myself. I didn't so much as fart! She really started to cry while she was wiping my face with a towel.

She said: He gave you quite a beating, Elder Brother Ears.

She said: Say something, Elder Brother Ears.

That stinky-mouthed girl disgusted me.

But tears slipped out of my eyes and down my cheeks.

They were so cool!

That night Second Master slipped into my room like a ghost on the prowl. He lit a match to find the lantern on the windowsill, then lit it with a second match. After looking down into my face, he dragged my homemade bamboo chair over to the wall; it creaked when he sat down. In the lamplight, his gauze-swathed face was scary as hell. But his good eye sparkled and sent out daggers of light, scraping the flesh right off my bones.

I shut my eyes and ignored him.

There wasn't a sound in the room for the longest time.

Something heavy, like a snake, dropped onto my quilt, and scared the hell out of me. Then I realized it wasn't a snake, it was that weird whip of his. I held my breath and waited for him to say what turned out to be the last thing I expected to hear.

He said: It's your turn, Ears.

The silence that followed was broken by a bunch of talk not meant for me or for anybody else.

He said: I'm a piece of shit. I can't do anything right. I was born to be a plaything for somebody to destroy, put on this earth to disgrace other people. Worthless! Nothing I've tried to do has turned out right. What good am I? Why should I suffer like this? I worry about other people, people as useless as me. They look like human beings, but they're a bunch of two-legged beasts! So what am I supposed to do? With those two-legged beasts running wild across the earth, where is there any justice? And what good is justice anyway? Why let crap like them have their place in this world? I'm going to obliterate them! I'm the number one piece of crap in the whole world! What to do with me? Why don't I just immolate myself? Or grind myself to bits? Or blow myself sky-high! Because

I don't have the guts, Ears, I don't have the guts. I don't deserve to possess a body, not even a shadow. Use that whip on me, Ears. Beat the breath out of my body! I'm a beast, so put your hand to it, you and all the others. I beg you! Why is everybody ignoring me? Come on, do it!

Even if I'd been the biggest fool on earth, I couldn't have kept myself from opening my eyes and gaping at him. He wasn't shouting or anything, just mumbling, like talking in his sleep. His head was bowed and he was leaning forward, holding on to the back of the chair with one hand and slobbering. He was staring at the floor, as if there were a deep well right in front of him and he was afraid of falling into it. He was racked by tremors. That's the bizarre sight that so often greeted Young Mistress. The glint in his exposed eye was anything but human. Maybe, like he was saying, it was the eye of a beast. In his madness, the first person he'd gone after was himself. For a moment there I really toyed with the idea of getting out of bed, picking up his whip, and lashing him mercilessly. But then tears gushed from the eye of the beast. With his ranting, it was like he was flaying the skin from his own body, and I had no inkling what was going on inside that head of his. But all that crazed talk seemed to make him happy, and his tears silently washed away whatever was stuck in his heart.

The whole business was so disgusting I felt like throwing up.

If I went ahead and beat him, I'd just be satisfying his masochistic desire.

I couldn't use that whip on him.

So I decided to attack him with my mouth.

I couldn't act the fool any longer.

I said: Second Master, who are you putting that act on for?

I wanted to hurt him as cruelly as possible.

My comment was ten times worse than a lashing. It had a devastating effect.

Still sitting in the bamboo chair, he thought about what I'd said and quaked from head to toe.

Whatever dream he'd been caught up in vanished.

He just sat there holding his head in his hands until the lamp went out. Then he picked up his whip and limped over to the door. He'd probably have calmed down and come to his senses even if I hadn't said what I said. His voice filled me with emotion.

He said: I'm sorry, Ears.

Then he said: I'm a worthless human being. Just ignore me.

He walked out the door and into the night.

That night he paced the veranda like a restless horse. He was still there when I woke up the next morning. In the midst of his agitation he'd torn the gauze off his face, ripping away the newly formed scabs and exposing the pink, blood-streaked flesh beneath them. The look of madness was stronger than ever.

Second Master was beyond help.

He was finished.

March 29th

One day during the twelfth lunar month, the Cao family assembled in the main dining room to eat the traditional eight-treasures porridge. During the meal, Young Mistress got up from the table and left the room. I watched through the window as she slipped behind a post on the veranda, bent over, and threw up. Later, when the meal was done, she was the first to leave the table, rushing back to her room in the left-hand corner. But she didn't quite make it: on the path home, she stopped, squatted down, and threw up again; this time it was nothing but white, sticky stuff, since she hadn't really eaten anything after the first time. As Second Master walked past, he stopped and looked down at her.

He asked: What's the matter?

Young Mistress said: It's nothing. Something caught in my throat.

So Second Master walked up to the steps. But then he had a thought, and turned to take another look. Young Mistress didn't have the strength to stand up, so she rested there on her haunches, her shoes splattered with vomit. Without saying anything, Second Master turned and walked off. I asked Wuling if Young Mistress had eaten anything but the eight-treasures porridge, and she said she hadn't. Wuling was pale with fright. Young Mistress had stopped throwing up, but her head was still drooping and her mouth was wide open; she was waiting. Her back arched as she was racked with dry heaves.

Just then the three of us heard some whistling; it was Big Road. Young Mistress's eyes lit up, and with her hand propped against the wall, she struggled to her feet. When he saw us, Big Road waved with his fan, the one decorated with a large bunch of dates, which Old Master had just painted for him. From where I stood they looked like oversized fingerprints.

Big Road said: Dates! They were in the porridge!

He showed us the dates proudly.

Young Mistress nodded.

She smiled weakly. She was absolutely beautiful.

She said: They're wonderful. They look real.

Big Road couldn't tell there was anything different about her. We all walked through the gate, and then went our separate ways when we reached the pond. As Young Mistress stepped onto the veranda, she looked as if nothing at all were wrong. I took it all in and wondered why she was putting up a front. Of course, she'd looked ghastly when she was throwing up, with her neck thrust out in front and her mouth open, like a duck, and making that terrible noise. It bothered me the way she tried to cover that up in front of Big Road.

I said: You should have Steward Bing go get the doctor.

Young Mistress said: I'm fine, Ears. Now don't go off half-cocked. There's a chill in the air, so put a little extra charcoal in Mr. Road's brazier. And tell him to leave his window open a crack, so he doesn't choke on the smoke. Now go on, Ears, I'll be fine. And be careful in your room too.

Be careful of what? For a slave, except for a few minutes after dinner, there was no burning charcoal, day or night. The little bit of heat from the meal was enough for us. And there was no need to tell me what to do about Mr. Road, since I always made sure he had plenty of charcoal and that his room was properly ventilated. It bothered me the way she was making such a fuss over him. She was able to conceal everything but this, and that upset me.

Nights were still the same where Big Road was concerned: he took a bath nearly every other day. I heated two big braziers and placed one on either side of his tub. I also kept a brass water jug on top of the brazier to add to his bathwater while he was bathing. Adding water was my responsibility. Since I couldn't keep going in and out of the room, because that would just let the steam out and the cold air in, I hunkered down next to the wall across from the tub. When he said to add hot water, I got up and went over for the jug. He'd be sitting there, only his head showing above the rim of the tub, eyes closed and saying nothing, immersed in his thoughts. So I'd study his face, trying to guess what was running through that head. His already large face seemed even larger floating on the surface of the water. His nose and chin looked puffy to me, and so did his eyelids. He was not a good-looking man. But that was the face that had been up against Young Mistress's face, and those were the lips that had nibbled hers. And that body, it was the one that had lain on top of her!

His body was covered with dark hair.

And what about Young Mistress's body?

It was a fair lotus root, not stained by any muck.

It was enough to depress anybody. But what really hurt was Big Road's nonchalance. During the first few days after Second Master's return, he wore a glum, stiff expression. But then he brought out the chessboard and went looking for Second Master.

They played on the veranda, in the main house, on a stone table or an octagonal table, or wherever they happened to be. The smell of charcoal and the fragrance of Young Mistress's rooms clung to him the whole time, and there was always a reassuring smile on his face. I couldn't tell if he was reassuring himself or Young Mistress. I didn't figure it was there to reassure Second Master.

The face below that forehead was a mask.

The face in the bathtub was real.

Deep creases ran from his nose to the corners of his mouth.

Steward Bing's wife called them lines of bitterness.

She said the man's heart was filled with bitterroot.

Big Road's body peeked over the water in the tub, like a toadstool. With his rear end facing me, he pressed up against the far end of the tub, leaving space behind him for me to add water. He turned to look at the jug, worried about being splashed by the scalding water. Did the evil thought of dumping it on him actually cross my mind?

I don't think so.

He said: Ears, pour half of it in.

Another thought crossed my mind. Envious, not evil. I was thinking how wonderful it would be if that big, strapping body were mine! And for one reason only: I wanted it to carry me to conquest in my endless daydreams!

Where Young Mistress was concerned, my thoughts were wicked and debased!

I told Steward Bing that the rats in the book storeroom were running wild and eating the glue that held Old Master's books together. He asked what had happened to all the poison he'd given me before. Had I eaten it? He handed me the key and a jar of poison, which I took out to the rear garden. I wasn't lying about rats in the storeroom, just exaggerating the extent of the problem. I opened the door and went straight to the bookshelves. I saw scattered traces of little footprints on the dusty floor between them, like embroidered patterns. At the end of each of these patterns, where there was either a hole or a crack in the wall, I put down some poison, then went over to the hardwood shelves to pore over my favorite book. I turned to the illustrations, picking out the most interesting positions to enjoy at my leisure. There was no brazier in the book storeroom, but before long it felt as if the storeroom were one big brazier and I was a lump of charcoal burning inside it; either that, or a date tree limb, turning transparent in the flames and stretching out hard and straight, refusing to crumble even after being burned to a crisp.

I turned to cinders along with the men and women in the pictures.

I didn't realize anyone had come into the storeroom until I heard a noise behind me. I looked up and saw Young Mistress standing at the head of the stacks, dressed simply, a faint smile on her face. I turned beet red and nearly dropped the book in my hands. It was like a dream. How had she chosen this very moment to appear in this place? In that instant, the men and women in the pictures turned unbearably ugly, unbearably dirty. And I turned into a spider, spinning its stinking web in the storeroom corner. I had ceased being human, inside and out.

Young Mistress said: I was strolling in the garden, and when I saw that the book storeroom door wasn't locked, I decided to take a look. I didn't expect to find you here. What's that you're reading? The tip of your nose is all dusty. Why don't you wipe it off. I'll just look around in here. Go ahead, keep reading.

Breathing a sigh of relief, I replaced the book on its shelf.

Young Mistress stopped in front of the medical book section.

I could only see segments of her body and the profile of her face. I was having trouble catching my breath. Death would be too good for me! There I was, looking at an erotic book again.

She stood in the same place for a long time.

All I wanted was to get out of there.

I said: I'm leaving now, Young Mistress. Lock the door behind you. It's awfully cold in here. You shouldn't stay long.

She asked: Who gets the key?

I said: Steward Bing.

She said: All right.

She'd been standing in the cold a bit too long, and didn't look well, seemed completely drained. I assumed she was tired; I didn't know there was another reason. Why was she so interested in those medical books? The answer never came to me. That erotic book had scrambled my brain and sucked all the energy out of me. I saw how degenerate I'd become.

A few days later she learned that I was going to Willow Township and came looking for me. I'd just finished helping Big Road with his bath and was out in the yard with the empty water jug and bucket, on my way to the kitchen to put the pots and pans away. Young Mistress, who was standing on the path, called to me softly. She said, Come here, Ears. I detected a quaver in her voice, and could tell she'd been standing there for quite a while. A hard wind was blowing as I followed her to the far end of the path and stood so I could block the wind for her. I guessed she wanted to ask me something, but I was wrong. She handed me a slip of paper rolled into the shape of a straw. Her icy fingernails brushed my palm when she put it in my hand.

She said: You don't need to look at it. It's a prescription my family gave me. I want you to go to Willow Township to fill it. Don't tell anybody who wants it or who it's for.

I asked her: Is it for you?

No questions, she said. Ears, you're a clever boy, and you know what's what. Can you do exactly as I say?

I said: Don't you worry about a thing, Young Mistress.

I could tell this was pretty important, and was surprised she'd be willing to put so much trust in me. I was all choked up. I'd lowered my voice to match hers, like a sneak thief. At that moment, if she'd asked me to kill someone, I'd have done it without a second thought. I knew she must be in some sort of trouble. The quake in her voice and the way she hunched down in the cold wind nearly had me in tears. She put some silver coins in my hand and closed my fingers around it. My poor soul flew off along with her instructions, and I seemed to float in the air, like a drunk.

She said: This is for the medicine. You can keep whatever's left over.

I said: I don't have anything to spend money on.

She froze.

I quickly added: It's enough for me just to do something for you. I don't need any money.

She reached out and touched my face.

The left side, just above the jaw.

She said: You're a dependable boy. I'm sorry to have to ask you to do this.

Your health is the most important thing, I said. You must get well.

She said: No questions, Ears.

I felt terrible.

Young Mistress had touched my face!

To me it was a mother touching the face of her child.

My heart was in shreds.

She said: Mr. Road has a persistent cough. Tell him to smoke less. We don't want his lungs to suffer. I've noticed the past few days that he seems to have developed a limp. See if there's a nail in his shoe. If there is, take care of it for him. If not, get him to change his shoes. Ears, take good care of the medicine. Don't spill any.

There I was, up in the clouds, and she had to bring up Mr. Road. I quickly came back down to earth. But my heart still hadn't cooled off as I stood alone now in the cold air on the path. I got down on my haunches, next to the water jug and bucket. I was squeezing the slip of paper in my hand. Slowly but surely, my head began to clear.

I gulped down a mouthful of cold air.

The medicine she wanted me to buy couldn't be poison, could it?

If so, who was it for?

Second Master?

The foreigner?

The slip of paper in my hand grew into a snake.

I wanted to throw it away, but couldn't.

I took out the prescription on my way to Willow Township and read it. I recognized some of the ingredients, such as safflower and angelica, but most were new to me, things like some kind of rhizome and ox-knee root, altogether five or six things. The fellow who ran the pharmacy was tickled by what he read.

He said: After all these years of taking restoratives, I see your old master has restored himself right into a sex change. This is a prescription for stimulating menstrual flow. Does your old master have a blood clot in his belly he wants to dissolve? Or has he been ingesting too much cinnabar tonic lately?

To hell with you! I said. This is for one of the female servants, so no more stupid comments please.

The pharmacist said: Oh, forgive me! Maybe I should slap my own face.

His playful apology put my mind at ease.

What didn't put my mind at ease was Young Mistress's flat belly.

Did she have a blood clot in there?

The thought of her being pregnant never crossed my mind.

Talk about stupid!

March 30th

A matchbox porter brought Second Master a letter, turning lights on in his dead-fish eyes. As Second Master was leaving, he said he'd be back in time for Chinese New Year's in a few days, but at Willow Township he sent his sedan chair back before boarding a ship headed downriver. Elder Master had hoped he'd take the sedan carriers along to serve and look after him. But they returned empty-handed, to his angry displeasure. As luck would have it, there was a lot of New Year's shopping yet to do, so Elder Master left Elm Township and followed the Green River into town. The absence of the two brothers put a damper on the family's year-end festivities. Another Blue Kerchief insurrection had broken out, this time at Stone Tower Bay, near the prefecture capital, and government troops had sealed the Green River in both directions. A few intrepid souls tried to sneak across the water, but were invariably caught, and bloody gourds began to appear above the pier again. With New Year's rapidly approaching, the atmosphere at the Cao estate was decidedly unfestive. An opera stage was erected in the open space in front of the gate tower, but then was taken down before it was finished. Steward Bing and I took turns going to the pier at Willow Township, but neither of us was able to bring good news back to Old Master, who spent his days in front of his brazier and medicinal cauldron, a silver-handled knife in his hand the whole time, ready to cut paper, slice flora, kill fauna, whatever was needed. We were all worried that the gloom might prove too much for him, and that with a flick of the knife, he'd wind up facedown in the watery mixture.

I said: Let me help you, Old Master.

I took the knife from him and began shaving the rolling pin the family cook had used for years, dumping the shavings of both it and the dried flour stuck to it into the cauldron. I knew what I was doing. This wasn't the first time Old Master had ingested this stuff, called thousand-day powder. But he was in a bad mood. There was too much heaviness in his heart. He snatched the rolling pin away from me.

He said: Everybody says Guanghan beat you senseless. Is that true? He rattled your brain. I told you to shave the flour, not chop up a piece of firewood.

Some time passed before he looked at me again with those ewelike eyes of his, and I reacted by gazing at his gray old head with the look of a good little lamb. I knew he was on the verge of losing it altogether.

He said: My grandfather and my father died at the end of the year. Both my brothers died just before the end of the year. We Caos have trouble getting through the end of the year. Year-ends have been the bane of this family for generations. I'm afraid that Guangman and Guanghan will have more bad luck than good.

I said: Don't worry, Old Master. They'll be back as soon as the piers reopen.

He said: It won't make any difference. The end of the year is almost here.

He walked back to his table to finish painting a fan. During that period, he painted only dates. Sometimes, when his mind was elsewhere, each date was the size and shape of a road apple: the big ones were donkey droppings; the smaller ones were goat droppings. None of them remotely resembled a date.

As soon as I wrapped up my duties with Old Master, I rushed over to the commune. Since I could no longer work in the mixing shed, that became Young Mistress's responsibility. The hardest part wasn't mixing the chemicals, it was the adhesive base. It had to be just right, not too wet and not too dry. And stirring it in the vat was hard work. During the last few days of the lunar year, Young Mistress worked like a woman possessed. She put Wuling in charge of the matchboxes, while she assumed all the hard, tiring jobs in the granary. The waist-high stirring paddle was strapped to a wooden rack, the wide end buried in the vat, with the other end serving as handle. Stirring the adhesive base was hard, sweaty work that usually required two people. But Young Mistress refused all offers of help—from me, and from Big Road. She wanted to do it alone. Even in the muted light of the mixing shed I saw him grab her wrist. She shook his hand off, really flung it!

You've got things to do, she said, so go do them!

Big Road didn't know what to do then.

He asked me: What's going on, Ears?

He couldn't figure out why Young Mistress was acting like this. Nor could I. At night, up on the roof, I detected a medicinal smell coming through the skylight. Given the way she was throwing herself into her work, she didn't look like someone with a serious illness. She prepared the medicine I bought for her. But did she take it? Or did someone else? During those few days, Wuling was like a girl whose soul had fled her body. If anyone was sick, she was the more likely candidate.

What's wrong with Young Mistress? I asked her.

She said: There's nothing wrong with her.

If there's nothing wrong, I asked, why's she taking medicine?

She said: She's not.

If she isn't, I said, maybe it's you.

She said: Elder Brother Ears, I don't know a thing.

I said: You know, all right.

I don't, so stop asking me, she said.

Since she seemed on the verge of tears, I stopped grilling her.

The day before the commune closed for the holiday, Young Mistress swooned in the granary compound. She was pushing some chopped wood over to the base of the wall when she keeled over, sending empty bamboo baskets beside the wall flying into the air. The mute, Hole in the Ground, carried her back to her compound on his back; Big Road, not daring to come too close, just followed quietly behind the crowd into town. By looking over the people's heads, I could see her seemingly lifeless back, wood chips and pieces of bark stuck to her clothing and hair. She looked barely alive.

Slow down, Big Road said. Not so fast!

He said it so softly that no one could possibly hear him. No one but me, that is. Hell, I could even hear his heart beating. As I looked into his sunken blue eyes and listened to the quickened beating of his heart, I thought he might be trying to send it straight into the unconscious body of Young Mistress.

Slow down, he said again. Not so fast!

I thought I heard his heart sobbing.

That night Old Master Cao summoned me to his room and asked what had happened to Young Mistress. I told him it was nothing serious, that she was just tired and had tripped and fallen. Then he asked what she was doing to get so tired. I told him she was doing man's work. With Second Master off somewhere, she could do what she wanted. Old Master sighed and said: That daughter of the Zheng family is something special. Guanghan got a real bargain in her.

He was experiencing one of his attacks.

He was consumed with a fear of dying.

He was lying in bed, the quilt pulled up to his ears, until only the top half of his head showed. His eyes looked like black holes in the light of the nearby lantern. He hadn't even undressed before climbing into bed. His shoes peeked out from under the quilt at the foot of the bed, barely touching the carved sandalwood footboard. The brazier stood cold. There was nothing simmering in the cauldron, over which a thin wisp of steam floated. The smell of stewed hoof lingered in the air; if not goat's hoof, then pig's hoof; the third possibility was sliced horse's hoof, first charbroiled, then stewed until it turns pasty. When it cools, you apply it to your navel, the soles of your feet, or your armpits to treat a variety of discomforts.

This latest problem involved Old Master's urinary system. At first, he had trouble urinating at all. Then, once that symptom subsided, he felt he was losing something each time he urinated, that instead of urine, he was passing blood.

He said: Ears, I'm going to die.

I told him: No you're not.

Ears, he said, I can't go on living.

There's nothing wrong with you, I said. Tell me what you'd like to eat, and I'll get it for you. Once you've eaten whatever it is you want, you'll be fine.

He said: Ears, I want to drink an infant's urine.

I'll take care of that right away, I promised. Wait for me.

Did you summon a doctor for Young Mistress? he asked.

I said: There's nothing wrong with her. She's back on her feet already.

No more than a hundred days, he said. If the child is over a hundred days old, it's useless. Less than a month old is ideal. Has anyone in the township had a child within the last month?

Yes, I said. Wait here while I go take care of it.

Rather than use a chamber pot, I went into the kitchen, found a little bottle, and washed it out. Then I went to ask Steward Bing's wife if there'd been any babies born in town within the last month. She said that the wife of a man named Big Frost had recently delivered twins. Bottle in hand, I went calling.

Big Frost was a tenant farmer, dumb as a post. When he heard that someone from the Cao estate had been sent over for infant's urine, he could barely contain himself. Since outsiders were not permitted in the confinement quarters, I handed him the bottle and waited outside. He asked if an adult's urine would do just as well. I said no; if an adult's urine was all I needed, why would I have come to him? What if the baby won't pee? he asked. I told him not to worry about it; I could wait all night if necessary. The kids were better than their father. As soon as one had finished peeing, the other took over.

Big Frost said: This stuff stinks. What's it for?

I said: To water the plants.

It was a cold night, and the bottle of urine felt as if it were icing up. So instead of handing it to Old Master when I walked in the door, I warmed it up by placing it against the brazier. Old Master said it was getting late, and sent me off to bed. So I handed him the bottle and left. Winking stars filled the sky, and there was just the barest sliver of a moon. As I stood on the veranda I heard gulping noises on the other side of the window, the sound a parched person might make when drinking at the edge of the Green River.

Old Master Cao drank down the infants' urine, every drop of it.

He put out the lantern. There was no way of knowing what he was doing there in the dark.

I headed quietly over to the left-hand compound. There were no lights on in either Young Mistress's or Big Road's room. What they might be doing was anyone's guess. I was too tired to even think about going up to the roof. Urine is urine, I was thinking, and that includes infants. And the way Old Master gulped it down made me think I might like to give it a try.

I was dying of thirst.

Why wouldn't I be, after running around all night?

I knew there was nothing wrong with Old Master's urinary system.

His sickness was in his bones.

Maggots were growing in his marrow.

March 31st

The first day of the lunar year. The holiday passed quietly in the Cao household. But sometime before midnight, I heard the screams—some long, some short—of a woman in the compound. It was the wife of Elder Master, Guangman, about to present him with his ninth child. Exploding firecrackers here and there in Elm Township accompanied her screams, which lasted way past midnight. The labor was intense, the end product a stillborn child. A girl. Her passage through the Cao household was like an air bubble on a watery surface. Pop! It's gone.

On the second morning of the lunar year, Big Road and I headed over to the granary to relieve the watchmen. On the way there we met up with some male servants from the right-hand compound. One was carrying a hoe, the other walked along with the stillborn baby slung over his shoulder, holding on to it by one foot, not unlike the way a hunter would carry a skinned rabbit. Big Road sucked in his breath when he saw it.

He said: They didn't even put clothes on it.

It was born dead, I said, so it doesn't count as a person.

What are they going to do with her? he asked.

I said: Take her out and bury her.

In the cemetery? he asked.

I said: No. She wasn't a person, so she'll wind up in the woods.

I continued on to the granary, while Big Road followed the burial team up the mountain. I watched as he took the tiny corpse down off the man's back and swaddled her in his robe, a New Year's gift from the wife of Steward Bing, made especially for him. The outer layer was made of black satin, the lining was of blue cotton; for padding she'd used fluffy imported cotton. He seemed bigger and taller in the Chinese robe than in his Western suit. From the back he looked like a bear standing on its hind legs, about to disappear into the woods with a stillborn infant. The servants sang a light-hearted funeral song. It went something like this:

Young one, go on now, so you can come back soon.
Don't dally along the way, 'cause your mother's making rice porridge.
When you step through the door, it'll be ready to eat.

Big Road may have understood the lyrics, and as he disappeared over a rise, his back bent, it wouldn't have surprised me if his nose was beginning to ache a bit. It was a song I knew well, but it was far from my favorite. You see, since I had no mother, who was going to make me rice porridge while I was on the road? Big Road's mother was waiting for him in France, and it was hard to say just how long he was going to dally along the way.

Having nothing better to do, I hunkered down at the base of the granary wall to soak up some sun. Big Road spent a long time burying the child in the woods, and when he finally reemerged, the lining of his robe was missing, that and a large chunk of the padding. He told me they'd buried the baby on the top of a rise, with a big tree behind and the whole valley spread out ahead. He said it was a better place than the Cao family cemetery on the other side of the Black River.

I said: Now you've done it. You buried her in wolf territory.

What? he said.

I said: You've gone and fed her to the wolves.

He said: No we haven't.

He smiled and flicked my ear with his finger as he told me they'd put a big rock on top of the grave. He made a wide circle with his arms to show me how big it was.

He said: That big!

With nothing more to say, he walked off to grease the machinery, whistling a melancholy tune. I stayed where I was, lazily soaking up the winter sun, as my thoughts turned to the baby in the ground. Was she lying in a comfortable position? Was it her good luck that she'd come and gone so fast? She'll sleep the winter wrapped in Big Road's liner and cotton stuffing, and by the time spring rolls around, there shouldn't be anything left of her, right? I started thinking about all the ways people die, and it seemed to me at that moment that Old Master Cao Ruqi's fear of dying was both realistic and very interesting.

Big Road and I were spelled so we could spend the night at home. We got back just in time to witness Old Master deal with a fellow by the name of Zhao, who was in charge of the paper mill. One of his assistants had found him smoking opium in the mill storeroom and reported him. According to the rules of behavior imposed upon Elm Township by the Cao family ancestors, smoking opium was a form of suicide, as bad a crime as robbery or adultery. Zhao, it appeared, would have to start putting his affairs in order.

A fat man in his forties, he was sprawled facedown in the main hall, his pants around his ankles, exposing his light-skinned, girlish rear end. Two house servants were taking turns lashing him with bamboo switches. *Splat splat!* It sounded like someone smacking a stuffed burlap bag. Old Master Cao and Old Mistress were seated at the head of the room, while the people who were supposed to be standing were arrayed on all sides. By the time Big Road and I strolled into the room, the man's rear end was bright red. Big Road and I spotted Young Mistress in the crowd opposite us at the same time. Her eyes were shut, her face waxy white; every time one of the bamboo switches landed, she would shudder. And she wasn't the only one who was having trouble bearing up. With a pop, the thin skin covering the man's red rear end split and blood spurted out like a blossoming chrysanthemum. Some of the observers gasped. Steward Bing heard the sound and rushed forward.

He said: Stop! Stop it!

Old Mistress, who was enjoying the spectacle, gave Steward Bing the evil eye.

Old Master was slumped in an armchair, eyes nearly shut, a satin blanket draped over his shoulders; he appeared to be dozing. But he awoke as soon as the whipping stopped. Fearfully, it seemed, he looked down at the bloody mess at his feet. Not knowing what to say, he opened his mouth, and kept it open, sucking back the slobber that oozed out. Steward Bing was waiting for the master of the house to say something, but when nothing came, he stepped up to give the target of the lashing a way out.

He said: All right, Zhao, it's time to beg. Beg Old Master to spare your life!

I beg the old master to beat me to death! said the manager.

Steward Bing said: Are you crazy? Are you just asking to die?

The manager said: I'm too humiliated to keep living. Please, Old Master, beat me to death!

Steward Bing, seeing no way out, looked over at Old Master and Old Mistress, then looked around, hoping someone would step forward and speak up for the man asking to be killed. But no one did. They were stupefied. Then Old Master stirred. Slipping one of his legs under him, he pulled the blanket around him. Although he looked discouraged, he uttered words that shocked everyone.

He said: Grant him his wish.

Old Mistress added: Don't worry about your wife and children. The Cao family will take care of them. Man or ghost, face is important, so I'll burn incense for you.

Old Master said: Enough of that prattle. Take him out.

With a wave of Steward Bing's hand, two servants walked up, one on each side, and recommenced whipping the manager at a leisurely pace. Now, rather than a burlap bag, they were pounding a pile of soggy laundry, a wet sound accompanying every hit.

The manager's rear end had become an overripe watermelon. Blood soaked the servants' shoes; the floor tiles, too, were turning red.

I sensed Big Road moving forward, and quickly grabbed hold of his robe. He looked back at me. His face was ghostly white; his lips were quivering. He looked scared to death.

He said: This can't be!

What can't be? I asked.

They'll kill him! he said.

He broke free of my grip—I couldn't hold him—and walked into the middle of the hall, next to the servants and the manager. Raising his arms in the air, he looked funny standing there. But no one was laughing. They were too stunned.

Big Road begged: You'll kill him! You're going to kill him!

The servants stopped and looked over at Steward Bing, who didn't know what to do. He in turn looked to Old Master and Old Mistress. Old Master was slumped in his chair again, but obviously feeling better. Seeing a living, breathing man at his feet being beaten to death must have lightened his own fear of dying considerably.

Big Road said: You'll kill him!

Everyone ignored him. Old Mistress stood up and was helped back to her meditation room by her girls in waiting. The rosary in her hand clicked loudly. Old Master said nothing as he looked down at the fat, silent manager, then walked out of the room. The rest of the people in the room grew fidgety and began filing out of the room in orderly fashion.

Big Road said: They'll kill him!

Steward Bing said: He's already dead.

Big Road stood there stupefied. Another group of servants lifted the manager by his four limbs and carried him out facedown, blood dripping on the floor. All of a sudden, I realized that Young Mistress was looking at me. Dressed in green, she was leaning up against a post like a wandering soul. She said: Ears, take Mr. Road back to his room for some rest. The holiday season isn't over yet.

Big Road and I were the last to leave the hall.

The ground was blood-spattered the whole way.

Servants were on their knees wiping up the blood.

I stepped on a piece of flesh the size of a walnut.

My heart nearly stopped.

Big Road quickened his pace as he followed the blood trail out of the compound.

He was a man who had lost his way.

He couldn't find his way home!

I couldn't sleep that night, so I got dressed to climb up onto the roof, in spite of the cold winds. Although there was just a sliver of moon in the sky, it was enough to light up the compound. I'd circled the stone-bordered pond and was headed toward the man-made hill when I heard strange sounds coming from the water. It wasn't the fish, but whatever it was, it was alive. It broke through the thin layer of ice. I stopped in my tracks and looked at the water. Something black and blurry was standing in the broad expanse of water, like a boulder sticking up in the middle of a river. Before I had a chance to figure out what the strange rock formation was, it began to move, producing loud cracks in the ice.

Who's there? I said.

Then I yelled: Who are you?

No answer. I was scared. I ran over and knocked on Big Road's door. He lit his lantern, throwing his ghostly, dancing shadow on the window covering.

He said: What's the matter, Ears?

I said: Get up, quick!

The dark figure in the pond, startled by all the commotion, headed for the far edge, cracking the ice at a frantic pace. At that moment, I knew it was a person, and that knowledge was quickly followed by the realization that it was Young Mistress. I didn't know what she was doing there, nor what I planned to do about it, but seeing her stumbling around, I jumped in instinctively. By the time I realized what I'd done, I was already up to my navel in freezing water, with one hand around Young Mistress's waist and the other clamped tightly on her shoulder. Fearing she might fall face-first into the water, I did everything I could to hold her up. She was freezing from head to toe, like an ice sculpture. Her teeth chattered when she spoke, like bowls crashing together.

She said: I can get out by myself.

I asked: What are you doing?

She said: I'll get out by myself.

Did you stray off the path and fall in? I asked.

Ears, she snapped, mind your own business!

By the time we'd waded over to the edge of the pond, Big Road was rushing up from the veranda with a lantern. Young Mistress was so numb by then she couldn't drag herself out of the water, so I lowered myself until only my head was showing and wrapped my arms around her knees. As I lifted her into the air, the water around me seemed superheated, burning the skin right off my bones.

Even after she was out of the water, Young Mistress couldn't stand. So she knelt on the ground with one knee. Big Road, completely undone by the whole situation, just stood there with his lantern shining on her face and body and asking over and over: What's going on? What's going on? What's going on?

I figured the look in Young Mistress's eyes had thrown a terrible scare into him.

That look held but a single word: death.

I found I couldn't move after I was out of the water either.

I said: Hurry up and carry her inside. She'll freeze to death out here!

Big Road put down his lantern and picked up Young Mistress by her arms and legs, then carried her back to her room. I wanted to follow, but couldn't get my legs to work. My clothes and my skin were as hard as sheet metal, and the water I'd brought out of the pond with me stuck like glue. I heard Big Road's footsteps as he walked up to the veranda, then I heard him kick open the door and stumble over some chairs inside the dark room. I waited for a light to come on. Finally I heard Wuling say something. The lazy little bitch was awake at last. One of them lit a lantern, and a soft gasp escaped from Wuling. She muttered something before bursting into tears.

So many figures were moving behind the window, I couldn't tell who was who.

I also didn't know what they were doing.

In the soft red light of the brazier, Wuling appeared to be helping Young Mistress out of her wet clothes. The door squeaked, and Big Road emerged, his head sagging. I guess that's when his thoughts turned to me, and he shuffled over my way, obviously distracted.

What was that all about? he demanded.

I don't know, I said.

What was she trying to do? he asked.

I said: What do you think?

He replied: How would I know?

Of course you know, I said.

All of a sudden I hated him, hated him so much my teeth ached. It was all because of him, I was thinking. He'd driven her to the brink of self-destruction. Young Mistress had been unfaithful to Second Master, and her guilty conscience had nearly forced her to pay with her own life. And he had the nerve to ask, What was that all about? How could I not hate him? The way I saw it, if he wanted to prove he was a man, he'd go over, stand in the pond himself, and let the freezing water end his life!

I felt like cursing him for all I was worth, but my tongue was a heavy weight in my mouth, choking me. Not a single word emerged. I walked over to my room—it wasn't easy, but I made it—where I took off my clothes and underwear. The room was cold, and so was my cot, even under the covers, and I thought back to how warm the water had been when I was in it. I began to regret going to Big Road for help. If I hadn't, Young Mistress and I would have frozen together in the icy pond, actually merging into a single being. At the very least, after I'd gotten her out of the water, the person who picked her up and carried her would have been me, not him. Me, carrying Young Mistress in the cold night, two bodies pressed together—the thought was more beautiful than anything I had ever dreamed before!

Big Road brought his brazier over for me, then pulled up a stool and sat down. He was planning to stay a while. I could see he had something to say, so I waited. As he sat there with his pipe in his mouth, I saw fear and anxiety written all over his face. Whatever he wanted to say, it had to be important. You can imagine my dismay when he opened his mouth and out came the same stupid question.

Ears, what was that all about? he asked.

I just shut my eyes and ignored him.

At the time I didn't know that he was thinking much further ahead than I.

He understood women.

He was, after all, a sinner.

And what did I understand?

Nothing, not even a dog's fart!

The seed had quietly begun to sprout.

April 1st

At first, Young Mistress tried to fight the effects of her icy experience, but eventually she spiked a fever and took to her bed, where she was racked by convulsions. That was a bad sign. Wuling kept the truth hidden from Big Road and me, not letting on whether Young Mistress was worsening or improving. She would only tell us that she was keeping warm in bed and moving as little as possible. But as her condition continued to worsen, Wuling panicked and came looking for me, her eyes red from crying. She told me she didn't think Young Mistress was going to get well.

I asked: What have you been doing all this time?

She said: She didn't want to bother the doctor.

If you had any sense, I said, you'd keep your mouth shut. What good does crying do?

She said: You think it's my fault. I'm not the only person in that corner of the compound. What have you people been doing? Young Mistress says to stay out of her room, so you stay out, just like that. I wonder if you care about her at all. Elder Brother Ears, I'm really at the end of my rope.

So I followed her over to Young Mistress's room. She was lying there unconscious, and for some reason, all I could do was reach out and slap Wuling across the face. She started to cry, but forced herself to hold back and just looked at me, her eyes begging me to do something. I bolted out of the room and, instead of skirting the veranda, cut across the lawn and jumped over the juniper hedge. Big Road, who was just then coming out of his room, stopped and gave me a strange look from the other side of the pond. Worried that he might decide to go into Young Mistress's room to see what was going on, or meet up with people coming into the compound from outside, I yelled to him: Go back to your room!

He didn't know what I was getting at.

I said: Her brother's coming here!

That's all it took for him to slip back into his room.

He had a very guilty conscience.

I went to get Steward Bing, and then went with him to town to summon the doctor. When the townsfolk saw the two of us—one old, one young—heading down the street, looking as if we'd just wet our pants, they wondered what was wrong at the Cao estate now. The doctor's ancestors had been tenant farmers to the Cao family, so he was, for all practical purposes, the family doctor. Although he treated townspeople when they were sick, he was on call for the Cao family. He always came as soon as he was summoned. Fortunately, Old Mistress chose the Buddha over medicine and Old Master chose medicine over doctors, so there were few occasions when his services were urgently needed, and he spent most of his time taking care of the complaints, major and minor, of local residents. He was tired when they found him, but when he heard that Young Mistress was seriously ill, he grew visibly nervous, and wake up fast.

He knew his stuff, that's for sure. His first diagnosis was that Young Mistress had caught a bad cold. His second diagnosis was that she was pregnant. Steward Bing and I were waiting out on the veranda when we saw the steward's wife emerge in the company of the doctor, who wiped his sweaty forehead with the sleeve of his robe. A broad smile decorated the walnut-shaped face of the steward's wife. She held a prescription high over her head. She's with! she shouted. She's with!

Steward Bing asked: With what?

His wife said: With child!

Steward Bing asked: Are you sure there's no mistake?

His wife said: Even if he misread her pulse, I felt her, and there's no mistake. It's her first time, so I'm not surprised she didn't know. But I should have known better. All I noticed was how much nicer a figure she had than other women, and didn't spot the change. Go tell Old Master. I'll tell Old Mistress. I hope there's plenty of *yang* in the womb; that way the Cao family line will continue. Ears, stay by the gate and don't let anyone inside.

The doctor, on the other hand, was anything but happy, and he sighed to Steward Bing as he was walking out. He said: I wrote a risky prescription that should drive out the cold and anchor the fetus. We can't neglect either one, but if the two medicines collide, I can't be held responsible for the consequences.

Steward Bing said: Prescription or not, if the worst happens, it's still on your head.

I guess you're right, the doctor said.

The doctor wiped his forehead with his sleeve again. His goatee was quivering like a rat's tail. After seeing him out of the compound, I stopped at the gate to keep people from entering, as Steward Bing's wife had told me to do. In no time at all, servants and cooks from the main house came over to poke their heads in the gate and ask: What happened in there?

I said: Somebody died.

They asked: Who?

I said: The person who was supposed to, who else?

I closed and bolted the gate so I could go back to my room to rest. But I changed my mind when I reached the door, and headed over to Big Road's room. He was on his haunches, his back up against the bedpost, taking apart a machine shaft and cleaning it in a bowl of kerosene. About half a foot in length and as thick as his thumb, it clanged loudly each time it bumped the side of the bowl. He knew it was me, but didn't look up, as if that way he could avoid talking to me.

I said: She's with child.

He didn't understand.

I said: She's pregnant.

What? he asked.

I said: There's a baby in Zheng Yunan's belly.

I think he finally got the picture after I made a sign with my hand over my own belly, though he went back to cleaning the part a while longer. Then he just sort of blanked out. His brazier was lit, but the room wasn't very warm. After cleaning the shaft, Big Road put the bowl down in the middle of the floor, where he struck a match to burn off the last of the kerosene.

I moved up close to warm my hands over the fire.

I said: She didn't even know.

Who didn't know? Big Road asked.

I said: Young Mistress.

He lost himself in the flames as they died down, then he held out his oily hands, not knowing what to do now. He was like an old potter in his studio who refuses to admit that he's lost the touch. He was talking to himself, in that foreign language of his, and since I didn't have anything more to say to him, I turned to go.

He said: Ears, boil me some water tonight.

All right, I said.

He then squatted down on his haunches, holding his head in his hands, his nose barely inches from the kerosene flames in the bowl. Back in my room, I lay down on my cot to think things out, trying to find a connection between the pond bath and the pregnancy. But it was too much to expect from a sixteen-year-old who'd lived a cloistered life, with no experience and very little courage. I actually thought that if Young Mistress had known she was pregnant, she wouldn't have done something so rash as to bathe in the icy pond. In my view, she had wanted to end her life because she'd been unfaithful to Second Master, but had wavered at the last minute, and wound up making a fool of herself. Now any thoughts she had about doing herself harm had to be weighed carefully against the fact that she was pregnant. There was no doubt in my mind that the child was Second Master's. Sure, I knew Big Road had lain with her, but I didn't believe that one or two awkward encounters could bury foreign seed in the belly of the Cao family's daughter-in-law. My thoughts just never went in that direction. How was I to know?

I also never got a handle on Big Road's nervousness. I figured he was afraid of the haunting look in Young Mistress's eyes. The reason I ran over to tell him she was pregnant was to console him, to take some of the pressure off him and let him know he didn't have to worry that she'd do anything like that again. I also wanted to give him a reason not to have any more funny ideas, to make him understand that enough was enough. I had no way of knowing that, little by little, this foreigner had figured everything out, and that I hadn't the slightest idea what was bothering him.

What turned the light on inside my head was medicine.

Steward Bing asked Old Master to read the prescription the doctor had left behind, and then gave it to me. He told me to make a run to Willow Township because we'd run out of some of the ingredients. I went first to see Big Road and tell him that if I was late coming home, he should get somebody else to boil water for him.

He said: Wait up. I'll go with you.

He was already dressed to go to the church at Acacia Township. Certainly there was nothing unusual about praying to God at a moment like that. If you don't have anything to say to people on earth, there's always the chance you can find something to say to Heaven. As I saw it, his inconsolable worries were his retribution, and if the foreign god didn't come to his rescue, as far as I was concerned, he was lost. On the way over, he kept turning to look at the valley we were leaving behind us, and walked very slowly.

He forced a pained smile on his face. After passing Jade Mountain, we picked up the pace. With nothing to say to one another, we rushed along like a couple of refugees.

At the Willow Township pier we said good-bye. I said I'd meet him where we always met after I'd bought the medicine. He patted me on the head without saying a word. At the Eastern Avenue intersection, he turned to look one more time and gave me a smile. He was still putting on an act. His smile wasn't much different from crying.

He must have known that God was waiting to give him an earful!

At the pharmacy I sat on the hard bench and watched the pharmacist fill the prescription. Young Mistress's illness was on my mind, and as my thoughts turned to daydreams, she walked up to me, took my hand in hers, and placed it on her belly.

I asked: Who's inside there?

She said: Feel with your hand.

When the pharmacist banged the scale on the counter, I nearly jumped out of my skin. All of a sudden I was reminded of the other time I'd been here to get medicine for Young Mistress. That time, too, I was wrapped up in my thoughts when a banging on the scale brought me up short. She hadn't been sick that time, but she'd sent me for medicine, and then taken it. This time she was sick, but tried to hide it from everybody. Why was that?

She said: Feel with your hand.

I said: I feel it! I feel it!

I could feel a head. I turned it around to face me. It was Big Road! Young Mistress giggled in my ear. Big Road was laughing.

The pharmacist asked: What are you laughing about?

I said: I'm not laughing. Who's laughing?

He asked: Which mistress is in a family way?

I said: I don't know. They told me to pick up some medicine, and that's what I'm doing. I didn't ask any questions.

Did the medicine you bought last time do the trick? he asked me.

I said: I didn't take it, how would I know?

He asked: Who did?

I said: The adopted daughter of one of the amahs.

He asked: Did it do the trick?

What trick? I asked.

He said: The abortion!

They're country folk, I said. Who knows if she even took it?

He said: I'll bet it was for your girlfriend.

Watch what you say about the Cao household! I protested.

I slap my face! he said. I wouldn't dare to presume. Take it easy, I really wouldn't dare. I value the Cao family's business too much. Tell your old master that some new antler chips from the north just came in, and I'm holding them for him, whether he needs them or not.

I said: How nice of you to think of him.

I went to the Lucky Teahouse for a cup of tea, where I watched the soldiers walking up and down the pier through the window. After all the time the river had been sealed, they still had murderous looks on their faces, as if they were just itching to cut down the next man they saw.

I felt that I was not only the world's number one idiot, but the world's number one candidate for extinction. A bolt of lightning had crackled through my head as I was conversing casually in the pharmacy; and that had led to a brainstorm. Medicine, matches, pond, ice, belly, yellow hair, blue eyes—they were all connected. I may not have known what was going on between Young Mistress and Second Master, but I had a pretty good idea what had happened between Young Mistress and the foreigner. When he carried her into the drying room, they did something that made Heaven weep and the earth groan. Now they had their backs up against the wall, with nowhere to turn and no place to hide, as thunder rumbled all around.

Young Mistress had been trying to injure herself in order to save herself. Big Road had not only seen death in her eyes, but had likely detected the smell of death on his own body as well. I was thinking about the smiles he kept forcing on his face and the frequent backward looks into the valley, and was increasingly troubled by them. On the day manager Zhao was beaten to death, he'd stepped

on the bloody flesh, and his pure blue eyes had dimmed. He'd
watched the woman throw herself into the icy pond with that same
pair of eyes, and his own sinful heart had been immersed in the
icy water. I suspected that he wanted to escape death, which was
bearing down on him. He wanted to flee!

The foreigner wanted to run away!

The lousy son of a bitch wanted to run away!

I slipped out of the Lucky Teashop.

Lucky called after me: Ears, your change.

Save it for next time, I said.

I crossed the pier, went down Eastern Avenue, and ran out of
Acacia Township like a galloping horse. I guessed that by now
Father Ma had already put Big Road on the church boat and sent
him down the sealed-off Green River.

I burst through a stand of dead trees, and there was Big Road,
head bowed, walking my way. I stopped in my tracks, and when
he spotted me, so did he. He had a loaf of bread from the church
bakery; his pipe was in his mouth. He wore the look of a calm man.
Apparently, his God had told him what he wanted to hear.

He said: You?

I said: I got tired of waiting and decided to meet you halfway.

He asked: Why are you running?

I said: I was in a hurry.

He asked: Hurry to do what?

I couldn't answer him. My cheeks were burning. We stood there
a while longer before he started walking, with me following close
behind. I knew I was being ridiculous, afraid he'd see through me.
When he asked if I wanted a piece of bread, I said no, and that
ended the conversation. He was hurrying toward the Elm Township valley, as if it were a refuge from disaster. We skirted Jade
Mountain as the sun set, and he slowed down. Then he stopped
altogether, lost in the sight of the setting sun. So was I. I was reminded of that autumn day when Young Mistress had gone up in
flames in the sun's dying rays.

Big Road muttered something in his language.

And then I knew who he was talking to.

If Young Mistress was fated to be his, she would understand what he had on his mind.

And what was that?

I can't tell you.

No one can.

April 2nd

On the eleventh day of the new year, the Green River reopened. Elder Master Cao Guangman returned to Elm Township two days later, bringing with him dozens of packages, large and small, filled with New Year's gifts. For Young Mistress: several bolts of silk and satin, one in her favorite color—pastel green—and an imported cuckoo clock about the size of a Buddhist altar, to hang on her wall. Big Road was given a box of imported tobacco and an imported umbrella. When he opened the box and saw that it was filled with real cigars, he immediately tossed away his pipe. The umbrella was black, slim enough when rolled up to double as a walking stick. At first he used it to pace the narrow area of the servants' quarters, but after a while, he took it out on the street with him. He wore the look of a clown having fun at his own expense. Townspeople, who had gotten to know him, saw him carrying his umbrella in the middle of winter, looking like a big, dumb bear in his tentlike robe, and couldn't help but laugh at him. Children would grab hold of the back of his robe and follow him, as if they were holding up a long swishing tail. He hadn't looked this happy in a long time.

Wuling got an embroidered handkerchief.

I got a large white towel.

Wuling said: Let's swap.

I said: Why?

I have such oily skin, she said. I can use that as a pillow cover.

I said: No swap. You can have it.

She said: All right. I'll think of something to give you later.

That's all she said, but gratitude showed in her eyes as she took the towel and walked off. She'd grown up a lot in recent days, ever since the Caos learned that Young Mistress was pregnant. Immortals were summoned, divination lots were cast, and it was determined that the baby-to-be was a boy. Overnight, the left-hand corner became the gilded section of the family compound. Old Mistress ordered Steward Bing's wife to move in with Young Mistress; she shared the outer room with Wuling, the two of them taking turns looking after Young Mistress. The steward's wife was a very attentive woman whose observant eyes recorded everything Young Mistress did. If Wuling forgot to take Young Mistress's arm when she stepped over a threshold, she was sure to get a scolding from the old woman. This was no aging slave; she looked and acted like an unrelenting mother-in-law. Now that Young Mistress was no longer in charge, there was precious little joy in Wuling's life.

The joy soon drained from Big Road's life too. Since it was improper for Young Mistress to be out on the veranda, he was reduced to gazing up at her room from across the pond. It was hard enough to see anything, especially since he had to pretend to be watching the fish or the ripples on the water and, from time to time, toss in a pebble or a shard of tile. Then, too, he could look all he wanted and still never see what he was looking for, since Young Mistress hardly ever emerged from her quarters; her familiar pale face was nowhere to be seen. Looking out the window of my little room, I could see him standing there. He always looked livelier somehow in Western dress; in his thick Chinese robe he seemed clumsy, someone to be pitied, a man in a daze.

Without being conscious of it, he wiped his nose with the sleeve of his robe to rid it of the snivel brought on by the cold. He'd never have done that in a Western suit. When he folded his hands in his sleeves, he looked exactly like Steward Bing or, for that matter, any of the men in Elm Township, and I wouldn't have been surprised if he'd had trouble deciding just what the hell he was.

I took pity on him, and on myself. I longed to see Young Mistress's smiling face in the sunlight, yearned for an air of tranquillity and relaxation to settle over her face and her heart. In my daydreams, I was forever asking her: How are you doing, Young Mistress?

What troubled Big Road was the look of death in her eyes.

What troubled me? I couldn't say for sure.

Elder Master's return swept away the pall of death that hung over the compound and breathed new life into the Cao household. He walked with an air of confidence, back straight, head up, as if nothing but good things had happened around the place. His ninth child was dead, and so be it. He'd keep trying, for he refused to believe that he could not produce the son he longed for. While waiting for the river to reopen, he'd put the family's business interests in order and straightened out some of the more chaotic accounts. If not for the river blockade, he probably wouldn't have found the time to sit down and take care of these matters. He wasn't all that worried about Second Master. The way he saw it, Guanghan still had money in his pocket, and if he wasn't worried, why should anyone else be? Besides, what good would worrying do? Elder Master was content to wait and see what happened.

Since the New Year's holiday had been such a muted affair in the Cao household, Elder Master took it upon himself to make sure that the Lantern Festival on the 15th was much more raucous. He took some bamboo paper out of the paper mill storeroom and distributed it free to the tenant farmers, telling them to make paper lanterns in any shape they desired. Concerned that more was needed for the family's prestige, he had the servants bring out a basketful of candles, which they handed out on the steps outside the gate tower. On the afternoon of the 15th, children poured into the streets with handheld lanterns before the sun went down. Then, when stars appeared in the sky, lanterns hanging from the eaves were lit. People in twos and threes lined the Black River, waiting for the Cao family to show up and set the river lanterns adrift. Steward Bing sent me on ahead to check the wind and the flow of the water. What I found was a slight northern breeze and no countercurrent. The waves were not breaking on the bank. It was one of those days arranged especially by Heaven.

Both the front and main compounds were packed with servants and domestics busy making lanterns.

Wuling picked up some bamboo and paper and put some paste in a bowl. She said that Young Mistress was bored to tears and wanted to try her hand at making a lotus-shaped lantern.

At around midnight, the Cao family assembled in the dining hall for the traditional rice dumplings. Present were Old Master and Old Mistress, Elder Master and his wife and concubine, and Big Road, the only outsider at the table. Just before the dumplings were boiled and ready to eat, Young Mistress arrived, supported by Steward Bing's wife and Wuling. I hadn't been this close to her for days. She'd put on weight and was paler than ever. I was surprised to find the trace of a smile on her face. After all the necessary courtesies, she lowered her head and took a seat. Elder Master's wife and concubine gathered round her to whisper and giggle.

One of them asked: How many months?

The other said: About three months, I'd say.

The first said: With your pretty figure, it doesn't even show.

The other said: Was it conceived when Guanghan was recuperating that time? Take good care of yourself, little sister. Eat plenty of honey and fish skin. If you don't, the baby will have the same burn scars as its father.

Choosing not to reply, Young Mistress sat with her lips pursed into a faint smile. When the dumplings were brought out, steam filled the air above the table. I was standing behind a column, and while everyone was laughing at Big Road, who was trying to pick up one of the dumplings, I saw a dark cloud settle over Young Mistress's face. She looked up, and our eyes met; quickly she looked away. I moved over behind another column to stare at her some more. For some reason, I figured that if I kept it up long enough, I could see what was behind that smile.

Old Master looked healthy. He was blowing on one of the scalding dumplings.

Old Mistress had half a dumpling in her mouth, which she was chewing so slowly I wondered if she'd ever finish it.

Elder Master was regaling everyone around him with auspicious comments, while the people at the table laughed politely. The servants were having a great time laughing behind their backs.

I couldn't hear what he was saying.

I was still looking at Young Mistress. When she put her red lips around one of the white dumplings, two rows of spotless white teeth flashed through the steam. The round little dumpling disappeared behind her thin red lips. My God! my heart cried out.

At that moment, Big Road said something everyone found puzzling.

Old Master Cao, he said, I like the people in your family.

Then he said: Me—that is, I . . . miss my mother.

That was met with silence at the table. Everyone's eyes were on him.

Mr. Road, are you planning to return to your own country? Elder Master asked.

Big Road said: Yes, yes, I like you people, but I want to go home.

He was so nervous he twisted his chopsticks, and his dumpling fell to the floor. When he bent down to retrieve the spoiled dumpling, I scooted over, snatched it off the floor, and retreated with it. Big Road's nose was beaded with sweat; his face and neck were red. Elder Master politely put some food into his bowl. There wasn't a sound from anyone at the table. Young Mistress kept her eyes on the bowl in front of her.

Elder Master said: Guanghan hired you, but since he's not here, it would be awkward for us to let you go. You know my brother's temperament as well as anyone, so let's wait till he gets back before we do anything. What do you say?

I couldn't tell whether Big Road understood him or not, but he sort of stammered for a moment, and then out came a stream of foreign words. Quickly realizing that no one at the table could understand him, he sighed and shook his head in embarrassment, shrugging his shoulders like a fool. Young Mistress asked him something in the foreign language. At first he was shocked, but then he began talking to her, accompanied by hand gestures. In the conversation that followed, neither of them looked at the other; most of the time, they kept their eyes on the large porcelain bowl on the table. But when she interpreted what he said, she looked at Old Master and spoke with respectful elegance.

She said: Mr. Road says that the workers are well trained on the machinery and that his departure would have no real effect. He says his mother is getting on in years and isn't in the best of health, so he must get back to her before too long. He is asking you to arrange for him to leave Elm Township as soon as possible. He says he cannot sleep at night for worrying.

Old Master nodded slightly and glanced at Elder Master.

Elder Master asked: What do you say, Father?

I'm impressed by his filial piety, Old Master said. Let him do as he wishes.

Big Road seemed to understand this, but Young Mistress interpreted anyway, and they were soon engaged in another conversation that excluded everyone else at the table. I didn't understand a word of it, but I knew, even if no one else did, that they were using this opportunity to talk of other things. They spoke in short sentences, at a relaxed pace, although I could see that there was tension beneath the surface. Young Mistress stopped the conversation and smiled respectfully at Old Master.

She said: Mr. Road says he is an only son. She paused and looked over at Big Road.

She went on: Mr. Road says he will never forget the people here as long as he lives. But he needs to get back to his own home as soon and as quickly as possible. If it's convenient, he'd like to leave tomorrow. That's what he said; that's all of it.

Big Road had to know that not all of what she said came from him, but he could only let it go.

He said: Me—that is, I like you people!

Old Master said: Go if you must. The match commune has been Guanghan's plaything all along, and I can see it's taken its toll on you. Guangman, make the arrangements for him. For now, it's getting late, so everybody dress warmly and let's go down to the river to set the lanterns adrift.

His wife said: Yunan, you needn't go. You might catch cold.

They left the table, with the older generation leading the way. Old Master stopped in front of Young Mistress and looked her over. I could tell he held her in high regard.

He said: You've been very helpful to Guanghan, but I never guessed you also spoke fluent French. You did not do well by marrying Guanghan.

Young Mistress replied: It's English.

Old Master said: Whichever it is, I know it's not the sort of thing you normally hear from a Chinese. Mrs. Bing! Mrs. Bing! Take good care of her. If anything were to happen to her, we'd never be able to face the Zheng family.

Before he had finished speaking, Old Mistress was already walking slowly out of the dining hall.

All those candlelit river lanterns in the main compound looked like stars in the sky. Shouts, some loud, others not so loud, were rising into the air on the bank of the Black River, where the townspeople were growing impatient. Young Mistress called me over to say she'd made a lotus-shaped lantern, which she wanted me to set adrift. I accompanied her back to the left-hand compound. She and Wuling walked in front, with Big Road and me bringing up the rear. Mrs. Bing didn't come along, since she'd been sent off on an errand by her husband. Wuling and I held our tongues as we walked, listening to the indecipherable conversation between Young Mistress and Big Road in the night air. For all we could gather from the tone of their conversation, they could have been talking about the weather or they could have been pouring out their hearts to one another. But whatever they were saying, I was sure it couldn't have been as bland as the expressions on their faces. That was all an act, one that fooled Wuling, but not me. When we reached the veranda, I tactfully quickstepped my way up in front of Young Mistress, causing her to stop in her tracks.

She said: Wuling, take Ears in to fetch the lantern.

Inside the room, I dawdled as much as possible, telling Wuling
to scare up some thread to secure the lantern base. The lantern itself was glued together nicely, with three lotus blossoms propped
up with bamboo; two were in full bloom, the third had yet to open.
A thick candle stuck on a bamboo spike could easily stay lit for at
least three miles down the river. Once we'd given them enough
time, I carried the lantern out onto the veranda, where Young
Mistress and Big Road were standing on opposite sides of the stone
table. Neither was moving and neither was speaking. Whatever
they had to say had apparently already been said.

I said: The lotus bud on the side seems a bit too heavy. It might
flip the lantern over.

No it won't, Wuling said. We'll just move the spike a bit.

I said: It's worth a try.

After laying the lantern on the table, I asked Big Road for a
match. He didn't reply, as if he hadn't heard me. I tried again, and
this time he handed me a match. When I lit the candle, the others
came closer to get a good look, and when they did, I noticed that
there were tears in Young Mistress's eyes. Very nice, she said, very
nice. Then she blew it out. As Big Road and I set out for the river,
I heard him speak softly to Young Mistress. It could have been
something like Take care of yourself, and it could have been Good-
bye. It was a sad moment. All that had happened gave me a strange
feeling and really upset me.

Young Mistress said: Ears, after you put it in the water, walk
along with it and don't let it float up onto the bank. We want it to
travel as far as it can. My luck and fortune are riding on that lantern, and the last thing I want is for it to flip over close to home. If
it's going to flip, let it be far downriver. Ears, send it off for me,
and be careful.

I said: I think you should go back inside.

It was dark all around us, and my eyes filled with tears. By the
time we reached the riverbank, the Black River was awash in lanterns, like swarming fireflies. Big Road and I sought out a quiet bend
in the river to release our lantern and then followed it downriver. It
kept edging up to the riverbank, where it spun around, as if reluc-

tant to continue. And each time, Big Road reached down and nudged it on its way, wetting his shoes and pant cuffs. I scared up a bamboo pole to keep the lantern out in the middle of the river, floating along, not stopping. Ahead and behind, nothing but floating lanterns. Some flipped over, while others, unattended, nestled up against the bank, where their candles eventually burned out. There were even some that ignited in the middle of the river.

We accompanied Young Mistress's lotus lantern downriver; after passing the slaughterhouse, the flow picked up until, at the dam at the head of Jade Mountain canyon, it turned into a roaring white-water rapid. Instead of flipping over, the lotus lantern shot past like a meteor and disappeared from view.

That's it, I said. Let's go home.

Big Road said: That's it. It's over.

He stood on the bank of the river and lit a cigar.

We didn't start back to town until he'd finished his cigar.

We just stood there with nothing to do but count.

Altogether, forty-six lanterns flipped over.

The lotus lantern was far ahead of the others when it flipped.

Part Three
April 1992

April 3rd

I was in the habit of daydreaming, but never in my wildest dreams could I have imagined that the Cao family would actually put me in charge of the match commune. Such a wonderful assignment was beyond the grasp of most slaves. And I was barely seventeen at the time—in the eyes of Elm Township tenant farmers, little more than a calf. I didn't tell anyone, but I was thrilled. All of a sudden, my life had meaning.

Elder Master summoned me that day, and I could tell by the look in his eyes that something was up. When he told me what he had in mind, his attitude was courteous, his tone cordial; he wanted me to understand how he valued me. How could I not be grateful? The words were no sooner out of his mouth than I was on my knees at his feet banging my head painfully on the floor.

I said: Thank you, Elder Master!

He said: Mr. Road is going to leave us, and Second Master shows no concern for the family, always off doing something, while his wife is carrying a child. Steward Bing and I have discussed this from every angle, and can think of no one better suited to the task. You are clever beyond your years, and we expect you to do a fine job. Take advantage of Mr. Road's last few days here to familiarize yourself with the ins and outs of the commune. Just do the best you can, and we'll be happy, no matter how things turn out. Your monthly spending allowance will be raised to six ounces of silver. As soon as Mr. Road leaves, you can move into his room. If there's anything you need, let Steward Bing know. Turn your present duties over to other people. What do you say?

I stayed as calm as I could, and kept knocking my head against the floor.

I said: Old Master needs me to do things for him sometimes, and I don't think anyone else can take over.

He said: You'll have to continue taking care of Old Master's needs, because we could never feel easy with anyone else. Fortunately, his demands are not heavy, and you should be able to handle both tasks.

When I took leave of Elder Master, my heart blossomed. A bright future came rushing at me, and I couldn't have hidden from my good fortune even if I'd tried. I lay on my cot, too excited to sleep. How would the residents look at me the next time I went into Elm Township? I knew I'd be carrying myself differently.

I was so pleased with myself I put all the chaos of the left-hand compound out of my mind, so I could concentrate on taking over at the commune. I held my head high, as if I were the master, ignoring Big Road's taciturn demeanor as he strolled aimlessly through the old warehouse or sat in the reclining chair Young Mistress favored, his arm resting on his forehead. He gazed at the spot where he'd taken Young Mistress and at the spot where he and Young Mistress had knocked over the rack. I could guess what he was doing, but I didn't let that spoil my happiness.

I was in charge of the match commune, me and me alone!

Me!

My happiness was premature.

On the evening of the nineteenth day of the first lunar month, a sedan chair pulled up to the gate of the Cao compound. The passenger seemed reluctant to show himself, but someone spotted a constable from the county government among the sedan bearers. After the sedan chair had rested there a few moments, the passenger was spirited away. Every lantern in the Cao estate was lit, as residents scurried from one pocket of the compound to the other. We servants had no idea what this was all about. Young Mistress, too, was alarmed. She came over to the main compound behind Wuling, who lit the way with a lantern. Just before dawn the next

Elder Master was waiting for me in the main hall, and that I was
to rush over there immediately. In response to my question of what
it was all about, he told me not to ask anything, that I'd know when
I got there.

A sense of impending doom settled over me.

My first thought was of Big Road and Young Mistress.

There didn't seem to be any way out of the trap of adultery.

But were lives going to be lost?

I didn't dare let my thoughts go any further.

Elder Master was alone in the main hall, seated in the chair normally reserved for Old Master. His eyes were puffy, as if he hadn't
slept all night and he was struggling to stay alert. When he saw me
enter the hall, he sat up straight and assumed a carefree attitude.

Ah, you're here, he said. Have a seat.

I remained standing.

He said: Have a seat. You're the man in charge now.

So I sat down.

He asked: Ears, tell me, how does Old Master treat you?

I said: I'll never be able to repay him.

He asked: Ears, how about me?

I said: I'll never forget what you've done for me.

He asked: Ears, how have you treated us?

I said: I am but a brick in this house.

He nodded as he picked up a liquor flask and took a sip.

He asked: Have you been hiding anything from us?

No, I answered.

He said: Think hard, now.

No, I haven't, I said. If I have, may lightning strike me dead.

Without so much as blinking, I pinched myself on the thigh. I
was afraid I couldn't bear what was happening, and that the blood
would rush to my face. Elder Master was staring straight into my
eyes; I met his gaze as if nothing were wrong. He sighed heavily.

He said: Guanghan has been arrested by the garrison command.

An explosion went off in my head. The end has finally come,
I said to myself. But at the same time, a stone in my heart fell softly

away. There was no immediate danger; the left-hand corner of the compound wouldn't be the site of disaster, at least not for a while.

Elder Master said: Guanghan might be involved with the Blue Kerchiefs. You've been at his side most of the time since he returned from abroad. Do you know anything at all about that?

I said: I know that he and his brother-in-law are friends. But that's all.

He asked: What do you know about Zheng Yusong?

I said: Nothing, really, except that he's a merchant who deals in local products.

He said: Tell me everything you know about Guanghan's secretive comings and goings. Holding back won't do anyone any good. If we don't find a way out of this, his head will no longer be attached to his body. And so far I'm completely in the dark. You won't be repaying me by holding anything back.

The look in his eyes turned cruel all of a sudden, something I hadn't seen before.

I considered falling to my knees in front of him.

Should I tell him about the explosives?

I fell to my knees.

I didn't say anything about the explosives.

But I did tell him about the chemicals.

I told him about the strangling incident.

Elder Master's face paled before I'd even finished.

He said: That shameless wretch!

If you hadn't asked, I'd have let the incident rot in my guts, I said. Second Master is to be pitied. It's not his fault.

He said: Ears, you're a decent youngster. On behalf of Old Master, I want to ask a favor of you.

Whatever it is, I'll do it, even if it kills me! I vowed.

He said: The Cao family will be forever in your debt.

My heart froze when I heard that, and I shuddered. The calamity I'd feared for so long was about to come crashing down on my head. My daydreams were about to all turn up empty, leaving nothing behind. Later on, I realized that the person who had come in secret on the nineteenth day of the first lunar month was a county garrison command inspector, a personal friend of Elder Master's father-in-law. They had planned everything, and were using me as a pawn, to be kept or discarded, however they saw fit.

The next day an officer arrived with a dozen soldiers. They searched the commune, and planned to search Second Master's quarters as well. Everyone had a role to play in this little drama. First they put samples of all the chemicals into little glass vials, then they carried out baskets of matches with the barrels of their rifles. Inside the family compound they didn't even go through the motions of making a search; they went straight to the dining hall, where they ate and drank their fill. They didn't so much as set foot in the left-hand-corner quarters. I played my role, saying my good-byes throughout the compound, dressed in new clothes.

Young Mistress was suffering from swollen legs, and Steward Bing's wife wouldn't let her out of bed. So I knelt in the anteroom facing her bedroom and spoke to her past a dividing screen. I caught an occasional glimpse of her form behind the mosquito netting. Her face was a blur, but her voice was crisp and clear.

She said: Ears, take good care of yourself.

I asked: Is there anything you'd like me to say to Second Master?

She said: Remind him how important his health is.

Anything else? I asked.

There was a momentary silence, during which I waited. I loved the way the room smelled, and was reluctant to leave. I figured the chances were eight out of ten that I wouldn't return.

She said: Don't worry him about family affairs. Just tell him I'm doing well, that everything is fine at the match commune, and that I look forward to his return.

Young Mistress, I said, take care when you walk. I'm leaving now.

I took one last look at her. I could see the swollen shape of her belly under the bedding. Everything looked normal, and I hoped that all my recent conjectures were nothing but groundless suspicions. If not, then Young Mistress was in for unimaginable torment. That thing in her belly would prove to be more worrisome than any mixture Second Master had concocted. It could provide the biggest explosion any of us had ever witnessed!

How worthless was I?

Could I save Second Master?

Who could I save?

If I could save anybody, it would be Young Mistress.

But I couldn't save a single one of them.

Death was inevitable.

Before I started out, Old Master sent for me. He rubbed my head, but didn't say anything for a long while, as if he were very sad. His cauldron was uncovered. A small, rusty brass bell was immersed in the bubbling liquid. I'd climbed a ladder to take it down from an old pavilion south of town a few days before. The water gurgled, the bell reverberated, but the man remained silent. If this went on much longer, I'd be in tears for sure.

Old Master said: I never thought the Cao family would one day use you like this.

I said: I'm happy about it. It is my great good fortune.

He said: Ears, come closer. I want you to do something.

I said: Just tell me what it is.

Old Master lowered his voice, and his breath on my neck made it tickle. His mouth stank. All those weird things he ate had combined to produce a strange, noxious odor. But when he'd said his piece, the confusion in my heart melted away.

Old Master probably believed that I was someone who could turn bad luck to good.

He asked me to get him some spiders and spiderwebs.

He told me to get them from inside the prison, and from a condemned cell if possible.

I don't care what's stuck to them, he said, bring it all.

At that moment I felt totally relaxed.

Big Road, who was waiting for me outside my door, couldn't figure out why I was so happy. Second Master's arrest had hit him so hard he'd delayed his departure. But we both knew the real reason for the delay. Nonetheless, I couldn't be sure what was on his mind at this moment.

Big Road said: Do me a favor and give him my best.

Then he said: Tell him I'm planning to leave.

He looked like a listless old Chinese gentleman, his hands tucked into the sleeves of his gown. His runny nose had soiled his moustache and one of his eyes was nearly closed by cigar smoke. He looked truly down-and-out, a man overwhelmed by his own sorrows.

I said: Ask your God to look after him.

Surprised by my comment, he merely laughed hoarsely.

After the garrison soldiers had ended their feast and taken their silver offerings, they bound me with thick, heavy rope. Once that was done, Steward Bing came quietly up behind me and said: Tell them only what they need to know. Now's your chance to see just how clever you can be. It was a hard-hearted thing for him to say, but I saw that his eyes were moist.

Wuling was the only person who shed tears for me. As I walked down the steps of the gate tower, she began to cry. She said: Elder Brother Ears, come home soon. With all the people out on the street to gawk, I felt she'd caused me to lose face. So instead of looking at her, I held my head high and walked off.

I wasn't despondent.

I was thinking about spiders and spiderwebs.

About all the little insects and moths caught in the webs.

Old Master had saved me!

I didn't give a thought to dying.

And I was right.

April 4th

Second Master Guanghan had been arrested in a little village called Water and Fire Camp, not far from the county seat. Renowned for its blacksmiths, it boasted no fewer than ten smithies. It was also home to a clandestine weapons manufacturing and repair shop for the Blue Kerchiefs. When the garrison command raided the place at night, the people working inside scattered like a stampeding herd, forgetting all about Second Master, who was in a storage room for Black Dragon matches on the village outskirts. He told his captors that he was a manufacturer of matches and that he'd rented the room as a distribution center for his product. But his explanation fell on deaf ears, especially after they discovered a pistol, manufactured in another province, tucked into his waistband. When they asked where he'd gotten it, he said he'd traded a hundred baskets of matches for it. Why had he found it necessary to carry a firearm? As protection against pirates and highwaymen. He gave all the right answers, but that didn't stop one of the soldiers from thumping him in the mouth with the butt of his rifle, knocking out several teeth. He was bundled off to prison, where he was beaten some more, and if not for the fact that one of the investigating officers recognized him as the second son of a wealthy family, they might have beaten him to death then and there. Sometime after all this happened, we heard that Second Master, who was little more than skin and bones, had laughed and cursed the whole time he was being beaten. He quickly became the number one prison hero. The men who inflicted the beating said they'd never seen anyone stand up to punishment like that—and, even more unusual, someone who had grown up in the lap of luxury. I also heard—afterward, of course—that in order to keep the garrison troops from searching the Cao estate and perhaps arresting more members of the family, Elder Master had parted with several thousand ounces of silver. I was to be the sacrifice, an object to be tied up and taken away in order to get the rest of the family off the hook. But there was a difference between me and other objects: I could talk, and I knew exactly what to do and what not to do for the sake of my master. But it was silver, not the sacrificial lamb, that was handed over that made the difference. At the time I thought that the Cao family had raised my status so that Second Master's crimes would be on my head, and that, if it came to that, I would die in his place. What a joke!

Me, a proper human being?

I was a lowly dog being dragged away from the Cao estate.

All I was good for was to gather spiders for Old Master!

Before leaving Elm Township, I asked Elder Master what I should say and do in prison. Wearing the unfamiliar look of someone resigned to his fate, he told me not to worry about what to do. Just go, he said. You'll be told what to say when the time comes. After we arrived at the county seat, I was tossed into a cell, where there was no one to tell me what to say. I felt like a worthless bedbug that had been tossed into a clump of grass in the prison grounds.

There were spiderwebs all over the cell's high ceiling.

But I didn't know to get them down.

I shared a cell with fourteen other men.

I fell asleep sitting up.

They crowded around me and asked what crime I'd committed.

I said: I killed a man.

They asked me: Who?

I said: An enemy.

The savage-looking men quickly lost interest in me and returned to their empty bowls. I'd been given a bowl too, and when the guard came by with the food, I followed the others' lead by sticking it out through the bars. I waited for the guard to say something, but he ignored me. I also waited for the night duty guard to talk with me, but he ignored me too. There was no one to tell me what to say. I was a forgotten man. The guard reminded me of a groom as he walked up and down the corridor, between two rows of cells, like stables. For days on end, an unbroken stream of men were taken out of their cells and returned to them. They were standing when they went out, but carried back in. Some left and never returned.

The torture room was at the rear of the prison. Even without a window in the wall, we could hear the sounds of the beatings, especially at night. The prisoners' screams rose and fell, and we could hear them shout for their fathers or for their mothers.

I was fast asleep late one night when a loud noise on the other side of the wall awakened me. At first I thought I'd been dreaming. But, no, I was awake, and there was the noise; it was softer now, but there was no question whose voice it was.

I traded places with a convict next to the wall and pressed my ear up against it to hear what was happening on the other side. Something was landing heavily on flesh, though I couldn't tell if it was hard or soft. The man being beaten was Second Master! Every shout was like a peal of thunder.

He shouted: Dogs!

He shouted: Dogs! Ow!

He shouted: Ow!

He shouted: Ow! Ow!

Then he shouted: Dogs! Dogs! Dogs!

Whatever was hitting him kept an uneven, unhurried pace.

It was landing on his flesh.

It was landing on his bones.

The sound of something landing on flesh continued, even when the shouts stopped.

I was pressed up against the wall, stunned.

I said: My master's money went to feed a pack of fucking dogs!

A convict said: He's got balls, that one. A rarity.

I asked: What are they beating him with?

He said: A rattan switch.

I asked: Does it hurt?

He said: You'll know when the time comes.

I asked: Can it do any real damage?

Not even a water buffalo can take beatings like that, he said. Who in his right mind would dare shout insults? Can calling your torturer a dog make things easier? No, it's death he's looking for. Hear that? No more shouts.

The words *no more shouts* still hung in the air when Second Master recommenced hurling insults.

The convict said: That guy's not fucking human!

Fuck you! I snarled. You're the one who isn't human.

He asked: Who is he, your father? Your grandfather?

I said: He's your worthy ancestor.

The convict, unable to figure me out, lay down and went to sleep. I went back to the wall and stayed there listening until there were no more sounds. After taking money from the Cao family, the garrison people must have killed their prisoner anyway. Things couldn't have been worse. I didn't know what I had to look forward to, and there was no one to tell me what to do. The men in here had put me out of their minds. But what about Elder Master and Old Master? The lamp in the cell shone on the walls and its spiderwebs. I spotted a little spider hanging motionless by a long, thin thread, and I figured the only way I was going to get any spiderwebs was by standing on someone's shoulders. But whose?

The guard came for me in the middle of the night. He followed me with a lantern. The courtyard was a maze of twists and turns around hidden walls. Before we reached the torture room, he stopped me.

He said: Don't say more than you have to. If you do, the investigator may be in a forgiving mood, but others won't.

I asked him: What should I say?

He said: You'll know. Just remember, no more than you have to.

He shoved me into the torture room.

There was Second Master. He was hanging by his arms from a rack shaped like our gate tower, his toes barely touching the ground. His head hung down, as if he were gazing into the brazier in the middle of the floor. When I got up closer, I saw that his eyes were closed, and I assumed he was unconscious. His hair and body were blood-spattered, and his queue was missing. A man hanging by his arms looks just like a rag doll. Sitting at a desk on the other side of the brazier was a weary-looking officer in an official hat, complete with feathers. He looked at me gloomily. I fell to my knees before anyone said anything.

He asked: Know who he is?

I said: Yes.

He asked: Who is he?

I said: Second Master of the Cao family.

He said: Rubbish!

Terrified, I started to tremble. I kept my mouth shut.

He said: This person is a leader of the Blue Kerchiefs. You didn't know that?

I said: No.

He asked: What do you know?

I said: He's the head of the Elm Township Match Commune.

He asked: What's a commune?

It's a family, I said.

A family? he asked. Like how?

I said: With a father and mother. And it's licensed by the provincial industrial promotion office. If I'm lying, Venerable Master can rip out my tendons.

Someone snickered.

Venerable Master and his subordinates all looked over at Second Master.

It was he who had laughed, not them.

I couldn't see his eyes.

But I could see the gap where his teeth had been knocked out.

Venerable Master said: Rip out your tendons? That's a new one. You'll have to teach me how. You've got quite a mouth, you little whelp. String him up. Then I want you to tell me everything, what you know and what you don't know. I'll be the judge of whether or not you're lying.

They hung me up about two feet away from Second Master. But the rope was tied badly, and I twisted in the air, since my feet didn't quite touch the floor. Second Master laughed again. The glare in his eyes, filtered through hair that had fallen in front of his face, terrified me. My arms felt as if they were about to snap off, and every joint in my body creaked and groaned. I tried to stretch far enough to touch the floor with my toes, and was rewarded with a stinging blow across my calf. It felt like a piece of red-hot steel had snapped my leg in two. I screamed in pain—I couldn't help myself. I screamed every time they hit me, as my legs recoiled and the ropes sent me twisting again. I didn't think there was any way I could stop.

I screamed: Aiyo!

I'd never screamed like that before.

And I screamed: Venerable Master, spare me!

I screamed: It hurts! Please, Daddy!

My screams grew so chaotic that not even I knew what I was shouting. I wanted to hold out, but I couldn't. So I kept shouting, and pretty soon I was crying. Tears and snot ran into my mouth, and still I kept shouting, as if the mouth weren't mine at all. I knew that Second Master was still laughing—I could hear the air whistling through his teeth.

He was like a madman, afraid of nothing and no one.

Venerable Master asked me: Who is he?

I said: He's Second Master.

Venerable Master asked: Is he the leader of the Green River Branch?

I said: No!

He asked: How do you know he isn't?

I said: I don't know.

Beat him! he said.

I said: I just know, that's how. Venerable Master, put me out of my misery! Aiyo! Venerable Master, spare me! You're killing me! I know he isn't, because I am! How's that, Venerable Master? Daddy! Daddy!

I was crying and shouting so much I nearly choked myself.

The interrogator and his man with the whip were tired. They looked at me impatiently. Someone kicked me. I didn't realize it was Second Master until he spoke to me. His voice was as soft as the buzz of a mosquito. He said: How you holding up, Ears?

I said: It hurts. It hurts something awful.

He said: Keep your mouth shut and think about other things.

Second Master, I said, I want to die! Aiyo!

That *aiyo* startled even me. It was loud and high-pitched and had a weird, inhuman quality to it. The rattan switch ripped open my guts and broke my bones, until I felt that only my skin remained intact, that everything inside me was pulverized. Second Master said something, and the rattan switch immediately left me; it whistled in the air before landing on his body.

The officer said: Keep that mouth of yours shut, rebel!

Without making a sound, Second Master raised his head as if looking for something in the beams of the ceiling. I looked in the same direction, but saw nothing—nothing, that is, but a spiderweb the size of a food steamer. I couldn't see the spider, but I spotted a pair of black bugs, long since sucked dry.

Second Master said: Ears! Think of something else.

I said: Beat me! I beg you, Venerable Master, beat me!

They ignored me. Second Master's shredded clothing was flying everywhere. His head tilted backward, and he squinted to look at something mortal men could not see. His gap-toothed mouth hung slack. He was in a different world, his mind a million miles away. He was far more terrifying than those strong-armed men with their switches.

Ears, he said, I'm thinking about Paris!

He said: I'm thinking about her!

He shouted: I'm thinking about her! About her!

Then he shouted: Come! Come here!

I didn't know who the *her* was.

But I did know that Paris was a land across the ocean.

As he continued to shout, he began speaking in that foreign tongue.

The officer just looked at him nonchalantly.

I'd been hanging there so long that my toes touched the floor and I stopped spinning. The officer told his men to stop the beatings and had them put two pieces of charcoal into small braziers inside the larger brazier, one under Second Master's feet and one under mine. Panic-stricken, I tucked my legs up as high as they would go. So did Second Master.

I sobbed: Venerable Master, our Second Master is an innocent man. Spare him, please, and spare me!

The official was tired, too worn out to bother with me. He kept yawning in his seat behind the desk, his eyes fixed on our feet. I kept my mouth shut and did as Second Master said, trying to think of something else. I thought about a horse I'd tended as a child. It had loved to gallop on the banks of the Black River. Then I thought about Wuling, whose eyes were swollen from crying as I was taken away. She watched me through hot tears. Finally, I thought about the first time I laid eyes on Young Mistress. She was standing on the steps of the corner compound, dressed all in green, and Big Road and I nearly crashed into her holding our big fish. Such a big fish! she said.

The naked fish struggled in my arms, trying to break free.

It moved, it squirmed, and soon turned into the sleek body of a human being.

I embraced the laughing and shouting Young Mistress.

Second Master sucked in a mouthful of air.

The official jumped to his feet.

I smelled the odor of burning flesh. I felt my coiled legs begin to sag. I tried to think of something else, but it was useless. I watched as Second Master's feet touched the red-hot coals in the brazier. Blue smoke coiled upward, following the contours of his legs; his tattered pant legs caught fire. Second Master stared at the ceiling and made a strange sound. He'd wanted to laugh, but that's not how it came out.

Dogs! he said. Dogs!

The official said: Bastard! Bastard!

I couldn't hold my legs up any longer. The men bumped into me as they rushed up with their switches to beat out the flames on

Second Master's pant legs. Heat from the coals burned my soles. There was no way out—all I could do was step down. As if sliced by a razor-sharp knife, one layer at a time, my feet disappeared in a blaze of pain. I screamed a time or two before everything turned black. I have no recollection of what happened after that, except that the official jumped to his feet and bellowed: You'll never get out of here alive, I promise you that!

And Second Master said: I thank you for that.

I wanted to tell them to kill me too, to not let me live any longer. I don't know if I actually said it before losing consciousness.

April 5th

During the days Second Master and I were being tortured in prison, Elder Master was running back and forth between the capitals of the county and the whole prefecture. The official who interrogated us belonged neither to the county nor to the garrison command, but was a newly assigned prefecture magistrate. Having never received any of the Cao family's silver and seeing that the officials were lukewarm over the case, he was particularly cruel in his treatment of the accused. But he soon softened, thanks mainly to the intervention of money. Rescuing his brother was Elder Master's sole concern; to that end he sold off a considerable portion of the family's commercial holdings. And although we remained in prison, a medical officer was sent to treat Second Master's wounds and, while he was at it, tend to my burns. Second Master and I were transferred to a secluded little cell, all to ourselves, where we were given decent food.

Second Master, whose injuries were more serious, spent most of his time in bed. With so much on his mind, he wasn't interested in talking. Once again I was his servant, devotedly tending to his needs and, observing him watchfully in the process, careful not to say more than was absolutely necessary, given his dazed state. I knew he was thinking about what had happened on the Green River. He was a Blue Kerchief. And so, of course, was Zheng Yusong. I'd come to that realization back when I was leaving Elm Township. But I kept my curiosity in check and refrained from asking any questions. By not asking, I remained his personal servant; if I'd asked, I'd have been an outsider.

One day during the second lunar month, just after sunset, prison guards came and took Second Master. When he didn't return right away, I began to worry. In order to keep busy, I stood on my cot and held the flames from the prison cell lantern up to a black spider spinning a web. It scurried into a crack in the wall. I tried to catch it, but it got away, leaving behind only its ragged web. I took down the net by coiling it around a piece of straw, knowing that the spider would emerge to spin a new one before long. Nothing had been caught in the old web except for several bedbugs. Now what were bedbugs doing that high up on the wall? A real mystery.

I waited for the spider to reappear, so I could burn it up. But Second Master returned before the spider emerged. He didn't look good, but since he went right to bed without a word, I blew out the lantern and lay down. He tossed and turned—slowly, because of his injuries—before finally quieting down. I thought he'd fallen asleep, and was surprised to hear him call to me in the gloomy voice of a lost spirit.

What are you doing, Ears? he asked.

I said: Just lying here. Is there something I can do for you?

He said: Guangman came to the prison to visit me.

Is everyone okay? I asked.

He said: They're fine. We're going to be released in a few days.

Really? I cried out. Have they closed the case?

He said: Yes, it's all over. Ears, you suffered a lot on my behalf, and I'm in your debt. But everything's okay now.

I said: I only did what's expected of me. I'm happy just to be with you, whatever the circumstances.

I felt my nose tighten as my emotions got the better of me. But Second Master just let out a long sigh, as if he'd die if he held it in any longer.

He said: Tell me, did you know about Yunan?

What about her? I asked.

He said: Be honest, now. Did you know she was pregnant?

I said: Yes.

Why didn't you tell me? he asked.

I said: You had so much on your mind, I didn't want to worry you.

How would that have worried me? he asked. I'm going to be a father. Did you people think that wouldn't make me happy? Or did you think I wasn't worthy of it? Say it. What were you afraid I'd do?

I said: Second Master, I deserve to die!

Shut up! he snapped.

I climbed out of bed and fell to my knees. I didn't know what I could say to smooth things over. He didn't stir, ignoring me completely and not saying another word all night. Worn out from kneeling, I got up to try again for the black spider. Quickly raising the lantern, I caught it by surprise. Seared by the flame, it fell to the floor, where it struggled vainly to get away on roasted legs. As I held it in the palm of my hand, an image popped into my mind of the spider's black juices squishing through Old Master's teeth as he bit down.

I thought about Second Master's heart.

And about Young Mistress's belly.

And about the dark hair on Big Road's body.

And about myself.

I didn't want to leave this place.

Winter had already passed when we left prison. Little blue and yellow flowers bloomed on the muddy banks of the Green River. We sailed upriver toward Willow Township on a virtually empty double-decker boat. At Duckweed Bay we stopped to give a government boat the right of way downriver. It was a medium-sized steel-hulled steamship, sleek and fast, a rooster-tail wake in the water behind it. The passengers on our ship, wanting to avoid trouble at all costs, quickly went belowdecks. But out of curiosity, I leaned up against the railing and stood very still. Something was hanging from the government ship's mast, like a drooping flag. But as the ship drew nearer, I saw that it was a man, his arms stuck out to the sides, as if he were about to fly away. He was covered with blood, from head to toe, still alive, but beyond speech. As the two ships passed, the man's bright eyes looked down at me. But though they were bright, I'm sure he saw nothing, for his face was devoid of expression. Then it hit me—I knew who he was. I didn't dare shout to him, for fear that the armed men on board the ship would open fire on me.

The man hanging from the mast was Zheng Yusong.

I didn't need to be told that he would not live long.

I went belowdecks to tell Second Master. Elder Master was there with him. They rushed up to the main deck, but by then the government ship was maybe a hundred yards downriver. All they could see was the outline of a man hanging high up on the mast. They stood there looking until the ship disappeared around a bend in the river. Second Master was deeply saddened. The color drained from his face as he stared blankly at waterfowl on the river.

Elder Master asked me: Are you sure it was him?

I looked him right in the face, I said. There's no mistake.

Elder Master said: People who have been tortured all look about the same.

Second Master said: It was him. I recognized the robe he was wearing.

None of us said anything more on the subject. Elder Master kept a close eye on his brother and brought up other subjects to take his mind off the incident. But there was no change in Second Master's expression. It was the one he'd worn the whole time in prison: indifferent yet cynical, making it impossible for anyone to guess what was going through his mind.

But I assumed he was thinking about bombs.

Then I assumed he was thinking about his child.

He was thinking about the child in Young Mistress's belly!

The ship docked at Willow Township sometime before mid-night. The Cao family sedan chair was waiting on the deserted pier. Since the burns on my feet hadn't completely healed, I was allowed to ride in a sedan chair for the first time in my life. It was well past midnight by the time our little procession reached the Cao estate. Both the surrounding area and the residence were quiet. We were met by Steward Bing and some family servants. Lantern in hand, Steward Bing led the way to Second Master's quarters, without a word to me, so I went straight to my little room, which was exactly as I'd left it, except that my bedding and pillow had been washed and dried in the sun; they gave off a sweet odor. I heard some movement in the main quarters, then the same in the side rooms. I wanted to get up and take a look—how I'd missed the left-hand compound! But I was so tired I couldn't keep my eyes open.

I slept straight through to the next afternoon.

When I stepped outside, I was greeted by a host of familiar sights. Big Road and Second Master were on the sun-drenched veranda, seated across from one another at the stone table, all the chess pieces in place. Young Mistress was sitting off to the side watching the battle, resting her head in her hand. Wuling was standing behind her. She cried out when she saw me.

Elder Brother Ears, she said, did you get enough sleep?

I was so embarrassed by her reception, I felt like slinking back into my room. But the others turned to me with strange looks in their eyes. Big Road stood up—probably a reflex action—and, after mumbling something, sat back down. He looked very tense.

Good to have you back, he said. Welcome home! Oh, sorry, would you like to come watch us play?

I said: In a while, maybe. I have things to do first.

Young Mistress gave me a smile, a wan, dreary smile. She was pale, and I could tell that watching the chess match brought her little pleasure. But for reasons that escaped me, it was important for her to be there, whatever her mood. Her face was unusually round, sort of puffy, and dotted with dark spots. It made me terribly sad. In prison, it was she I'd thought about, but she would never know that. I'm thinking about her at this very moment, but no matter how hard I try, I can never make those blotches go away.

You've gotten taller, Ears, she said.

I said: I know. It's all that good prison food!

She and Big Road laughed. Second Master didn't, yet he was clearly the most relaxed and composed person present. He spoke harshly to me, worse even than in prison, probably for the benefit of the others. He was playing chess not because he enjoyed it, but to make the others uncomfortable, since he'd had to endure a bellyful of shame.

What are you doing hanging around here? he asked me. My father's waiting for you!

Yes, I replied. I'm on my way.

He said: When you're finished there, bring me a bowl of eggdrop soup. I'm hungry.

I said: Yes.

The look on his face convinced me not to ask Young Mistress and Big Road if they wanted anything from the kitchen. Besides, that would have to come from him, not me. Wuling stood there with her lips parted. The stupid girl was smiling!

Big Road gobbled up one of Second Master's chessmen.

Second Master said something in the foreign language.

It sounded like cursing to me.

Big Road's expression didn't change.

I went to see Old Master Cao, taking along the paper packet with the spider and its web. He was in a good mood. He was always in a good mood in the spring. After asking how I was doing, he praised me right and left as he opened the packet, picked up the dead spider, and studied it closely, as if it were a precious gem. He chewed up the spider raw, then dumped the rest of what I'd brought into his cauldron. He told me he'd once eaten a whole plate of spiderwebs as a youngster, as if it had been a plate of noodles.

Now I'm old and useless, he said, just like that spider. See how its web falls apart when it hits the water. Everything in this world is getting worse and worse.

Old Master asked me: Ears, does Guanghan look like a rebel to you?

I said: No.

Me either, he said. They made a mistake.

I said: Second Master is tough as nails.

He said: He's hard as a rock when something sets him off. Harder, even. He got off lucky when they decided not to kill him. From now on, keep a close eye on him. The next time he runs off on one of his insane escapades, follow him.

He's an upright person, I said.

He said: Who in this prefecture isn't? Aren't you? Keep a close eye on him. If anything happens, and I can't find him, I'll come looking for you.

I will, I said. I won't forget.

That satisfied him. Old Master loved that time of the year. When spring rolled around, he became a happy man, unafraid of death. That's not to say he didn't keep up his weird diet, but in the spring he wasn't as particular about what he consumed. He swirled his chopsticks in the mixture to fish out threads of spiderweb, but nothing came up. So he tried again. Still nothing. But instead of getting upset, he merely dumped the liquid into his bowl and drank it all down. Death was the furthest thing from his mind.

Not bad, he said, not bad at all.

The air was, in fact, permeated with a pleasant aroma.

I wondered what strange occurrences the black spider, now an invisible spirit, would cause as it made its way through the Cao household. For a short while, at least, I'd feel its presence, feeding on my blood. But the child in Young Mistress's belly was my greatest concern. In my daydreams, tragic scenes came and went, eating away at the unborn infant, until only a puddle of blood and a few broken bones remained.

The left-hand compound became a fearful place.

I couldn't say why.

I guess I was afraid of a total loss of face.

Because then a person stops being a person and becomes a ghost.

April 6th

Porters stopped coming to Elm Village after Second Master's run-in with the authorities, which brought a temporary halt to our match operations. Back in the prefecture capital, when Elder Master was working to free us from prison, he'd called upon friends in the chamber of commerce to secure permission to sell Oolong matches in outlying provinces. Back in Willow Township he rented some sheds near the piers and hired porters to carry our matches over on a daily basis. Then, whenever a ship docked, he was ready with thousands of baskets of matches to be transported up or down the river for sale. Whether it made Second Master happy or not, or me, for that matter, the operation was running more smoothly than when we were in charge. Even Elder Master had to admit that they had the foreigner to thank for that. He could have left when the family fell on hard times, but he hadn't; instead, he stayed on and worked harder than ever. That sort of devotion was a rarity. And so, Elder Master decided to reward him with a cash bonus. Second Master neither objected nor gave his consent—he reacted to the news with a blank expression. But I saw him bite down hard on his lower lip. Of course, I might have been mistaken; hard to say. What I can say for sure is, he said something that took us all by surprise.

He said: He can leave now if he wants.

Then he turned to me and spoke coldly.

He said: Go tell Mr. Road that if he wants to leave, he should make preparations now. The nights are long, the dreams are many. No one can predict what might happen on the Green River.

I said: The commune will fail without him.

Are you telling me that I don't count? he said.

I said: No! But you have wounds that need to heal.

And you? he asked. What about you?

I said: I count for nothing. I'm totally inept.

He said: Yes, you are. But you're one hell of a liar.

Second Master! I cried out.

Shut up! he snapped. Shut that mouth of yours!

He wouldn't look at me, as if afraid to note my embarrassment. Since he wouldn't permit me to speak, I didn't dare make a sound, no matter how cluttered my mind was. I knew exactly what I was hiding from him, and that I'd take some of that to my grave. I would never acknowledge that I'd lied to him, just as I never said a word about the explosion, even when they were burning my feet with hot coals. That had been for Second Master's benefit, and so was this. I couldn't drive a knife into his heart. He'd already done enough of that himself.

The first time he'd told me to shut up was in prison. News of his wife's pregnancy should have made him happy, and when it set him off instead, my heart leapt up into my throat. I was gripped by a fear I couldn't shake. So the last thing in the world I expected was to hear him say matter-of-factly, He can leave now if he wants.

Big Road understood perfectly well that he could leave now and avoid harm.

What kept him from doing so was the will of Heaven.

Heaven held him in its hand and wouldn't let go!

The year's first rain fell that day, bringing with it talk that Zheng Yusong had been beheaded in the prefecture schoolyard. Confirmation was not long in coming, as his head was paraded all along the Green River, on its way to Willow Township, where it was to be hung up for public display. Not long after, a small sedan chair arrived from Mulberry Township to fetch Young Mistress to see her father, who was on his deathbed. We had kept the news of her brother from her as long as we could. But even after she found out, Old Master and Old Mistress would not let her return to her parents' home. Being with her father was, they felt, less important than protecting the continuation of the Cao family line, that invisible piece of flesh in her belly. So the Zheng family sedan chair returned empty in the rain. But something strange occurred later that night. A letter was pinned to the main gate by a dagger. A servant took it to Steward Bing, who gave it to Elder Master. None of us knew what the letter said, but we couldn't help but notice how Steward Bing's legs trembled as he walked. When I got up in the middle of the night to relieve myself, I spotted some servants lying concealed in the left-hand compound. I asked them what was going on, and they stammered something about someone out there vowing to murder a member of the Cao family. Everyone was sleeping with one eye open that night.

The main house was dark.

So, too, were the side buildings.

Second Master had been staying in one of the side buildings ever since his return; he seldom set foot in the main house. Steward Bing's wife said that the pregnancy had weakened Young Mistress, who needed plenty of rest and nourishment. Out of a sense of concern for her, Second Master was willing to sleep alone, something few men would be capable of. Steward Bing's wife was a fool. Many people in the Cao household were fools. Those who knew the truth concealed it, but they didn't know much, since they had no way of getting inside other people's heads. I wanted to cry! I wanted to run away! Did they know that?

For a long time I'd felt that someone had murder on his mind.

My daydreams were awash in blood.

What I didn't know was who wanted to murder whom.

I later learned that the letter comprised but four words:

Death to the rebel.

Death—to—the—rebel!

I'll remember those words till the day I die.

Death!

Just think about it.

A bullet hit one of the cooks on his way to the slaughterhouse to grade some meat. Coming from the woods on Jade Mountain, it merely grazed the back of his head. After rolling and crawling around on the gate tower steps, he felt his wound and pulled back a blood-smeared hand; once he realized that it was only a flesh wound, he let loose with a hair-raising howl. The man's build and face were similar enough to Second Master's that everyone knew who the real target was. Elder Master kept Second Master from going to the left-hand compound and told the servants to watch him closely. But when Second Master heard what had happened to the cook, he decided not to hide any longer. With mounting agitation, he walked out of the compound on his way to town. They stopped him at the gate.

He demanded: Let me go! I'll teach them a lesson!

He shouted into the road: Come on, you blind bastards!

He nearly broke free, frightening Steward Bing into falling to his knees. Even after they managed to drag him back to the compound, he refused to go inside, and simply camped out on the veranda like a man waiting for somebody. I knew who that somebody was. Big Road and I sat with him, silently, but after a while we got up and went to the old granary to do some work. I was still in charge of the commune. Big Road and I were going over some last-minute details when we heard a shot out by the gate. We ran over, ducking and crouching to avoid stray bullets. Big Road did his best to keep up with me.

He said: Ears! Cao! What's going on?

I don't know, I said.

He asked: Who hates Cao?

I don't know, I repeated.

He smiled wryly and stopped asking questions.

There were a lot of things I didn't know. Since being informed of Zheng Yusong's tragic end, Young Mistress had taken to her room and stayed there. Wuling told me that she neither cried nor spoke. She spent the whole day, every day, in bed. Before, she had listened to Steward Bing's wife, eating what and when she was told to. But now she ignored the old servant, as if she were deaf and dumb, which brought Steward Bing's wife to tears on several occasions. Given her condition, I wondered what Young Mistress would say to Second Master if he came to see her. I guessed they'd each just go to their own room and talk to themselves. Whether that meant cursing or pitying themselves was not something for mortal men to know.

Later that day, after work, the sedan chair from Mulberry Township reappeared in front of our gate. As Big Road and I were walking down the path heading to the left-hand compound, we heard an argument somewhere off in the distance. The voices belonged to Elder Master and Second Master.

Elder Master said: She's a member of the Cao family, so her people have no say in whether she goes to Mulberry Township or not! She's six months pregnant, and she's not leaving this compound, even if the sky falls. This comes straight from Father and Mother!

Second Master said: Let her go, for my sake.

Elder Master said: Guanghan, you don't owe anyone anything. If you care at all for this family, you'll let me handle this. I don't want you or your wife going anywhere. Stay put inside the compound so you won't get caught up in any of the troubles out there. That's my job.

Second Master said: You people won't rest until you suffocate me! Let her go. Her father's on his deathbed, so let her go home to be with him.

Elder Master said: Use your head!

Second Master said: If you won't let her leave, then I'll leave!

A flurry of footsteps erupted in the compound somewhere. Big Road and I quietly stepped over the threshold, where we saw a group of servants struggling with Second Master at the end of the veranda, just as Young Mistress emerged from her room. Everyone froze. Her face was unusually pale, and she walked slowly, hindered by her protruding belly. But she was as poised as ever, and still dressed in bright, colorful clothes. Holding a letter in her hand, she walked up to Elder Master, wearing a smile that nearly broke my heart.

She said: You can stop quarreling. I'm not going anywhere. Where would I go? Tell them to take this to my parents. Guanghan suffered in prison. So they won't get the wrong idea about him, I've written on his behalf. Please read it first and correct anything you find inappropriate.

That's not necessary, Elder Master said. We'll send it along to them, I promise.

He smiled a bitter smile and sighed, then signaled the servants to go back to what they were doing. After they stepped through the gate, only Second Master, Young Mistress, and Big Road remained on the veranda. Plus Wuling and me, of course, though we were outsiders. It was unnaturally quiet, with no one saying a word. Finally, Big Road, unable to endure the silence, said: Cao, I'm leaving.

Second Master sat frozen, as if he hadn't heard.

Big Road said: You've got Ears; he's quite good. I can leave.

Second Master exploded in a fit of temper.

He said: Then leave! Leave right now! Haven't you stuck around long enough? What else do you want to do here? And what were you planning to do if you didn't leave? Please, I'm begging you. Get out of here! Get lost!

Big Road shrank in front of our eyes, and his lips quivered. He couldn't say a word, not in Chinese and not in his own language. All he could do was swallow hard. Even Second Master himself seemed stupefied by his outburst. Looking down at his clenched fists, he seemed to be wondering what he'd done.

Young Mistress said: Guanghan, he's our guest.

Second Master said: I know exactly what he is.

With that he returned to his quarters, leaving Young Mistress and Big Road standing there looking at each other, apparently forgetting Wuling's and my presence altogether. She said something in his language, turned, and left. He watched her leave and then walked off. I had a pretty good idea what she'd said to him, which translates into three words—Time to leave.

She was all but begging him.

I assumed that he would pack his things that night.

But he didn't.

He said to me: Boil some water. I'm going to take a bath.

He soaked in the tub for what seemed like most of the night, whistling the whole time.

What I heard in that whistling was fear of neither earth nor Heaven. The sound came to me in my room and chilled my heart. I could picture the trustworthy, hardworking Big Road climbing out of his tub, dripping wet, as he once again became the big-nosed barbarian. He'd run around the place, stark naked, like a wolf baying at the moon, guaranteeing no peace for the Cao family or all of Elm Township.

His whistling breathed layers of heat on me, inside and out.

I was like a bag filling up with air.

I felt myself getting bigger.

I went looking for Steward Bing to tell him that the rats that had made it through the winter were back at work in the book storage room, and that something had to be done about them. He handed me the key and some rat poison and told me to stay inside long enough to spot their paths. If I didn't do that, he said, I could put down a whole basket of poison without doing any good. I told him I'd do it, then waited until the sun had nearly set before going over there. On the way, I ran into Wuling on the path; she was carrying a brass basin filled with clean laundry she was bringing back from the Black River. She'd washed her hair while she was at it and had tied her apron over her head. It flowed out behind her like a train. Normally, I never gave her a second look, but this time I thought of her crying over me, and suddenly felt terribly lonely. She called out Elder Brother Ears when she saw me, and smiled; in that moment she broke the dam in my heart.

I wanted to touch her.

I said: Wuling, I've been looking for you.

Really? she said. What for?

I said: Put down that basin and come with me to the garden out back.

Our first date.

She followed me without a word.

I led her into the book storage room, where I wanted to take out my favorite book. Not daring to light a match, I felt my way along. Afraid of the dark, Wuling followed close behind me. When she asked which book I was looking for, I screwed up the nerve to describe it to her in detail. She didn't believe me. Embarrassed and a little afraid, I felt my heart beating like crazy; I was eager to find her lips with mine. When I couldn't find the book I wanted, I made a little bed out of books, with Wuling as a book I was in a hurry to open. Scenes from my daydreams flashed before me. Dark little Wuling's body was white and womanly.

I read my book, page by page.

I was soaked in sweat.

She and I slipped into another world.

I asked her: Do you know what Young Mistress and Big Road have been doing?

Yes, she answered.

I asked: How do you know?

I saw them, she said.

Where? I asked.

She said: Behind the man-made hill.

I asked: Anyplace else?

She said: On the veranda.

What did you see? I asked.

She said: I'm not going to say. It was too ugly.

I said: You don't need to say anything. I'll show you.

I'd practiced for this in daydreams, but couldn't get the hang of it in real life. I was too eager, too rough, had too much on my mind. The way I moved around, it looked like I was trying to rip my new book up. Wuling was breathing so hard I really felt for her. But I couldn't put a damper on my frantic brain, and tried to turn my thoughts elsewhere.

I asked her: How far along is Young Mistress?

She said: Steward Bing's wife said six months.

I asked: Do you know whose it is?

I know, she said.

I asked: Is it Second Master's?

She said: No.

Are you sure? I asked.

I live in the room next to her, she said. Of course I'm sure.

I asked: How can you be sure?

She said: Second Master and Young Mistress have been living in the same quarters for a long time, but they sleep alone. The bamboo cot is not a recent development.

I asked: How come?

She said: Young Mistress is afraid of all the strange things he does. He even scares himself sometimes. After lying low so long, he's changed.

I asked: What kind of strange things?

She said: You know.

I said: No, I don't. Tell me.

She said: I don't want to say it, Elder Brother Ears.

I said: I might kill you if you don't.

Kill me, then, she said.

The moon was beautiful that night, and I was thinking maybe I ought to kill us both. But as I thought of death, I saw a face like the full moon. I was standing on a cloud, calling: Yunan! Yunan! Yunan! I was ready to jump.

All of a sudden, Wuling said: Elder Brother! Don't get me pregnant!

I froze.

I cooled off.

I saw Young Mistress. She was about to die.

Then I saw Big Road. He was also about to die.

I really cooled off.

I closed the book of Wuling before finishing it.

I had become someone who knew everything.

It was a terrible feeling.

I still didn't know what death felt like.

April 7th

Zheng Yusong's head had been put on display at Willow Township. Following a family discussion in the Cao household, they decided not to go look at it, but to send one of the slaves instead. First they went to Steward Bing, who begged off, saying that at his age he was not up to viewing dead bodies, let alone a severed head. So Elder Master came to me. All I had to do, he said, was give the head a quick look. I was not to do or say anything. I was willing, solely on account of the lighthearted comment Zheng had once made to me. He'd said that if they ever chopped off his head and hung it up for display, he hoped I'd go speak to it and see if he heard me. I'd wanted to go see him ever since that unforgettable last view I had of him, with his eyes shining down on me. More and more, I believed that he'd seen me at that moment, but wasn't willing to let on that he recognized me, a sign of what kind of man he'd been. You could chop off his head and let it rot in the sun, but you couldn't take away his magnificence.

Second Master slipped me some silver before I set out and told me to buy some spirit paper at a funeral shop, then burn it in some out-of-the-way spot. I wanted to ask Young Mistress if there was anything I could do for her, such as say some words for the soul of her brother. But Second Master wouldn't let me go to her quarters, wanting to avoid making her feel any worse than she did already.

Second Master's dejected look showed how bad he felt.

He said: Take note of everything you see and report back to me.

And, he added, remember everything you hear.

Finally he said: People who have me in their sights will also be targeting you, so be careful.

The pier at Willow Township was the same as always, with lots of boats and crowds of people. The flagpole where the head hung was also the same as always, with guards sitting at the base. The differences this time were that instead of a cluster of heads, there was only one, and instead of hanging there exposed for all to see, it had been put in a porous bamboo basket that resembled a birdcage. A queue hung down through one of the gaps in the basket, like a dead snake. Plump and dark, Zheng Yusong's head had not yet decomposed. He looked peaceful, his eyes reduced to slits, the corners of his mouth drooping; leaning to one side, it seemed to be cocked in a listening pose, the ears pricked up to hear more clearly.

I felt like crying.

I sat in Lucky Teahouse sipping a cup of Emerald Conch tea and spoke to Zheng Yusong through the window. I could neither see nor hear anything else around me. What I saw was that robust young man slipping into his sedan chair and taking off like the wind, and what I heard were the sounds of our seemingly endless conversation.

I said: Elder Brother Zheng, I've come to see you. Can you hear me?

I can hear you, he said. Thanks for coming.

I said: You don't look very good.

He said: I'm in pain.

I felt like crying.

He asked: How's my sister?

I said: She's pregnant.

How about my brother-in-law? he asked.

I said: He's going to be a father.

He asked: And how about you, Ears?

I'm great! I said. I finally slept with a woman!

I was nearly in tears.

I asked: How could you have wound up like this, Elder Brother?

A friend betrayed me, he said.

I asked: Who was it?

He said: I don't know.

I said: How terrible that was for you, Elder Brother.

He said: I know what you mean, Ears.

I could hardly keep from crying.

He said: Ears, you're a man!

I said: Elder Brother, as a man, how should I live my life?

Remember, he said, death to all those people who don't deserve to live.

I asked: Anything else?

He said: If you like a woman, be sure to get her in bed.

Elder Brother, I said, when you come back as a hero, roaming the world, take me with you.

He said: I won't be coming back, not with my body gone.

I said: You can have my body.

He said: Ears, you'll be worthless if you keep talking like that.

My eyes were moist. Zheng Yusong's tilting head was all a blur. But he was still listening, or at least still straining to listen, even if he couldn't hear me any longer. His dried-out queue fluttered in the wind, making the basket appear to have a tail.

Lucky said: What are you thinking about, Ears?

The cunt of a white horse! I replied.

He said: That's not what I expect to hear from the mouth of the new man in charge!

I said: It's not my mouth, it's my asshole!

Lucky spat on the floor, turned on his heel, and left.

I lit a bundle of paper under the table.

Zheng Yusong looked at me serenely.

Tears gushed from my eyes.

No matter how you try, life isn't worth living!

Death is always waiting for you.

Young Mistress's father died not long after my visit to Zheng Yusong. Young Mistress was sunning herself under a wisteria trellis in the left-hand compound, a loose white filial overgarment

hiding her green clothes from view. Under strict orders from Old
Master, the servants maintained a close watch on the compound,
charged with keeping outsiders from entering and Second Master
from leaving. At first, Second Master spent a lot of time in the compound yard, even sitting on the man-made hill when he was in a
relatively good mood; but later on, he stayed in his room and refused to come out, except on occasion to go see his mother in her
meditation room. He hardly ever went to see his father. Old Master had no time for anyone else's affairs, and little understanding
of what others in the family were doing. I once heard him arguing
with Elder Master in the main house. He was shouting: Take some
money to the Blue Kerchiefs and find out when this is going to end.
Tell the Zhengs that if Guanghan did in fact sell out his brother-
in-law, then they can do what they want with him. He'll get exactly what he deserves. But can you ask them how much his head
is worth if we buy back his life?

I'll handle it, Elder Master said. Don't worry.

Old Master said: And remind Guanghan that a man's actions
are limited by his abilities. If you know you're not somebody else's
equal, then tuck your head down between your shoulders. This
family isn't counting on him, and all we ask is that he not cause us
any more trouble.

Elder Master said: Don't worry. One stay in prison taught him
a lesson.

Old Master said: If he loses his head, that lesson will have come
too late. He wanted to go abroad, so we sent him. Then he wanted
to set up a match commune, and we took care of that too. Now what
sort of craziness is he trying to get away with? We hoped we'd keep
him home by finding him a good wife, but he's proved to be nothing but an annoyance to her. This family isn't finished, but if one
day it is, it'll be his doing! I can't do much anymore, and the family's
going to be yours sooner or later, so work things out.

Ears! he shouted.

Sir! I replied.

He said: Go out and dig me up an earthworm.

Red or white? I asked.

He said: Red, with blue rings.

Old Master had plenty to worry about. So did every other member of the family. Old Mistress prayed to her gods day and night, and was getting ready for another period of fasting for the Buddha Bathing Festival in the fourth lunar month. The master who taught her how to fast had already instructed her on several occasions. Elder Master was nearly worn out dealing with his wife and his concubine, and whatever energy he had left went into managing the family's financial and miscellaneous affairs. Young Mistress, Zheng Yunan, spent her time staring at her swelling belly as if possessed, trying to figure out what was waiting on the other side of that thin layer of skin. The foreigner soaked in his tub every night, lost in his thoughts; before going to bed, he got down on his knees beside his bed and muttered something to God. I could hear him from my room, and the sound was no different from the intoning of sutras in the meditation room upstairs; both gave me a creepy, edgy feeling. I had my worries too. Ever since winning over Wuling, I'd pretty much lost interest in prowling the rooftops. So many important things were going on in the left-hand compound, but none could wipe away the memories of the secret rendezvous in the book storage shed; there were still things about her body I didn't understand, and I ached to clear them up. So I invited her back to the same place, where we could enjoy each other on top of the Confucian Analects and books with erotic pictures. But every time we got to the climactic moment, she hit me and said: Don't get me pregnant! That was her biggest worry.

All she could think about was her belly.

Not a thought for me.

At the height of my pleasure I pinched her with my fingernails.

She bit me.

What was the point in going on like this?

I said: You're just like the young sow Old Barren is raising!

She said: And you're a young boar on the make!

She thought I was just joking around.

I was itching to smack her one!

I forced myself to hold back.

each other, Second Master was up to his old tricks in his room. Bottles
and cans crowded his windowsill, all filled with chemicals for his
match heads. He'd forced me to fetch them from the old granary. I
reported this to Elder Master, who didn't stop me. All he said was:
If we don't let him play with that stuff, he'll find something else to
do, just as bad or worse. So go ahead. But to guard against fire, put
a vat of water outside his window, and keep a close eye on him.

Bright red flashes through his window at night were enough to
scare anyone, while the smell of sulfur and phosphate in the air was
thick enough to choke you. Sometimes, I detected the fragrant smell
of burning pine or candle wax. There were also flashes of green, blue,
and purple, and it was clear that he was not only hard at work, creating these colors and smells, but more stubbornly dedicated to his
task than ever. Unhappy over how his life had turned out, he was
incredibly lonely. I had no way of knowing if he thought of strangling himself during this time. But all those lovely flashes of light
late at night reminded me of the kids who were always running up
and down the streets in town, no matter what Second Master was
doing on the other side of the window, whether it was strangling
himself, or whipping himself, or whatever. I liked seeing those
flashes of light, the way the air in the compound and above the town
itself was lit up with all those colors. It's impossible to describe the
feeling it gave me, but I could see all sorts of things because of it,
including the tilted head of Zheng Yusong. I could also see the figures of Big Road and Young Mistress, crushed together in the sunset. I'm sure Second Master could see that too.

Every time those chemicals flared up, I lay in my room, sensing
that Second Master was throttling himself over and over, while his
tears flowed unchecked.

After his return, Second Master took his meals in the family
dining room for a while, but later had his meals sent to his room.
He stopped eating with the others because he had several missing
teeth, and he thought he looked funny when he ate; by eating alone
in his room, he didn't have to worry about other people watching
food slip through the gap in his teeth into his bowl or seeing how

hard it was for him to slurp up the porridge or hearing the weird noises in his throat. He ate like a thief, permitting no one to watch him, not even those closest to him; maybe this was just an excuse for him to avoid contact with other people.

On sunny days, he occasionally stood next to Young Mistress under the wisteria trellis or sat with her on the veranda, but hardly a word passed between them. Wuling said they acted more like guests or distant relatives than husband and wife.

Young Mistress, still in her white filial overgarment, and Second Master were standing by the pool, separated by a distance of five or six feet, as they looked out at the water.

You can imagine what that looked like.

Have the burns on your feet healed? Young Mistress asked.

Second Master said: Yes. They no longer bother me.

Young Mistress said: You should have Steward Bing find a dentist to replace your teeth.

There's no hurry, Second Master replied.

What was out there in the water? Nothing.

Don't stand out here too long, Second Master said. Maybe you should go back to your room.

I will, Young Mistress replied. In a minute.

Second Master said: Then I'll head back, all right?

Young Mistress said: Go ahead.

He left to go back to his room, leaving her standing there alone. There was so much they had to say to each other, but it all went left unsaid; they had a tacit agreement, but weren't sure what it was. It was as if all they had to do was poke a small hole in the paper covering of a window to bring the sky crashing down to destroy the earth. I don't have to tell you how we slaves agonized over this. We were left in the dark, not knowing what they were thinking or what they might do. Young Mistress's belly grew visibly bigger nearly every day, and we could sense the emptiness of the joy felt by most members of the family.

Steward Bing hired a dentist to fit Second Master with several silver teeth. Although he seldom smiled, now, with the silvery glint emerging from his mouth, he appeared to be smiling even when he wasn't, and that illusory smile was especially captivating. Eating was no longer a problem, but he had become an ugly man, someone to be pitied. When people talked to him, they looked away to keep from embarrassing him. The truth is, he couldn't have cared less, since his mind was on other things.

His heart was not in Elm Township.

It had grown wings and flown far and high.

People underestimated him.

Several days remained before Big Road's scheduled departure. I was out sweeping the gateway one morning while Big Road was brushing his teeth by the pond. Young Mistress was on Wuling's arm, strolling along the opposite edge of the pond. Steward Bing's wife had taken lunchboxes over to the kitchen to fetch breakfast.

A shot rang out somewhere outside the compound.

Then another.

The echoes merged in the valley and hung lazily in the air for the longest time. I waited instinctively for the next sound, but everyone around me was quiet, as if the gunshots had scared them into silence.

I forget who first realized what had happened, but I took off running. A gasp escaped from Young Mistress, who tottered and nearly fell. Big Road was right behind me, followed by family servants. The little path rocked from all the footsteps. The first thing we saw as we ran through the gate was Second Master sprawled on the cobblestone street. He was trying to stand up, but there was blood on the ground all around him, and for a moment it wasn't clear where he'd been hit. He was alert and showed no fear. When I bent down over him, he smiled.

They got me this time, he said. Everything's settled.

Who said you could come outside? I asked him.

He said: I was going stir-crazy. Now I've given them what they wanted.

I asked: Where are they?

Everyone ignored me.

A puddle of blood the size of a small table covered the cobblestones. The lower half of his body seemed bathed in his own blood. He was looking up at a patch of sky and smiling, acting as if he couldn't hear Big Road, who was screaming Cao Cao Cao right next to him. I was sure he was going to die.

I demanded: Where's the person who did this?

Someone pointed to Jade Mountain, behind the town. My brain seemed to swell with anger. Letting go of Second Master, I ran toward the tree-lined mountain, shouting like a madman.

I said: You bastards! Are you blind? Shoot me if you've got the guts. I was in prison alongside him! They couldn't kill him, so you decided to do it for them! If you're so good, go get one of his interrogators and ask what sort of stuff Second Master's made of. Compared to him, you're a bunch of old ladies, turning tail and running away. Zheng Yusong was like an elder brother to me, and he sent me a message, vowing to get revenge against anyone who takes matters into his own hands! Heaven will strike you down, you blind goddamned pigs! Here I am, just waiting to see if the next bullet's got my name on it. Anybody who doesn't shoot is a chicken-shit bastard, lower than the dogs at our house!

Wind whistled through the trees.

I honestly believed that Second Master wouldn't survive this time.

Poor Second Master, with his silver teeth, wasn't going to survive this time.

Second Master, the cuckold, wasn't going to survive this time.

I didn't believe he was a rebel. Somebody had made a mistake. Killing him was like killing a mouse that had just climbed out of its hole. You couldn't help feeling sorry for him or breathing a sigh of relief at the same time. His blood looked like a lovely flower as it congealed on the cobblestones, changing from red to purple, and finally turning into a big black stain.

As it turned out, the bullet had only hit him in the arm. His assassin either had bad eyesight or had lost his nerve at the last minute. Five days later, on his feet again, his arm in a sling, he'd been transformed.

Elder Master said: You were spared this time. Now it's time to really start living.

Second Master answered: Don't treat me like a living person. I'm dead.

Elder Master said: Stay home and get ready to be a father.

Second Master said: I'm waiting. Since I can't seem to die, that's about all I can do.

He burrowed back into his room. Multicolored flashes of light reemerged from his window in the deep of night, when I detected inauspicious odors in the air. Sulfur, charcoal, and phosphorus. The odors came to me through my brain, not my nose. I thought about the bomb at Oxhorn Valley. Sometimes there was movement in his room, sometimes there wasn't, and I preferred to think of him as a corpse lying on the cobblestone street!

Cao Guanghan was a remarkable individual.

April 8th

For the Buddha Bathing Festival on the eighth day of the fourth lunar month, everything that wasn't nailed down in the meditation room was moved out to the main courtyard, filling three sides of the veranda. The servants carried out basins of salted water for Old Master and Old Mistress, who dipped fresh pine switches in the water and sprinkled it on all the Buddhist icons: not just the gold, silver, brass, and iron, but also those made of wood and stone. Then younger members of the family did the same, followed by houseguests and slaves in managerial positions. I didn't know who all those Buddhas were, but by the time it was my turn, they were covered by a layer of salt.

Unlike the others, who bowed to the icons when sprinkling them, Second Master merely brushed them with his switch, as if smacking them in the mouth. Young Mistress, who followed him, stood a while longer than expected in front of the Goddess of Mercy, brushing it from head to toe with her pine switch. Then she bowed grandly. Second Master turned back to look at her, and when she caught up to him, he gave his statue a vicious smack, nearly knocking it over. Big Road and I were wedged in the middle of the slow procession. He pointed to the Goddess of Mercy and asked me: Who's that?

I said: I don't know.

He dusted the statue carefully, then sprinkled water on its back and the lotus flower the bodhisattva sat on. His shoes were wet with saltwater. After sprinkling the statues with saltwater, they repeated the process with freshwater, after which they formed a human chain around the veranda, going round and round, over and over. Once the Buddhas were bathed, everyone sat down to a sumptuous meal in the dining hall. More food was served than at major holidays, a symbolic send-off for Old Mistress, who was to begin her fast and forty-nine days of seclusion. At the banquet, she asked her son: Has your wound healed?

Second Master replied: I'm much better. It wasn't serious to begin with.

Old Mistress said: You mustn't get into any more trouble. You're the only one in the family I'm worried about. I say the Diamond Sutra for you every day in my meditation room, to protect you and Yunan and your child. You must take care of yourself, Guanghan.

He walked up to his mother and knelt on one knee, leaning his head toward her. She took him to her breast. Everyone but Old Master laid down their chopsticks and waited for them. Old Master finished gnawing on a drumstick before mother and son separated. The scars on Second Master's face were dark red, and his eyes looked like those of a man in a dream. Old Mistress turned to Young Mistress and said: Yunan, Guanghan has always been a worry to me, so your devotion to him is very important. You must

take care of yourself too. I'm not worried, with Steward Bing's wife
there to watch over you. After I come out of my fasting, I'll be
waiting for the new addition to the family.

Young Mistress said: I won't forget what you've said.

Old Master said: Eat, everybody, eat!

He put a duck's foot in Old Mistress's bowl.

Old Mistress put a mushroom in Old Master's bowl.

Everyone at the table lowered their heads and continued eating. We stood up when Old Mistress rose to return to her meditation room, as if we were at a wake. Finally, we left the banquet through the veranda and returned to our own quarters—again, just like at a wake. I went first to the left-hand compound, where I watched Young Mistress, Second Master, and Big Road disappear into their respective rooms. To me, the compound felt like a cemetery, and my little room a stifling coffin. I couldn't sleep that night, so I went out to look at the lights by the pool. Both the main house and side rooms were lit up; a strange sound emerged from the side room, like wood striking wood, and I wondered what Second Master was up to now. I'd heard that same sound for many days in a row. Unable to curb my curiosity, I removed my shoes and climbed onto the roof. Pieces of broken tiles hurt the tender soles of my feet, which hadn't completely healed. But I didn't dare put my shoes back on, for fear of slipping and falling to the ground.

Since the side room didn't face the sun, the skylight was opened wide, revealing eight glass panes in two rows. Streaked by the rain, the glass was blurred, but I could see Second Master standing in front of a table, swaying gently back and forth. The oil lamp was in the corner, so I couldn't see what he was holding. But when he tired of what he was doing and sat down, I saw black powder on the table and a medium-sized rolling pin in his good hand. I could tell that the powder was charcoal. Second Master straightened the sling on his arm with his teeth and stayed in the chair a while longer before getting up and going back to the table to rock some more, rolling his pin back and forth, back and forth. The sound of wood on wood seemed endless. Second Master's shadow flickered on the wall behind him, like a soul in a coffin.

I then moved over to the main building, but the light went out before I got there. So I squatted down by the skylight, where I thought I could see Young Mistress seated in the center of the room, listening to the thud and grind of the rolling pin. Either that or she was lying in bed rubbing the layer of flesh covering a child that was more terrifying than any ghost. Steward Bing's wife, her eyes sharp as a cat's, was watching from the other side of the mosquito net. What was Wuling doing? She had to be sleeping soundly in the room next door, her milky little rear end peeking out from under the covers, just waiting for me to attack it! Wuling was destroying me!

And I was destroying my daydreams.

I had betrayed Young Mistress.

I left the main building and shinnied back down to the courtyard at the usual spot. As I passed the side room I suddenly sensed that I was not alone. It couldn't be any of the servants, I thought, since they had moved to the outer wall and the path a few days earlier. Then I thought of Big Road. Sure enough, it was him, but he still startled me so much I nearly cried out. He was standing beside the man-made hill, his shadow looking like an indentation on one of the famous rocks from Lake Taihu. He watched me lower myself catlike from the wall.

I said: Not asleep yet, Big Road? You should go to bed. How come you're standing there? You gave me a fright. It was so stuffy inside, I decided to cool off up on the roof. It was very refreshing. Well, I'm off to bed. It looks like rain tomorrow, so don't forget to take your damp shoes off the windowsill. Then, not caring if he'd understood me or not, I turned to go inside.

He said: Ears, listen.

I didn't feel like listening. I was sleepy. But he walked over quietly and went straight into my room. He was waiting for me to light a lamp, but I just lay down on my cot fully dressed. He struck a match, found my lamp, and lit it. That gave me a clear view of his pale, worry-drawn face. He'd spent several days packing, including an entire trunk filled with fans. But for the past few days he'd been dawdling, with no clear purpose. He kept

He said: Ears, listen.

I said: That's not a new sound. I've heard it before.

Cao, he asked, what's he doing?

I replied: Mixing chemicals for match heads.

He leaned against the window frame and stared at me for a long time, until I started getting edgy. He's weird, I said. We don't have to worry about him. He'd die of boredom if he didn't have something to do.

Again he asked: Cao, what's he doing?

I said: Whatever he wants.

He said: Making bombs, right?

Something thudded into my heart and kept me from answering. This was something I didn't dare talk about. Once spoken, it would be clear to all how frightful it was. The rolling pin never stopped thumping in the left-hand compound. It wasn't a loud noise, but so constant it felt as if the rolling pin itself had entered my head to pound and flatten my brain.

Big Road continued: To blow up whom? Who does Cao want to blow up?

Still I had no answer for him, as that thing was now smashing into my heart. He was bringing up things I didn't dare think about. But I couldn't help asking myself: Just who was Second Master pounding that rolling pin for?

Was he planning to blow up Young Mistress?

Or was it the foreigner?

Or maybe this compound and everyone in it!

The noise was becoming unbearable. Who was he planning to blow up? That's the question I wanted to ask, what I'd wanted to get to the bottom of for a long time. But if it had been up to me to supply an answer, even if I knew, I couldn't have said it. So I avoided Big Road's eyes and just started blankly at a crossbeam. With a sigh, he collapsed heavily into my bamboo chair, nearly breaking it in the process. He dug forcefully and noisily in his tobacco pouch with his pipe. He was becoming more and more like a local, smacking his lips when he smoked and holding his thumb over the top of the bowl. He even spit like a local. The burning tobacco was so dry it sizzled.

Big Road asked softly: Who does he want to blow up?

I forced myself not to say, You! I wanted to say: Now you've got the picture! And I wanted to say: Heaven will not forgive you, and even if your God wants to, it won't make any difference! I wanted to say: You'll get what you deserve, Big Nose! But I couldn't say it, none of it. I lay on my bamboo cot and waited for my heart to stop thumping.

I said: He doesn't want to blow up anybody. He's just playing around.

Big Road looked at me glumly. He'd seen through me.

I thought for a moment before saying: He wants to blow up the garrison command.

Big Road understood me, but didn't say anything. He was thinking his own thoughts. When his pipe went out, he knocked the tobacco from the bowl and stood up slowly. He sighed, having reached some sort of decision.

He said: Ears, I'm not leaving.

He left to return to his room, where he neither lit a lamp nor whistled. Not a sound emerged from the cavelike darkness of his room. My head was filled with images of him sharpening the blades of the slicing machine in the old granary. Cold, glinting knives flashed before my eyes, while my ears rang with the pounding of a rolling pin. A soft light emerged from the side room, and I was praying that nothing bad would happen, hoping that Big Road and I had misread Second Master.

Second Master had wounds on his face.

He had a wounded arm.

And he had a wounded heart.

Second Master was no more than half a step from insanity.

And yet he grew noticeably more peaceful every day. He took strolls in the misty mornings, his eyes fixed on the fish in the pond, a rare smile on his lips. The sight had me feeling that I'd been led astray by the pounding of the rolling pin, and believing that the guilt-stricken foreigner and I had misread him.

He didn't want to blow up anybody.

He couldn't blow up anybody.

There was no doubt about it—he was just playing around.

But then night would fall, the sound would emerge again, and my mood would change. I'd grow tense in anticipation of the sky's falling on me. Wuling was scared of the sound too, but she didn't know that it was caused by a rolling pin. She thought it was the sound of someone's bones scraping against the back of a chair, so loud it made her bones ache until her whole skeleton seemed about to shake apart. She told me that every time the sound from the side room reached her, Young Mistress lay quietly in bed, not sleeping and not saying a word, her eyes wide open in the night air, and that's how she would remain until the sound died out well after midnight. I was thinking: This is a payback.

I asked Wuling: What's Young Mistress afraid of?

Wuling said: She's not afraid, she's worried. She's worried that Second Master might burn the place down one day. She's also worried about the foreigner not leaving.

Does Young Mistress tell you what she's worried about? I asked.

She said: I'm with her all the time. How could I miss it?

You could, I said, so tell me what you think she's most afraid of.

Cocking her head to one side, she thought hard about it.

She said: She's most afraid that Second Master will kill her.

I asked her: Why would he do that?

She said: Do you have to ask? It's clear as day.

I said: You're a dumb little sow!

She said: Elder Brother Ears, don't get me pregnant.

We were getting bolder all the time. Under the moonlight, we'd trampled the grass at the base of the wall in the rear garden, and Wuling's naked back had already crushed a bunch of snails on the wall. There were lots of them, and a flick of the finger sent them falling to the ground like walnuts. Crushed, they gave off a sweet, fishy smell that made you feel hot all over. I squeezed Wuling's thin, sleek neck.

She said: Don't get me pregnant!

I said: If you get pregnant, I'll make you more afraid of me than ever.

Afraid of you how? she asked.

I said: Afraid I'll kill you!

Wuling peeled my hands away, lowered her legs, and arched her body toward me. I put everything I had into it, but when she was quaking with fear, I eased up. Realizing that I was toying with her, she drove her head into my gut and burst into tears. She told me she was worried that something bad was going to happen, that one day a ghost would appear in the left-hand compound. I told her I was doing this to her to keep the ghosts away. It wasn't much of a joke, and only I knew how frightened all this made me. I draped myself across Wuling's back in order to help put this fear to rest. And in that way, she and I were able to forget everything, whether we feared it or not.

A green nimbus filled the sky above the Cao compound.

Nothing like that had ever been seen there before.

It must have been one of Second Master's new creations.

It turned Wuling's fair skin green.

She turned into a frog.

A spread-legged frog.

I wanted to skin her alive.

April 9th

There was something wrong with my ears—either that or with my brain. The sound of the rolling pin was very faint, I could hear it was very faint, but still it got to me eventually, and I couldn't stand it any longer. It was like summer thunder, and my head was an overripe watermelon, slowly splitting open. One night I climbed down off my bamboo cot, walked across the veranda in my bare feet, and knocked on the side room door. The brass knocker was so loud that the rolling pin noise stopped immediately. I must have startled Second Master, who quickly put out the light. But he could tell it was me, and that it was urgent, whatever it was, so he relit the lamp and opened the door for me. I knelt down as soon as I was inside and banged my head against the brick floor. I stayed like that as Second Master asked me what I wanted, not once, but several times. Not knowing how to tell him why I was there, I began to tremble. It felt like little bugs were brushing my face, and I knew that I was crying. I'd known what I wanted before I got there, but all of a sudden I was a blithering idiot.

I said: Second Master, forgive them, please!

What in the world are you talking about, Ears? he asked.

I said: Open your heart and forgive them!

Then he figured out what I was saying and looked at me calmly, a cold smile on his face. Finely pulverized phosphorus powder lay on the table, like ground mustard seeds. He scooped it up with a spoon, filling one transparent glass bottle, then another. He gave a sinister laugh. I was almost sure he was going to hit me with one of the bottles of phosphorus, so I covered my head and waited. And I waited. His sinister laugh grew louder, turning into a strange guffaw. But it stopped when he began to choke on fine particles of phosphorus in the air, and doubled over coughing.

I quickly got to my feet and thumped him on the back. He'd grown terribly thin, and the gentle thumps from my fists produced a hollow sound somewhere inside him. A chemical odor clung to his long, uncombed black hair, which fell scraggily to his shoulders. Since the bullet wound in his arm hadn't completely healed, he wore a filthy gauze-wrapped bamboo splint from the elbow down, suspended by a strip of cloth around his neck.

There was something pitiful about Second Master's sinister laugh.

He said: You want me to forgive them, you say. Who are you talking about? And what did they do that requires my forgiveness? Tell me, Ears, who are they? The cooks who make the mushroom soup? Or the servants who guard the compound? Give me their names.

He was like a cat, waiting to pounce on a mouse—me. I realized then that the grinding had rattled my brain. There was nothing wrong in my coming to him to ask a favor, but I shouldn't have said it like that. Yet the words were already out, for good or ill, and all I could do now was say what I'd come to say.

Who are they? he asked. I'm asking you.

I replied: I beg you, please forgive them! Let the devil take them, let them be struck by lightning! Be lenient and forgive them! If you must kill someone, Second Master, kill me. Tie me up and take me over to Oxhorn Valley to blow me up. For the sake of Old Master, let there be peace in the Cao household. Second Master, your slave begs you!

I fell to my knees and wrapped my arms around his leg.

He said: Who are they? You're really not willing to tell me, are you?

I said: No, Second Master. I don't dare.

All right, don't tell me, he said. What did they do to me?

He said: Ah! Then why should I forgive them? And what difference would it make if I did or didn't forgive them? I want to hear what you think, Ears.

He had his claws in me now and was playing with me. My head was spinning, and I didn't know what to say. I was faced with nothing but absurd choices. Besides, how could I, a slave, have any effect on the outcome? I watched as he reached out for his rolling pin and I tucked my head down between my shoulders as everything turned black in front of me. I didn't protect my head with my arms. He could hit me if he wanted. But he didn't. He stuck the rolling pin between my arms to pry them from his legs. He didn't blow up when he found he couldn't do it, he just laughed warmly. I looked at him and saw him rest his face against the tabletop. All sorts of feelings welled up in my heart. Bits of powder stuck to his sweaty face, increasing the look of unbearable exhaustion. His abrupt switch to tranquillity made me sadder than ever, for some reason

I said dully: Forgive them, please.

Second Master said: I know, I forgive them.

I said: I've betrayed you. Do what you want with me.

He said: Crush this phosphorus powder for me, Ears, and don't say anything more. If you say another word, I'll make you eat this rolling pin. Do it gently, so the powder won't fly into the air. Now go ahead.

He spread several ounces of phosphorus out on the table and then went over to sit down in the chair by the wall to rest, not uttering another word after telling me what to do. As I pressed down on the rolling pin with both hands, a crunching sound oozed up through my fingers. I worked hard, and the sound was more rapid than it seemed before, and heavier. I wondered what the people in the other rooms were thinking when they heard me, but I found nothing terrifying in the sound. I quickly got the hang of it, while Second Master sat against the wall serenely, not making a sound. His face was like one of the icons at the Buddha Bathing Festival—expressionless, unblinking eyes staring straight ahead.

Before long, he fell asleep. Sometime after midnight, I scooped up the powder and bottled it, then cleaned off the tabletop before leaving quietly. But when I reached the doorway, the sleeping Second Master called my name.

He said: Ears, no blabbing.

I said: No, sir.

My affairs are my business, he said. And don't you worry about them.

I said: Yes, sir.

He said: I'm willing to forgive them, but let's see if they're willing to forgive themselves. I can't be bothered about other people's problems. I've got my hands full with my own. When you feel up to it, Ears, come over and give me a hand. And remember, no blabbing.

I said: Yes, sir.

He added: Don't worry, I forgive them. And I forgive you. You're a lying little bastard, but I know how much trouble you've gone to, and I forgive you. But no blabbing, or I won't forgive any of you. You understand, Ears?

I said: I understand everything, Second Master!

I said I understood, but I didn't, not really. Second Master's hair covered his face, so I couldn't see if his eyes were open. He appeared to be sleepy, dull and lifeless, but his words showed he was still alert. I could still picture how he'd looked in Oxhorn Valley, when he'd used his comb to mix the explosive chemicals, but I wasn't sure if he was doing the same thing now. If he was, then I had no idea who he, a man who had recently gotten out of prison and a cuckold, planned to blow up. But I knew I'd have to help him. I knew I couldn't go blabbing. And I knew that the cat had its claws in this mouse and wouldn't let it get away.

Back in my room I pondered whether or not to tell anybody. It wouldn't do any good to tell Old Master, so it would have to be Elder Master; he was the only one who had any chance of preventing what might happen. I thought it over till dawn, ultimately deciding to keep my mouth shut.

Keeping my mouth shut was a lot safer than blabbing.

I'd keep the crunching sound to myself.

Yes, I'd keep it to myself.

I felt better already.

Steward Bing's wife was so hard-of-hearing she was oblivious to what was going on in the side room. But she had a keen nose, and could smell just about everything. If they were making dumplings in the right-hand compound, she could tell what kind of vinegar they were using from way over in the left-hand compound. One morning she ran over to the main house and reported to Old Master: Second Master spends all his time preparing elixirs. Send someone over to take a look. I think he's mixing his own gall with some chemicals. It's rank! Old Master sent Elder Master, and when he got there, all he saw were some bottles filled with powder. He said: Don't play with this stuff, it's dirty. If it gets in your wound, it'll never heal.

Second Master said: It'll heal sooner or later. I'm just doing this for my own enjoyment. Come back tonight for some fun. Ears and I will put on a show for you.

Elder Master left with a grave look on his face. He was not interested in his brother's hobby. I didn't know what sort of show Second Master had in mind for us, and I didn't know what his nightly activity was all about, which made me very nervous. The commune was closed that day, and I spent it in my room, doing nothing but keeping an eye on the activity in the left-hand compound and holding my breath.

It was a clear day, with the sun filtering through the wisteria trellis and falling on the people around the chessboard on the veranda. Second Master and Big Road played one murderous game after another; they even took their lunch at the chess table. They were having a great time, drinking and conversing in the foreign tongue. They sounded happy, especially when they started singing foreign songs, and that scared me. Wuling and Young Mistress came out in the afternoon. A leather cushion for young Mistress was placed on the stone bench between Second Master and the foreigner. She was her old self again as she studied the chessboard, her fair face like a large flower, her eyes like a pair of butterflies resting on its petals. She sat there until they finished their last game. Thanks to what they were drinking, the gay mood of the two players never flagged, although there was a significant difference in how they played this last game. Apparently, Second Master began it, and after a momentary shock, Big Road took his cue. Each time one of them took a piece, he turned and flung it several yards into the pond, accompanied by a hearty laugh. The chess pieces floated in the water amid the lotus plants like little fish. Exhausted by their furious playing, they stayed on the veranda to rest quietly after the last game. Young Mistress, her face paler than usual, kept her head lowered and her eyes fixed on the empty chessboard. I walked out of my room with the net I normally used for trash to scoop the chess pieces out of the pond. Second Master smiled when he saw me, but said nothing. Big Road also spotted me, and when he saw that my arms were too short for the job, he ran over enthusiastically to help. Second Master mumbled something; Big Road grunted a reply and snatched the bamboo handle out of my hand. His face, neck, and nose were bright red.

Second Master said: Wuling, go inside and get me a comb.

Wuling brought out a box of combs.

Second Master shook out his hair.

Young Mistress lowered her head even more.

Yunan, Second Master said, will you comb my hair for me?

Do you want a queue? she asked.

Yes, he replied. I want to look presentable.

She said: Your hair's a little short for that still.

He replied: That's all right, just do your best.

Young Mistress stood behind Second Master, her big belly nearly touching his back, and combed his hair carefully, stopping to ask if it hurt or if it was pulled too tight. He told her no, that it was just fine. That was the extent of their conversation, so the only sounds anywhere in the compound were of a comb swishing through hair and a net swishing through the water in the pond. Big Road didn't so much as look back at the veranda. He concentrated on fishing the chess pieces out of the water, as if they were actually fish which, if he wasn't careful, would swim away.

Young Mistress combed Second Master's hair into a queue. Though not very long, it was beautiful.

By chance I discovered that there were tears in both their eyes. Wuling had moved off the veranda, and I also stayed as far away as possible, wanting to look over in their direction, but not daring to. I gathered up the chess pieces Big Road had fished out of the pond and laid them out on the windowsill of my little room. But not neatly enough for Big Road, who arranged them in two rows by color, a meaningless task that took him a long time. He didn't stop until Steward Bing's wife called out from the doorway.

She said: My little ancestor, you're going to wear your wife out, letting her stand there so long! Yunan, my little lady, come inside right this minute. As for you, Wuling, I ought to throttle you. Why couldn't you do this for her?

Teary-eyed, Young Mistress turned and walked off.

Second Master got up and went to his room without a word.

After nightfall, Second Master had me make a trail of chemical powder on the brick floor of the veranda with a little funnel, all the way to the man-made hill at the far end. When all the curious members of the Cao household had come up to see what was going on, he touched a match to this dragon's tail. Sparks flew as the flame slithered along, a rainbow of colors, until it seemed to consume the hill. Like an excited little boy, Second Master ran after the trail of sparks, all the way to the foot of the hill, but without making a sound. The sight of him, with one arm in a sling and sparks flying all around him, upset me terribly. But all the others hooted with delight, and even Elder Master liked what he saw. As he was leaving, he told me to make sure the water vat outside the window was full, alternating between cautioning me to be alert to the risk of fire and remarking on how beautiful it all was. With the sparks lighting up the sky, I had a good look at Young Mistress's and Big Road's faces, plus those of lots of other people. But when the sparks died out, the faces disappeared. I carried a bucketful of water over to the vat; when I returned with the second bucketful, I discovered that I was the only one left in the yard.

Second Master called out from his room: Come in here, Ears.

My shoes were wet, so I just stood in the doorway. He was sitting in his chair, his face flushed. With his jacket off, his white gown looked like mourning clothes, except for the blue sash around his waist, which was tied with a nice little knot right above his navel. That knot meant something to members of the Blue Kerchiefs. Naturally, I'd long thought that he was one of the Blue Kerchief ringleaders, but I never dreamed that in the wake of the slaughter of society members he'd continue to decorate himself with these worthless objects.

He asked me: Everything okay?

I said: Great!

He said: It's been my dream for a long time to spread powder all over Jade Mountain and light up the whole valley. But I guess I won't be able to do it in this lifetime.

You're strong-willed, I said. You can do anything you want to.

He said: Me, strong-willed? There's no one in the world more useless than I. Ears, come take the cotton batting out of this vest.

His vest, with bits of cotton poking through a ripped-out seam around the neck, lay on the table. Using a pair of fireplace tongs, I began pulling out pieces of cotton batting. The vest had two layers of batting between layers of durable imported cotton, and as I carried out this baffling task, I wondered what he had in mind. Now that the powder had all been ignited out in the courtyard, the floor and windowsill were cluttered with empty bottles. Second Master massaged his injured arm, looking like a man who had pulled off something spectacular. Reaching out for the batting I'd retrieved, he crumpled it into balls, with which he wiped his hands, both sides of his nose, the arms of his chair, and the lamp shade.

Out on the street a night watchman's gong rang out.

Second Master blurted out: What are they going to do?

Who? I asked.

Them, he said.

I blushed.

The cat was on the prowl for mice again.

He pressed on: Tell me honestly, what are they going to do?

I said: They only have one option. Don't get mad if I say something you don't like, Second Master.

What's the option? he asked.

I said: Run away.

He asked: Where to?

I said: As far as they can go.

How will they manage that? he asked.

I said: I don't know.

With a frown, he laughed.

I could sense that he'd caught me again.

That made me very unhappy.

I blurted out: Second Master, why did they try to assassinate you?

He said: I should never have come out of prison alive.

Getting bolder by the minute, I asked him: Are you a rebel?

The scar on his cheek twitched.

He answered with a question: What do you say? Do you think I am?

I said: No.

He said: You should tell that to the man who fired the shot.

I said: People in Elm Township believe the rumors they hear. They're blind as bats.

Let them talk, he said, since I'm a worthless human being anyway. No one believes I'm capable of doing something extraordinary. They all think I'm someone who belongs in a dog's cave. In the eyes of the foreigner I'm Chinese. In the eyes of the Manchus I'm a Han. But in the eyes of my family I have no claim to being a normal human being. I couldn't talk to them, so when I had something to say, I went looking for someone who'd listen. I went looking for Zheng Yusong. There's something I can't wait to do, and if they'll let me live long enough to do it, I'll die happy. Wait and see! Just wait and see! Don't pull so hard. You'll tear a hole in it.

Once I'd removed all the cotton lining from the vest, excitement gripped Second Master, as he reached under the bed, pulled out an earthen jar, and ripped the waxed paper seal from the mouth of the jar, which was filled with explosive powder that looked like sesame paste. Telling me to hold up the vest, he spooned the powder in through the opening; gradually, the vest puffed up the way it was before, and I finally realized what he was up to. But I kept my questions to myself and said nothing, doing exactly what he told me to do, and in such a way as to please him. He scraped the bottom of the jar with his spoon like a greedy little boy scraping the bottom of his rice bowl. He forgot all about me, forgot even about himself, as he was caught up in a scheme that was like a bottomless pit.

My nose began to ache and my eyes burned.

I said: They really are blind dogs.

Second Master didn't say anything.

I said: Second Master, be careful.

He just smiled.

I said: Second Master, Heaven is looking after you!

He said: Go get some sleep, Ears. Good-bye!

He put on the powder-filled vest, which turned him into a plump, hefty-looking man. His eyes were bloodshot and a kindly smile adorned his face; his mind was cleared of all mortal suffering and misfortune. I was immediately reminded of Zheng Yusong's date-red face, and the blood ran hot in my veins. At that moment, all I wished for was the chance to follow someone, anyone, to cut a murderous swath through the world! I didn't try to stop Second Master, although I couldn't say why. Maybe I was hoping he'd do something that shocked the world and cleanse himself of all stigmas. And maybe I was hoping that by leaving he would bring peace to others and to himself. There was nothing crafty about my thoughts. He was the cat and I was the mouse; there were things he had to do, and there were things I had to do. I felt I was helping him. In that moment, when Second Master put on his vest, in my heart he became a hero, and the images of bad things he'd done were driven out of my eyes and my heart for all time. Standing in the midst of a blazing pan of fire, he was transformed into a superman.

All the other residents of the left-hand compound became inconsequential.

One night several days later, Second Master went to visit his fasting mother in her meditation room. As he passed in front of my room he gave me a long, meaningful look, but said not a word. His arm was no longer in a sling; he filled out the simple clothes he was wearing, and I knew at once what was about to happen. I went back inside and lay down on my cot to wait. The footsteps of laborers moving stones out on the path sounded way past midnight. I never heard Second Master return to his compound; he'd slipped out by blending in with the workers as they returned from the rear garden. He'd managed to evade everyone, including the servants. I waited for him until daybreak, when I finally fell asleep. I was able to breathe a sigh of relief.

I dreamed of someone spreading open steaming legs!

It was like a big white bird spreading its wings.

It was a woman.

It wasn't Wuling.

Cao Guanghan was never seen in Elm Township again.

April 10th

I don't recall what day it was. All I remember is that tassels had appeared on new rice in the fields, so it must have been a few days before the period known as "grain fills," which would put it somewhere around the middle of the fifth lunar month. It rained during the night and continued raining after sunup. It was wet all day long. Planning to go to church in Acacia Township, Big Road took out his umbrella and galoshes. But then the rain turned heavy and he decided to stay put. Umbrella in hand, he went over to the old granary instead. Since I had things to do, we parted on the path. As I think back now, I don't believe we said anything meaningful. He went to make some repairs on the slicing machine; for some reason it had begun turning out uneven strips of matchstick material.

I said: Why not rest for a while. I can come over and give you a hand in a little bit.

I'll go first, he said. If you come, that's good. See you later.

I said: Wear your galoshes.

Too hot! he replied. Okay, see you later.

He followed the slope down the path. He was still dressed in the Western clothes he'd put on to go to church, except, that is, for his galoshes, having changed into leather shoes with toes pointed like ships' prows. He walked off with his pant cuffs rolled up, the green smoke from his pipe leaving a trail behind him. He sloshed his way to the far end of the path.

I went to see Old Master in the main compound.

He'd been laid up in bed for several days. After dismissing all the other servants, he told me to stay with him. I spread a rush mat on the floor beside his bed and sat with my legs crossed as he prattled on and on about life and death. There was an unusual twist to this particular illness—it was a result of his fan painting. He'd had a special fan made; open, it nearly filled one entire wall. He had to climb a ladder to paint a wisteria trellis, and in the process he'd missed a step and nearly crashed to the floor. Actually, a fall might have been better, since his near accident cost him his appetite and his ability to sleep. Unremarkable though the incident was, it got him thinking about death again.

He lay in bed not wanting to move.

He watched the rain outside his window, a bright curtain of water cascading down off the eaves. Rain-spattered leaves on the clove tree sang out. That he was overcome by desolation on such a day was not surprising, because I was too.

Old Master said lethargically: Ears, I have a headache.

I said: Let the doctor have a look at you and take some proper medicine.

Tucking his blankets under his arms, he said: It won't do any good. I know nothing will. My head is splitting. It feels as if someone is pinching my brain with a pair of fireplace tongs and won't let go. It's killing me! There are some things I've been thinking about since I was a child of seven, Ears. And I still don't have the answers. But with my brain being squeezed like this, I can't think at all. Tell me, Ears, do you think it's possible for someone not to die?

I said: Old Master, that's something that's never occurred to me.

What is death, anyway? he asked.

I don't know, I answered. Maybe it's going down to the nether region and keeping King Yama company.

He said: Nonsense! Are you mocking me? There's nothing at all on the other side. What could there be for someone who's dead? My head hurts. I'm going to die, Ears! The other side is nothing but a bottomless pool of ink. Our ancestors want the living to accompany them to the grave because they're afraid of the dark. For all these years blackness had been crushing me down, forcing the breath right out of me. I ask you, Ears, if I really do cross to the other side and want someone to talk to, are you willing to go with me?

A shudder racked me as I sat on the rush mat.

Old Master said: I've shocked you, haven't I? I just want you to understand that human beings have nothing to fear, except for this. It's the one thing no one can escape. I've searched for the perfect plan, but it's not to be found, and in the meantime I've just about used up all the time I have. My God, it hurts! My head is splitting!

He opened his old eyes wide and curled up in bed. He wouldn't let me touch him, but had me sit where I was to keep talking with him. I felt cold all over. The thought that he'd actually considered having me accompany him to the grave and serve him as I did in life made me feel that he and I were already in Hell. Steam rose from the little medicine cauldron gurgling over the brazier, and all signs of life seemed to disappear from this aging, rain-splashed room!

I said: The fortune-teller said you'd live to be a hundred. Fortune will always smile on you! There's no need for you to have such crazy thoughts.

What fortune do I have? he asked. Do I look like someone who enjoys good fortune to you? If I did, would the Cao family be in the shape it's in today? Besides, good fortune or bad, what's the difference? Do you have any news of Guanghan, Ears?

I replied: No. It looks like he's gone farther away this time than before. But don't worry, he'll lose interest in a while and come home, that's for sure.

Old Master said: I think he's the one who enjoys good fortune.

If he does, I said, it's all thanks to you.

Old Master sighed and stretched out his neck to spit. I hurried to bring over the spittoon. He smelled like bean curd sediment. I sensed that I also had a body odor of some sort. The rain wasn't letting up, and the floor under my mat was getting wet, turning the bricks moldy. My joints felt mildewed.

Out in the courtyard, someone was running this way through the rain puddles. When whoever it was came straight past the corridor, I knew it was on urgent business. It was Steward Bing. His clothes, his shoes and socks, were soaked, and he was staring straight ahead. With a shiver, he said: Old Master, there's trouble in the other compound. Guanghan's wife is going into labor!

Old Master received the news indifferently. He blinked for a while as he pondered the news, then said: So she's in labor, what's the problem?

Steward Bing said: It's only the end of the seventh month. That's a bad sign!

Old Master asked him: Are they in danger?

Steward Bing replied: Hard to say. For mother *and* child. Old Master, tell us what to do. The slaves can't make this kind of decision.

Old Master said: If you don't do everything in your power, Heaven will never forgive you. Other things take care of themselves. Success or failure is all up to Fate, and there's nothing you can do about that.

Steward Bing ran back out into the rain, his old arms and legs flopping around like a marionette's. I was dumbstruck. As I sat on the mat, I didn't know what to do. How could she be ready so

soon? No one expected that, especially Young Mistress and Big
Road, I suppose. They thought they still had time to think things
through and come up with something. Who'd have thought that
the sword hanging over their heads would suddenly come slicing
down?

Second Master had asked me: What are they going to do?

I'd told him: They have only one option. Run away.

I was telling the truth. Since Second Master didn't hold it against
me, I knew his question was genuine. What were they going to do?
On the night he left, he had passed my room with a smile on his
face. He hadn't said a word to me, but, thinking back, I read a great
deal in that smile. It was clear that he was saying: I've got my own
affairs to take care of, and can't be bothered by other things. Not
by them, not by the family, and not by you. I can only take care of
myself. I'm to be pitied, and so are they. Everyone is. I don't want
to see any of you again. I've had all I can take, all I can take!

There was much more to it than that.

Deep down I knew.

As long as I stay calm, there's nothing I don't know.

Run!

Run away!

Big Road had to have thought of this.

But now it was too late. The sword had already sliced down.
The rainwater coursing through the courtyard was getting thicker
and was about to turn into bright red bloody water. Old Master,
who was lying down again, grunted suddenly and his eyes lit up.
He signaled me to come closer, like King Yama summoning one
of his little devils. It was something I was used to, and I knew what
he wanted. He wanted to ingest something he didn't like to talk
about. But even though this wouldn't be the first time, I tensed up
as Old Master's lips quivered. I drew up so close to him I was afraid
he might actually take a bite out of me. He didn't, but what he
wanted was nearly the same as demanding my life from me. His
words were like the buzzing of a mosquito, so soft as to be all but
unintelligible, but it landed on my ear like a bomb that blew me to
pieces.

Old Master said: Ears, I want to eat afterbirth.

You want to eat what? I asked.

He said: Afterbirth. My grandson's afterbirth.

I asked him: How am I supposed to get that for you?

Old Master said: Stand in the doorway holding a large platter, and when the baby comes out, put the fresh afterbirth on it and bring it to me. But first, add water to the cauldron and fetch the knife and whetstone from the drawer for me. Now go on, and don't dally. If you don't get it for me, I'll eat you instead!

Old Master threw off his blankets and sat up.

He felt that salvation was on its way.

But I was done for.

I handed the platter to Wuling, who took it inside with her. Elder Master and Steward Bing were sitting on the veranda, surrounded by several servants. Steward Bing was working on the problem of a wet nurse. He said that old Brother Cang in the southern part of town had a child who'd died within the first month. His wife's breasts were bursting with milk, and they should waste no time in bringing her over. Elder Master was very composed as he poured wine from a gourd and asked the older servant women if a child this premature could survive. They hemmed and hawed to avoid answering him; it was up to Steward Bing to supply the answer: The odds are against them, and it's all up to their collective fate.

He had barely finished saying this when a loud *waaah* emerged from inside.

We could tell at once it was a strong baby.

The cry drowned out the sound of the rain.

Rain bubbles on the surface of the pond popped open like flowers.

Steward Bing called out to his wife: Hey, old lady, is it a boy or a girl?

No one answered from inside.

The baby's cries were too loud.

Before long, Wuling appeared in the doorway carrying the platter. I didn't even glance at what was on it, because I was too busy looking at Wuling's face. She was very pale, like a frightened rabbit. In that brief instant, all I wanted to do was turn and run, to sneak out of there without gods or ghosts knowing about it. But I turned so weak I could barely stand. I watched as Wuling walked down the veranda in the rain, and I ran after her. We stopped in the middle of the path and let the rain fall on us like a couple of statues.

I asked softly: Well?

She didn't answer, and it looked like she was almost in tears.

Steward Bing, who was still on the veranda, called out: Wuling, is it a girl or a boy?

Wuling shouted back: It's a boy!

Shouts of joy erupted from the veranda, first from the servants. I took the platter from Wuling, but as I turned to leave, I heard her say softly: Blue. Then I heard her footsteps running back into the house. Blue! As I headed back to the main house, I was walking on a cloud, with complete silence all around me.

Back on the veranda, Elder Master was so happy you'd have thought *he'd* just had a son. Servants ran past me on their way to report the news to Old Master and Old Mistress. I was still lightheaded. As I walked through the gate of the corner compound, I headed south down the path, all the way to the main gate. Realizing with a start where I was, I turned and headed back.

A servant asked me: What's that?

Meat, I replied.

The servant said: It looks like a pig's heart.

I said: It's a human heart!

The rainwater caught in the platter turned the thing red. It resembled a meat patty, about the size of a bowl and as thick as a chopping board, but with a tail that was about a foot long. It looked a lot like some mountain critter or something from the sea, but with no eyes and no legs, and it seemed to move all by itself.

Old Master, his beard sticking straight out, was sharpening his knife.

The lid was off the cauldron; the black soup inside was roiling and producing rank-smelling steam. I set the platter down on the table. Old Master wiped the blade of the knife with a sheet of stationery, then used it to flip the thing in the platter over.

I said: The fortune-teller was right on the mark. It's a boy.

Old Master said: So I heard. Has it been washed?

I said: Not yet.

Good, he said. Are your hands clean?

Yes, I replied.

He said: Come here and slice it. Thin slices, like you would pork belly. But first go to the kitchen and get some condiments. Don't forget the shrimp oil and chili paste. If there's any coriander, bring back a few stalks. Now go on. Take your time, there's no hurry.

He rubbed his hands together and exhaled heavily. On my way to the kitchen, I toyed with the idea of running away; the same thought occurred to me on the way back. Run away! I spent the rest of the afternoon slicing the thing for Old Master. My mind was blank the whole time, except for a single word: blue! I knew, of course, what the word blue meant, but I wasn't willing to think about it. Every time I started, the back of my neck turned cold, as if the sword were slicing down on top of me.

Old Master wanted to eat the thing by blanching it, but the meat was too thick, so he decided to boil it instead. When it still wouldn't cook up, he picked up his chopsticks and shook them angrily at me and at the cauldron. Since it wasn't going to soften, he'd eat it hard. Staring wide-eyed at the steam rising out of the cauldron, he waited for the afterbirth to become edible, all the while swallowing mouthfuls of saliva. Steward Bing came by once during all that time. Elder Master came by twice. Both were turned away loudly and impatiently.

Old Master's face had a purple cast, something I'd never seen before. The blood that had rushed to his head seemed ready to spew out of his eyes at the slightest touch. I didn't dare look at him. I kept slicing away, wishing I could slice it as thin as human hairs. So much was going on inside my head I couldn't think of anything else.

It seemed that the rainy sky was falling slowly to earth.

softened, which made him happy.

With my eyes wide open, I believed he was capable of eating a
human being!

He would chomp away at me.

In my daydream I ran away so fast I was nearly flying.

I fled.

Old Master said: Taste it.

I tasted it.

It was delicious.

It was heavenly!

Old Master said: I'm sweating.

I said: Take off some clothes before you eat any more.

Old Master's face was bathed in sweat as he ate.

I fanned him.

In my daydream I began to fly.

The sky fell.

April 11th

In the rain, the Cao estate was quiet; the rain was so loud I couldn't
hear anyone moving or speaking. I sat with Old Master while he
consumed the afterbirth, a process that lasted until sunset. He finished it off by drinking down the soup in the cauldron. When I left
his room and went into the courtyard, the silence around me was
terrifying. I scurried into my little room, not wanting to see or be
seen by anyone. The only sign of life in the main room of the left-

hand compound was the yellow light from lamps that had been lit earlier than usual; in the rain the place looked warm and bleak at the same time. I waited for Wuling to come out, but there was no trace of her. The only person I saw was one of the cooks, who carried a meal into the main room, then returned empty-handed. I didn't see anyone taking food to the side room. I didn't know if Big Road had returned or not; his room was dark—no lights and no sounds inside. I didn't feel like seeing him, and he probably didn't feel like seeing me. Quite possibly, he didn't feel like seeing anyone. I lay down on my bamboo cot, gradually sensing that something wasn't right. I felt he should have returned by now, and that I should be taking him his meal and getting his bathwater for him.

Hugging the wall, I walked over to his room. It was pitch black, which meant there was no one home. But when I lit the lamp, my heart leaped into my throat and nearly soared out the door.

Except for the furniture, the room was cleaned out.

The baby's cries came over on the wind.

Big Road's stuff was all gone.

Not even a scrap of paper on the floor.

At first I assumed he'd left town in a hurry, kicked out by the family. Back in the courtyard, the silence of the Cao estate was unnerving. Something was definitely wrong. Opening my oilpaper umbrella, I walked down the path, racked by shudders. I couldn't help thinking that the end had come.

A servant in a palm bark rain cape was guarding the main gate.

He said: Elder Master has sealed the compound. No one is to leave.

I said: I have to run an errand for Old Master.

He said: Hurry back. And be careful out there. We're expecting floods.

On the edge of town, water rushing down the Black River produced a dull roar that echoed in the valley. The rain seemed to be swallowing up Jade Mountain. I walked through town as if everything were just fine, but as soon as I reached the outskirts, I took off running toward the old granary. The umbrella slowed me down, so I threw it to the side of the road. The cover of the pulley platform was tossing violently in the rain. Inside the granary, I looked all over for the watchman, but couldn't find him. Lighting a lantern, I ran crazily around the place shouting: Where's the watchman? Get the fuck out here, you bastard!

Hearing something in the drying room, I screwed up the courage to go see what it was. There, behind a rack, I spotted the mute, Hole in the Ground, confusion filling his eyes. He was scared, and he looked at me as a penitent begging for forgiveness. Along with a flurry of hand gestures, I asked him what had happened. He just shook his head. But he kept shaking his head even when I didn't ask him anything or make any gestures. I knew he was a good twenty years older than me, but I kicked him anyway. I was the man in charge, and the man in charge was free to hit an employee anytime he wanted. I wanted to hit him, no matter who he was. Instead I shouted in his ear: You fucking bastard! How dare you try to hide something from me. I'll boil you in oil!

Hole in the Ground couldn't hear me. His eyes looked like those of a mouse.

Lantern in hand, I went into the machine room. The roof had sprung a leak, leaving a water stain on the wall the size of a woman's scarf. A chunk of wood was stuck in the shaving machine; stripped of its bark, the naked wood looked like a human bone. The slicing machine looked normal; I couldn't tell if it had been broken down, but it shone of oil, as if covered with a layer of wax. I turned it on to see if it would run, and without much difficulty, the pulley belt began to turn and the machine sputtered into action. The blades moved up and down smoothly, making a chopping sound as they cut through the air. That's when I spotted something strange dripping from the blades. At first I thought it was machine oil, but when I held the lantern up close to it, it didn't look like oil. I turned the machine off and touched the liquid with my finger. My heart nearly stopped.

It struck me like a bolt of lightning—it was blood!

Human blood.

The foreigner's.

I spotted large drops of blood on the machine casing. There was also blood on the floor; it had merged with oil that had soaked into the ground. Getting down on all fours like a dog, I pressed my face against the ground, trying to find a trace, even a smell, of Big Road. In one of the gaps in the base of the machine I found one of his shoes. It looked like a little rabbit hiding from a predator. There was no blood on it, but it was hot to the touch, as if not wanting to give up Big Road's warmth. In fact, it looked like it was about to incinerate itself. I carried it back into the drying room, where the mute greeted me with more frantic head shaking, so intense it made me feel that all was lost. Mr. Road had postponed his departure, and postponed it and postponed it, until he'd finally destroyed himself.

I hit the mute across the face with the shoe, how many times I don't know. His head stopped shaking as, his eyes filled with tears, he pointed to the Black River. I was completely spent; light-headed and dizzy, I sat down to rest. The mute was still gesturing, but he didn't need to do that, since I already knew what had happened.

They'd thrown him into the Black River.

Before that they'd carved up parts of his body.

His hands.

Maybe other parts as well.

They'd murdered him.

Only a slave who has disgraced his master deserves to end up like that.

They had given the foreigner no immunity.

Mr. Road's deep blue eyes hadn't saved him.

I followed the Black River home. Water from the mountain filled the riverbed; it overflowed its banks at a number of spots, inundating rice and vegetable crops. I began to wonder if I'd read the mute's gestures correctly; I knew my doubts were superfluous, but they spurred me to call out over and over.

I shouted: Big Road! It's Ears! Can you hear me?

I shouted to him: Mr. Road! Don't hide; come home with me.

I shouted myself hoarse. A heavy night rain fell in the blackness of the valley, the only whiteness coming from the whitecaps

on the Black River. The sound of rushing water cloaked me like a
shroud. Wading through the muddy water, I walked to the spot
where we'd released the river lanterns around New Year's. At the
mountain path, where Young Mistress's lotus lantern had disappeared, the floodwaters had formed a wall, and I had a feeling
that Big Road's dismembered body had already passed over that
wall and was being carried by the Green River to the ocean, floating all the way to the far-off homeland he was forever pining for.

Back at the Cao compound I met up with Elder Master, who was
making night rounds. This was normally a job for Steward Bing,
but tonight the master had taken over, clear evidence that something was troubling someone. Standing in the rain with him glar-
ing at me, I was surprisingly unruffled. I was actually giddy, taking
notice of absolutely nothing.

Elder Master asked me: What have you been up to?

I said: I was out getting some water scorpions for Old Master.

He asked me: Where are they?

I said: It was dark out there and the rain kept blowing out my
lantern. A bunch of water grass has piled up at Three Path Bay, so
I'll go back when it's light out.

Go to bed, he said. You shouldn't be out running about at night.
It's not safe out there. There's been more trouble on the Green
River, and it might find its way to Elm Township before long.

With malicious intent, I asked him: Has Mr. Road returned? I
didn't see him at dinnertime. Did he work on the machinery right
through dinner?

Elder Master looked at me through eyes narrowed to slits and
said: He left.

Left for where? I asked.

He said: Where else but where he was supposed to go—home.

I asked: Without even saying good-bye?

Elder Master smiled and said: We all have our priorities. He can
do what he pleases!

I said: He owes me thirty-five ounces of silver! He said he'd pay
me back, so how could he have just up and left? Everybody says
foreigners are all bastards. I guess that includes him.

Elder Master said: Steward Bing will give you the silver you've got coming. Let that be the end of it. Stop worrying about who owes what and who pays whom back. Now go on!

In the lamplight his phony smile made my skin crawl. Always considerate and understanding, Elder Master was not a man to scowl. But after he told me to leave, his face darkened. It was as if the skin had peeled away to reveal the naked skull beneath! With the weight of family affairs on his shoulders, maybe his carefree exterior hid an inability to bear up under it. I could no longer trust that man. And he could no longer trust me. Maybe there was no one in the whole family he could trust. I walked down the rain-swept path; he followed me a short ways. Ears, he said, did you hear any talk out there?

I stopped and said: No. Talk about what?

He didn't answer right away, and the rain beat down on his umbrella.

Then he said: Plug up your ears for the next few days, and keep your mouth shut. I'll come get you if I need you. Now get some sleep. I want you to be with me tomorrow to accept the congratulatory offerings. Forget about the water scorpions for the time being. By sunup tomorrow, he might have decided to eat something else altogether.

I said: Whatever you say, Elder Master.

He walked through the gate, heading for the right-hand compound. I stood in the middle of the path for a long while. Earlier that morning, Big Road had strolled leisurely up the slope of that very same path, his pant legs rolled up, his pipe in his mouth, a trail of green smoke in his wake, carefree as can be. What had he been thinking? At first he'd planned to go to church. If he hadn't changed his mind, maybe God would have warned him what was about to happen. What was on his mind while he was working on the machinery and then when disaster struck him? What did he say? He'd walked along feeling so carefree, prepared for nothing out of the ordinary, straight down to Hell. I was pretty sure that during his critical last moments, he'd understood completely.

And I was pretty sure he'd shouted for help. But who would he shout to?

Zheng Yunan was one possibility.

His mother was another.

And maybe he shouted for his son.

As I stood in the rain, I heard him call out to me from the far end of the path. He was smiling warmly. He said: Ears, I want to take a bath. Have them heat some water for me. I replied: Mr. Road, there is no bathwater. And you don't need any more water, you've got plenty. I heard the resonant sound of his whistles.

I was crying as I walked down the path. Big Road's shoe was still tucked under my jacket. It was pressing painfully against my ribs. I heard the baby's cries when I reached the steps of the left-hand compound. It sounded to me as if the shoe pressed against my skin were crying, but then the cries seemed to be coming from Big Road off in the waters of the Green River. Big Road hadn't died, after all; he had made his way into Young Mistress's belly, a chunk of flesh the size of a rabbit, and then had come back into the world with a swagger.

A pair of blue eyes opened wide in the sky above Elm Township.

I wondered if Big Road was looking down at his woman and his son.

I took the shoe, which was as big as a small boat, and locked it up in my trunk.

Many people came rushing into my daydream.

I flew into the air to watch them.

I was spellbound as I looked down on figures as tiny as ants.

That very night I put Big Road out of my mind.

I also forgot myself.

I couldn't figure out what all those two-legged creatures were.

They covered the earth.

Bastards!

Fucking bastards!

They weren't worth worrying about.

April 12th

For three straight days an unbroken stream of people arrived with congratulatory offerings. The posts and beams of the gatehouse were hung everywhere with bright yellow satin banners and local weavings, all decorated with similar congratulatory messages to the Cao family for having gained an heir. People who were especially close to the family had been told privately that Old Master had given his grandson a name, and they included that on their scrolls. All of Elm Township quickly learned that the crying little devil was named Cao Zichun, Son of Spring. Old Master hoped that Young Mistress would subsequently bring to the family sons of summer, autumn, and winter, I suspect.

Like everyone else, most members of the Cao household knew the infant's name, but had yet to lay their eyes on his face, a privilege accorded only a very few. And those people never stepped out of the compound after the birth of the child, remaining inside to attend to Young Mistress during the monthlong lying-in period. Old Cang's wife, who had been brought into the compound as a wet nurse, was put up in the side room where Second Master had lived; during this period, of course, she was not permitted to leave the compound. Not even Old Master or Old Mistress had seen their grandson. Old Mistress was still fasting, coiled up in her meditation room like a hibernating snake, and, in order to protect the child against the elements, he couldn't be taken to her. With the cries of the baby swirling around her, Old Mistress held firm to her determination to remain a recluse. The old nun who watched over her seclusion said: Old Mistress was born under a lucky star and will one day become an immortal.

After consuming the afterbirth, Old Master seemed invested with nearly supernatural energy. All day long he climbed his footstool to paint and calligraph the enormous fan on the wall in his underwear, like a monkey hanging from the wisteria trellis created by his brush. Wisteria flowers blossomed as if the brush were guided by a divine hand. I don't know what the realization that his grandson could not be brought to him and that he could not enter his daughter-in-law's lying-in chamber meant to him, if anything, for after he'd chosen the name, he didn't bring up the subject of the child again.

Elder Master had a blood red curtain hung from the gate to the left-hand compound, making it off-limits to all males except for him, Steward Bing, and an aging cook who brought in the meals. Even I was kept out. Four days after Young Mistress had the baby, my bamboo cot and I were moved in to share Steward Bing's quarters in the front compound. I no longer heard the baby's cries. Elder Master said I could move back after the lying-in period, but I didn't care. Steward Bing's place suited my mood just fine. I didn't want to be alone. Back in my own room, the sounds of whistling and roaring water came to me in my sleep. The foreigner's soul had me in its grasp, and I really didn't think I could take being alone much longer.

There were many things I didn't understand, but I avoided bringing up the subject of Big Road with Steward Bing, or anyone else, for that matter. During the days I went to the commune, as usual, but I never asked any of the workers about what had happened that rainy day. And since I never asked, no one said a word about it to me. But they all appeared to know something. I, on the other hand, knew nothing for sure, which was unnerving. I never learned whether or not they were around when disaster had struck. If they were, had they taken part? By my not mentioning Big Road's name, they assumed that I knew everything. And the fact that they never mentioned him convinced me of what they had done. With their sweaty faces and dumb expressions, they did what I told them to do, without a murmur. But I was afraid of them. There's no deny-ing that the foreigner had taught them their jobs—how to run the machinery and how to repair it—and that they had used this knowl-edge and machinery to chop the barbarian to pieces. I knew that if someone were to tell them to do the same to me, they'd do it. Then they'd pick up the pieces and toss them into the rushing waters of the Black River.

I didn't have the nerve to even think about what happened on that wretched rainy day.

It was unthinkable.

As the man in charge, I could move against the fearful men first. One day, when I was preparing chemicals in the mixing shed, I found a whip buried in the dirt under the corner of the wall. Sec-ond Master had never used it, nor had I. All the men in charge of things in the Cao household owned little leather whips like this. Some used them, some didn't. The man who ran the slaughter-house used his just about every day. The backs of some of the men who wielded the knives were covered with welts. They had ap-parently lost sight of the fact that the knives they carried had more than one use, but I assumed that the slaughterhouse boss would get what was coming to him one day. I knew I'd get what was coming to me one day too, but I had no time to think about that. What was in my heart steeled my nerves, telling me to move first.

Without warning I used my whip on one of the men.

With a sharp crack, the tip of the whip left a white mark on his back.

I said: That'll teach you!

Then I turned and hit another man.

It opened a tear in his shirt.

That'll teach you! I shouted again.

The workers didn't know what I was doing, and probably didn't know what I was talking about. Hell, *I* didn't know. They threw themselves into their work, the slicing machine running full steam—*ke-cha ke-cha*—spewing the white matchstick material into bamboo baskets like sliced potatoes. From where I stood, on top of the woodpile, I tried my best to instill fear in them. I said: By your doing

evil instead of working at your jobs, Heaven is going to smash your
rice bowls! Now get to work and mind your own business. On
behalf of Second Master, I'll fire any of you who slack off! Don't
underestimate me. Second Master isn't around, and neither is the
foreigner. But I am! Look down on me, and you've got my word
that I'll never forgive you, not as long as I'm in charge. Try me
and see!

I scared the hell out of those workers, but it made no difference—
I was still afraid. I couldn't shake the feeling that at any minute
they'd stop working and come at me, all of them. They'd stick me
under the knives of the slicing machine. I don't know if Big Road
begged them to spare him or not, but I knew I would.

Spare me!

I wonder what it would have sounded like in that foreign tongue.

That phrase could turn into a look.

I could spot someone with that look in his eyes.

I'm one of them. I worked during the day and spent the nights
holed up in Steward Bing's quarters. Elder Master's coughs
and the servants' footsteps made my heart race and my flesh
crawl. Big Road's soul hid under my cot, venturing out when the
lamp wasn't lit, and then going back into hiding when it was. I
didn't know what to do with it, or with myself. Whether I was
dreaming or awake, two words kept getting caught in my throat:
Spare me! I begged Heaven to spare my worthless life. I couldn't
be sure if there was anyone in front of me or behind me with
murder on his mind, but I had the feeling that somebody had me
in his sights.

Steward Bing was very busy during those days, often coming
in late at night. Rather than light a lamp or let me light one, he
groped his way to bed, where he tossed and turned and sighed
from time to time. One night, after one of his long sighs, I heard
him call out softly, over and over, like a man with a headache or a
stomachache. I said: Are you all right, Steward Bing?

He said: I'm fine. Go back to sleep.

Where does it hurt? I asked.

It doesn't, he said. Everything's fine.

A long silence followed. I was about to fall asleep, and I assumed he was already asleep. But then he began to moan, as if a snake had latched onto his toe. I got out of bed and lit the lamp, which I carried over to his bed to see what was wrong. I saw that look in his wide, staring, and moist eyes. He pointed to the lamp, a sign that he wanted me to put it out. I did. Then he sighed again and began to sob.

Ears, this is bad karma! he wailed.

I said: What do you mean?

He said: There are a lot of things I can't do at my age. Ears, I'm not afraid of Heaven or earth. But I am afraid of retribution in my next life!

Steward Bing, I said, I don't understand.

He said: Don't pull that on me. You understand perfectly.

I said: Steward Bing, you're confusing me.

Then stay confused, he said. Confused is good.

He didn't say anything more to me that night, or for several nights after that. A fine rain fell in the valley. Not much was happening around the estate, and few people were out anywhere in town. No one went up the mountain, and there was no real news from the Green River. There were, of course, rumors, lots of them. One rumor had it that insurrections were breaking out everywhere. Besides the Blue Kerchiefs, there were the Red Kerchiefs, the Green Kerchiefs, and the White Kerchiefs, each active on one particular mountain or one particular river. The way it looked, imperial land was being chipped away by the rebels, piece by piece. There were also conflicts between the rebels and the religious converts. Dead Christians floated down the Green River, while one church after another was put to the torch. Missionaries and converts alike were fleeing to outlying provinces. Wealthy families were running off to the provincial capital. But in Elm Township the days were as peaceful as ever. We heard that was the case in Willow Township and Acacia Township as well. Black Eagle and White Horse were still peddling flesh in Willow Township, day and night. Father Ma at the church on Eastern Avenue could still be seen riding his donkey everywhere. But good times were not to last long, and some of the more courageous were already out on the streets causing disturbances and filling the air with their shouts of Down with the Emperor! Fuck the Emperor's mother!

Mildew was cropping up all over the Cao compound in the unending rain and moss began to cover the stone path, fresh and delightfully green in the fine rain. It was the green of Young Mistress's clothes and felt like soft satin under my bare feet, which I imagined to be the fair skin under her skirts. Nights were unimaginably boring. I didn't dare climb onto the rooftops, and was reduced to walking along the path by hugging the wall like an alley cat. Holding an umbrella in one hand and my shoes in the other gave me a strange feeling I find impossible to describe. I didn't think much about Wuling, but when I did, I got hot all over. I was fond of her soft, white legs, which looked like a pair of fragrant boughs when she raised them in the air. And those boughs took the place of the person I was thinking about; when I shuddered against them as I would a pair of Chinese date trees, all I thought about was the face stamped on my heart. When the little bastard in the left-hand compound laughed, I thought of his mother rolling over! But those thoughts brought me nothing good, and I could only feel myself rolling over, tossing and turning on my bamboo cot in Steward Bing's room. I couldn't sleep, and was no longer visited by daydreams.

Steward Bing couldn't sleep either. The look in his eyes carried those two words: Spare me! Heaven was pressing him, demons of death were chasing him, and even he had turned into a self-destructive monster. One night, when thunder roared but no rain fell, he could hold it in no longer and told me everything, stammering slightly. What I heard scared me so badly my face was awash with snot and tears. I stayed as calm as I could. Although he was at least fifty years older than me, in my eyes he seemed like a frightened little boy, far less experienced than I. As I heard him out I made up my mind on the spur of the moment. In that instant I became someone to reckon with.

Steward Bing said that Young Mistress had given birth to a bastard, and Elder Master had told him to secretly get rid of it. Even if he'd been willing to do it, he didn't know how, and was so shaken by the duty that he thought about killing himself instead.

I said: What's the big deal? They've already gotten rid of Mr. Road, haven't they?

Stunned by my comment, he began crying piteously. It was as if King Yama had grabbed him by the leg and he had given up all hope. I loved seeing him like that. I said savagely: There's a pond in the left-hand compound and a water vat alongside the wall. Why not just toss the little bastard into one of those?

Steward Bing said: I can't go on living. All I want is a decent life the next time around. If he tries to force me to do something that evil, my life is over. Ears, one of these days I'm going to drown myself in that water vat. For me there's no escape!

I said to myself: You get what you deserve, Steward Bing! But I knew that the poor wretch was falling apart, and even though I had an idea, I wasn't about to tell him, not yet. I'd wait till he'd exhausted himself, then I'd tell him.

I said: Don't worry, Steward Bing. I'll do it for you.

You? he blurted out. You'll do what?

I said: Don't ask. I'll take care of him.

You're not just saying that, are you? he asked.

I said: Ears has always done what he's said he'd do. You haven't forgotten, have you?

Tripping over his words, he said: You'd do that for me?

As I said, there was plenty of thunder that night, but no rain. Lightning flashed on the far side of Jade Mountain, lighting up the whole valley. I could hear the little bastard crying off in the distance, and all of a sudden my heart felt empty. I tried to imagine what he would look like when he grew up—his mouth, his hands, his feet—and when I got to his toes, it felt as if they were kicking me in the belly and tickling me all over. I was only seventeen at the time, but I liked kids. Like Steward Bing, in my heart I knew I couldn't go on living after doing what he was talking about. I thought I could kill the little bastard, but I was wrong. And so

I formed a plan. As the sun rose after a night of thunder but no rain, I entered a dream with my eyes wide open.

Second Master was gone.

The foreigner was gone.

I was now the little bastard's father.

April 13th

I waited in the scrub brush beside the Jade Mountain path, watching Steward Bing walk down the stone path in the compound and out onto the township street. There was no lamplight in town, but the moon was bright enough to see his every movement on the white roadway. He was carrying a bamboo basket about twice the size of a pillow, covered by an old shirt. He was quaking, and his teeth were chattering. At first he didn't say anything. So I took the basket and turned to leave. But he reached out and grabbed me, then held on real tight, his old hand like steel talons.

Do it fast, he said. Don't make him suffer.

Then he said: Ears, I really can't go on living.

I had nothing to say. The basket was very light, and I wondered how the little whelp had kept from putting on any weight in twenty days. He weighed no more than a handful of vegetables. At first I wondered if he was even in the basket, and then I wondered if he was already dead. But as those thoughts ran through my mind, the basket got heavier.

Steward Bing added: Make it clean. Don't leave any traces.

I said: Don't worry.

Then he asked: How do you plan to do it?

I said: If you don't trust me, come along.

He let his hand drop and said: Ears, don't get cute with me. I know you pity me. You won't suffer retribution over this, but sooner or later, I will. In serving the Cao family, we slaves have nothing to be ashamed about. Go on now, Ears, and come right back. Don't dally. Cao Zichun, you little bastard, I'm truly sorry.

Steward Bing touched the basket, but before he could say any more, I walked off in a hurry. I was fed up with the old man. He said he couldn't go on living with the dead on his conscience, but was worried I might leave traces and wanted me to make a clean job of it! No sound emerged from the basket, so after I crossed Jade Mountain, my curiosity got the better of me and, reaching a spot where the wind was behind me, I lit a match, opened the basket, and looked inside. What I saw shocked me. The pink little object inside looked like a skinned rabbit. His eyes and mouth were shut, and he didn't look much like the foreigner to me. I lit another match, but still saw nothing much except for a little head not much bigger than a wine bowl, covered with downy yellow hair. I was tempted to pry open his eyelids to see the blue Wuling had told me about. I resisted the temptation. I was worried that would wake him up, and that that would open the floodgates. With moonlight to guide me, I hurried in the direction of the church at Acacia Township. I avoided Willow Township's Main Avenue and the piers, skirting the stony hill south of town and walking through rice paddies, which took me directly to Acacia Township. Concerned about the town's dogs, and terrified of the paranoid Christian converts who lived there, I hesitated outside the gate until I'd screwed up the courage to enter town. To my surprise, I made it all the way to the church gate without incident. Everything might have been fine if I'd laid the basket down then and there and walked off. But I couldn't bring myself to do that. As if possessed, I just had to see his blue eyes; I owed myself that much. So I lit a match with one hand and pried open one of his eyelids with the other. And there was Mr. Road's eye, staring straight at me. No doubt about it, it was blue. When I pried open his other eye, out came a loud wail.

Cao Zichun woke up Acacia Township's dogs.

Acacia Township's dogs woke up the meddlesome Christian converts.

Quickly dropping the basket to the ground, I turned and ran as fast as I could, the chorus of barking drowning out the baby's cries, but not the shouts of the Christians or the sound of rifles being cocked. *Bang!* A bullet whistled high in the air above my head. *Bang!* Another shot, followed by the loud peals of the church bell. Damn! I said to myself. I won't get away this time!

I cut across the rice paddies, heading toward Jade Mountain. About halfway up the mountain, I realized that quiet had returned to Acacia Township, all except for the cries of a baby not yet a month old. I thought for a minute that my ears were playing tricks on me, but even after I'd crossed to the other side of the mountain, I could still hear him crying. Mist over the Green River carried his cries into the Jade Mountain villages and straight into my heart. All I could think was that I hadn't let Mr. Road or his offspring down; nor, for that matter, Young Mistress. The baby's fate lay in the hand of Heaven; whether he lived or died depended on whether or not he was blessed with good fortune. The priest ran a tiny orphanage behind the church, normally populated by seven or eight unwanted children. People outside Acacia Township said that Father Ma fattened the children up so he could cook them like beefsteaks and feed them to his local converts as part of the prayer ritual. I didn't believe a word of it. But even if it had been true, would the priest really cook a baby with blue eyes? None of this worried me. My only concern was the Acacia Township dogs. I was afraid they'd converge on the basket and rip him to pieces. Running right into Acacia Township was like tossing them a chunk of meat. But the baby's frightful cries probably terrified the dogs as well. And if I delayed them long enough, Father Ma would emerge from his church, find the basket, and take it inside. With one pair of blue eyes looking into another, no matter what difficulties might lie ahead, I knew I didn't have to worry.

I returned to Elm Township well after midnight. Steward Bing was waiting anxiously for me at the main gate, where he'd spent the night. Spotting me quietly make my way up to the compound not only failed to comfort him, but made him more nervous than ever. He watched me fearfully, as if I might walk up and kill him on the spot.

He asked: How'd you do it, Ears?

I said: I stuffed him into a catfish hole.

He asked: Won't the current pull him out?

I said: No, I put a rock on top.

He said: That makes me feel better.

With a sigh of relief, he told me to go get some sleep. I was worn out, but keyed up from all that activity, I couldn't sleep. I'd probably appeased Mr. Road's soul enough that it would stop coming out from under my cot to enshroud me. But I could still hear his son's cries, and that drove all thoughts of sleep away. My head was filled with a welter of thoughts, but none of them led anywhere. The wails gradually became the cries of a woman. I climbed out of bed to listen more carefully, but as soon as I did, the sounds vanished.

Wuling told me afterward that the source of the ghostlike cries that came and went that night was Young Mistress. First old Cang's wife took the baby from her to feed him. After that, Steward Bing's wife took him out of the left-hand compound under the pretense that Old Master and Old Mistress wanted to see him. But when she didn't return, Young Mistress reacted as if struck by lightning, knowing at once that something awful had happened. Although still weak from the birth, she burst out of the room. Wuling tried to hold her back, but failed, and had no choice but to follow her. She was surprised to see Elder Master Guangman sitting on the veranda as if waiting for them to come out. His face was round and full in the light of a lamp on the stone table. Even from where she stood, behind Young Mistress, Wuling could smell alcohol on his breath.

Young Mistress demanded: Elder Brother, where's my baby?

Elder Master said: Zheng Yunan, if you're smart you'll turn around and go back inside. You have no right to ask me questions, when I never asked any of you. The Cao family has treated you fairly. And look how you've repaid us! You know what I'm talking about. We don't plan to do anything to you, so leave the child to us. He's a Cao, and as such, of no future concern to you. Don't cause a scene—that won't do anyone any good. Once your lying-in period is over, we'll send you back to your parents' home. They wanted you home, didn't they? Well, now they'll get their wish.

Young Mistress demanded: What about my baby? Where's my baby?

Elder Master said: I'll say this one more time. We don't plan to harm you. We residents of Elm Township don't want to provoke an incident with the Mulberry people. Our loss of face has been total. I am now the head of the family, and I'm not going to argue with you. You must let me salvage what face I can. I don't want Father or Mother to learn about this, do you understand? I want them to live a while longer. Do you understand, you rotten whore?

He swirled the liquor around in the little gourd as he grumbled. He was drunk. Young Mistress began to shake when he called her a rotten whore, but she held her tongue. Wuling helped her back inside, and the moment they entered the room, she saw that Young Mistress's pale face was wet with tears. That quickly led to sobs. Steward Bing's wife came in just then and joined the tearful scene. When Young Mistress asked what had happened to the baby, the old woman refused to answer; by then she was sobbing more pitifully even than Young Mistress. As I listened to Wuling's report, I concluded that while the women were crying their eyes out, I had probably been scurrying down Acacia Township's Main Avenue. Had the baby wailed while dogs were barking all around him because he knew that his mother was crying at that very moment? Whatever the answer, that was surely the moment when the bond between mother and son was broken for all time. They were both destined to a bad end. Fate would dictate how their lives turned out, and there was nothing either of them could do for the other. No one could presume to know what Young Mistress was feeling then. She was drowning in a deep well, had been for a long time, and was the only person in the world who knew just how much suffering that entailed.

Wuling told me: Young Mistress is as soft as clay. She's not going to make it.

I said: If she grits her teeth and gets through this, she can still be saved.

Wuling said: She can't get through this—she's about to crumble.

A woman who had been so full of life only a year before, carried into the compound in a swaying sedan chair and flooding the household and the streets outside with her crisp laughter, had been brought low and had lost the will to endure. The thought was more than I could take. It broke my heart. And as the world seemed to lose all meaning, I thought of Wuling, of her soft, fair legs. Finding no opportunity to take pleasure in her body, either at sunset or late at night, I had begun taking her over to the wall next to the path and pressing up against her, my hands roaming over her body. With thoughts of nothing else, I'd lift up her skirt or take her hair in my hands as if I wanted to tear her to pieces.

I said: She'll have to get through it, whether she wants to or not. Be careful and make sure she doesn't take the coward's way out.

Wuling said: Let her end her own life if she wants to. I'll accompany her in death.

I said: I'll kill you myself if I hear any more of that nonsense.

Wuling said: Elder Brother Ears, don't get me pregnant!

I said: So what if you're pregnant? Maybe I'll kill you anyway!

I was going mad.

Crickets were chirping on the footpath.

Someone was crying in the distance.

People were crying everywhere.

I didn't know what they were crying about.

I was afraid I'd die the next day.

But before I did, I was going to make trouble.

Wuling was crying.

So was I.

I thought of death.

I wanted to find someone who had died before me.

My heart—empty!

April 14th

Steward Bing was sure I'd killed the bastard child. Elder Master believed that Steward Bing had done it. That brought matters to an end. Elder Master ordered that a skimpy coffin be made and that Steward Bing lead a procession to go bury it. So one rainy morning just after sunup, the residents of Elm Township saw the yellow-draped casket and knew that the Cao family had lost its heir. Before long people everywhere learned that the tiny thing had died of yellow fever. Everything the child had touched was burned, raising a pall of black smoke over the walls of the left-hand compound, one that hovered above all of Elm Township and floated up over Jade Mountain, where it merged with the clouds. Wuling told me that Young Mistress sat on the veranda watching Steward Bing's wife lead servants in burning the child's clothing and bedding. Saying that wasn't enough, Young Mistress had them take the furniture out and burn it too. When they balked, she picked up the heavy wooden chairs Second Master and Mr. Road had sat in and tossed them out the gate; she then removed her jewelry box and a picture frame and threw them onto the steps of the main house. It took such little strenuous effort to reduce her to gasps and bring an end to her attempts. The redwood picture frame was unbroken and the photograph inside was not damaged. But the glass was shattered. Wuling retrieved the photograph, which she later showed me. I'd seen that picture frame before, but had never gotten a good look at the photograph inside. Now I saw that it was a group photo of girls at the normal school in the provincial capital. A dozen or more of them were arranged in two rows, those in back standing and those in front kneeling or sitting. They wore carefree smiles. Young Mistress was in the front row, her flared skirt spread out on the grass like a day lily to cover her legs. She wore a beautiful smile, and her hair was done up with a sprig of peach blossoms; she looked like a girl without a care in the world.

The photo disturbed me, producing a void behind my ribs, as if someone had removed everything inside and taken it away. I had trouble catching my breath. Wuling wanted to return the photograph to Young Mistress, but I said no, she should give it to me. When Wuling balked, I told her that if she gave it back, Young Mistress might tear it up. Then I grabbed it out of her hand and tucked it into the pocket of my undershirt. Everything that had been taken out of me suddenly returned. My body was pressed up against Young Mistress's face, which brought me warmth. I vowed to protect her with my life! She'd given up all hope, had crumbled like a pile of mud, while from that moment on, my backbone grew stiffer by the day.

The day the clothing was burned turned into one of the Cao family's worst days. After taking care of everything, Elder Master reported the death of Cao Zichun to Old Master and Old Mistress. Old Mistress's seclusion had by then entered a new realm: not only was she fasting, but she had taken a vow of silence. Her face, devoid of expression, made her look as if she were in the world of the living dead. The old nun who was leading her to immortality lay her soft white hands on the top of her head, as if trapping a locust, to help her take in and expel energy. Even after she'd gone so long without eating, Old Mistress's skin was as healthy-looking as always, although she appeared somewhat numb. But the servant attending her in the meditation room was grumbling that while Old Mistress didn't eat during the day, at night, after the lamps were put out, she could hear the sounds of chewing and swallowing. So she was eating after all, but not enough, which is why she was so lethargic and absentminded. Elder Master knelt at her bedside and told her everything, how Second Master's son

had fallen sick and died, and how they had buried him and burned
his clothing. Not a flicker of a response from her. The old nun grew
impatient and asked Elder Master to leave. She said: Don't bother
her with all these petty affairs. Your mother is already halfway to
immortality!

So Elder Master left the room and went to see his father. Old
Master was up on his footstool, painting butterflies amid the wisteria blossoms. Elder Master knelt by him and told him what had
happened. Calm and composed, Old Master finished the wing he
was working on.

Old Master said: I heard someone crying. Was it Yunan?

Elder Master said: Yes.

Old Master asked: What was the child's name?

Elder Master replied: Cao Zichun. It was the name you gave him.

Old Master turned thoughtful as he climbed down off the footstool. Elder Master rushed over to help him. Old Master stepped
back to admire his fan proudly.

Old Master said: A few more strokes, and they'll be able to fly.
After the child died, you buried him without letting me see him,
is that right? I was his grandfather, but I never laid eyes on him.
And you went ahead and buried him. Guangman, what were you
thinking to come up with this scheme? You were jealous over the
fact that Guanghan had produced an heir when you couldn't,
weren't you? Go get Cao Zichun and bring him to me. I want to see
him! Then send someone down to the Green River, find Guanghan,
and bring him back. The father must see the son. Do you hear me?

Elder Master, unable to reveal what was eating at him inside,
got down on his knees and kowtowed to his father.

He said: I held back telling you one thing to keep from worrying you. The child died of yellow fever, and we are burning things
in the left-hand compound.

Yellow fever? Old Master asked.

Elder Master said: We don't know where Guanghan has gone,
and even if we did, we couldn't get him back here in time.
Guanghan's son was my son too, since he would have carried
on the Cao family line. But since he died, it's up to me to make

arrangements in Guanghan's stead. Don't worry, everything will be taken care of.

Old Master sat down heavily. All other thoughts were purged from his mind as he mumbled over and over: Yellow fever yellow fever yellow fever! Elder Master got to his feet and left the room with tears in his eyes. Old Master called out from behind him: Burn it well! Show no reluctance. If there's any doubt, burn it. Then Old Master told Steward Bing, who had been standing in the doorway the whole time, to take the rush mat Elder Master had knelt on outside and burn it. A while later, he took off the gown Elder Master had touched when helping him down from the footstool and had it taken outside to be burned. Finally, since he had stepped in the same spots as Elder Master, he removed his shoes and socks and had Steward Bing take them out to be burned also. Steward Bing was on pins and needles, since at the rate Old Master was going, he'd be consigning himself to the flames before he was completely satisfied. After burning the shoes, Steward Bing returned to the room and discovered there was nothing left to burn. Old Master was on the footstool in his bare feet, wearing a red satin vest. He had a brush in one hand and a plate of ink in the other. But instead of painting, he had his head buried in the white porcelain plate, and was lapping up the ink.

Steward Bing shouted: Old Master!

Old Master just looked up and smiled at the butterflies.

I was asleep in Steward Bing's quarters. Mr. Road's soul was no longer causing me any trouble. Now it was Steward Bing, who was very much alive. Tormented by a guilty conscience, he could not escape the feeling that it was he who had stuffed Cao Zichun down the catfish hole. And now, added to that, he felt responsible for Old Master drinking ink. Worried that I wouldn't believe him, he related the ink-drinking episode from start to finish, over and over again. Me? Not believe that? Consuming ink was nothing, nothing at all. Steward Bing was really getting on my nerves, but I let him ramble on and on in the dark. With a sigh, he said: The Cao family is doomed! What a pity! And there isn't a thing we slaves can do about it. If it would help, I'd beg them to take me with them. What are these old bones worth anyway? I might as well follow them down that fateful road.

I didn't interrupt him. Let him talk, I thought. But some of what he said found its way into my heart. I was thinking what it would be like when I got old. I'd be just like Steward Bing, a scrawny old dog hanging around the master's house shedding tears of anguish. What a miserable life. So while Steward Bing talked on and on, I was thinking my own thoughts. I held Young Mistress's photograph up against my chest and belly, so that her face was touching my skin. I counted the days of her lying-in on my fingers, knowing that when the time was up, she and Wuling would leave Elm Township. They said they'd be going on a visit to her parents' home, but anyone with an idea of what had happened knew they wouldn't be coming back. I'd never see them again, and would be all alone in the left-hand compound; I didn't know how I'd get through the days after that. The Cao household would be the same as always, but I wouldn't be the same old me. I didn't want to be in charge of anything anymore and had no interest in going back to the old match commune. In my eyes, matches were the most evil things in the world. My head felt as if it might explode every time I heard the slicing machine make that *ke-cha ke-cha* sound; it nearly drove me out of my mind. Now I knew why Second Master had run off to the other side of the mountain to wander like a lost soul. And I knew why he'd done all those terrible things, like a man possessed. I wished I could turn myself into a bomb and blow the Cao compound and all of Elm Township sky-high, turn the valley into a wasteland! I'd blow up everything that deserved destruction, with Young Mistress, Wuling, and me floating on a cloud together. My daydreams would then be perfect. By adding a few people I liked to our cloud, plus those people I still thought about, my daydreams would be absolutely perfect. I held Young Mistress's photograph up to my lips and kissed her. Of course, the photo was so small and the room so dark I might have actually kissed one of the other girls. But that didn't matter, because in my eyes, all those girls were goddesses, the only sisters I had anywhere in this world. Lying on my bamboo cot, I turned to the wall and lit a match; Young Mistress's girlish face burst into view, and no matter how hard I tried to hold them back, hot tears filled my eyes.

Oh, if only I could die for her!

I'd no longer have to look at this rotten world.

Just die!

Old Master was reaching the end, at last. He sent for me. He lay under the covers blinking up at me for the longest time before sputtering that he wanted to eat shit. I hesitated for a moment, not because I was shocked—I wasn't—but to size up the situation. While his eyes were on me, I bent over and spit into his little cauldron. No reaction. Then I knocked some mud off my shoe and dumped it into his teacup. Still nothing. His eyes were fixed on the chair legs, fear written all over his face, as if a poisonous snake were slithering up to him. Besides fear, there was a crazed look in his eyes, as if he hoped that rather than bite him, the snake would crawl into his mouth so he could swallow it down.

Old Master, I asked, whose should we eat?

His face reddened as he replied: Old Mistress's.

I said: Can't be done. She hasn't eaten anything for days.

I don't care, he said. Find a way, Ears.

How about your own, Old Master? I asked.

He said: Do I have any?

I replied: Yes, I know you do.

Old Master said: What do you know? I have diarrhea the year round.

I said: Don't worry, I'll think of something.

Old Master said: Ears, I can't think of any reason why that should be a problem. I've managed to get through the days all this time, until my hair has turned gray, and in the end I've spoken about the things I wanted to do. I feel good at this moment. I'll wait while you go to the kitchen and find a pretty porcelain bowl. I feel good all over, no fears at all. I'll wait here. Hurry up. Do you hear me, Ears?

I said: I hear you. Wait for me.

I spit again into his cauldron, and still no reaction from him. I pretty much knew what was happening. So I went to the kitchen, where I found a blue and white porcelain bowl and a piece of fried rice cake. I had the cook cut the cake into slices and sprinkle some brown sugar over the top. After putting it in the bowl, I covered it with a piece of paper and carried it back to Old Master. When he saw me approach his bed, he tensed like a tiger, but then relaxed as soon as he raised the bowl to his mouth. Neither over-eager nor unhurried, he closed his eyes and finished off the entire bowl of fried rice cake shit. It would have been impossible for him not to know what he was really eating, but he turned to me and said that it wasn't bad at all. With a long string of saliva hanging from his mouth, he asked: Whose was it? That really threw me. As I was leaving his room, he said: Ears, be sure the door is closed. I don't want the butterflies to get out. They were hard enough to catch the first time. If they fly away, I'll never get them back!

I ran away, not daring to look up at the fan.

Early one morning, Young Mistress had Wuling take down the red curtain by the compound gate, then went over to the main compound to say good-bye to Old Master and Old Mistress. Several days still remained before her lying-in period was over, but she was eager to leave. From the very beginning, Elder Master had refused to let her depart before the end of the lying-in period. That would have been tantamount to the Cao family's driving her out or mistreating her. But she was adamant in her decision, and Elder Master lost interest in stopping her. He finally relented. I was assigned the task of escorting her and Wuling across the Green River. I couldn't decide whether that made me happy or sad. I went along when she said her good-byes to the family elders, but didn't have a chance to speak to her, and certainly had no chance to get cozy with Wuling. I was burning up with anxiety. Young Mistress spent a little time in Old Mistress's meditation room and then spent a little time with Old Master. The rest of us waited outside each time. Surrounded by all those people, I reached out and squeezed Wuling's hand; she squeezed back, really hard, almost cruelly. Our fingernails clicked against each other's. We could hear Young Mistress and Old Master talking; we were talking too.

Old Master said: The child's dead and there's nothing you can do about it. In Elm Township, it's considered good if three out of ten children survive. The ones who die are supposed to die. In fact, it's bad luck if the ones who are supposed to die don't. Guanghan ought to be back when you return from your parents' home. I said long ago that that dissipated whelp wasn't good enough for you, and it is the Cao family's good fortune that you accepted him. You've suffered much and deserve a rest at your parents' home. The good days now belong to your generation; ours are all behind us. Today I'm talking to you, but for all I know, I might not wake up tomorrow. Yunan, I want you to take a good look at those butterflies on the wall. Are they flying?

Young Mistress was silent for a moment before saying: Yes, they are.

I whispered to Wuling: I honestly feel like killing you!

Wuling snorted and said: Go ahead! I don't want to leave!

Our fingers were intertwined so tightly our knuckles cracked. Young Mistress emerged from Old Master's room perfectly calm. She was dressed in her most eye-catching green blouse and skirt, and even her shoes and her hair ornaments were green. I found her calmness chilling. In accordance with Elder Master's instructions, few people came to see her off. But many pairs of eyes were on her as she strode slowly through the gate—some out of tribute, others to bid good riddance. Elder Master was unchallenged as the most ferocious representative of the latter group, but he treated her courteously as he saw her into the sedan chair. I also found his courtesy chilling. Several tenant farmers standing in the open space beyond the gate observed the smile on the faces of the family members, but were too far away to hear what was said. I, on the other hand, heard it all, most notably two comments made by Elder Master. The first was: You take care of your own affairs as you see fit. I say this to you for Guanghan. The other was: Take care of yourself. The Cao family owes you nothing!

I heard no response from Young Mistress.

The sedan chair was carried speedily up Jade Mountain, Wuling and me following with an assortment of bundles. I couldn't shake the feeling that evil intentions were hidden behind Elder Master's courtesies, and when I thought about Big Road's blood, I grew wary of servants with daggers or rifles. Leaving Wuling behind, I ran to the front of the sedan chair, feverishly turning over in my mind the possibility that I could save Young Mistress from the same terrible fate. But as we crossed the mountain and headed down the opposite slope, I began to sense that my fears were unfounded. Then, as we were crossing the suspension bridge over the valley, another worry entered my mind. I couldn't bear the image of Young Mistress's calm face. I was afraid she might leap from the bridge into the Black River. She got off and let the sedan chair cross the bridge first, then followed it over. I was about two paces away from her when she leaned down and looked at the river below. I nearly ran up to throw myself on her!

Young Mistress said: I wonder if my lotus river lantern got this far.

If it did, I said, by then it was probably falling apart.

Then she said: I wonder if my lotus lantern made it to the Green River.

I said: Probably not. Even a lantern made of tin would break apart.

She was spellbound by the sight of the river below.

I was ready to rush up and grab her around the waist.

But she floated across the bridge, a vision of green.

I could see that my worries were groundless.

Totally groundless.

We were held up at the pier at Willow Township until the ferry arrived. So I took Young Mistress and Wuling over to Lucky Teahouse for some tea while we waited. The sedan chair was sent back. We sat at a table by the window. The other patrons, who were exchanging ribald stories, clammed up as soon as they saw women enter the shop. Lucky knew who Young Mistress was, and was disgustingly attentive. She didn't feel like talking, however, and neither did I, so he lost interest and quit slobbering over her. But he couldn't stop himself from pulling me to the side and, with a frown of concern on his gray brows, asking: The poor thing, did her baby really die?

I said: Yes.

He asked: Has Second Master returned?

I said: No.

He said: The poor thing! After you board the ferry, be sure to have her cover her head and face. It's windy out there on the water. Just because it's nearly summertime, don't be fooled. Those are ill winds blowing down from upriver. They can really mess up your head, even paralyze you.

I said: Don't try to scare me.

That may be what I said, but when I got back to the table, I passed on the news to Young Mistress, who just smiled indifferently and gazed out the window at the river. The Green River was swollen this year; if it rose another foot it would swamp the pier. Ships tossed about on the surface, carried swiftly on the waves as if made of paper. I was drinking Emerald Conch tea, but was so light-headed I might as well have been drinking liquor. There was an important decision I had to make, but for the life of me I couldn't pull the threads together. I didn't know if I should tell Young Mistress that her child was at the church in Acacia Township. And if I did, should I take her there? What would that accomplish? I didn't even know if he was still alive. But dead or alive, taking her to see and acknowledge him would be about the stupidest thing I could do. So then I thought about going myself after I'd seen Young Mistress across the Green River.

I was starting to miss Cao Zichun, the little bastard.

His eyes were inlaid with Big Road's blue irises.

I wondered where Mr. Road had floated off to.

Maybe all the way to his hometown.

Could he have floated up his hometown river and crawled to shore soaking wet, the same way he used to climb soaking wet out of his tub in the Cao estate? He filled a tub that could have accommodated a great many fish, sending water splashing all over the brick floor. The Green River is much wider than that tub of yours, Mr. Road. Did you have a nice soak? I know it's cold, but what can you do, when there's no one to add hot water for you, no one to secretly consider pouring boiling water over your naked skin? As I drank my Emerald Conch tea and gazed out at the clear water of the swollen river, my ponderings left me with a building sense of dejection. Wuling stepped on my foot under the table; tears were welling up in the poor girl's eyes. I ignored her—she could step down as hard as she wanted. I was too busy studying Young Mistress's face. Earrings as big as the mouth of a teacup hung down through her hair and swayed beside the fair skin of her neck. Her eyes hadn't changed, nor had her mouth and nose; but she was a different person. With a smile on her face, she'd fallen into a well of bitterness, and when she'd floated to the surface, she'd gazed up at the opening above her. I wished I could take her hand, for no matter where she was, I could lift her out, even if I took her place. Her hand rested on the table: fingers like bamboo shoots, palm like a flower petal, fingernails like glossy wax. I wanted to lay my hand on top of hers, and my heart fluttered at the thought. Wuling could stomp on my toes as hard as she wanted to; all I could think about was laying my hand on top of Young Mistress's lonely hand. I wanted to lift her out, I wanted to save her, hoping that in the process she could save me. I was a slave, a slave dog, but in my daydreams, it didn't matter whether someone was a master or a slave. I was the emperor, the old master, a man whose head held up the sky, and I was going to turn that sky upside down!

Kwang-dang. A ship thudded into the pier. Not a ferryboat, it was a coal-burning passenger ship from upriver. We emerged from the Lucky Teahouse as people boarding and disembarking from the ship formed a crowd on the pier. Several heads stuck out of the portholes in the two decks, gaping curiously at the shore. Those unwilling to fight the crowd on the gangplank shinnied down one of the docking hawsers, like monkeys descending a mountain. Young Mistress held her hand over her eyes and squinted in the bright sunlight. To me, she was looking up at the square of sky at the top of the well to see if she could rise out of the water. She didn't notice me and couldn't see the power hidden in my body. I could turn the sky upside down, but I was powerless to change what had been branded on my body. I would always be a slave, no matter where I went. She didn't favor me with the look I sought, and certainly didn't allow me to touch her as I so often did in my daydreams. Her heart was the shell of a river snail, and I couldn't have bored my way in, even if I'd been a tiny insect.

I wished the ferry would sink before it got here and leave us standing on the Willow Township pier, day and night, always together, until we were transformed into stone pilings, never to be separated.

The ship was taking on no new passengers and the deckhands were preparing to get under way. All of a sudden, Young Mistress ran over and started up the gangplank, leaving Wuling and me standing there dumbstruck, watching her float up on deck. In her green clothing, she looked like a tree with a canopy that blotted out everything else around it.

I shouted: That ship doesn't cross the river, Young Mistress, it's headed downriver! That's not the ferry!

She replied: I know. I want to go to the capital. I need a change of scenery to work things out. Take Wuling across the river, Ears, then you can go home. Wuling, you go ahead to Mulberry Township and tell my family I went to the capital to visit friends from school. I've been thinking about them a lot lately. Don't worry about me, I'll be there in a few days. And as for you, Ears, don't get all worked up. I just want to visit my schoolmates. I'll only spend a day or so there. I won't be gone long. You're a good boy, Ears. Wuling and I won't forget you. Wuling, stop crying! Wuling! Ears will see you across the river, and if you want him to, he'll go with you to Mulberry Township. So stop crying, you silly little girl. It only makes you ugly. Even Ears won't want to look at you. I'll go see my friends in the capital and then turn around and come back. So don't worry about me, either of you. Stand back, Wuling. Ears, move her back.

Crying loudly, Wuling said: Young Mistress, I've got your luggage.

Young Mistress said: I have enough money on me.

Suddenly I had the feeling that something was terribly wrong.
Young Mistress had said a whole lifetime of words.

She was not a talkative person.

Something terrible was going to happen.

The docking ropes were thrown off and three of the five gang-planks taken in. A fourth gangplank rose shakily from the pier. Grabbing Wuling by the hand, I ran up onto it. Terrified female passengers began to scream, and the noises coming from the frightened Wuling no longer sounded like crying. I wasn't afraid of falling into the river, nor was I worried about being crushed between the ship and the pier. I'd often dreamed of dying in front of Young Mistress. She was looking straight at me. Heaven was looking down at me. With no thoughts for my own safety, I wanted to fly over and rescue her. Wuling and I negotiated the foot-wide gangplank onto the deck, like crossing a narrow footbridge. Wuling had no sooner flung herself into Young Mistress's arms than the ship pulled away from the pier and the water below began to churn. High up on the mast, the ship's whistle sounded and thick black smoke billowed out of the smokestack. The belly of the ship seemed to be on fire. It swayed so little, it didn't feel as if we were moving at all, but rather that the pier itself was moving away from us; even the distant Jade Mountain appeared to be floating away. The sight of Young Mistress holding on to Wuling sent tears gushing from my eyes. Quickly looking away, I gazed down at the muddy waters of the Green River.

A man on the prow was trying to make his way toward us, all the while cursing—the word fuck came through loud and clear. At first I didn't know who he was cursing, but it quickly became clear that he was screaming at Wuling and me, mainly me. He appeared to be the bosun's mate, and might well have been coming over to slug me. The deck was crowded, not just with passengers, but with their luggage as well, plus some tied-up pigs. Unable to shoulder his way through them, he brandished his fists at me.

He said: You motherfucker, are you and that little slut tired of living? You got off easy this time. Next time I'll grind you both to pulp! I'll squash you until they can't tell where the man begins and the woman ends! Motherfucker! You brought the angel of death onto our ship! Shit!

Since he couldn't force his way through the crowd, he turned back and accidentally stepped on a pig, which squealed as if it were being slaughtered. The passengers laughed. Except for Young Mistress and Wuling, the passengers were either looking at the pig or at me and having a good laugh.

I shouted at the top of my lungs: Pig!

My shout was louder even than the pig's squeals, and I heard the echo of my voice bounce off the surface of the river. Suddenly no one was laughing anymore. My shout bounced off Jade Mountain, beyond the far bank. I was nearly mesmerized. Like a crazed man, I shouted again, and raised another whirlpool in the Green River.

Pig!

Pig!

The ship's whistle bellowed after me. We were moving farther and farther away from Elm Township. As we went around a bend, the river widened; the houses on the banks looked like matchboxes. We went belowdecks and found a spot to sit amid the crowd of passengers; with our knees and faces nearly touching, we'd never been that close before. Young Mistress had a serene look on her face as she talked about her student days at the girls' school. We'd never heard her talk about such things before. She recalled everything in great detail and with great delight. Every now and then she'd stroke Wuling's face, then she'd stroke mine. Her eyes were soft and deep; it was like she was our mother.

Young Mistress said: There's a stone threshold set in the ground at the school gate. I tripped on it so often I was afraid to even walk through the gate. What to do? My schoolmates told me to march over the threshold, like a goose-stepping soldier. But I knew how funny that would look, so I did something else: I wrote the word threshold on the cover of all my textbooks to remind me. After a while, I stopped tripping on the threshold, but the other girls thought I was foolish, and Threshold wound up being my nickname. Up to the day I graduated, my schoolmates always called me that. Threshold! Isn't that terrible!

She giggled.

She was transformed into the girl wearing a sprig of peach blossoms in the photograph.

I said: Threshold.
Young Mistress said: Yes.

I'll never forget the look of pleasure on her face that day. I was a worthless slave. All I knew for sure was that she looked at me with motherly affection, and that my mind drifted farther and farther away with the boat. What I didn't know was that I'd never return to my home in the valley again and that this would be the last heartfelt smile Young Mistress left behind.

She said: Yes.

I can hear that sound anytime I want to. It's like a flower that blooms once and then is gone forever. But anytime I feel like hearing it, so long as these big, fleshy ears don't turn deaf, that flower will bloom in my heart. I said: Threshold! Young Mistress laughed at that.

Ai!

Ai!

Threshold laughed.

April 15th

The ship sailed down the Green River all night, stopping at a couple of small piers along the way, but not at the county seat. Lanterns formed lines on the mountains behind the city, where gunfire could be heard. Bullets whizzed over the city wall, followed by streaks of light; some of the bullets landed in the river, in front of and behind our ship, encasing it in echoes as they thudded into the water. Rebels were still rebelling, defenders were still defending the city, and the knots of enmity between them were impossible to untangle.

Not daring to dock, the ship's captain stayed the course. Moonbeams streamed in through portholes, illuminating stacks of luggage and rows of passengers, some sleeping, others wide awake. Wuling and I sat in front of Young Mistress, who was resting against the bulkhead. I stayed awake to watch over them as they slept. Wuling was curled up on the deck like a silkworm. Young Mistress slept with her head on her knees, turned to one side, her arms hugging her shoulders. She didn't make a sound, not even the sound of breathing. I felt terrible that she'd suffered so much. But if not for what had happened, I'd never have had the chance to be this close to her. The perfume of her body struggled against the stench of the compartment. My nose inched closer to her hair, and I kept breathing it in. My wayward hand crept toward her like a mouse, but I lost my nerve just before it reached her. I didn't touch her leg or her shoulder, settling instead for the chance to rub her skirt, which was spread out over the deck, and the embroidered flowers on the edges. My hand then moved around Young Mistress's foot and made its way up the lapel of Wuling's jacket and settled on her breast, which was about the size of a pomegranate. Wuling was fast asleep, her head lying between Young Mistress and me, and breathing deeply. As I stared at Young Mistress's nose in the moonlight, I let my hand roam over Wuling's sleek body. Eyes wide open, I began to dream, and before long, I fell asleep with my head cocked to one side.

It must have been sometime after midnight that Young Mistress threw herself into the moonlit waters of the Green River. Neither Wuling nor I witnessed it, so we have no proof that's what happened. But I have no doubts at all that she gathered her green dress around her and tumbled into the river like a felled tree. On the steps of the Cao estate, she'd said: What a big fish! And that is ultimately what she too became. Lying beneath the swells of the Green River, heading somewhere.

Wuling wouldn't stop believing that Young Mistress was still alive, but not me. Not from the moment I opened my eyes that next morning. The ship was moving slowly through a fog bank. When I awoke, I realized that my hand was still inside Wuling's

was vacant. The air was gray in our compartment; I was the only
person awake at that hour. The deck above us was perfectly still,
with no footsteps; the only sound came from the propeller below
the compartment, a very dull sound. My heart skipped a beat; I
knew something was terribly wrong. I stepped on several people
as I rushed up to the main deck, which was packed with sleeping bodies, seemingly lifeless, sprawled this way and that. The
water of the Green River appeared murky in the fog, about the
consistency of blood. The pain that stabbed my heart was so excru-
ciating, I had to shout.

I screamed: Young Mistress! Young Mistress! Where are you?
Young Mistress! Young Mistress! Young Mistress! Where are you?
I knocked luggage out of my way and bumped into sleeping passengers as I ran crazily up and down the deck. It was a moment of
total despair. I, a seventeen-year-old boy, wept worse than a girl,
louder than Wuling, with passengers cursing me and calling me a
madman.

Wuling, holding our belongings tight to her body, followed me
in my wanderings around the ship, as if I'd grown a tail. We searched
and we searched, hoping desperately that we'd find Young Mistress,
maybe hiding in the iron coal bin. But we failed. The ship hadn't
made any port after I fell asleep, and Young Mistress wasn't anywhere on the ship. Could she had flown up into the sky? The
bosun's mate who had leveled all those profanities at me was at it
again. He said: You motherfucker, what are you crying about?
What are you looking for? Three people went overboard during
the night. Don't ask me which of them was the person you're looking for. And even if I did tell you, you'd have to fish her out yourself. If fishing passengers out of the river was our responsibility,
we'd be so busy we wouldn't have time to run the ship! Every trip
we make on this river we lose more passengers than we can count.
Go ashore at our next port and prowl the riverbank. If you're lucky,
the corpse will wash up for you. If you're not, maybe some fish
will give back a little of what you're looking for. I guarantee you'll
be lucky if you wind up with as much as a leg, but I doubt you'll

ever see even one of her hairs. I said you were the angel of death. And I was right. See that pier up ahead? That's where you get off.

I committed the man's face to memory.

I planned to murder him one day.

I planned to feed him to the fish.

The waters of the Green River were murky. I had the powerful urge to jump in.

After being put off the ship, we walked upriver, asking everyone we met if they'd seen Young Mistress. Had they seen a woman dressed all in green? They said they hadn't. I knew it was hopeless, but Wuling refused to give up. So we turned and walked downriver, nearly all the way to the county capital, asking in every town and village we passed if anyone had seen a beautiful young woman all in green. They said they hadn't. So we stood on the riverbank the whole day, staring at the water, hoping that something green would float by. By then we'd used up nearly all the travel money Young Mistress had left behind and wondered dully where to go now.

I didn't feel like going back to Elm Township.

She didn't feel like going to Mulberry Township.

So we decided to try to make a life for ourselves in the county capital.

We were free.

I found work as a porter at the rice granary. Wuling got a job making paper streamers at a funeral shop on the west end of town. We earned enough to rent a hut outside of town and put food on the table, and settled into the uneventful life of man and wife. It was hard work carrying rice, and I often thought about Elm Township, the people there and all that had happened. I discovered that I missed them all. So I did have a heart after all. I was concerned about Old Mistress, wondering if she was eating or not, and about Old Master, wondering what he was eating; I was concerned about Elder Master, if he was still drinking more and more every day; I was concerned about Steward Bing and his wife, and concerned about the old granary, about all those slaves who had learned how to make matches. But I had no plans to go back. My only worry was that Elder Master would have someone open my locked trunk.

There they'd find Mr. Road's shoe and the sanitary pad that both Young Mistress and I had used. The first object would puzzle them, but their opinion of me would surely plummet because of the second one. I'd be shamed. But then, when I thought about it more calmly, I didn't think it meant all that much. And if I didn't think I'd shamed myself, how could anybody else shame me? Putting the sanitary pad in my trunk was very much the same thing as putting Young Mistress in my heart. I was a good person, and while this might have been considered obscene, I was in no way disgraced.

White bloated corpses frequently floated up onto the banks of the Green River, and each time I heard the news, I rushed over to see for myself. Even knowing that it couldn't be the person I was looking for, I couldn't stop myself from going over, as long as it wasn't too far, to look at the latest face and body. Once I assured myself that it wasn't the person I missed so badly, I walked away in high spirits, even given the tragic circumstances. But I'd wake up in the middle of the night in our little hut, my head filled with heartbreaking thoughts of how the river had turned Young Mistress and Mr. Road white and bloated, and how fish had fed on their eyeballs.

Wuling was different. She often spent her idle moments out walking, certain that one day she would run into Young Mistress on the street. I did my share of walking too, but I didn't dare think that I'd actually meet up with the eccentric Second Master. Born in the year of the rat, he'd been a master of secret dealings, and would never have put himself in the position of running into me or anyone he knew. Wuling and I made a special trip to the girls' school in the city's northern district, where we saw that the threshold Young Mistress had told us about was in fact very low, almost worn through, until it was little more than a stone shuttle. But because it was so low, people often overlooked it, which made it the potential hazard it was. If it had been much higher, it would have invited high-stepping. After that visit, I returned often to look at that threshold. The rice granary wasn't far, so I made a habit of walking by the school after work, and each time, long before I reached the school, I felt I could see Young Mistress, all in green, strolling out of the gate; my heart would race and some damned object would block up my throat.

I shouted inwardly: Threshold!

She smiled and said: Yes.

The threshold was still there, but the person was gone. I wanted to cry. I went on rainy days too, even if I was soaked to the skin, for then I could hear the sound of her sloshing through the puddles. Sometimes I felt that by my going over to look at the school she had recalled so fondly, Young Mistress would emerge from the Green River, one step after another.

Wuling worked hard to save money. She knew that Cao Zichun was being raised at the church in Acacia Township, and it was her hope that we could save up enough to bring the little bastard home and raise her for Young Mistress. She also went around asking street corner snake-oil peddlers if they had a preparation that could turn blue eyes black. It didn't matter if it was pills or an ointment or a patch, she'd buy it. When she did, I could only make her realize how absurd she was being by yelling or threatening to hit her. But reality had no chance of conquering her foolishness when she thought of the misfortunes of mother and son. She was convinced not only that Young Mistress was still alive, but that the bastard infant was alive as well. It wasn't until she and I set up house in that little hut that I truly understood the meaning of a one-track mind.

I can't recall which day it was toward the beginning of the ninth lunar month, although I'm sure I've got the month right, probably sometime around the autumn equinox. The local officials were planning to carry out some executions at Old River Bay outside the city gate. Strangulations rather than beheadings. Bored with decapitations, the city's residents turned out in droves to get an education in a new way to kill. The condemned men were to die the slow death of suffocation, which was more appealing to spectators than seeing heads lopped off in a matter of seconds. Since the execution ground wasn't far from where we lived, Wuling and I went along, deciding to take a quick look and then return home. We never expected to be caught up in the crowd ringing the site and carried right up to the execution posts. Six men stood at the bases of six poles, and as we watched, they were hoisted up by the ropes around their necks. As the second condemned man's toes left the ground, he cried out.

He said: Ears!

I broke out in a cold sweat.

It sounded like Second Master's voice.

He looked barely human.

He was spinning in the air, his gaunt body looking like the stem of a sunflower. He was staring at Wuling and me, the trace of a smile on his lips. Then his lips parted slowly, as if he were about to laugh, but they quickly began to twitch to make way for his thick purple tongue, which blotted both his lips and his chin from view. His hair was a mess and his face scarred and dirty; but it didn't take long for Wuling and me to recognize him. There was no question—it was Second Master, Cao Guanghan. I couldn't breathe; I felt like I was being strangled right along with him. All I could think of was running up and wrapping my arms around his legs. The idea that a master could be strung up like a goose or a goat in front of one of his slaves was unimaginable. I wanted to grab him by the legs and lift him down so he could pull that ugly tongue back into his mouth. Foamy bubbles oozed from his mouth. All six men turned into bubble-spewing fish caught on hooks, unable to get away. Our noses picked up the smells of emptied bowels and bladders. Filth slid down Second Master's pant legs and dripped from his toes to the hard, dry ground below.

Wuling was quaking, her head buried in my chest. Since we couldn't shoulder our way out of the crowd, we had to listen to the strange gasps from the six men. Creaks and pops emerged from somewhere on Second Master's body, like the snapping of taut strings on a lute. From somewhere behind us a strange cry flew over the heads of the crowd: Fifth Brother! In twenty years you'll be back as a true hero. Now fly up to the heavens. Fifth Brother, luck is with you!

My throat began to itch and I joined in the shouting.

There was still a light in Second Master's eyes.

I ran up to him and shouted: Second Master, you are a hero among heroes! They've done you a favor by hanging you up there! Second Master, go in peace. Everybody, cheers for our Second Master!

A confusion of shouts of every imaginable kind erupted from the crowd.

I heard a pop from Second Master's body.

He hung limply in the air, like a pile of laundry.

Had his spine snapped?

I weighed the possibility that he'd heard me flatter him.

A commotion arose at the execution ground; there was gunfire off in the distance and shouts nearer by: Down with the Manchu monarchy, and Long live the Republic and the masses! The execution officials and guards quickly retreated to the city gate, where troops pointed their rifles at the bellies of civilians and opened fire. I don't know how many people died in addition to the six condemned men. Dazed by a blow from a rifle butt, I let Wuling drag me home. I was temporarily deafened in one ear and couldn't hear what Wuling was saying to me. But I could see that her face was bloodless and that her eyes had glazed over. So I turned my good ear toward her in time to hear her say: I've seen him hanging like that before. In the past, he was able to free himself from the rope, but not this time. What was he doing that for? It scared me out of my wits. And he was smiling. When you called him a true hero back there, I saw him smile. That scared me out of my wits too, Elder Brother Ears!

I said: I'll kill you if I hear any more of that nonsense! He was in agony!

She asked: Does a madman really know what agony feels like?

I said: I'm a madman too. I'll show you what that's like!

She said: I'll yell for somebody to come and throttle you!

I said: We'll see who throttles whom!

The execution at Old River Bay had put dread in our hearts, and we were frantic to find something to do to calm ourselves down. So we held each other tightly in our little hut and did what came naturally to let our pleasure drive away our fears. I raised Wuling's legs almost to the roof beams. She squirmed like an oversized fish. We were doing what came naturally, but sorrow surged up in us and drowned our pleasure.

From Second Master, my thoughts turned to Young Mistress.

Young Mistress jumps over the threshold at the girls' school gate.

Giggles erupt all around her.

I put my hands around Wuling's neck!

I cried out.

Yunan!

Yunan!

Oh, Yunan!

Wuling burst into tears.

She said: How can I compete with her?

I said: The dead can't compete with the living.

She said: Elder Brother Ears, get me pregnant!

I said: All right, I'll give you the seeds of a dragon!

Wuling cried with abandon.

Second Master was hanging at Old River Bay. I was hanging from the naked back of Wuling. There was no breath left in Second Master, nor in me. After all the commotion died down, some corpses were snatched away by enemies, others taken by the victims' families, leaving only Second Master on the execution ground. The strangling posts were taken down and burned. The waxed nooses were also taken away to be used somehow. The once upright body of Second Master was now laid out on the deserted bank of the bay, completely naked; obviously, some little pricks had stripped him of his tattered clothes. The sun baked down on his emaciated body all day long, and as night was falling, it had begun to bloat up. Somewhat against my will, I went over to take a look. A crowd had gathered, including children, who were throwing dirt clods at the body. They were generally wide of the mark, so each thud against the belly or the head was met with a resounding cheer. Not worrying about whether or not their behavior was sinful, the kids started throwing rocks they scooped out of the riverbed; now when they hit the belly, the thuds were much louder, and the adults' scolding shouts quickly turned to cheers. I walked up and kicked one of the kids in the ass. Lucky for him it was a glancing blow; otherwise it might have split him in two.

I said: The next person who hits him with anything will answer to me! Do you hear me? The next person who torments that body will be tormenting me, and while he might forgive you, I won't!

Now tell me what the fuck you're all gawking at! The ghosts of hanged men are back at your homes just waiting to get their revenge on you!

I took off my jacket and draped it over Second Master's belly, which was turning blue and gave off a strange odor. Then I stepped back and sat on the ground with my legs crossed to watch over his body. I wasn't sure what I had in mind, except to get as close to him as possible. But the terrible smell and the hideous look on his face kept me from tending to him. The gawkers kept their eyes on me from a safe distance. They must have felt that there was something very strange about this man sitting there without a jacket and staring blankly ahead. But I didn't care. At least I'd scared off those damned kids. People started heading home when the sun fell behind the mountain, and the evening winds chilled my back. That's when I discovered something both more loathsome and more fearful than the stone-throwing kids. The shadowy forms of wild dogs came into view on all sides of Old River Bay. Some prowled the area in front of the city gate, while others were running around in circles on the Green River bank. They were waiting for it to turn dark, when they would become the masters of the bay. These soon-to-be masters were stretching and limbering up in anticipation of the meal that awaited them. I shuddered—maybe from fear, maybe from the cold air. At that moment I knew what it was that had drawn me to this spot of land. I couldn't leave now, because the moment I did, Second Master would truly be finished.

He was a man to be pitied.

A proclamation posted around town listed his crimes. He really hadn't done much at all. When he was captured in his secret hideaway, they'd found a dozen or more homemade bombs. When asked what he planned to do with them, he'd said he was going to blow people up. When they asked who, he'd said the people in the local government office, the provincial governor, and the Emperor. He'd ended by saying he wanted to blow up everybody who deserved it, to kill them all and send them up to the heavens. People who read the proclamation spoke of how pitiful this son of a wealthy family, Cao Guanghan, was: after skillfully preparing all those bombs, the poor man had never had a chance to use any of them. If he'd been able to make news by blowing up even a few of the men he'd targeted, they said, things would be much different today. But by letting himself be strung up before he'd made his move he'd probably lost the chance for his eyes to be closed in death. And, sure enough, the eyes of the naked corpse being buffeted by the winds of Old River Bay were still open. I knelt near him and could sense that his eyes were beginning to bulge, so I turned to look at him, and what I saw were armies of ants swarming over his face and throwing a veil over his eyes. The sight pained me so much I thought my heart was going to break. One of the wild dogs swaggered up near Second Master. I screeched and bounded over like a lion.

I said: Get out of here or you're dead meat!

Another one slinked my way.

I said: Get out of here or I'll flay your hide!

Now several of them advanced at once and crouched nearby, watching and panting. The moon had risen in the sky but didn't seem to be moving; the dogs weren't moving either, although their shadows kept getting bigger and bigger. The stench of Second Master's body lay heavy in the air, the dogs' lapping tongues flickered in the moonlight—they were getting impatient. I wanted to run! I couldn't protect Second Master, probably couldn't even protect myself. I was afraid they'd eat me too. Then I saw some clusters of human beings—local citizens coming to watch the show. I shouted at the top of my lungs: Come help me! Somebody bring me something to use as a weapon! You people there, help me!

Nobody moved and nobody replied. Having come to watch the theater of the dead, they were even happier to watch the theater of the living. I was really scared! My skin tightened, as if the dogs were already burying their fangs in me. Now what? I could run, but then Second Master would be at their mercy, and if Elder Master brought people over from Elm Township to claim his body, there wouldn't be anything left; the dogs would eat every last vestige of him, even what little excrement was left. I couldn't leave. It was as if he were saying: Ears, I'm suffering. Stay a while longer. I said: All right, I'll stay with you. I was having a silent conversation with a dead man, and as it continued, I actually began to howl out loud.

I said: Ow! Oh! Ah! Ah!

I had turned into a nameless beast. But it didn't do any good. The dogs weren't fooled. They'd take one step back and two steps forward. I pleaded with the gawkers: I beg you, help me drive these bastards away and let the Second Master of the Cao family be buried whole!

They ignored me, hoping that the dogs would kill and eat me. Why help me? My only thought was: life is meaningless, and this is to be the end of me. Well, so what! I looked straight at the clusters of human shapes and hurled curses at them: Fuck you and eight generations—no, sixteen generations—of your ancestors! Is any one of you worth the trouble to beat? While I was screaming, I made another lunge at the wild dogs to drive them back, and then ran over and picked Second Master up off the ground. Hauling bags of rice had been good training. I was only seventeen, still a child, but I was nimble and quick. Bending at the waist, I hoisted the pile of rotting meat over my shoulder, then made a mad dash for the Green River. The water was several yards away, across uneven ground, and I wasn't sure I could make it carrying such a heavy load. I howled for all I was worth. The dogs and people quickly saw what was happening and took out after me, the dogs barking madly. The people were shouting frantically. Now it was time to get their revenge for all the obscenities I'd hurled at them.

Eat him! they shouted.

Eat him!

Eat that foul-mouthed little slug!

Eat the rebel's accomplice.

Eat him!

The dogs leaped up to take bites out of Second Master's head and arms, which dangled to the ground. One or two of them even nipped at me. I flung them away, but they kept coming back, so I dragged them along as I ran down to the overflowing Green River. The murky water was flowing so fast that the dogs barely got wet before they hightailed it back to dry ground. But Second Master

and I floated on the surface. He came to life, rolling over and over.
I couldn't hold him, but he kept drawing me out to the middle of the river. A big eddy swirled toward us, fracturing the watery moonlight and causing Second Master's head to bob like a fish before abruptly diving beneath the surface, his bare feet sticking straight up briefly, then slipping under the water. The stink from his body clung to my shoulder. It spread throughout the Green River. He really was a fish, slicing through the water and disappearing from view. As I felt him slipping from my grip, I clawed at him, and I think I caught hold of his genitals. Second Master was a little boy, I was thinking. All of a sudden I realized that the spongy thing I was holding was a dead man's tongue. I promptly opened my hand and let him get away, as if I were releasing a fish.

As I stood in the chest-high water, I couldn't decide what to do next. I hadn't let Second Master down. I may not have been able to keep him with me, but I had managed to keep him whole. And I hadn't let the Cao family down either. Their slave had done everything expected of him. What else was left for him to do? The dogs were raising a howl on the riverbank and wouldn't let me come out of the water. The clusters of human beings came crowding forward, chirping like angry birds: Drown him drown him drown him!

Wuling called out from the distance.

She shouted: Elder Brother Ears, where are you? Elder Brother Ears, are you deaf? Dearest Ears, are you dead or something?

I could tell she was crying.

I couldn't decide what to do next. When I looked up at the churning waters of the Green River, I suddenly understood where Second Master had gone. It was the same place Mr. Road had gone. And the place where Young Mistress, Yunan, had gone. Second Master had rushed off, hugging the muddy riverbank, in search of those who had left before him. So what was I doing punishing myself in the moonlight? A big ship was steaming down the river. It had an iron paddle that churned up the water, as if digging a hole in the river to suck up everything around it and swallow it down. I wasn't much of a swimmer, and had no intention of trying for the bank. The one who had gone before was summoning me, and I was prepared to let the river carry me away to a beautiful place I'd never seen before. As I stood chest-high in water thick as blood, I entered a dreamworld I'd never see the end of, not in this life, and stayed there until Wuling came up to the bank, where she leaned out and gave me a tongue-lashing. She shrieked: Dog's ear pig's ear cat's ear, are you deaf? Donkey's ear maggot's ear corpse's ear, are you stone deaf? You're deaf as a post!

Without pausing in her cursing, she entered the water. We wrapped our arms around each other.

I said: Let's go, what do you say?

She asked: Go where?

I said: To find Young Mistress.

She said: I'm not going. You owe me some dragon's seed!

I said: I'll give it to you right now. Floating!

I fulfilled my promise to Wuling there in the middle of the Green River.

We flopped around like a couple of fish.

The people?

The dogs?

Fish?

Shrimp?

Gather round, all of you, and watch.

My dream turned into reality.

We were floating on the Green River.

We left.

For a beautiful place far away.

We wouldn't be coming back.

Youngster, I've come to the end of my story. I think a lot of you, because you're a good lad. The fact that you've been willing to come to the old-folks home and listen to my drivel has extended my life span. I'd be happy to talk forever if it improved my health. I know the people here hate listening to me. Lots of them call me an old deadbeat. They're right, I'm going to beat death. And the older the better. As long as I'm alive I'll keep talking. I'll talk about anything and everything, and if people get tired of it, so what? They can curse me if they want to. I'm afraid that the attendant who hears me talking all the time will say I've got a mental problem and plug up my mouth with one of her nylon stockings. But my story might only have happened in a dream, not in reality. I like watching you listen to me, and don't like this tape recorder. It's like a dustpan, like a latrine. But I like it more since you first came. I'll pretend it's you when you're gone. I wipe it off with my facecloth every day.

A youngster here by the name of Wang died. He was seventy-seven, and on his birthday that year I gave him the nickname Seven Seven Incident, after the July 7th beginning of World War II. He called me an old deadbeat. But he wound up being the dead one. He died sitting on the toilet. He sat down in the morning and was still sitting there at noon. In the afternoon, someone gave him a bump, and he toppled right into the guy. It turns out he didn't have either diarrhea or constipation. It was just another July 7th Incident. The old guy loved to sit on the toilet. But after this latest July 7th Incident, I stopped dawdling in the can. Dawdling doesn't do anyone any good. Not like telling stories, which I can do nonstop. But I have to stop sooner or later. Sitting on the can too long can make for trouble. The youngster's eyes were closed and he had a smile on his lips. But as soon as somebody bumped him, he toppled right over. That was a good lesson for me. I know I can tell stories forever, and that will keep me from dying.

Youngster, it's now a quarter to midnight. An airplane just passed overhead. It was a good one, right on time. I wait for it every night. It's become an obsession. I worry that it will fall from the sky. I listen to the news, and every few days one of them crashes, with dozens burned to death and dozens more missing. If they know they're going to crash, why do they take off in the first place? But a plane has to take off. You can't take off on a table, can you? So I worry all for nothing. For some it's a wonder they don't crash. Our planet is a ball hanging here in space. And just like an airplane, if you don't keep it in good repair, sooner or later it'll come crashing down in some latrine. People are airplanes too, each and every one of them. If something goes wrong, they come crashing to the ground. If everything's in good shape, they can fly to the very end, but sooner or later they too come crashing to the ground. Airplanes all have airports for their safe landings. People don't. I've been traveling the earth all my life, and I've never found a safe place to land. That's something I can't get off my mind. Where am I going to come crashing down? The best would be some deserted spot, either that or in town someplace—*plop*, right in the middle of a bunch of people, like pouring a pot of boiling water down an ant-hill! All people like to take a few others with them. Youngster, send me a note after you get this tape. Don't keep me on pins and needles. Think about what I said regarding airplanes when you've got some spare time. I won't crash down on your head. But I really don't have much time left!

Huang the accountant is always talking about you. Are you really going to write her a letter? I know what's going on between you two. I urge you to break it off as soon as you can. The director here makes a visit to the accounting office every day to pinch her cheeks, top and bottom. All the old farts here are unhappy with them. We're jealous. Accountant Huang will send the tape to you tomorrow, and I've been wondering if I ought to try to cop a feel. Hundred-year-old claws are still claws, and just thinking about copping a feel breathes life into these old fingers. We bachelors have got it all over you, because you have a wife and children. Morality is important to you. You understand what I'm saying, youngster?

Lately I've been having trouble pissing.

The doctor says I've got an enlarged prostate.

He says that at my age I ought to be happy it works at all.

He says a dribble is still a dribble.

I am not optimistic.

My airplane is running out of fuel.

Youngster!

My airplane will soon be out of fuel.

Out of fuel . . .

All out.